**Praise for *New York Times* bestselling author
Lori Foster**

"Count on Lori Foster for sexy, edgy romance."
—*New York Times* bestselling author
Jayne Ann Krentz

"Foster's writing satisfies all appetites with plenty
of searing sexual tension and page-turning
action."
—*Publishers Weekly*

"In *Mr. November*, Lori Foster delivers her
trademark blend of sentiment and sensuality."
—*RT Book Reviews*

**Praise for *New York Times* bestselling author
Brenda Jackson**

"Brenda Jackson is the queen of newly discovered
love… If there's one thing Jackson knows how to
do, it's how to pluck those heartstrings and stir up
some seriously saucy drama."
—*BookPage*

"[Brenda] Jackson is a master at writing."
—*Publishers Weekly*

Lori Foster is a *New York Times* and *USA TODAY* bestselling author with books from a variety of publishers, including Harlequin, Berkley/Jove, Kensington and St. Martin's. Lori has been a recipient of the prestigious *RT Book Reviews* Career Achievement Award for Series Romantic Fantasy and for Contemporary Romance. For more about Lori, visit her website at lorifoster.com, like her on Facebook or find her on Twitter, @lorilfoster.

Brenda Jackson is a *New York Times* bestselling author of more than one hundred romance titles. Brenda lives in Jacksonville, Florida, and divides her time between family, writing and traveling. Email Brenda at authorbrendajackson@gmail.com or visit her on her website at brendajackson.net.

New York Times Bestselling Author

LORI FOSTER

MR. NOVEMBER

H HARLEQUIN® BESTSELLING AUTHOR COLLECTION

ISBN-13: 978-1-335-46821-5

Mr. November

Copyright © 2018 by Harlequin Books S.A.

The publisher acknowledges the copyright holders of the individual works as follows:

Mr. November
Copyright © 2001 by Lori Foster

Riding the Storm
Copyright © 2004 by Brenda Streater Jackson

Recycling programs for this product may not exist in your area.

H HARLEQUIN®

www.Harlequin.com

Printed in U.S.A.

CONTENTS

MR. NOVEMBER

Lori Foster

To Lt. Espinosa for incredible inspiration, insight and research information.
Not only does he risk his life for the community, he went one further and organized a charity calendar to benefit others—and still found time to answer all my questions. I'm sure I'm not alone in my sincere gratitude to him for all he does.

Here's to firefighters everywhere—
a truly heroic service. Our thanks!

Chapter 1

With great interest, Amanda Barker peeked into the locker room. She'd been at the fire station—hounding him—many times, but she'd never ventured into this private area.

There was a partitioned-off shower area adjacent to the room, and steam from recent use still crept around the ceiling, leaving the air damp and thick. A few of the lockers stood open and empty. Discarded white towels littered the floor, the benches and an array of varnished wooden chairs. Amanda wrinkled her nose. The room smelled of men and smoke, soap and sweat.

Except for the smoke, it wasn't an unpleasant odor.

On the far wall, opposite the door she'd entered, a framed copy of the *Firefighter's Prayer* hung slightly askew, droplets of water beading on the glass cover. Next to that, a plaque reading Always Loved, Never

Forgotten, listed local firefighters who had died in community service.

Amanda drew a shaky breath and crept inside. The prayer drew her and she found herself standing in front of it, reading words she already knew by heart.

Enable me to be alert, and hear the weakest shout, and quickly and efficiently to put the fire out. She touched the glass covering those incredible words, wiping away the moisture. She dropped her hand and turned away, troubled as always whenever she remembered.

With self-taught discipline, she shook off the familiar feelings and surveyed her surroundings.

The locker room and connecting showers appeared empty, but she knew he was in there. The watchman had told her so—had even given her permission to go in, smiling all the while, ready to conspire with her to get their most infamous lieutenant to finally cooperate.

Behind her in the main rooms, she heard firefighters talking, laughing as the new shift arrived and the others headed home. They were a flirtatious lot, sometimes crude, always macho and fun loving to counteract the heavy responsibilities of their jobs. They were also in prime condition, lean and hard, thanks to rigorous physical training.

They all looked good, and they all knew it. With only one exception, they were willing—even eager—to help her out with the charity calendar by posing for various months. The money they made selling the calendar would benefit the local burn institute.

Amanda hoped none of the men came in behind her; it was past time she and Josh Marshall got things settled. Since the start of the project he'd refused to take part and avoided her whenever she tried to convince him. He even failed to return her calls.

The man was bullheaded and selfish and she intended to tell him so, but she didn't want an audience. Confrontations were not her thing. In fact, she avoided them whenever possible.

He wouldn't let her avoid this one.

Much as she hated to admit it, she needed Josh Marshall. She needed him to understand the importance of what she hoped to do, and then she needed his agreement to take part in her newest charity effort. While it was true all the men looked good, Josh Marshall looked better than good. He looked great. Sexy. Hot. He'd make the perfect Mr. November and the perfect model for the cover. They'd use him in advertising in local papers, bookstores and on the Web.

One way or another, Amanda intended to get his agreement today.

A muted sound, like the padding of bare feet on wet concrete, reached her ears. She turned and there he stood, all six-feet-plus of him. Casual as you please, a man without a care, he leaned in the doorframe. His blond hair was wet, his muscles were wet and the skimpy towel barely hooked around his lean hips was wet.

Slow rivulets of water dripped over his chest and through his body hair, slinking down his ridged abdomen and into the towel. He had his arms and ankles crossed. The towel parted, and one bare hairy thigh was exposed all the way to the lighter skin of his hip, up to the insubstantial knot in the towel. It wouldn't take much more than a very tiny tug to remove that towel.

She'd seen him in his lieutenant's uniform, she'd seen him hot and sweaty fresh from a fire, and she'd seen him relaxed, sitting around the station, on duty but not occupied.

She'd never seen him mostly naked and it was definitely…an eye-opener.

Amanda stood a little straighter and met his gaze. She had to tip her head back because he stood so much taller than she did. At only five feet four inches, she was used to that and refused to let it bother her now, just because the man was mostly naked and *trying* to bother her. She said, "Lieutenant Marshall."

His dark green eyes, so often remote in her presence, now looked her over, starting at her dress pumps and advancing to her soft pink suit and up to the small pearl studs in her ears. He gave a crooked smile and sauntered three steps to a locker. "Ms. Barker." He opened the locker and pulled out a bottle of cologne, splashing a bit in his hands, then patting his face and throat.

His scent overrode that of the smoke, and Amanda breathed him in, all warm damp skin, clean soap and that dark, earthy scent he'd just added. She recognized it from previous contact, but now was different. Now his big body was mostly bare.

Her nostrils quivered and she took an involuntary step back, bumping into the wall.

Of course, he noticed; his smile told her so, the glitter in his dark green eyes told her so. She held her breath, waiting to see what he'd say, how he'd mock her, and instead he reached for a comb. He turned to face her fully while tidying his hair. "How'd you get in here, anyway?"

Never in her life had she watched a man groom himself. Josh Marshall…well, it was unexpected. The heavy muscles in his raised arms flexed and bulged as he dragged the black comb straight back through his wet hair. She could see his underarms and the soft, darker hair there. Her heart bumped into her ribs with startling force. Somehow, that part of Josh seemed more intimate than his exposed thighs and abdomen.

"Cat got your tongue?" He reached for a T-shirt, which he pulled on over his head with casual disregard for the hair he'd just combed. The front of the shirt read: Firefighters Find 'em Hot—and Leave 'em Wet.

Her pulse raced and she had to clear her throat before she could speak coherently. "The watchman let me in so we could talk."

"You're a persistent little thing, aren't you?"

She ignored the sexist comment even as she acknowledged it for truth; she was persistent, and she was most certainly little. "You haven't returned any of my calls."

"No, I haven't, have I?" His deep voice held only mild interest in her visit. "Ever wonder why?"

As he asked that, he lifted out a pair of black cotton boxers and she just barely had time to avert her face before he pulled the towel away.

Cheeks scalding, Amanda gave him her back. "You're being stubborn."

"Actually, I was trying to be direct. I don't want to do the calendar, so there's no point in wasting my time or yours."

"But I need you."

Amanda felt the pause, his utter stillness in response

to her words, and wanted to bite off her own tongue. Instead, she asked impatiently, "Are you decent?"

He gave a short laugh. "Never."

"I meant…" She wanted to groan, she wanted to ask him why he had to taunt her and be so impossible. But that wouldn't win him over so she drew a breath and asked instead, "Have you got your pants on?"

"Yeah."

She turned, and saw he'd only been half-truthful. He wore his boxers and the T-shirt, but that was all. Even sitting on the bench, his jeans next to him, he looked more manly than any man she knew. His large hands were braced on the bleached wood of the bench at either side of his hips, his powerful thighs casually sprawled, his gaze direct.

Amanda could see the bulge of his sex in his underwear and found herself staring. It was a contrast, the sight of that soft, cuddled weight when the rest of him was so hard and lean.

"Should I take them back off?"

She jerked her gaze to his face and asked stupidly, "What?"

"The underwear." His voice was silky, the words and meaning hot. "I can skin them off if you wanna get a better look."

She started to laugh to cover her embarrassment over being caught, except that he looked serious. Was he enough of a reprobate to do as he suggested? One look into those intense green eyes and she knew the answer was an unequivocal *yes*.

In fact, he looked…anxious to do so.

She'd allowed things to get way out of hand. "Lieutenant—"

"Why don't you call me Josh? Being as you just stroked me with those pretty brown eyes, I feel we're on more personal terms now."

"No." Amanda shook her head. "I apologize for the staring. It was dreadful of me, I admit it, and I promise you it won't happen again. But I prefer to keep things professional."

"Oh, but that won't do." Josh stood and that damn crooked smile warned her that she wouldn't like what was about to come next.

She edged to the side, ready to escape him, and banged into an open locker. Her high heels threw her off balance and she nearly fell before catching herself. Josh didn't give her time to be embarrassed over her lack of grace. He stalked her, his gaze locked onto hers as he closed in, refusing to let her look away.

He came right up to her and crowded her back until the only air she could breathe was heated and scented by his big body, until the only thing she could see was his broad hard chest in that dark T-shirt.

Flattening his hands on the locker at either side of her head, he caged her in. His thick wrists, incredibly hot, touched her temples.

"Lieutenant..." Amanda seldom panicked anymore; the feelings had been tempered by seven years of distance. But at the moment, panic seemed her wisest choice.

"Uh-uh," he murmured, "none of that." Very slowly, suggestively, he leaned down, making her think he might kiss her and bringing her very close to a scream.

She froze, her heartbeat skipping, her pulse racing. One second, two... The kiss never came and a riot of emotions bombarded her, none of them easily distinguishable except relief and a faint feeling of disappointment. He made a small sound of surprise, as if she'd somehow taken him off guard, and her damn knees went weak.

His nose touched her neck and he inhaled deeply.

Amanda quivered. "*What* are you doing?"

"I've decided how I'm going to handle you, Amanda." His hot breath brushed her ear, sending gooseflesh up and down her spine. She was aware of the cool contrast of his damp hair grazing her cheek.

Handle her? She couldn't move a single inch without touching him somewhere. She held very still. "What are you talking about?"

He tilted his head away to smile into her shocked face. Watching her with heavy eyes and a load of expectation, he said, "I want you in my bed."

Her mouth fell open.

No, surely he hadn't just said… But he had! He'd actually suggested… Amanda laughed. Such a ridiculous, ludicrous…

Shaking her head, she managed to say, "No, you really don't."

He looked a little confounded by her reaction. He tilted his head and narrowed his eyes to study her. "Now there's where you're wrong, sweetheart. You've been pursuing me—"

"For a charity event!"

"—for over a month now. I decided it was time I did the pursuing. And once I thought of it, I couldn't think of anything else." His gaze wandered over her face, and landed on her mouth. He leaned in again. "Damn, you smell good."

Of all the bizarre things that could have happened,

Amanda hadn't expected this one. Josh Marshall coming on to her? A man who wouldn't normally look at her without frowning, a man who only told her "no," when he bothered to tell her anything at all?

Her reserve melted away, replaced by the unshakable facade of apathy she'd built years ago. Josh Marshall didn't matter to her, so he couldn't hurt her. No one could.

Her heart now safely concealed, her mind clear, she put both hands on Josh's chest to lever him back.

He allowed her the small distance.

Hoping she sounded reasonable, she said, "Lieutenant, you can trust me on this one, okay? You don't want me. You're not in the least interested in me."

"I didn't think so at first, either." His hands covered hers, keeping them snug against his chest. Under the circumstances, she barely registered the firm muscles, the heat of his skin through the soft cotton and the relaxed thumping of his heart. "But as I said, I've changed my mind."

Gently, because she hoped to nip his outlandish plan in the bud without causing any hard feelings between them, she said, "Then unchange it, Lieutenant. Really."

He looked a little baffled by her response to his come-on. She nearly smirked. No doubt most women would have been simpering, eager to get to know him better, excited by the prospect of sharing his bed.

Amanda shuddered. She didn't waste her time on impossible dreams, and she definitely didn't waste it on men. Not in that way.

The reasons behind her behavior didn't matter. What mattered was that Josh Marshall not pursue her. That scenario would only agitate them both.

He lifted a hand to her cheek and gently stroked with his fingertips. His gaze appeared troubled, concerned and sympathetic. In a voice barely above a whisper, he asked, "What are you so afraid of?"

Amanda almost fell over. Her throat closed and her knees stiffened. No! He couldn't possibly see her fear. She kept it well hidden and buried so deep, no one, not even her family, ever saw it. Men accused her of being frigid, gay, a total bitch...but none of them ever noticed the gnawing fear she lived with.

"Shh. It's all right. I just didn't know." Josh continued to touch her, and then he stepped away. Not far, but at least she could breathe. He stared into her widened eyes and said with a mix of gentleness and determination, "Whatever it is, Amanda, we'll go slow. I promise."

"We won't go at all!" Her heart thumped so hard it hurt and her stomach felt queasy. She pressed a fist to her belly and sought lost composure. "I'm not in the least interested, Josh... Lieutenant Marshall."

He smiled. "Oh, you're interested. I wager you've even considered things between us a time or two. Maybe a hot fantasy late at night?"

"You'd be pathetically wrong." The bite in her words was unavoidable; she did not, ever, delude herself with fantasies.

Taken aback by her vehemence, Josh whistled low. "An abusive ex? Poor home life?"

"No and no."

Rubbing his chin, he said, "You might as well tell me. I'll get it out of you sooner or later."

The man was impossible! "Why do you even want to?"

He shrugged. "It's obvious there's a problem, and we can't get on to the lovemaking until it's solved."

Her mouth fell open again. "My God, your conceit is incredible."

"Confidence, not conceit." He lifted one massive shoulder. "I know women, inside and out. You're hiding something, something that scares the hell out of you, and now I'm doubly intrigued. All in all, I'm beginning to think this is going to be fun. Not at all the chore I'd first envisioned."

His every word, every action, threw her. She caught herself barking a very unladylike laugh. "A chore? *A chore.* You expect to ingratiate yourself with me using comments like that?"

He winked as he pulled on his jeans and sat on the bench again to don socks and lace up black boots. "I don't want to win you over, sweetheart. I just want you in my bed."

Tension prickled her nerve endings, started the low thrum of a headache. Amanda rubbed her temples, trying to think. "We've gotten off course here somehow." She drew a steadying breath and dredged up a vague smile. "All I want is for you to agree to have your picture taken. An hour of your time…"

Josh stood and began threading a thick black leather belt through his belt loops. "Have dinner with me."

An audible click sounded when her teeth snapped together. "No. Thank you."

He buckled the belt and pulled out a black leather jacket, slinging it over his shoulder and hooking it with his thumb. He looked her over, the epitome of male arrogance and savage resolve. "I thought we'd discuss the calendar."

Indecision warred with hope. Would he relent and allow her to get the photographs she needed? Was he just leading her on to get his way?

The biggest question was whether or not she could handle him—and she had serious doubts on that issue. In a thousand different ways, she knew Josh Marshall was unlike any other man she'd encountered. He was persuasive, a lady's man in every sense of the word, walking testosterone with an abundance of charm. To top it off, he had a killer body that got double takes from females of all ages.

They *wouldn't* end up in bed, of course, so that wasn't a real worry for Amanda. His confidence and past successes were irrelevant. The worry was how much hell he'd put her through before he accepted defeat. Somehow, she didn't think he took defeat very well.

In her case, he'd have to learn.

But if he would agree to the calendar, did it really matter if she had to put up with his seduction tactics first? She would resist because she had to, and in the end, she'd get what *she* wanted.

With a sense of dread, in spite of the pep talk that she'd just given herself, Amanda nodded. "All right."

Josh's expression softened. "I promise it won't be near the degradation you're imagining."

"Not at all." She needed his agreement, and antagonizing him would gain her nothing but his continued refusal. "The dinner will be fine, I'm sure."

Without her permission, he walked up to her and put his large muscled arm around her back. She felt the heat of his hand as it opened on her waist. Before she could react, he urged her forward.

"I have a few rules we can discuss on the way out."

"Rules?" She felt vague and uncertain with him touching her so much.

"That's right. And rule number one is that you have to call me Josh. No more 'Lieutenant' formality."

She could live with that. "If you insist."

"Rule two—no discussions of any actual fires. I like to leave my job behind when I'm off duty."

"Agreed." Amanda realized she'd answered a tad too quickly when Josh stopped and looked down at her. The last thing she wanted to discuss, now or ever, was a real fire. "I… I understand," she stammered, trying to keep him from looking inside her again.

For a long moment, he just stood there, considering her, and then he nodded. "Let's go."

As they walked through the station, firemen looked up. A few laughed, a few called out suggestions and Josh, without slowing, made a crude gesture in their general direction and kept going. But when Amanda peeked up at his face, she saw his satisfied…maybe smug, smile.

Ha! Let him be smug, she didn't care. All she cared about was her project.

And that meant she had to care about him. But just for a little while.

Josh watched Amanda as they stepped outside into the cool October night. He was just coming off a twelve-hour shift, and after two emergency calls that day, he should have been tired. He *had* been tired, clear down to the bone. He'd thought only of getting home and falling into bed. But now he was…expectant. And a little horny.

For Amanda Barker. He grinned.

There'd been a recent drizzle and the station's lights, as well as a bright moon, glistened across the wet pavement. The cool air was brisk, stirred by an uneasy breeze.

It matched his mood.

With his hand on Amanda's back, he could feel the nervousness she tried so hard to hide. It wasn't a reaction he was used to from women. But then Amanda wasn't what he was used to.

She also wasn't what he wanted, not even close.

Not that it seemed to matter tonight.

Once he'd made up his mind to turn the tables on her, he'd found himself thinking about her a lot. About getting her out of her perfect little feminine suits and letting down her perfectly coiffed hair.

He wanted to see if Amanda Barker could stop being so sweet and refined and classy. He wanted to see her wild, unreserved.

He wanted to hear her screaming out a climax, to feel her perfectly painted pink nails digging into his back as she bucked beneath him.

Josh stopped and drew a deep breath. He put his hands on his hips and dropped his head forward with a laugh. Damn, he'd let his lust get out of hand.

He hadn't expected her here tonight, had in fact been too wiped out from the emergency calls to do much thinking at all. Yet, she'd surprised him by hanging out in the locker room, waiting for *him*.

A pleasant surprise and a very nice distraction.

He'd made his decision a week ago and had been thinking about it ever since. At least a dozen different ways, he'd imagined their encounter, how he'd approach her and what he'd say, how she'd react to his come-on.

Not once had he imagined seeing fear on her face.

"Lieutenant Marshall?"

He whipped his head up and snared her gaze, making her brown eyes widen in startled reaction. "Josh, remember?"

"Sorry." She licked her bottom lip, apparently undecided, then that iron determination of hers came to the fore and she stiffened like a sail caught in the wind. "Josh, is something wrong? Because I want you to know if you've changed your mind—about dinner I mean—that's fine with me. We can just set up a time for the shoot and part ways here."

She really, truly, wanted nothing to do with him.

Josh hated being forced to face his own ego, but... he was stunned. Oh, he'd known women who hadn't wanted to be involved with him. He was twenty-seven years old and he'd had his fair share of rejections. Women who were already involved or those who didn't like the risks associated with his work. Women who'd been looking for marriage and those who'd just gotten divorced and needed time to regroup.

Most recently, he'd been rebuffed by two incredible women who'd chosen his best friends instead. He smiled at that, thinking how happy Mick and Zack were.

Oh, Wynn and Delilah liked him, they even doted on him occasionally, but only as a friend.

Other than Amanda, he'd never suffered complete and total disinterest.

Why she was so disinterested was something he intended to find out.

"I haven't changed my mind." Josh saw her delicate jaw tighten and felt just perverse enough to add, "I was imagining how you might be in bed. If you'd be so prissy and ladylike then, or if you'd really let go. Maybe do a little screaming or something."

A variety of expressions crossed her face in rapid succession—mortification, incredulity and finally, fury. She turned away from him, her arms crossed under her breasts.

The first words she spoke took him by surprise. "I'm *not* prissy."

A slow grin started and spread until he almost laughed out loud. Had he managed to prick her vanity? "No?" He drawled the question, just to infuriate her more. "Seem prissy to me. I can't know for sure, but I'm willing to bet even your toenails are painted, aren't they?"

"So?"

He'd love to see her feet. They were small and narrow and forever arched in sexy high heels. She had great calves, but the skirts she wore were too long to see her thighs, more's the pity.

"It's cold." She stared up at the glowing moon, rubbed her arms briskly and shivered. "Do you mean to stand here and insult me all night?"

Amanda had pulled on a soft, cream-colored cashmere coat with matching leather gloves. The outerwear was fashionable, but probably not very warm.

He could warm her, but she didn't look receptive to that idea. "I didn't consider it an insult. More like an observation."

"Then I'd hate to hear your idea of an insult."

Even miffed, she looked picture-perfect…and about as approachable as a china doll.

The woman stymied him. But then, he was up for a challenge.

Holding out his hand to her, Josh said, "My car's this way."

She slanted a suspicious, sideways glance at him. "Just tell me where we're going and I'll meet you there."

Hell, no. Now that he had her, he wouldn't take any chances on her changing her mind. For some reason, being with her tonight mattered more with each passing second. "Nope. We ride together."

Her face fell. "But I have my car with me." She gestured toward the street to a powder-blue Volkswagen Beetle. Not the new spiffy version, but an older model.

Josh did a double take. That car most definitely did not fit her image of refined ladylike grace. The car looked…playful.

Amanda Barker was chock full of secrets. First, that disbelieving laugh when he'd propositioned her. Then her indignation at the suggestion she might be prissy, which was a bona fide fact as far as Josh was concerned. And now that fun car. He shook his head.

He could discuss the car with her later, Josh decided. "So? I'll bring you back here for it after dinner." She looked ready to refuse, and he added, "We can discuss the calendar along the way."

That easily, she gave in. "Very well." She stepped closer, but stayed just out of reach of his extended hand.

Challenged, Josh snagged her arm and held on to it. She didn't pull away, but her nose did go into the air.

She had a beautiful profile, especially with her features softened by the shadows of the night and the opalescent sheen of the moon. Her neck was even graceful, and looked very kissable with tiny tendrils of tawny hair teasing her nape.

"Do you always wear your hair up?" He tried to imagine it loose, to guess how long or thick it might be.

In a voice snooty enough for a queen, she said, "My hair has nothing to do with dinner or the calendar."

"It has to do with my fantasies though." He tightened his hold when he felt her preparing to slip away. He lowered his voice and said, "I close my eyes at night and imagine your hair hanging free. Sometimes I can almost feel it on my stomach, or my thighs."

She stopped so abruptly he nearly pulled her off her high heels. Gathering her poise and clutching her purse in front of her like a blockade, she said, "This is sexual harassment!"

Actually, it had turned into a wet dream a few nights ago, but Josh thought it might not be a good time to share that with her. "I see you're out of practice."

Indecision and frustration tightened her features. "What do you mean?"

Leaning close, Josh touched the end of her reddening nose and said, "Seduction, sweetheart. Not harassment."

"I don't *want* to be seduced!"

A couple of passersby stared, then laughed before hurrying away.

Josh took her arm and started her on her way again. "Take deep breaths, Amanda. It'll be okay."

One gloved hand covered her mouth. "Oh God, this is just awful."

He didn't want to say it, but he couldn't let her start thinking of his pursuit as harassment. "You don't have to be here, you know. You don't work for me, I have no hold over you—"

"I need you for the calendar!"

"No," he said, giving her arm a gentle squeeze, "you *want* me for the calendar."

Miffed, she grouched, "I don't know why. You're absolutely—"

"Sticks and stones may break my bones…"

She looked like she wanted to scream again, but instead she stopped and straightened her shoulders, her spine. She pasted on a serene expression and even managed a smile.

Poor little thing, he thought. She worked so hard at maintaining all that elegant dignity when what she really wanted to do, what her nature demanded she do, was turn loose her temper and wallop him. He waited, anxious to hear what she'd say.

With shaking fingers she tidied her already tidy hair and smoothed her coat. "Where will we be eating?"

Josh waggled a finger at her. "That was way too restrained. I had myself all prepared and then, nothing but fizzle. I'd say I'm disappointed, but I think that's what you're after." He leaned down to his car, unlocked and opened the door. "In you go."

"This is yours?"

"Yep. Like it?"

She admired the shiny black Firebird convertible. "It's very nice. Very…macho." She settled herself inside, placing her feet just so, her hands in her lap. Amused, Josh reached around her to hook her seat belt.

"Oh!" She pressed herself back in the seat, avoiding any contact with him. "I can do that."

"I've got it." He liked buckling her in, taking care

of her. He smoothed the belt into place, and in the process, skimmed her stomach with the backs of his fingers. Even through her clothes and a winter coat, the simple touch aroused him.

Pathetic.

He'd have laughed at himself, but he was too busy inhaling her perfume. He'd first caught the soft, seductive scent in the locker room, and it had been all he could do not to kiss her. With his nearness, her shiny pink-painted lips had trembled, enticing him.

But the panicked look in her deep brown eyes—a look she didn't want him to see—had struck him deep.

Someone had hurt her, and he didn't like it.

Josh walked around to the driver's side, using the moment to come to grips with himself. Amanda wasn't a woman he should involve himself with. She appealed to him sexually, but she wasn't his normal type, wasn't the type of woman he'd come to appreciate.

She wasn't at all like Delilah or Wynonna. They were casual women, up front and honest and outspoken. He'd learned to appreciate those qualities.

Amanda, on the other hand, was so buttoned up she might as well have been wearing armor. And secrets! He was beginning to think everything about her was a mystery.

He'd meant to tease her, maybe teach her a lesson by turning the tables on her. He'd definitely meant to make love to her. Probably more than once.

But he hadn't meant to start delving into her past, discovering her ghosts, involving himself in her life.

Yet, he knew it was too late. Like it or not, he was already involved. And it hadn't taken any work on her part to get him there. No, she wanted nothing to do with him beyond using him for her damned calendar.

Josh intended to change all that.

But first there was something he had to know. As soon as he pulled into traffic, he girded himself, took a deep breath, and asked as casually as he could manage, "Are you afraid of me, Amanda?"

Chapter 2

"What?" Amanda's confused frown was genuine, relieving Josh on that score.

He shrugged. "We both know you're afraid of something. I just wanted to make sure it wasn't me."

She went rigid with indignation. "You do not frighten me, Lieutenant."

"Ah, ah," Josh chastised. He reached over and tickled her chin before she jerked away. "There you go again with that Lieutenant stuff. It's Josh. We have an agreement."

Silence fell heavily in the car, then she sighed. "Where are we going for dinner?"

He wasn't about to tell her, not yet. "Someplace nice and quiet, so we can talk. But nothing fancy."

"I'm not dressed for fancy anyway."

He glanced at her. Other than the lights of passing

vehicles and streetlamps occasionally flickering by they were held in a cocoon of darkness. Her nose was narrow and straight and aristocratic. With her wide eyes, that stubborn chin and the most luscious mouth he'd ever fantasized over, she was a beauty.

But that wasn't what drew him. That wasn't what had him suddenly hot with need. He'd known plenty of women, beautiful and otherwise. No, it was something else, something he couldn't put his finger on yet.

"Amanda, you could go anywhere, anytime, and be suitably dressed." As far as compliments went, it was subtle, not in the least aggressive, nothing for her to shy away from.

But she didn't respond, so he added, "You always look great."

She ducked her head, then bit her bottom lip. "Thank you." She quickly added, "Now, about the calendar. I'd like to discuss something special for your photo."

"Special?" He wasn't at all sure he liked the sound of that. In fact, the very idea of the calendar bugged him. Firefighters should, in his mind, be respected for the hard work they did, not just for their bodies. The whole beefcake approach didn't sit well with him.

"That's right. I want to put you on the cover and use you for the promotions."

If he hadn't been driving, he'd have closed his eyes with disgust. The cover. Damn.

With the new topic, Amanda had turned all businesslike on him, twisting in her seat to face him, her expression more animated, open. Because Josh liked the change and enjoyed seeing her less reserved, he didn't immediately disregard her offer.

"Why?"

She blinked at him. "Why what?"

"Why do you want to use me for the cover?"

Confusion showed on her beautiful face, then chagrin. She gestured at him, her small, gloved hand flapping the air. "Well…look at you, for heaven's sake. Out of all the firemen who agreed to take part, you're by far the most handsome, and you have a fabulous physique."

"You noticed, huh?"

Amanda rolled her eyes. "Because those assets will certainly help sell calendars—which is the whole point—yes I noticed. You're the obvious choice."

Josh drove in silence for a moment, his hands relaxed on the wheel, his thoughts hidden. Only the hissing of tires on wet pavement intruded. That, and her scent.

Her scent was making him nuts.

"I've got a question for you." He pulled into the parking lot of a take-out chicken joint. It didn't look like much, but he knew firsthand how good the food was.

Amanda looked around in consternation. "We're eating here?"

Josh ignored her question to ask one of his own. "If you think I look so good, why in hell do you refuse to get involved with me?" He pulled in to the line for the drive-thru. There were two cars ahead of him, so he braked and turned to face her.

She had her purse clutched tightly in her lap and that panicked look on her face again. "What are you doing?"

Because he knew she'd already figured it out, he said gently, "I'm buying some food."

Her chest rose and fell with agitated breaths. "For what?" She looked ready to leap from his car.

Josh reached across the seat and touched her cheek. His heart squeezed tight when she leaned away from him and that awesome fear widened her eyes and drained the color from her face.

His plan had gone horribly awry, he thought. He didn't want to tease her, didn't want to taunt her.

He just wanted her—sexually, and otherwise.

"For us to eat," he admitted, watching her closely, trying to better read her. "At my place—where as I said, it's nice and quiet and we can talk."

It was the last that got her. She jerked around, blindly, wildly reaching for the door handle. She yanked on it, but the door was locked.

"Amanda…"

She made a small sound, incoherent except for that damn fear.

Josh didn't know what the hell to do. Never in his blighted life had he dealt with a hysterical woman— hysterical because she didn't want to be with him!

Luckily, her seat belt restrained her so he didn't have to chase her through the parking lot.

Josh kept his tone calm and soothing. "What are you doing? I can take you back to your car if you don't want to have dinner after all. You don't have to walk." He sounded like an ass and hated himself. But she listened. "It's just that… I'm exhausted after two emergency calls on one shift. I want to relax, not sit in a public place."

That sounded plausible to him. Pleased with his excuse—entirely made up—he waited.

Amanda paused, facing the window, her shoulders

hunched. In a small voice, she said, "I don't see why we need to go to your place."

"We don't." Minutes ago, he'd have tried insisting, now he just wanted her to relax again. "Hell, we can eat here if you want. Or in the parking lot."

She looked at him over her shoulder. "You're really that tired?"

Enormous relief washed over him. "Yeah." He smiled. "You should have seen me in the shower."

Her eyes widened and he laughed. "Get those lecherous thoughts out of your mind, woman. I meant because I was so tired, I sat on a chair to shower. All of us did."

She shifted around, interested, calmer. The line moved at the same time, and Josh drove forward.

"Why?" she asked.

"I told you, exhaustion. We keep these old wooden chairs in the shower for such occasions." She looked fascinated, and he found himself breaking one of his rules. "After a fire, it's often like that. The adrenaline fades and you're left weary down to the bone, filthy with grime and soot."

His heart jumped when he felt Amanda touch his arm.

"I'm sorry."

He practically held his breath. Women touched him all the time, damn it, and in more interesting places than his elbow. But her touch…it meant something. And he liked it. "For what?"

"For acting so foolish. It's just that sometimes…"

Josh reached for her hand, laced his fingers with hers. When she didn't pull away, he felt as if the sun had just come out and shone on his miserable head.

"Sometimes you get afraid? You remember something and you find yourself just reacting?"

She stared at their entwined hands. "Josh, I want to be honest with you, okay?"

He waited.

She transferred his hand to both of hers. "I meant what I said." Her gaze was direct, unflinching. "I know lots of women adore you. I even understand why. But I really, truly, am not interested. I don't want you to understand me, I don't need your friendship or your affection. Of course I have…issues. Everyone does. But I like my life the way it is and I have no intention of changing a single thing." Her gaze implored his understanding. "All I need, all I want, is for you to agree to pose for the calendar."

Josh rested back in his seat and studied her. Whatever plagued her, he wouldn't find out about it tonight. Tactics that usually had women laughing and flirting back only fell flat with her. He needed a new plan, and he needed it now.

He made a sudden decision. "I'll do the pose."

She released him to clasp her hands together in excitement. Her face lit up. "You will?"

It was his turn at the drive-thru and he gave her a long look before pulling up to the order window. Despite everything she'd just said, he ordered enough for two.

After the food was handed to them and safely stored on the floorboards, Josh clarified. "I'll do the calendar, but I won't stop wanting you. And I won't stop trying to change your mind about wanting me."

He heard her gasp, but damn it, she couldn't expect him to just walk away. Not now.

As he eased back into traffic, he stared out the windshield into the endless black night. "It's your decision, Amanda. If you have me in the calendar, then you'll have to deal with my courtship."

"Courtship, ha!"

Josh hid his smile. At least now she wasn't squashed up against the opposite door, doing her best to put a mile between them. She was facing him, talking to him, and he chose to see that as progress. "Make up your mind, okay? You can either walk away now and use one of the other guys to fill up the calendar, or you can learn to deal with me. And understand, sweetheart, I would never force you, and I'd never hurt you." He took the turn off the main drag to the quieter, emptier street leading toward his place.

"But I am determined," he finished saying, "to have my own way."

Pigheaded lout.

Amanda stewed, unsure what to say next. Not only had she made a complete and total fool of herself, behaving like a spooked child, but she hadn't accomplished a thing with her honest, up-front admission to him. If anything, she was in deeper now that she'd spilled her heart.

True, Josh had listened. She'd felt his undivided attention. But then he'd disregarded everything she'd said.

She'd been truthful and so had he and now they were at an impasse. Amanda eyed him in the dark confines of the car and knew what she'd have to do.

Still, she gave it one more try. "It won't do you any good, you know."

"What? To chase after you? Hey, just call me an optimist." He smiled, looking so handsome and teasing. "Besides, I'm thinking you might be worth the trouble."

"I'm not."

"No?" He sounded amused. "How come?"

"Because you'll only be wasting your time."

"You think you're that boring, do you?"

Tension tightened her fingers on the strap of her purse and made her neck ache. "Josh, I don't date and I don't do…anything else."

He turned speculative as he asked, "Anything else like kiss or fondle or make love?"

Closing her eyes only made her more aware of him beside her, a large hard man who exuded energy and heat. He threatened the foundation of her existence. Everything she'd worked so hard for, including emotional peace, had to be kept in the forefront of her mind. She could not let him distract her from her convictions.

She forced herself to look at him. "I can't imagine you'd be content to just share a chicken dinner with me every now and again."

His big hand patted her knee, startling her. "It's a start."

"It would also be the finish."

He retreated physically, but not verbally. "Again I have to ask, Amanda—how come?"

With no streetlights on the narrower road, the night was black and all she could see of Josh was a faint outline and the glitter of his eyes.

"That's none of your business." The fragrant smell of fried chicken teased her nostrils and Amanda's stomach rumbled. She was hungry, stressed and still hopeful. "Tonight we can iron out the details and tomorrow

I'll bring a release form by the station. I'll leave it with the watchman. If you'd get it back to me right away, I'd appreciate it. We're really pressed for time—behind schedule actually."

"Because of me?" He turned down a cul-de-sac with duplex housing.

"I always try to do what's best for the project. I know you'll help sales, so yes, I held things up hoping you'd change your mind."

"Hoping you could change my mind."

"Yes. Everything's gone to the printers already, except the cover and the November photo, because those are what I'd like you to do. Once that's taken care of we can finish printing the first set of calendars and have them bound. They'll be ready for sale by early November, and we can cash in on some of the Christmas purchases."

Josh pulled into the driveway of a modern duplex home. He parked his car in an open garage spot, and with a remote, closed the garage door. "I'm to the left," he said, explaining which of the homes connected by the spacious two-car garage was his. He turned the headlights off and killed the engine, then turned to face Amanda.

Being in that closed garage made Amanda feel even more confined. Flustered, she started to open her car door, but Josh's long fingers closed around her upper arm. Panic, as fresh as it had been earlier, churned inside her.

What Josh didn't know, what he couldn't understand, was that her panic wasn't inspired by physical fear, but rather emotional. Her body didn't mind his touch at all, but her heart, her head, knew the danger in allowing him any familiarity at all. Seven years ago she had made a promise to herself, sworn to make reparations in the only way left to her, and she didn't want anything or anyone to sway her from that course.

She fought off the drowning emotions, drawing one breath, then two. She'd long ago learned that they came from memories and overwhelming guilt—she'd also learned to control them by isolating herself.

Josh wouldn't let her do that.

He caressed her arm. Through her outer coat, her suit coat and her blouse, his touch was still disturbing. Amanda could detect the seductive strength in his hand, the leashed tenderness that had likely lured so many women.

Just as it lured her.

"Even this upsets you, doesn't it?"

The overhead garage light, which had come on when he activated the door remote, now flickered off. A blanket of inky darkness fell that was both a comfort for what it concealed, and a threat for what it unleashed. Her voice shook when she said, "I'd prefer you quit touching me, yes."

She held her breath waiting for his reaction to that statement, but all he said was, "Sit tight while I get the light."

He left his car door open as he went to the door leading into the house from the garage. Light spilled out of the car and across the concrete floor, showing a tidy display of tools. It also showed a heavy ax, hung against a pegboard. For one brief moment Amanda imagined Josh swinging that ax, ventilating a burning house before the heat and smoke overtook him. She gasped with the image, hurt and fearful.

The sudden bright light nearly blinded her. She glanced up to see that Josh had unlocked the door and reached inside for a wall switch. Now that she could see her way, Amanda opened her own door and climbed out. She took a single step and then Josh was there beside her—the consummate gentleman, the pushy contender, she wasn't sure which.

He reached into the car for the bucket of chicken and the bag of side dishes, then maintained his hold on her elbow as he led her inside.

They walked directly into an informal dining room. Josh plopped the food onto a thick cream-colored enamel table edged in shiny brass and surrounded by cream leather chairs. He reached for her coat and she had little choice but to slip it off. He put it over the back of a chair and while she removed her gloves, he shrugged out of his leather jacket.

All the while he watched her, leaving her unnerved and uncertain.

To escape his probing gaze, she looked around his home. The sparse dining room opened into a modern stainless steel kitchen and to the right of the kitchen was an archway leading into a living room. She could just see the edge of a beige leather couch with brass-and-glass end tables topped with colorful deco lamps. A short flight of carpeted stairs went up, likely to bedrooms, and a flight went down, maybe to a den.

He wasn't much for decorating, she noted. Most of the tabletops were barren; there were no photos or knickknacks about. Everything looked clean and utilitarian—perfect for a bachelor. She turned back to Josh with a smile. "Your home is lovely."

Hands on his hips, he asked, "So what's it to be? You wanna eat first and then talk, or talk first?"

"Eat."

The corner of his mouth quirked at her quick answer. "Is that decision inspired by cowardice or hunger?"

It was a little of both, but she said, "I'm just starving."

Josh smiled. "C'mon. You can help me grab a few things in the kitchen." He strode to the refrigerator, peered inside and asked, "What do you want to drink? Wine, cola, milk, juice…?"

"A cola would be great."

Still bent into the refrigerator, he glanced at her and said, "I suppose you want it in a glass over ice?"

"Well…yes."

He grinned and straightened, pulling out a couple of cans. "Plates are in that cabinet if you want to grab a couple. Tableware is in the drawer below it."

Josh snagged two glasses and held them under the refrigerator's icemaker. Over the sound of clinking ice cubes he asked, "So what do you do, Amanda? Besides chase firefighters around and organize this charity-type stuff, I mean."

Amanda had to go on tiptoe to reach the shelf of plates. In her home, she stored only the most seldom used items so high, but she supposed for a man of Josh's height, it wasn't an issue.

She began saying, "I'm a buyer for one of the mall's clothing stores—" when the telephone rang. She and Josh both looked toward the wall unit. Neither of them moved. "Aren't you going to answer it?"

He shook his head. "The machine will pick it up."

He no sooner said that than the answering machine beeped and a woman began to speak.

"Josh." A wealth of disappointment rang in that utterly feminine voice. *"I was really hoping you'd be home. I miss you, baby, and you know exactly what I mean. After last week, well, let's just say I'm anxious to try that again!"*

A giggle, ripe with suggestion, made Amanda blink.

"I need an encore, Josh, and I'm not taking no for an answer. So whatever time you get in, I don't care how late, give me a ring. I'll be here—waiting." The woman said goodbye with a string of kissing noises and then the phone disconnected.

Amanda, feeling almost like an eavesdropper, looked at Josh.

He said, "So you're a buyer? Does that mean you get to help pick out which fashions will be most popular?"

Astounded that he intended to ignore the call, Amanda said, "Well…um…" Her mind was still back there on that *"I need an encore."* What had he done to the woman?

"I can see you being a buyer," Josh continued. "You always look really put together, so it makes sense I guess. Let's go eat. I'm starved."

Like a zombie, Amanda walked back into the dining room. Josh took the plates from her hand, held out her seat for her, and then left the room saying, "I'll be right back."

She sat there trying to gather her wits, then shook her head to clear it. She didn't care about Josh Marshall's sexual exploits! The man was such a rogue, there was no telling what the woman referred to, but no doubt it would be shocking.

With that tantalizing thought, her heart thumped hard, making her catch her breath. What type of shocking things did he indulge in?

A few seconds later a thrumming musical beat began to filter into the room from ceiling speakers. Josh reappeared just as a male singer started crooning. "You like Tom Petty?"

Since her brain was muddled, still pondering that phone call and the intimated sexuality, and she almost never listened to music anyway, Amanda merely nodded.

"Great."

Josh sauntered back to the table and began loading both plates with corn on the cob, stiff mashed potatoes and biscuits. When he reached for the chicken, Amanda said, "A breast please."

Josh glanced up, winked, and pulled out two crispy fried chicken breasts. "See, we're already finding things we have in common."

Amanda opened a paper napkin into her lap. "You think so?" After that phone call, she had serious doubts. While she avoided sexual conduct, Josh apparently embraced it.

"Absolutely." He saluted her with his glass of cola before taking a long drink. "Drinks, music and we both love breasts."

Amanda choked—and then amazingly enough, she laughed. Josh was so outrageous, it was impossible not to be entertained by him. He said and did things she'd never before imagined, much less experienced.

At the sound of her hilarity, Josh looked very pleased with himself. He sat down across from her, propped his head on a fist, and smiled. "I like your laugh," he said in a low, rough timbre.

Amanda struggled to collect herself. These spontaneous losses of decorum were not acceptable. She just couldn't seem to help herself with him. "Thank you."

"It's sexy."

Knowing she blushed, Amanda rolled her eyes. "It is not."

"Yeah," he said, searching her eyes and disconcerting her, "it is."

Refusing to be flattered, she scoffed, then shook her fork at him. "A woman can't believe anything from a man on the make."

Josh looked startled for only a moment, then he threw back his head and roared with laughter. Trying not to smile with him, Amanda ducked her head and primly, precisely broke her biscuit in half.

That only made him laugh more.

His lack of propriety was contagious, she decided, making *her* say outrageous things now. She shook her head but inside, she felt more lighthearted than she had in years.

She watched him continue to chuckle, pausing to wipe his eyes every so often and then bursting into new fits of mirth. And he kept looking at her, his expression tender and hot and happy.

No one had ever looked at her with quite that combination of feelings. Seven years ago, she'd been too young to inspire any real or complicated depth of emotion from males.

Since then, she hadn't been interested.

Finally, he dropped back into his seat, his laughter having subsided into occasional snickers. He rested his

as retaliation for the way she'd pestered him about the calendar. Kissing her now would only be the first step in his campaign to have sex with her.

It would be pleasurable, she had no doubts on that, but still meaningless. Never could she let that happen.

She ducked away.

Josh caught her arm and pulled her back. "Okay, I won't kiss you. But don't run from me, all right?"

She looked pointedly at his hand on her upper arm. "I can hardly run with you restraining me." She raised an eyebrow, waiting.

He had the grace to look sheepish. His hand opened wide and he held his arms out to his sides. "Sorry."

Amanda stepped aside to pull on her gloves. Her heart still raced from his nearness, from the close call. *What if she had let him kiss her?* No!

"We're not ending the night like this."

That sounded so ominous, his tone disgruntled, that she whirled around to see him, half expecting him to pounce.

Josh cursed. "Damn it, I didn't mean… Don't look at me like that. I much prefer your laughter." He ran a hand through his hair, putting it on end. "I just don't want you going home upset. I want you to understand."

"Understand what? That you intend to…to…have your way with me, no matter what it takes and no matter what I think of it?"

His eyes glittered, one side of his mouth curled. A second later he chuckled. "Have my way with you?" He laughed again and when she scowled, he said, "Okay, okay, don't get all riled. Truth is, I want you to have your way with me. I promise not to resist too much."

"You're impossible."

"Not so." His smile epitomized masculine charm. "Hell, most women think I'm easy."

"And do they call here around the clock?" Amanda snapped her mouth shut. She wanted to choke herself, to bite off her unruly tongue, to somehow call the words back. She'd sounded petulant. She'd almost sounded...jealous. Damn.

Hoping to retreat, she held up her hands. "Never mind. I don't want to know."

"Oh, but I want to tell you." He wore a taunting smile, which perfectly matched his mussed hair and the sinful twinkle in his beautiful green eyes.

"Take me home, Josh."

"Spoilsport." His sigh was exaggerated and profound. "All right." He pulled on his leather jacket, but she saw his satisfaction. The jerk.

Once they were on the road, Josh reached for her hand. She didn't have time to evade him. He squeezed her gloved fingers and said, "Tell me you at least enjoyed part of the evening."

She shouldn't. If she gave anything away, anything at all, he'd use it against her.

"Come on, Amanda. Stop being a coward. Admit it."

"If I'm a coward then you're a bully."

"Just meet me halfway. A little admission, that's all I want. For now."

"All right, yes." She made a feeble attempt to retrieve her hand, but he didn't let go and she wasn't about to make an issue of it. "I enjoyed myself. It was a novelty."

"A novelty? You calling me odd?" He didn't sound particularly insulted.

"No, I meant going out with a man at all, eating fast food, listening to music and…laughing."

"It's been a long time since you dated?"

Thinking the truth would make him understand her resolve, she said, "Seven years."

He almost ran the car off the road. "Seven years!"

"By choice, Josh."

He fell silent for a long time. "You'd have liked the kiss, too," he eventually predicted, "if you hadn't run scared."

She believed him. There were times when she craved everything he now offered. But she'd learned the hard way that sexual frivolity could mean disaster. And she already had one disaster to make up for.

"It wasn't fear, Lieutenant. It was self-preservation. I have no intention of becoming another conquest for you."

"Those women who called?" He waited, but she refused to reply. She could hear the smile in his tone when he said, "I don't consider them conquests. That's dumb. They're just women looking for a little fun, and I'm glad to oblige them. It's a good arrangement."

"A good arrangement?" she repeated.

He shrugged. "Yeah. Casual dates, Amanda, nothing more."

She looked at him in amazement. "Casual dates do not do unspeakable things!"

His face twisted as he tried hard not to laugh, but he lost the battle. *"Unspeakable things?"* he guffawed. "Is that what you thought? Were you imagining some type of perversions in that active little mind of yours? What? Tell me, Amanda. Did you think I dragged out the fire hose?" He kept laughing—at her expense.

"Shut up, Josh."

He couldn't. But he did lift her hand to his mouth to treat her knuckles to a tickling, chuckling kiss. "You are so funny. Unspeakable things." He shook his head. When they pulled up to a red light, Josh shifted toward her. "I can promise you this, Amanda honey, when I get you into my bed, you'll not consider anything we do perverted or unspeakable." His tone dropped. "You'll just enjoy yourself."

"And then I'll start calling your house begging for your favors? Don't hold your breath." She should have stopped there, but she heard herself ask, "How many women do you see anyway? A baker's dozen?"

"As of right now, only one."

Her heart plummeted. "Someone special?" Not that it should matter to her. It didn't matter to her. Her association with Josh Marshall was based strictly on the calendar. Once the photo shoot was finished she wouldn't see him again.

He pulled up next to her Beetle, put the car in Park, then tugged her just a little bit closer. Looking at her mouth, he said, "Yeah, she's special." He touched her cheek, drifting his fingers down to her chin, to the sensitive skin of her throat. "And very soon, she's going to tell me all her secrets."

Chapter 3

It had been the slowest morning of his life. The minutes had ticked by, and after a night fraught with erotic dreams of Ms. Amanda Barker, Josh's temperament was on the surly side.

What was she hiding?

In between those smoldering dreams of naked bodies and wet mouths and soft moans, Josh had worried. He didn't like to worry, and generally didn't waste his time with it. But that was before he'd gotten involved with Amanda.

He'd already considered every unspeakable thing that could happen to a woman and every one of them made him madder than hell. Somehow she'd been hurt, and he hoped whoever had been to blame was still around so Josh could get a piece of him.

That is, if she ever fessed up.

Just the fact that he wanted to avenge her, that he wanted to protect her, was strange for him. As strange as the damn worrying.

Whenever he'd slept, she'd occupied his thoughts. When he woke, he could think of nothing but her fear, her reservation. *Seven long years.* Incredible.

In the darkest part of the morning, when the chill air had kept him beneath the blankets staring at the ceiling, Josh had contemplated what he'd do if Amanda never softened toward him. What if she continued to refuse him, if she wouldn't let him help, if she went on in her isolated, cold lifestyle?

What if he never even got to kiss her?

No, he wouldn't think that way. She had softened already, and he'd build on that. Last night she'd even been enjoying herself, until...

He made a sound of disgust. It had been unfortunate, those two calls coming in when they did. Amanda had relaxed enough to chat with him, to even tease him some. Then the women had called.

He was cursed with bad timing.

The restaurant was mostly empty when Josh arrived ten minutes early. He peeked in, but since he didn't see Amanda yet, he decided to wait for her by the door. The day was cool, but not overly so and the sun shone brightly. It was a day full of promise—and he intended to take advantage of it.

He was deep in sensual thoughts when a soft female hand tickled the back of his neck. Josh whirled—and came face-to-face with Vicki, one of the women who'd called the night before. He started to scowl, but then she laughed and threw herself against him.

"Josh! I fell asleep waiting for you to call me back last night! What did you do, stay out all night?"

Josh said, "No, I—"

She kissed him, her soft mouth opening on his with determination. Josh held her back. "Vicki," he chided, "slow down." Her full-steam-ahead enthusiasm, which had first attracted him to her, now seemed a problem.

She leaned into him, pushing her full breasts into his chest, looking at him through her lashes. With one finger stroking his chin, she whispered huskily, "Come over tonight."

"I can't."

"I'll make it worth your while." Her smile made a number of promises, all of them heated.

Josh grinned. He truly loved women and the way they flirted and teased. "Sorry, babe, no can do."

Now she pouted. And Vicki's pouts were enough to bring a man to his knees. Luckily, Josh had become recently immune, thanks to Amanda.

"But why not?"

"Because as of yesterday—" he started to explain, and was interrupted from behind with a strident, *"Excuse me."*

Wiping the cringe off his face at that recognizable voice, Josh looked over his shoulder and sure enough, Amanda stood directly behind him, primly dressed in a soft gray business suit and matching cape, her arms stiff at her sides, her mouth set.

Despite Vicki's still tenacious hold on him, Josh smiled in pleasure at seeing her. "Amanda."

Her big brown eyes snapped with fury.

He tried to tactfully ease Vicki aside, but she held

on like a limpet. "Well," Vicki said with a predatory smile, "this is awkward."

Amanda's gaze shifted to the other woman and she said, "Not at all. You're welcome to him."

To Josh's surprise, she didn't turn on her heel and leave. No, she shoved her way around him and went into the restaurant.

It took him a few seconds and then he started chuckling. She was jealous! And not just a little jealous, but outright furious with it.

It was more than he'd dared hope for. The night before, he'd suspected, but her performance today left no doubts. He looked at Vicki and gave her a quick hard smooch on the lips.

"She's jealous," he said, still grinning like the village idiot.

Vicki peered at him askance. "I was…um, under the impression you didn't like jealous women."

"Amanda is special," he told her by way of an explanation.

"She is?"

"Yes." And then gently, "That's what I was just about to tell you. I'm officially out of commission. No more dating."

Her jaw loosened. "You're kidding."

"Sorry, no." It was all Josh could do to keep from laughing. Oh, some men might run from the sudden idea of getting pulled from the dating scene, but not him. Hell, he'd spent all his life playing around. He'd enjoyed himself and he was pretty sure the women he'd been with would say the same. He had no regrets. But now… Amanda affected him differently. She was different.

He thought of Mick and Zack, how they'd gotten

involved recently. Mick had already married Delilah, and Zack and Wynonna had set a date. But before that, both men had fought the inevitable tooth and nail, to the point they'd almost messed things up.

Josh considered himself smarter than that. He'd been with enough women to know what he felt around Amanda was different and unique. As he'd told Vicki, special.

He wouldn't blow it. No way.

Vicki frowned at him, looking like someone had just goosed her. He gave her an apologetic shrug. "I'm sure you understand why you shouldn't call anymore, and why we can't be standing here in the walkway like this."

"No, actually I don't understand." She searched his face, then put the back of her hand to his forehead. "You're not acting like yourself, Josh. Are you okay?"

Josh set her aside. He almost rubbed his hands together, thinking of his plans. More to himself than Vicki, he said, "There's a good chance this might work out with Amanda. I don't want to blow it by fooling around. As you just witnessed, she doesn't like the idea of me with other women."

"And that matters to you? Her likes and dislikes?"

"Of course it does."

Josh decided he'd make a few calls that night, let the women he still saw know that he wasn't available anymore. He'd give Amanda all his considerable concentration. It'd have to be enough.

Having made up his mind, he nodded to Vicki. "I need to get inside. The longer she sits there, the more she'll stew and the longer she'll want to make me suffer."

Still wary of his sudden turnaround, Vicki said, "Well, okay. But if you change your mind…"

"I won't."

She shook her head. "Good luck then." She gave him another brief hug and left.

Good luck indeed, Josh thought, peeking into Marcos and seeing Amanda staring stonily toward him. Had she watched the whole exchange in the doorway, and seen that last farewell hug? Probably. She sat at a round table in the corner, and she didn't look happy.

Josh shoved his hands into his pockets and sauntered in. He almost whistled, but he thought that might be overdoing it. When he reached the table, Amanda snapped open her menu, using it to hide behind.

Josh dropped into his seat. She was so adorable. And so damn vulnerable. And *so* incredibly hot. "I hope you're hungry, because I'm ravenous."

She harrumphed.

"Yeah," he said, trying to gauge her mood, "about that woman I was with outside…"

"Not my business."

Her words were brisk and cold and, damn it, he couldn't help himself. He liked it that she was piqued. He sat back in his seat, crossed his arms over his chest, and said, "I told her I was unavailable now."

Amanda slapped the menu down. "You did *what?*"

"I told her I was—"

"I heard that," she snapped impatiently. "Why would you tell her such an idiotic thing?"

Josh slid his foot over next to hers. The long tablecloths on the round tables hid their legs, and gave him the opportunity to play footsies. He rubbed his ankle against hers. Amanda's eyes rounded and she jumped, making him smile.

He was willing to bet Amanda had never played footsies under the table.

He was willing to bet there was a lot she hadn't done, *and thinking that would definitely give him a boner,* so he brought his mind back to more important issues. "I told you I was only seeing one woman right now."

She denied that with a hard shake of her head. "Not me."

"Yeah, you."

"Josh, no." The pulse in her throat fluttered and her hands flattened on the tabletop. "Once the calendar is complete, there'll be no reason for me to see you again."

He didn't like the sound of that at all. "Unacceptable."

She drew back like a verbal prizefighter, ready to go for the knockout—and luckily the waiter stepped forward. "What can I get you folks to drink?"

Amanda sputtered. Josh slid in smoothly with, "Coffee for me. Amanda?"

Her teeth clinked together. She glared at the hapless waiter, then muttered, "Ice water."

"*Only* ice water?" Josh questioned.

Without looking at him, she said again to the hovering waiter, enunciating sharply, *"Ice—water."*

"Yes, ma'am. I'll get your drinks right away."

Josh chuckled. "You terrorized that poor boy."

"I did not."

"Look at him."

She glanced toward the kitchen area where the

waiter whispered to another while gesturing with his hands. Both young men glanced at her, then quickly dashed away, trying to look busy, when they saw they had her attention.

Amanda moaned. She propped her head up with her hands and said, "You're such a bad influence."

"Blaming me for your nasty temper?" He pretended a grave affront. "*Tsk, tsk*. Not fair, sweetheart. In case you haven't noticed, I'm in a cheerful mood."

Rather than comment on his mood, and why he was cheerful, she said, "I am *not* your sweetheart."

"Not yet anyway. But I'm working on it." It was a good thing they were in a public place, Josh thought. He had no doubt she'd just mentally bashed him real good.

"I never had a nasty temper before meeting up with you."

"I noticed." He said it kindly, with a measure of sympathy. "You kinda worked in one gear, didn't you? Bland."

"Controlled," she grumbled through her teeth. "Polite. Mannerly, considerate, respectful…"

Josh laughed. Riling her was so easy, he could hardly credit that he'd ever believed her prudish or bland. "Okay! I get the picture. So I bring out the beast in you, huh?"

"Unfortunately, yes." Her fingernails, today painted a rosy almost-red, tapped on the tabletop. "Actually, I thought about that last night."

"About me?" Now they were getting somewhere.

"This is not a reason to be hopeful, Josh. I thought about how horribly I'd behaved, how I'm going to have to work doubly hard to maintain an even keel around you."

The bottom dropped out of his stomach. She sounded so serious, so self-castigating. "I wish you wouldn't." And before she could go into another cold explanation, he added, "I thought about you a lot last night, too. About how nice it was to hear you laugh and see you being just a little bit devilish. Much nicer than when you're working so hard to be refined and unemotional."

"I have my reasons."

"I wish you'd share them with me."

"I doubt they'd make any difference to a man like you."

Now that was an insult he couldn't ignore. "A man like me, huh? Why don't you explain that."

A stony expression had entered her eyes. "I care about the calendar, about those less fortunate who'll benefit by the proceeds. I would think with you being a firefighter, you'd be especially empathetic also."

His face muscles felt too tight to allow him to speak, but he managed. "What makes you think I'm not? What gives you the right to judge me?"

A moment of uncertainly flashed over her features. "You wanted nothing to do with the calendar."

"I see. And your project is the only way to help? Money and time can't be donated directly? There aren't other projects going on?"

Just like that, she paled. Guilt, heavy and ugly, visibly weighed her down. "You do all those things?"

He'd said too much. God knew, he hadn't wanted to upset her, to bring on such a pained expression. He flattened his mouth in self-disgust, and reached for her hand.

In turn, she reached for a leather case by her seat and he was left grasping air. Josh retreated as she extracted a folder. In a small, apologetic voice, she said, "I brought the photos you requested."

"Amanda."

"You can look them over and see which ones you like."

He ignored the glossy eight-by-ten photographs. "You're right that my job makes me more sensitive to some issues, especially concerning burn victims."

Face averted, she rushed to say, "We don't need to talk about this."

"I've seen the reality of what a burn victim suffers, how his life is affected."

"Josh, please." She looked around the restaurant as if seeking help.

Josh frowned, and pressed her despite her upset. *He had to know.* "Why are you so concerned, baby? Explain it to me."

She exploded. Hands flat on the table, voice elevated enough to draw attention, she all but shouted, "I am *not* your baby! I will never be your damned baby!"

So much bottled emotion, so much she kept repressed. Josh tickled his fingertips up her wrist to her elbow. "I figure your jealousy is a good sign. At the very least I know you're not being honest when you say you're uninterested."

Her face frozen, she fanned out the pictures, slapping them into place one by one, and growled, "As you can see, the photos are done in bright, eye-catching colors with natural backdrops—"

"The way I see it, once you tell me what your hang-ups are, we can work on getting past them." *God, let him be able to get her past them.* He now had a few suspicions and consequently his stomach was in knots and it felt like his heart had cramped.

Gently, with loads of reassurance, he added, "I'm willing to be patient, by the way, if you need some time for that. It'll make me nuts, because I want you really bad, but I figure you're worth the wait."

One of the pictures tore in her hands. She stared at it, appalled. "Look what you made me do."

"You have other copies?"

She nodded. "Yes. And it's already been sent to the printer anyway. But…"

The waiter cautiously approached. "Um… I have your drinks and if you're ready to order…"

Josh scooped up the photos. Amanda looked a little numb and he soothed her by rubbing his thumb on the inside of her delicate wrist.

She jerked back. "I'll have the soup and a salad with lo-cal Italian dressing."

"Yes, ma'am." The waiter hastily scribbled down her order, anxious, no doubt, to escape once again. The tension at the table was thick enough to choke on. He looked at Josh.

"A burger, loaded, double order of fries, and a choc-olate malt." He eyed Amanda. "You sure you don't want something more than soup?"

She appeared too dazed to answer, so Josh closed the menus and said quietly to the waiter, "That'll be it."

The waiter escaped with alacrity.

Josh sought her small feet out again and enclosed

them in both of his, making sure she couldn't escape. Amanda looked up at him.

"It's okay you know."

"No." She shook her head and her eyes looked shiny with dazed confusion. "It's not okay."

"Why?" He reached for her hand and amazingly enough, she let him enfold her fingers in his own. She even gripped him tightly.

"You're making me muddled, Josh. I don't want to be muddled."

"Muddled is good. It means you're maybe just a little bit as affected by all this as me."

"All this?"

She looked skeptical again. "Sexual chemistry, instant attraction, whatever you want to call it."

Regaining some of her old self, she scoffed. "Do I really look that naïve, Josh, that stupid? Or have you forgotten you already told me what you want and why? A little retaliation, a little payback because I was too persistent in getting you involved with the calendar."

"That is what I wanted—at first."

"Oh, and now you've suddenly got more altruistic motives?"

"No, now I know you a little better and I've smelled you and laughed with you, and I want you. Just because you're sexy as hell and you turn me on and because in some strange skewed way, your laugh is almost more exciting than sex with other women."

Her face flamed. She almost choked, swallowed a large drink of her water, then said, "You *smelled* me?"

Covering his grin, Josh pressed his thumb to the racing pulse in her wrist and said, "The smell of your skin makes me hard. I want to get you naked and smell you all over, everywhere. I want to rub myself against you until our two scents mix."

She went mute.

Josh leaned across the table and lowered his voice to a barely-there whisper. "Do you know what you smell like, Amanda?"

She shook her head and stared at his mouth.

Damn, he thought, seeing her skin rosy with warmth, her eyes darkened. He wanted to kiss her, right here, right now.

He had a feeling she'd let him.

So what did he care if they were in a public place, if other patrons saw them? *He didn't.* They'd already seen them arguing, so now they'd just think they'd made up.

Besides, he ate at Marcos regularly with Mick and Zack. Most everyone there already knew him, so they'd understand.

Josh slowly moved closer to her, watching her lips part, seeing her tongue move behind her teeth, and…

"Hey, Josh." A hard thwack on his shoulder almost took him out of his chair.

Josh straightened with a wince. Mick and Zack stood there, smiling down at him.

"Go away."

Amanda gasped.

Josh shook his head at her. "Don't worry, they won't think I'm rude."

"Of course we will," Zack disagreed, and pulled a chair from another table to join them. "Hey, Ms. Barker. How are you doing?"

"Fine." Her voice squeaked and she cleared her throat. "How are you, Mr. Grange?"

Josh stared at one of his best friends. "You know Amanda?"

"Sure I do. We've spoken several times."

Amanda looked flushed. "I wanted Mr. Grange to pose for the calendar, too. I know he's a paramedic, but he does work for the fire department. With his excellent physique and good looks, he'd have been perfect."

Zack chuckled. "Don't you just love how she states all that without leering? Too bad it never worked out." He said that tongue in cheek, because Josh knew exactly how Zack would feel about posing in a beefcake photo. "I had all that overtime, remember?"

Josh remembered that he'd volunteered for a load of overtime just recently.

Mick, too, pulled up a chair, turning it around and sitting with his arms braced on the chair back. "Hi. I'm Mick Dawson, a friend of theirs, too."

She nodded. "Hello." She looked Mick over with professional interest. "Hmmm. I never saw you at the fire station. Are you a firefighter, a paramedic? Either way, we could have really used you on the calendar, too."

Josh rolled his eyes. "Amanda, please stop telling all my friends how sexy and gorgeous you think they are. It's embarrassing."

Zack snickered. "For you maybe."

Amanda, red-faced with embarrassment, threw her spoon at him. It bounced off his chest. Josh caught it, grinned and handed it back to her.

"I'm with the police," Mick interjected, regaining Amanda's notice before a war broke out. "Undercover."

Amanda looked awed at that information. "Undercover!"

Josh spread his arms wide. "Gee, why don't you guys join us?"

His sarcasm was completely ignored. "Thanks," Zack said, then asked, "What's with the pics?"

Amanda cleared her throat yet again, though she kept sneaking peeks at Mick. Josh was used to that. Mick was so dark, an air of mystery just clung to him, attracting women for miles. Amazingly, Mick had been mostly oblivious to them all—until Delilah invaded his life. Then he'd fallen hard.

While peering at Mick, Amanda's blush intensified, but now her expression was clear of any sexual interest. If anything, she looked more remote than ever. "The lieutenant has finally agreed to pose for the calendar," she explained to Zack, "but he wanted to see some of the various shots first."

Mick snatched them out of Josh's hand and flipped through them. After he looked at each picture, he handed it across the table to Zack. Together they "hmmed" and "hummed" to the point of real irritation.

"They're all ridiculous," Josh grumbled, feeling a little ill at ease. "Firemen do not work without shirts or helmets. That's just plain stupid. Why aren't any of them in real uniform? Where's the turn-out gear? The steel-toed boots?"

Amanda made an impatient sound. "We wanted them to look sexy."

"Yeah, well no one cares how sexy they look when they're putting out a damn fire. There's no helmets, no Nomex hoods, and not a single S.C.B.A."

Zack shrugged. "The calendar isn't meant as a career description. It's just for fun."

"Fun? Did you see this one? The guy has his bunker

coat on, but it's hanging open to show off his *shaved* chest." Josh grunted in disgust. "Wouldn't do him a damn lot of good that way would it?"

Zack turned to Amanda and excused Josh's surly mood by saying, "Being the lieutenant and all, he has to take his responsibility to the crew pretty serious."

"You know," Mick interjected, putting the remaining photos aside, "I've seen Josh at a fire when he's pulled on his bunker gear right over his underwear." In a lower, confiding voice, he added, "You know—*no* uniform."

"Yeah," Zack said, nodding. "He does do that a lot. And after he finishes with the call, he has a habit of jerking off his jacket and strutting around all dirty and bare-chested with his suspenders loose enough that you think his pants are going to fall right off." Zack leaned toward Amanda, who leaned away. "Josh has a hairy chest, not like the Romeo in the photo. I think he likes showing it off."

"I do not strut," Josh said. Since Amanda had already seen him in the locker room wearing nothing more than a towel, she was intimately aware of his hairy chest so he didn't comment on that. "And I take off my jacket when the job is done because it's usually hotter than Hades and we're roasting in our own sweat."

"The civilian females are always whispering about him. They—*ouch!*" Mick reached beneath the table to rub his ankle. "Damn it, that hurt."

Josh thought about kicking him again. "Shut the hell up, will you?"

"Why?" Zack asked. "She already knows your reputation. Any woman who's been around you ten minutes sees how it is, and she's been around you longer than that."

Almost on cue, three women at another table laughed conspicuously and when Josh looked up, he saw they were staring at him. One even gave a flirtatious, three-finger wave.

Amanda shoved back her chair and threw her napkin on the table. "I think I need to visit the ladies' room."

Josh, Mick and Zack all lurched to their feet with gentlemanly haste.

"You *think?*" Josh asked, seeing that she once again looked jealous. It gave him hope, that very human emotion meant she cared. "You don't know for sure?"

"Oh…be quiet." Spine military straight, she marched away, and the men reseated themselves.

Mick and Zack peered questioningly at Josh, who just grinned. "She'll be back," he said, "after she composes herself."

Mick whistled low. "Wow. She looked ready to bite your face off."

Zack said, "I've never seen her in a temper. Whenever she's been around the station, she's always been so…" He searched for a word and finally settled on, "Cool."

Josh shook his head. "That's just a front."

"It is?"

"Yeah. She's actually a very warm woman. And she doesn't like other women flirting with me."

"Is that what set her off?" Zack lifted a mocking brow. "Because I thought maybe it was the way you harangued her about the calendar. After all, it's her pet project, and you, my friend, just ran it into the ground."

Josh froze. His stomach cramped, even his brain

cramped. For a man who professed to know women, he'd blown that one. He wanted to kick himself in the backside. *"Shit."*

Mick snickered.

As soon as Amanda presented herself again, he'd make it up to her. He'd explain why he was sensitive on the subject, and maybe, just maybe, she'd confide a little about her own sensitivities.

He saw Zack nudge Mick in shared amusement, and he asked, "What are you two doing here anyway?"

Zack held out his hands in a placating gesture. "We came for lunch. We haven't gotten together in a month."

Mick shook his head. "Hard to believe we used to manage a regular get-together, what? At least once a week, right?"

"We were pathetic," Zack agreed.

Because Zack and Mick had seldom dated, they'd had plenty of time to meet at Marcos. Mick was a natural loner who trusted very few people, and Zack had a four-year-old daughter who normally took up all his time. Until they'd met the right women, they'd made meeting at Marcos for lunch a highlight of the week.

Josh, as a once confirmed free-wheeling lady's man, hadn't been bothered with any commitments other than ones he arranged himself, so he'd been able to adjust his schedule around theirs. Being with his buddies had been important to him—then.

Now he wished they'd disappear.

"What's Delilah doing?"

Mick rolled his eyes. "She's interviewing a bunch of prostitutes down on State Street."

"What?" As a writer, Delilah Piper-Dawson engaged in a lot of strange research, but usually Mick

was at her side, protecting her whether she needed protection or not. At one point in time, Josh had entertained a secret infatuation for her. She was the type of woman who told it straight and charmed a man in the process. But then Mick had fallen in love with her, and she adored Mick from first sight, so Josh had forced himself to think of her only in platonic terms.

"It's all right," Zack assured him. "Wynn went with her and besides, the women are reformed prostitutes Mick busted months ago. They're nice ladies—with a wealth of information to share."

At nearly six feet tall with strength far surpassing that of most females, Wynn Lane could serve as protection, Josh supposed. But she was still a woman, still very female in the most important ways—ways he sure as hell couldn't help but notice.

He thought his two friends about as lucky as men could get. "One of you asses should have gone along."

"They wouldn't let us," Zack replied.

Mick nodded in agreement. "They said the women wouldn't be as open with us around."

Josh shook his head in pity. "You're both whipped."

Zack slapped a hand to his heart and sighed. "Happily so, yeah."

Envy gripped him. Josh wanted to be that happy, damn it, and he wanted Amanda. After meeting Delilah and Wynn, he'd thought he wanted a woman like them—tall with mile-long legs, outgoing, ballsy and honest to a fault.

Instead, he'd gotten thrown for a loop by a tiny, prissed-up woman with well-hidden secrets and a definite lack of attraction for sex.

What the hell was taking her so long?

Here he was, worrying again, and that was enough to make any man crazed. He heard himself mutter, "She doesn't want anything to do with me."

Mick and Zack shared a look. "Who?"

"Of all the stupid questions! *Amanda.*" They looked as incredulous as he often felt, so Josh nodded. "It's true. I've had to coerce every single second out of her. If it wasn't for her damned project, she wouldn't be here with me now."

"She's not attracted to you?" Zack asked, forcing Josh to admit the awful truth again.

"No. And I don't like it."

"No man would."

At that moment, Amanda came rushing back to the table. Her animosity had been replaced with excitement. "I just got a call!" She waved her cell phone at Josh. "The photographer had a cancellation. We can do the shoot today."

Josh was so stunned he forgot to stand. "Today?"

Mick held her chair out for her, and Zack took her arm as he seated her.

Josh thought about clouting them both.

"Yes. At six." She dropped back in her seat, all smiles again. "That'll give me enough time to finish up at work, and you'll be able to go to the station to pick up your gear."

Still feeling slow, Josh asked, "My gear?"

"Of course. For ambiance. You and I can meet at the park at five-thirty, by the nature trails. That way we can get set up before the photographer arrives."

She seemed to have everything all figured out and simply assumed he'd go along with her. As if he didn't have a life, as if he were at her beck and call.

Which, at the moment, he was.

Disturbed by that reality, Josh almost lied and said he had other plans. But one look at the excitement on her face, and he knew he couldn't disappoint her.

"I have the perfect image in mind," she told him.

Josh looked at Mick and then at Zack. They both shrugged, unable to offer any help.

"The perfect image?" he asked.

She nodded. "I know exactly what I want."

Josh closed his eyes. He knew what she wanted, too, and it wasn't him, damn it. But he liked seeing her smile too much to *not* do it. And this way he'd get to spend more of the day with her.

He opened his eyes, accepting his fate and not all that displeased with it. He grinned. "All right. I'll do it."

"Thank you."

"There's a small catch."

Chapter 4

Amanda crossed her arms and stared stonily out the windshield. What kind of stupid "catch" was this? "I don't know why we couldn't bring both cars."

"Because if I'm going to do this," he explained, not the least bothered by her mood, "I at least want to get to spend time with you."

She wouldn't explain to him again. Sooner or later he'd give up. Intimacy was not in her future, whether she wished it or not. That part of her had been permanently frozen seven years ago, thanks to stupid mistakes and irresponsibility.

She said, "I like your friends."

"Mick and Zack?"

"Yes." She twisted toward him. "Tell me about their wives."

"Mick is the only one married so far. Zack has to

work around his daughter and Wynn's nutty family." He glanced at her and smiled. "No easy feat that. If you ever met her family, you'd understand."

"He doesn't get along with them?"

"Sure he does. Everyone likes Zack. He's so easygoing and all. Well, he wasn't always easygoing around Wynn. In fact, she kicked his ass a few times."

Amanda said, "Right."

"No, she did. Wynn is a lot of woman." He wore a secret little sexy smile as he said that. "Almost six feet tall—with the longest most incredible legs you'll ever see. She's strong, and outgoing and athletic."

Admiration dripped from his tone, making Amanda want to grind her teeth.

"Zack got thrown to his back more than once. 'Course, letting a woman get you on your back isn't always a bad thing." He bobbed his eyebrows suggestively. "I personally think Zack knew exactly what he was doing all along."

Amanda couldn't conceive of a woman wrestling with a man. It seemed much too farfetched, like something out of a sideshow. "You sound very taken with her."

"Wynn? Yeah, sure. She's great. I suppose if Zack hadn't involved himself, I might have asked her out."

Amanda stiffened; he hadn't even bothered to deny it! "Does Zack know how you feel?"

"How I *felt,* and sure he did. I rubbed it in every chance I could, just to keep him on his toes." He smiled at her. "A little competition is good for a guy. Besides, Wynn never gave me a second look, except when she wanted to ask me questions about Zack."

Amanda didn't want to hear any more about the

amazing amazon who Josh respected and liked so much. "What about Mr. Dawson? You said he's married."

"To Delilah Piper. You ever heard of her?"

She shook her head. "Should I have?"

"She's a popular mystery writer. A real sweetheart with a twisted imagination, which I guess comes in handy when she's writing those awesome stories." He shuddered. "The stuff she does in the name of research is enough to make a man crazed."

Locking her teeth, Amanda ground out, "You sound rather partial to her, too."

"Yeah." He said that so softly, she wanted to thwack him. "I fancied myself in love with her for a while. But again, she set her sights on Mick and that was all she wrote."

"Do you make a habit of trying to seduce your friends' girlfriends?"

"Nope."

He didn't elaborate. Amanda stewed for a few minutes in silence until she realized why she was stewing. God, it was ridiculous for her to even entertain such ideas of envy. She'd learned the hard way that anything beyond casual acquaintance with a man was impossible.

Josh pulled into the entrance for the park and slowed the car. As he maneuvered the winding roads toward the walking trails, he reached for Amanda's hand.

"I used to think I wanted a woman like them. Just goes to show we never really know our own minds."

Amanda felt her heart flutter and called herself a fool. "What do you mean?"

He pulled up to a gravel lot and parked the car. Turning toward her, he said, "These days, there's only one woman plaguing my thoughts. And she's nothing like Wynn or Del."

Amanda drew her own comparisons. They sounded like wonderful women who led exciting, normal lives. They sounded like women who relished their sexuality and gave with all their hearts.

Her heart was encased in a layer of guilt, crushed under the burden of reparation.

She drew an unsteady breath. "Let's try to get set up before Jerry arrives."

"Jerry is the photographer?"

"Yes." Josh had picked her up at her home and together they'd gone to the station. One thing she'd insisted he bring along was his ax. He'd mumbled and grumbled and done as she asked.

She hadn't been quite so accommodating.

When he picked her up, he'd wanted to get out and look at her house, but she'd been waiting at the end of the long drive and hadn't invited him any farther. Because the trees on the property were thick, even when barren of leaves, and the driveway winding, he hadn't really seen anything at all. Her unusual little whimsical home was nobody's business but her own.

"Don't forget the ax," she reminded him when he left it behind on the floor of the back seat. He rasped something she couldn't hear, and she smiled. "Here, I'll take your pants. You can leave your bunker jacket and helmet behind for now." No way would she cover up his gorgeous face or magnificent body any more than absolutely necessary. "Bring your boots, though."

She walked away, not waiting to hear Josh's reaction to her directions. She peered up at the beautiful blue sky and hoped Jerry got there on time because the sun would soon be fading.

She found a spot on the ground with no grass and bent down, careful not to soil her suit. Josh reached her just as she finished rubbing the front and back and especially the knees of his once clean pants into the dirt.

He didn't ask, so she turned to look up at him and said, "They were too clean. We want you to look like you've been working."

"Firemen don't roll around in the dirt."

She hid a smile; he could be so prickly at times. "Believe me, I know exactly what it is firemen do."

Speculation darkened his green eyes. "Had firsthand experience have you?"

Rather than meet his gaze or answer his question, she stood and shook out the pants. They now looked well worn. "Here, put these on."

Allowing her the evasion, Josh looked around. There weren't many people in the park this time of year, certainly not so far back near the trails. He asked with sinful suggestiveness, "Over my jeans, or not?"

She knew he wanted her to gasp and blush, but she'd already made up her mind about the shot, so she said simply, "Not."

He cocked out his hip, bunched the heavy pants in one fist, and glared at her. "You want me to skin out my jeans right here?"

"There's no one watching. If you're shy, then you can step behind that large tree. But hurry. I want you ready when Jerry arrives." No way did she want to try to organize another session with Josh. More than anything, she needed to get away from him. He tempted her, when she knew from experience there was no point.

He didn't go behind a tree. No, not Josh Marshall. He stared her in the eye while he kicked off his shoes and unhooked his belt.

Now she blushed.

"No, don't run off," he taunted. "I'll need you to hold my jeans. That is, if you can refrain from grinding them into the dirt."

Amanda assumed a casual pose. "Fine. But hurry it up." She'd already seen him, she reminded herself. The shock of that first viewing still haunted her at night—so what was a little more haunting for such a worthy cause?

He shoved his jeans down to his ankles and stepped out of them. Luckily, the shirttails of his flannel covered everything of interest.

It had been dry lately, leaving the hard ground cold but thankfully not wet. His socks would have been soaked otherwise.

A car pulled into the lot. They both turned, but to Amanda's dismay, it wasn't Jerry.

Mick and Zack stepped out, identical expressions of hilarity on their faces when they spied Josh in his underwear. They laughed while trying to keep two women stuck in the car.

Amanda watched as one slender, almost fragile woman with incredible dark hair slipped out to stand beside Mick. She wore sloppy jeans, an unbuttoned corduroy coat over an enormous sweater, and a fat smile. She took one look at Josh and gave a loud appreciative wolf whistle—destroying the image of frail femininity.

On the driver's side of the car, Zack got shoved aside

and a veritable giant of a woman emerged. She wore gray sweats, no coat and had the fuzziest hair Amanda had ever seen. Raising her long arms into the air, she applauded, then yelled, "Hey, don't let us stop you, Josh! Keep going."

Josh laughed. "This is all I'm taking off, you lecher."

Amanda felt as if she'd faded into the background. An easy camaraderie existed between the five people, a nearly palpable friendship that excluded her. She crossed her arms under her breasts and tried not to feel resentful.

These people deserved happiness. Unlike her, these people hadn't committed any terrible transgressions.

Still without pants, Josh nearly felled her when he threw his muscled arm around her shoulders and urged her forward. "Wynn, Del, I want you to meet Amanda Barker. She's doing this crazy benefit calendar and I'm her newest victim."

The word *victim* echoed through Amanda's head with painful clarity. From somewhere deep inside, she dredged up a polite smile and met the two paragons who had nearly stolen Josh's heart. "Hello."

Del stepped forward and embraced her. "Hey, I'm Del, Mick's wife and a friend of Josh. Sorry if we're intruding, but Wynn and I finished our business and had the rest of the day free and Josh and Mick insisted on coming here to stick their noses in, so naturally we had to tag along, too."

She'd said all that without taking a breath and Amanda's brain whirled. "No, that is, I don't mind as long as Josh doesn't care."

Zack cuddled his big wife into his side. "Doesn't matter if he cares, we don't pay him any mind anyway."

With a beautiful smile, Wynn reached out her hand. "I'm Wynn, Zack's soon-to-be wife if we can ever get everything arranged."

"Where's Dani?" Josh asked.

Wynn said, "With my mother. They're doing some tie-dye. She'll have Dani looking like a hippie in no time."

Zack just laughed and explained, "Dani is my daughter, four years old going on forty. It took her all of about five minutes to get Wynn and her entire family wrapped around her little finger."

"And when he says little, he means little," Wynn added. "Dani is a tiny little thing. I feel like a giant around her."

Amanda wondered that the woman ever *didn't* feel like a giant. Not that her height mattered, because she was lovely even with that awful hair that kept dancing in the wind like dandelion fluff. The loose sweats couldn't quite hide all her curves—Wynn had a body like a model.

Amanda caught herself standing there stupidly with everyone looking at her, and she said, "Oh, I was just telling Josh how we'd do the shoot." She turned and shoved the soiled pants at him. "Here, you can put these on now." The man had absolutely no shame, lounging around without pants.

Grinning, Mick said, "It is kinda cool today to be out here in your drawers."

While Josh pulled on the pants, Amanda fetched his boots. She hated awkward silences and explained, "His is the last picture we need and we'll use it for the cover and other promo, too. I want a candid shot of him without a shirt, holding his ax, maybe with a small smile."

Wynn said, "Josh does have a very nice smile."

Josh blew a kiss toward her, then grunted when Amanda shoved the boots at his midsection, making him scramble to grab them. He looked at her and laughed—the jerk.

Realizing what she'd done, Amanda peered up at the women and caught them watching her with gleeful expectation, curiosity and consideration.

Thank God, Jerry arrived.

Amanda rushed to greet him and help him with his equipment while Josh donned the steel-toed boots. Normally, she knew, the boots were already in place at the bottom of the pants. The firefighters stepped into their pants and boots at the same time, making it easier and quicker to dress.

There was nothing "normal" about this particular day. "I'm so glad you're here, Jerry. I know you're not late or anything, but I was afraid we'd lose the light. And Josh is antsy. I don't know how much longer we have before he storms away. He's not always the most agreeable man about this stuff. Not at all like the other firefighters we've been working with."

Amanda realized she was babbling and snapped her mouth shut.

Jerry gave her a long look. "No worries. I take a lot of outdoor pictures in less light than this. Like most photographers—" he bobbed his bushy brows "—I have special cameras and lenses with me. It'll be fine."

She tried to busy herself by pulling a leather bag out of Jerry's car and he said, "Hey, hey, easy with that, okay? Just let me get it."

Flustered, Amanda moved out of his way.

Jerry was a large man, thick through the middle

with a drooping mustache and balding head. Though he seldom rushed, he always looked flushed with exertion. Even now, he wore only a pullover without a jacket yet he appeared overheated.

Laden with equipment, Jerry turned and surveyed the collection of people. He frowned. "So who's our model today?"

They all pointed at Josh.

Jerry huffed and lumbered across the lawn. "Off with the shirt then." He dug into a bag and pulled out a small can of something. "For the photo, Ms. Barker wants it to appear as if you've just been on the job. Very macho stuff, you know."

Josh's jaw tightened, but he did tug off his shirt and threw it toward Mick, who caught it handily. He stood there in only the pants and boots. His suspenders hung at his side, and the waistband to the bunker pants was loose, curling outward to show his navel and a downy trail of hair on his abdomen.

Amanda forced her gaze upward, to safer, but no less tempting ground.

Gooseflesh had already arisen on his arms. The air had a definite nip, but Amanda assured herself it would only take a few minutes to get the picture. Josh was a big man layered in muscle. He'd be fine.

"I've got some blackening here," Jerry announced. "We'll rub it all around on you, your chest, arms, neck, maybe even your gut, dirty you up a bit so you match those scruffy pants and then I'll spray you with baby oil to simulate sweat, and voilà, a hard workin' man."

Jerry carefully set all his equipment on a nearby picnic table then opened the jar. He started toward Josh and Josh said, "No damn way."

Jerry wavered. He looked at Amanda, one bushy brow elevated.

Amanda looked at Josh. He stood braced as if for combat, jaw jutting slightly forward, eyes narrowed, his arms loose but fisted at his sides, his feet braced apart, his stomach tight.

She stomped forward. Her high heels sank into the ground with the ferocity of her pique. "Josh," she hissed close to him, "you agreed."

Green eyes glittering, he said, "I never once agreed to have some guy smear black stuff on me."

"Only a little," Jerry explained, oblivious to the static tension in the air. "It won't take much."

Josh shook his head. "Hell no."

"I need you to look like you've been working," Amanda insisted.

He glared at Jerry while replying to her. "I've never in my life had a guy rub me down and I'll be damned if I'm going to start now."

Mick choked and Zack guffawed. Even Wynn and Delilah began chuckling.

Amanda wanted to shout at them all; their hilarity didn't help the situation. Despite Jerry's assurances, she wanted to make use of the remaining light. She could just picture Josh with a halo of crimson sunshine behind him.

She wanted everyone else to see him as she saw him.

She was in far too deep and she knew it.

"Fine," she said, refusing to dwell on her growing admiration for Josh. "You can rub it on yourself."

He gave one hard shake of his head. "No way. I don't want my hands in that goo."

Wynn shouted, "Oh for pity's sake, *I'll* do it." She

started forward, her long legs eating up the distance in record time.

Amanda whirled on her just as Zack snagged her by the seat of her pants. *"No,"* Amanda said.

"No," Zack said.

It was a contest who frowned more, Zack or Amanda. Left with few choices, Amanda snatched the jar from Jerry's hand and stuck her fingers into the greasy goo. No way would she let one of the paragons touch Josh's naked flesh, not now, not right here in front of her. The slick inky gunk went between her fingers and beneath her manicured nails. She wrinkled her nose in distaste.

Then she looked at Josh's magnificent chest.

"Hold still," she grumbled at him, seeing that he now looked triumphant.

"I won't move a muscle," Josh promised, and then he held his arms out to the sides, his muscles going all rigid and tight as he waited for her touch.

With a fortifying deep breath that did her no good at all, Amanda smoothed in the first dark smear, right across his pectoral muscle. Despite the late October weather and the lateness of the day, he felt warm. And hard. And…sexy.

God, she hadn't learned a thing. Every moral reparation that she'd fought to gain over the past seven years had been obliterated by Josh Marshall. Now what was she supposed to do?

Josh watched Amanda, knowing he'd end up aroused but not giving a damn. She looked adorable. With fierce concentration, she watched the movements of her hand on his body as she smeared the blackening here and there. It wouldn't take much imagination on his part to visualize her making love with that same degree of intense focus.

He shivered.

Amanda glanced up and in a low, slightly raspy voice, she asked, "Are you cold?"

He answered in kind, every bit as affected as she. "You're touching me, sweetheart. I'm getting hotter by the second."

Her lips parted.

Jerry said, "Put a little on his abdomen, around all those macho muscles. Highlight 'em a bit."

Amanda looked down at Josh's stomach and hesitated.

"Go ahead," Josh encouraged her, wanting her hands on him even if they had a damned attentive audience. Mick and Zack would give him hell the rest of the month, but he could live with it.

She swallowed, and dipped her delicate hand back into the can. Her fingers and the goo felt cool against his heated skin. Hoping she wouldn't notice too much, Josh put his hands on her shoulders in the guise of steadying her. Their foreheads almost touched as they both watched the progress of her fingers caressing him.

Jerry made an impatient sound. "Hey, you two. If we're not going to take pictures after all, then at least go get a room."

Mick and Zack howled with laughter—until the paragons hushed them into reserved chuckles.

Amanda sprang back, appalled, mortified and without thinking. She wiped her hands clean on the skirt of her suit. Josh thought about breaking Jerry in half, but then Amanda wouldn't get her damn photo.

He caught her wrist and pulled her closer. "Ignore them."

"I'm... I'm done anyway." She tugged her wrist free and began tidying her hair, making sure no strands had escaped the elegant twist.

Used to be, Josh hated to see her fussing around. Wynn and Del seldom did the feminine fretting that seemed so much a part of Amanda.

But now that he understood Amanda better, he knew that she used the busy little movements to collect herself. His heart wrenched, seeing her look so lost, so alone.

Jerry appeared with a spray bottle and began misting him all over.

"Damn! *That's cold.*"

Jerry paid him no mind. "Almost done," he said, and then, "Close your eyes." He gave Josh just enough time to comply before spraying the oil right in his face.

"There. You're dirty, sweaty, everything a *real man* should be."

The irony in Jerry's tone couldn't be missed, and Josh shared his sentiments on that one.

Amanda protested. "It's not about being a real man. I just want the illusion that he's been hard at work. I want to capture the..." she cast about for a word, and settled on, "*drama* of fighting a fire."

This time Josh didn't take exception. He had a few troubling ideas about Amanda's preoccupation with the benefit calendar and her reluctance to get involved sexually. He hoped like hell he was wrong, and tonight he intended to find out. Whether his suspicions proved true or not, he still wanted her. More so every damn day.

But until then, he would treat her with kid gloves. "Let's get this over with," he said.

Amanda rushed to hand him his heavy ax. "Prop this on your shoulder, and lean on the tree."

"Prop it... What? Like Paul Bunyon?" he teased.

"No, like Josh Marshall, firefighter extraordinaire."

He shook his head, but inside he was pleased with her description. He sauntered to the tree, propped the ax handle on his shoulder and lifted his brows. "Good enough?"

"No." She rushed up close to him again. "You need a sexy smile."

Everyone else stood a respectable distance away—Jerry adjusting his camera, Josh's friends huddled together by the car chuckling. Josh felt safe in touching her chin and saying, "I don't have anything to smile about right now."

"Bull. Your mind is probably crowded with thoughts of...physical things."

"My mind is crowded with thoughts of you."

She huffed. "Must you always be so difficult?"

"Yeah, because you're difficult." She drew up and he said quickly, "You know what would make me smile?"

"I'm afraid to ask."

Taking her by surprise, he leaned down and kissed her forehead. "Don't ever be afraid with me, okay?"

"I didn't mean... Okay, what? What does it take to make you smile?"

"Promise me a kiss."

Her eyes narrowed and her brows beetled. "You just took a kiss."

"Uh-uh. A real kiss. On the lips. Mouth open, a little tongue play..."

She started to turn away. Josh waited. She took half a step, crossed her arms around her middle, then propped her fists on her hips, then rubbed her temples. Such a telling reaction to such a small request!

Whirling back around to face him, Amanda asked in a low hiss, "Just what is it you hope to accomplish? I've told you I don't want to be involved."

"Even to a teenager," he explained gently, "one kiss doesn't equal involvement."

"But if I kiss you once…" Her voice tapered off like a fading echo.

"What?" Damn he wanted to touch her. He wished like hell that they were already alone. "You might want to kiss me again?"

Sounding tortured, she said, "Yes."

It felt like his knees got knocked out from under him. "Ah, babe…"

Jerry yelled, "Ready when you two are."

Josh touched the small gold hoop in her left ear. "Promise me, Amanda. Give me something sexy to think about, a reason to smile."

She closed her eyes, swallowed hard. "Okay."

The sexy little smile came of its own accord. So did the boner, but damn, he'd never in his life anticipated a kiss quite so much.

Luckily, the bunker pants were, by necessity, thick and insulated. It'd take an impressive man indeed to tent them.

Amanda looked at him, her eyes widened, and she quickly backed up. "There, Jerry! Take that shot."

Josh continued to watch her, their gazes locked and his imagination in overdrive, while Amanda backed away and Jerry's camera clicked enthusiastically.

Amanda blushed, her brown eyes darkened, her lips parted. Josh took it all in, all the signs of beginning arousal, and wanted to groan. He knew his own face was flushed and his eyes hot, but it was so much like foreplay, sharing thoughts with her this way.

Amanda kept backing up until she was eventually pressed to a wide bare tree trunk. Her arms were crossed over her middle and her chest rose and fell with her breaths. Josh thought about taking her right there in the woods, with the cool air around them, his hands protecting her soft bottom from the rough bark, lifting her, grinding her forward…

But Amanda, with her prissy suits and polished appearance, likely wouldn't appreciate a romp in the dirt.

He'd have to be patient—not his strong suit.

"All done," Jerry called out. "I think I got some good ones. I don't know what you said to him, Ms. Barker, but…"

"Nothing! I didn't say anything to him!"

"Then he's one hell of an actor." Jerry, not one for small talk, saluted them both and headed back to his car.

Josh called out, "When will the prints be ready?"

"It's a rush job," Jerry answered. "I can pull them up on the computer tonight. Amanda can have the disk to look over tomorrow morning. Once she chooses which shots she wants I can have 'em ready in a day."

Amanda, still looking tongue-tied, pushed herself away from the tree and rushed after Jerry. Josh approached Mick and Zack.

Without preamble, he said to both men, "Take off, will you?"

Mick grinned. "You got plans?"

Del elbowed her husband. "Of course he does. Did you see the way they were looking at each other?"

Zack edged in. "What happened with that business of her not wanting you?"

Wynn pretended to reel. "My God! You mean there's a woman who doesn't want Josh?" She shook her head, making her frizzy hair bounce. "No. I refuse to believe it. All my illusions will be destroyed."

Zack pinched her behind, and she jumped.

Laughing under his breath, Josh said, "Yeah, a few actually." He gave Wynn and Del pointed looks, because they had indeed made their sincere disinterest well known. Then he explained, "I don't know what's going on, but I hope to find out. Only I can't find out a thing with the curious quartet hanging around, watching my every move."

Zack leaned around his wife to see Mick. "Does he mean us?"

Mick nodded slowly. "I think he might."

Del swatted her husband, then went on tiptoe to kiss Josh's cheek. "We'll drag them away. And good luck."

"Careful," Zack told his wife when she went to kiss Josh, too. "You'll get all greasy."

Wynn was tall enough that she could reach Josh's cheek without bracing on him anywhere. "You'll win her over with your charm," she assured him, all kidding put aside.

Josh remembered a day when Wynn hadn't noticed his charm, but evidently she considered her resistance superior to that of most women.

Half a second later Amanda was at his side, scowling, furious maybe. Her normally arched brows were lowered in a dark frown and her mouth looked pinched. "What's going on here? Why is everyone kissing you?"

"Just saying goodbye," Mick told her, and he and Del turned to get in the car.

Zack said, "I hope you got some good shots, Ms. Barker. Thanks for letting us observe." And he and Wynn also got into the car.

Amanda just stood there, looking self-conscious and bemused. Together they watched the car back out and drive away, Jerry following close behind them.

Josh looked down at her, and said softly, "Alone at last."

She blinked several times, her nervousness so apparent that Josh wanted to just lift her and hold her and rock her in his arms. Instead, he caught her chin on the edge of his hand.

His heart thundered, surprising him with his over-the-top response. Amanda breathed hard, her hands fluttered, then settled on the waistband of the heavy pants, just over where his suspenders connected in the front.

He leaned down, touched his mouth to hers, heard her soft moan, and like a virgin on prom night, he lost it.

Chapter 5

Amanda's hands slid over Josh's oiled shoulders, up to his neck where she caught him and held on tight. Josh forgot about her nice gray suit and matching cape, about her styled hair and her reservations.

All his senses were focused on the fact of her kissing him, her taste, her indescribable scent, the feeling of rightness having her small body inching closer and closer to his own.

He tunneled his fingers through her hair, dislodging pins and clips to cradle her skull, to keep her mouth under his so he could continue to kiss her. Her mouth was hot and sweet and her tongue shyly touched his own.

Her breasts, discreetly covered by bra and blouse, suit and cape, brushed his abdomen with the impact of a thunderclap. Josh tilted his pelvis into her, lifted her to her toes, crushed her close.

She was such a petite woman, all softness and sweetness and femininity. She took his breath away with the need to devour her, the urge to protect her.

She bit his bottom lip and her nails sank into his shoulders. Slowly, in small degrees, Josh lifted his mouth. "Baby, you burn me up."

Her beautiful brown eyes, heavy and unfocused, stared at his mouth. She licked the corner of her lips and whispered, *"Yes."*

Josh groaned and kissed her again. He didn't know how long it had been for her, but he felt like he hadn't had sex in years and now he was at the boiling point. Even through the damn bunker pants, he was aware of Amanda's pelvis pressing into his swollen erection with blatant, yet probably unconscious, invitation.

Her cape was soft—and easily removed. Amanda didn't even seem to notice when it fluttered to the ground to land around their feet in a soft gray heap of material.

He slid his hand down her back, over her curvy hip to the bottom of her sweet cheek. He groaned low in his throat—damn, but she had a nice ass, firm and round.

He hadn't realized. Her suits did a lot of concealing, not that he minded. The last thing he wanted was every other guy ogling her butt. Or for that matter any part of her anatomy.

Edging his hand farther downward, he found the hem of her skirt and tugged it up enough to let his fingers drift over her nylon-covered thigh. Her breath hitched as he went higher and higher…when he reached the edge of a garter, he nearly collapsed.

"You little sneak," he murmured, his mouth still touching hers, but gently now. His fingertips encountered the warm, bare satiny flesh at the back of her thigh and he stroked her. "You came here today with sexy stockings, and you weren't even going to tell me."

Amanda went still, then she stumbled out of his arms so quickly she tripped over the cape and landed on her rump. Josh tried to catch her, but he wasn't quick enough. She'd taken him totally by surprise and now she was sprawled at his feet, staring up at him in horror, her face utterly white.

She'd landed more on the cape than off it. She had one hand braced on a clump of dirt, the other pushing frantically at the hem of her skirt. Her knees were pressed together, her feet apart, giving her an adorably posed look, especially in the high heels and prim suit, her hair more down than up, her lipstick now gone.

Josh felt hornier than ever, and more confused.

He knelt down in front of her, elbows braced on his knees, his hands dangling, hoping to appear relaxed when he was so tense a touch could shatter him. "What is it, sweetheart?"

She scampered back, her heels kicking up the hard ground and her skirt rising a little more, showing a sexy stretch of slim smooth thigh and the edge of a lacy garter. Damn she had nice legs. Before she could go entirely out of his reach, Josh caught her left ankle.

"Hold up. I just want to know what's wrong."

She started to smooth her suit jacket with busy hands, realized it was now covered in the baby oil that coated his chest and she grimaced. "My suit is ruined."

"I'll buy you another one."

Her head flashed up so quickly, she startled him. "You will not!"

"I ruined it," he pointed out reasonably, still with his long fingers wrapped around her ankle.

"You did no such thing. It was…it was me and my behavior…"

"We kissed, Amanda. There was no behavior, at least not the way you're saying it, as if you killed someone."

Her eyes widened and she gasped. Just as quickly, she turned her head to stare toward the woods. "Josh, please, let me go."

"Hell, no. Not until you explain."

"You have to be cold!"

"Not even close." She looked disbelieving and he shook his head. "Nice try, but after the way you kissed me, you gotta know I'm burning up."

Amanda pulled herself together. It was a visible effort, and Josh watched in fascination—and remorse—as her cold shell fell into place. "I told you this wasn't what I wanted. But as you just said, you got your kiss. So now we're through."

Josh thought about his options, letting them run through his mind in rapid order, sorting and picking until he decided on the only course of action that just might get him what he wanted—her trust. And ultimately, her.

Maintaining his hold on her ankle, he levered himself over her, moving slowly to cover her, not letting her draw away.

"Josh!"

"Shh," he soothed. "I just want to talk and we can't

say anything important when all you want to do is lock me out."

"We're in a public park!"

Raised on one elbow, she flattened a hand on his chest to ward him off. Josh released her ankle and caught her shoulders, then pressed her down to lie flat. "No one is around."

She turned her head so far to the side her nose touched the ground. "I don't want you to do this," she said in a voice gone thin and shrill.

"Oh? Is that why your pulse is racing?" He kissed the tiny telltale fluttering of excitement in her throat. "Besides, I'm not going to do anything to you. At least know that much, Amanda. I'd never force you."

She squeezed her eyes shut, and said, "I know it."

That was something, he supposed. Not much, but it'd have to do for now. "Amanda? Come on, look at me, honey." He knew she wouldn't so he cupped her head and brought her face around to his. "I want to ask you a few things, and I want you to know that no matter the answer, it won't make a difference about how I feel."

Her lips, swollen from his kisses, parted. "How do you feel?"

With a tiny smile he couldn't contain, Josh admitted, "Poleaxed. Dumbfounded. Smitten, bit, infatuated and so physically attracted I'm learning to live with a perpetual hard-on."

Her eyes grew round, her pupils dilated. "For me?"

Now he laughed out loud. He kissed the end of her nose and said, "Yeah, for you. And it isn't easy being here with you like this, on top of you, able to smell you—"

She scoffed. "There you go with the smell thing again."

He nuzzled his nose against her cheek and whispered in a voice gone husky, "I love how you smell."

Her lashes fluttered at the *L* word, and again she turned her head to the side.

"Amanda," he chided. "Don't hide from me."

She nodded, looked at him directly, and whispered, "Thank you."

"You're welcome." Josh wasn't at all sure what she thanked him for, and at the moment, he didn't care. He prepared himself and blurted, "Were you burned?"

Her whole body stiffened and jerked. The word, *"No,"* exploded from her and she began to struggle. "I wasn't," she said, still fighting. *"I wasn't."*

"Amanda, I swear it doesn't matter to me!" Josh easily subdued her, catching her wrists and pinning them beside her head. His own throat felt tight, making it hard to speak, even harder to breathe. Her legs shifted under his but he was so much bigger, she had no way to dislodge him. "It doesn't matter, honey. If you have scars…"

"No!" She shook her head hard, ruining her hair and bumping his chin. "I was never burned. You don't understand…"

She practically sobbed out those words and Josh, his heart breaking but needing to know, said, "Then explain it to me. Make me understand."

She stopped fighting him to press against him. He was so stunned he released her arms and she flung them around his neck, squeezing him so tight he felt it in his heart, in his soul. Her hot, frantic breaths pelted his throat and the wetness of her tears touched his shoulder.

He squeezed his own eyes shut. "Amanda?"

"I wasn't burned," she swore with raw guilt, her voice shuddering, her body shaking. "I wasn't even in the fire."

The fire. Discovering he was right, that there had in fact been a fire, gave Josh no satisfaction. Instead, it made his skin crawl and his stomach cramp with thoughts of what she might have gone through. He knew firsthand the damage a blaze could cause, both physically and emotionally.

At least Amanda claimed she hadn't been in the fire, not that it would matter to him now if she had been burned. He'd meant what he said. But then what *had* happened?

Josh knew he had to go slowly. Cradling Amanda close, keeping her tucked protectively to his chest, he sat up. He brought her into his lap and just held her.

Someone she loved had been burned? Another man? Questions raced through his mind, but he didn't dare push her. She was already at the end of her rope, and he knew how she'd feel once she regained control. She'd blame him, and he'd have to start over from scratch.

Josh nuzzled her cheek, seeking forgiveness, because despite what he'd just told himself, he needed to know.

Hoping to help soothe her, he coasted his hands up and down her narrow back and kept on kissing her, her temple, her hair, her ear. He didn't care where, so long as he got to kiss her.

Minutes slipped by and neither of them broke the quiet. The sun sank down behind the bare, gnarled treetops, leaving the park shadowed and cold. A breeze rustled the dry grasses and brush, chilling his naked upper body.

Sounding sleepy, Amanda rubbed her fingers over his chest and muttered, "You're all slippery."

He smiled. That wasn't at all what he'd expected to hear from her after her emotional display and the lengthy silence.

She lifted her face and he saw her cheek was shiny with tears and baby oil. Around her right eye the blackening made her look wounded, bruised. A thin smear decorated her chin, the fine line of her delicate jaw, the edge of her nose.

It seemed the rightest thing in the world to lean down and kiss her mouth.

She kissed him back, letting the touch of their mouths linger, long and soft and caring.

"I'm sorry," she said on a sigh, snuggling close again, unmindful of the mess their embrace had already caused to her appearance. "I don't usually carry on like a deranged woman."

"Not deranged," Josh corrected. "Upset. We all get upset sometimes. It's nothing to apologize for."

Amanda nodded and then started to rise. His arms tightened. "Hey," he asked gently, "where do you think you're going?"

"Just to get your shirt. I don't want you to catch a cold and it's getting nippy."

True. Chills roughened Josh's skin and made him shiver. Still, he didn't want to move. With Amanda in his lap, he felt more content than he had in weeks. But because he'd been forward enough for her to bring sexual assault charges against him, he helped her to stand.

She tottered for a moment, her legs unsteady as she looked around to locate his discarded clothes on the picnic table. Her steps methodical, a bit too slow, Amanda fetched the jeans and his T-shirt and flannel.

Josh rose, too, brushing off his backside and wishing he could read her mind. With most women, his confidence was iron strong, but Amanda was an enigma and he never knew for sure where he stood with her.

He watched her lift his flannel to her nose and inhale for just a second, before crushing it close and strolling back to him.

"Here," she said, acting as if nothing had happened, as if she hadn't just lost control in front of him.

As if she hadn't kissed him to the point of no return—and then backed down.

Josh accepted the clothes and yanked his shirt on over his head. It stuck to him, thanks to the oil and blackening. As a fireman, he'd had many occasions where soot had coated his body, even getting beneath his gloves to cake under his nails. By comparison, a little oil could be ignored.

He shrugged the flannel on while Amanda watched, her expression distant, impossible to read.

"If you don't mind," Josh said, "I'll change pants, too. These aren't exactly the best to drive in."

"All right." She bent to get her cape. Dried leaves and twigs stuck to the material so she shook it out, then gave him her back.

Josh noticed a run in one of her stockings, dirt on her dressy high-heeled shoes, blackening and oil streaks on her once-impeccable clothing.

He felt like a marauder, like a ravisher of innocents. But damn it, he didn't know how to deal with her. It was like floundering in the dark. He had to push her, or give up on her, and giving her up wasn't an option.

Her back still to him, Amanda put her fingers to her hair and discovered how he'd wrecked it with his impatient hands. Personally, Josh thought she looked sexy as hell rumpled—even with the grease streaks on her face—but he knew she wouldn't agree.

He watched Amanda as she fussed with her hair for a few moments, then her head dropped forward when she realized there was no way to repair it, not out in the park near the woods with only the diminishing sunset and a tugging breeze to help her.

One by one, she began removing pins, and with each silky light-brown lock that fell over her shoulders, Josh's heart punched hard. He skinned out of his bunker gear and steel-toed boots, and tugged on his jeans, awkwardly hopping on first one foot then the other while keeping his attention on Amanda. He stepped into his shoes, slipped his thick leather belt through the loops and bundled up the rest of his gear.

By that time, Amanda's long hair was free and she combed her fingers through it, trying to bring some order to the tumbled mass. Her movements were innocently seductive and sexual. Unable to stand the physical and emotional distance between them, Josh approached her.

He clasped her shoulders. "Amanda, are you ready to talk now?"

She reached back and patted his hand in a distracted, almost avuncular way. "Why don't we talk in the car?" Even as she asked that, the wind picked up, tossing her hair so that the silky strands brushed his chin and throat.

He shuddered with raw need.

Amanda shivered with cold.

The park was dark now, cast in long eerie shadows. Josh hadn't realized how quickly the sun would set once it began its decline. But with the tall trees surrounding them, little of the fading light could penetrate.

He didn't want to leave, but then he was aroused and equally concerned. With the odd combination of emotions, he knew he wasn't thinking straight.

"You're cold," he said, giving himself a reason to stroke her, to rub his hands up and down her arms under the guise of warming her. What he really wanted to do with her and to her would no doubt make her hotter than hell. It was certainly making him hot just thinking about it. But for now, he had to content himself with a little arm rubbing.

Amanda patted his hand again, then turned to face him. "I just think it's best if we get on our way."

Her eyes looked luminous in the dark, her skin pale.

"You're not afraid of me?"

She shook her head. "No."

"You're going to talk to me, to help me understand?"

"Yes. I'll try."

Josh searched her face, trying to read the truth there, but Amanda always did a good job of closing down on him whenever she wanted to. He tucked his extra clothes under his arm and hefted the ax. "Let's go."

Once they were in the car she said, "I still need you to sign the release."

"Sure." He started the car, flipped on the headlights, and drove out. "As soon as I approve the pictures you'll be using."

Her sound of impatience turned into a laugh. "You

are so impossible, Josh Marshall. What am I going to do with you?"

Love me. The wayward thought scared the hell out of him, making his hands tighten on the wheel, his heart pound, his stomach roil and his brain stutter. He'd never before wanted a woman to really care.

His throat burned with the need to curse, to rage at the fickle hand of fate that had shown him a woman he wanted more than any other, only to keep her out of reach because she didn't feel the same.

After so many women had admired him, women who were attracted to him, some of them a little in love with him, he was deathly afraid he'd gone and stupidly fallen for Amanda.

"Talk to me," he said. "That's what you can do."

"All right." She seemed very small and still in the car beside him. Her tone was hesitant, but she continued. "First, the reason I don't want to get involved with you is that there's no point. Beyond what we just did, things can't progress."

Having no idea what she was trying to say, he asked only, "Why not?"

"I'm not…capable of it."

He swung his head toward her, then forced himself to watch the road. *Not capable, not capable, not capable…*

"I'm a little slow here, babe. Can you explain that?"

"Quit calling me babe and I might try."

He shook his head. Damn, she could make him nuts. "Go ahead."

"I'm twenty-four years old, Josh."

"So? I figured you to be somewhere around there. I'm twenty-seven."

"I've never been intimate with a man. I'm still a…a virgin."

His heart lurched. Before his sluggish brain could assimilate that confession and make sense of it, she continued.

"That's not by choice. I tried a few times, but…"

Her voice turned cold, remote. It was as if she'd gone on automatic pilot, telling him things he'd insisted on hearing, but not allowing them to hurt her again.

Josh blindly reached for her hand. It didn't matter whether or not she needed the touch, because *he* needed it.

"Sometimes stuff happens in our lives and it affects us. When I was younger I did some really horrible things."

"Just a second here, okay?" He tried to keep his tone reassuring. "Are we talking physical reasons why you can't, or emotional reasons?"

She laughed. "I've got all the same parts as any other woman, they just don't work right. And the doctors call it mental, not emotional."

"I don't give a rat's ass what they call it."

She squeezed his fingers. "It's all right. I've accepted my life."

"Well good for you, but I'm not accepting it." He'd be damned before he'd accept this as anything other than an emotional setback. "And you're only giving me bits and pieces of stuff here. Amanda, I *care* about you."

Her next words were choked. "I'm sorry. I wish you didn't. I don't want to hurt anyone ever again. Not for the rest of my life." She dug in her purse for a tissue and blew her nose. After a shuddering breath that ripped out his heart, she said, "All I want to do now is try to make up for things in the only way I can."

"The calendar?" he asked.

"Yes. And other projects, other ways to help those who've been hurt or killed. Some things, well, there's no way to make up for them. They happen and you have to live with the consequences."

It was a good thing, to Josh's way of thinking, that her home wasn't far from the park. Otherwise, he'd have pulled over on the side of the road. But he reached her driveway and rather than stop at the end as he was sure she'd prefer, he drove right up to the front walkway.

Then he sat there in stunned disbelief as his headlights landed on the front and side of her home. Would Amanda just keep knocking him off balance?

"Is this a schoolhouse?" he asked.

"It used to be, yes."

The tiny rectangular building of aged red brick had two arched windows on each outer wall and an arched double front door of thick planked wood. The steep roof had slate shingles and a small chimney protruded off the backside. It looked like a fairy cottage, set in the middle of towering trees and scraggly lawn with dead ivy climbing up the brick here and there, waving out like a lady's hair caught in the breeze.

Other than the driveway that ended at the side of the house where he could see her Beetle parked under a shelter, and a short path to the front door, there was no relief from those tall oaks and elms and evergreens. No neighbors, no traffic, no real lawn to speak of, no…nothing.

She'd isolated herself so thoroughly that Josh wanted to get out and howl at the moon.

He wanted to take her back to his place where it was noisy and busy with life.

He wanted to keep her.

Amanda opened her car door and stepped out. Josh followed, fearful that she'd skip away from him and he'd never get his answers. No way in hell could he sleep tonight with only half the story, and her hanging confession about virginity.

Looking at her over the hood of the Firebird, he said, "Ask me in."

She tipped her head back and looked up at the treetops, swaying against a dark gray sky. "I suppose I might as well," she said with little enthusiasm. "We can finish this, and you can sign the release and it'll be done."

So saying, she found her key in her purse and walked on a short cobblestone path to the front door. Josh listened to the hollow echoing of her high heels on the rounded stone.

Finish it? Ha! Not by a long shot.

Tonight, to his way of thinking, was just the beginning.

Amanda watched as Josh stepped into her quaint little eclectic home. She flipped on a wall switch, which lit a tiny side-table candle lamp. While he stood in the doorframe, she went on through the minuscule family room and into the kitchen to turn on the brighter fluorescent overhead lights. Whenever she needed light to work by, she used the two-seat kitchenette table.

Even now, it was filled with photos and contracts for the calendar.

Her home was barely big enough for one, and with Josh inside, it was most definitely crowded. Especially when he closed the door. He looked around with a sense of wonder, then said the most unexpected thing.

"I thought you were rich."

After all the emotional upheaval, Amanda burst out laughing. She peered at Josh, saw his look of chagrin, and laughed some more.

His expression changed and he stalked toward her. "I do love it when you laugh." She stalled, realization of their situation sinking in, and he said, "I also thought you'd be immaculate."

Shrugging, Amanda looked around at the clutter. "No time. I work a regular forty-hour week like most people, then put in another twenty hours or more a week on projects. My place is never really dirty, but yes, it's usually messy."

Dishes filled the small sink and an overloaded laundry hamper sat on the floor. Amanda shrugged again. She did what she could, when she could. If Josh didn't like it, he shouldn't have invited himself in.

"I wasn't complaining," he said. "It just surprised me. Will you show me the rest of your place?"

Amanda gathered herself. She'd explain things to him, but there was no reason for more hysterics, no reason for an excess of the pitiful, useless tears and dramatics fit for the stage.

What had happened to her was the least tragic thing that had occurred that awful night. She wouldn't allow herself to pretend otherwise.

"There's not much to show, only the four rooms.

You've already seen two of them, the family room and kitchen."

"No television," he noted.

"It's in my bedroom, along with a stereo, through here." The house measured a mere fifty feet by thirty feet. The front double doors were centered on the overall width of the house, which put them into the far left of the family room. An open archway, draped with gauzy swag curtains in lieu of a door, showed her bedroom. The curtains weren't adequate for privacy, but since she lived alone, it had never mattered.

Straight ahead of the family room was the kitchen. The two rooms seemed to meld together, with only the side of the refrigerator and the location of her tiny table to serve as a divider.

The kitchen was just large enough for a stacking washer and dryer, a parlor table, an apartment-size stove and her refrigerator. The cabinets were almost nonexistent, but open shelving and one pantry offered her all the storage space she needed.

At the back of the house, opposite the kitchen, was the minuscule bathroom that opened both into her bedroom and into the kitchen.

A bare toilet, a pedestal sink and a claw-foot tub filled the room with elegant simplicity. Other than the creamy ceramic tile in the bathroom, the whole house had original rich wood flooring.

Josh peeked into each room. Her bedroom had a full-size cherry bed and one nightstand that held an alarm clock, phone and lamp. A large ornate armoire held her clothes and a TV-VCR combination. Her modest stereo sat on the floor beside it.

One narrow dim closet was situated next to the door

for the bathroom. It wasn't deep enough to accommodate hangers, so she had installed shelves and stored her shoes and slacks and sweaters there.

The tall, wide windows and cathedral ceilings made the house look larger than it was. The absence of doors gave it a fresh openness, while natural wood furniture and earth tone materials brought everything together.

"I like it," Josh said, and she could see that he did. His eyes practically glowed when he stared at her old-fashioned bathtub. "How old is this place?"

"An engraved stone plaque, embedded above the front door, says it was erected in 1905. I had to do some work to it before I could live here. Some of the windowpanes were busted out and the roof leaked. The floors all had to be sanded and repaired."

Hands on his hips, Josh looked around again and shook his head. "A schoolhouse."

"A hunter had converted it into a cottage years ago. He's the one who put in modern plumbing and electricity. When he passed away, his kids just sort of forgot about it for a long, long time. I'm glad they finally decided to sell because I love it."

"Lots of charm," Josh agreed. "You know, you need a school bell."

"I have one. It's in the back, next to the well."

"A bona fide well?"

"Yes." She smiled at his enthusiasm over that bit of whimsy. "It even works, though I can't bring myself to drink anything out of it. I guess I'm too used to tap water."

They still stood in her bedroom, and Amanda began to feel a little uncomfortable. "Should I make some coffee? Not that I think this will take long, but…" She headed out of the room, assuming Josh would follow.

Of course, he didn't. "I'd rather talk."

"Fine." She clasped her hands together. "Let's at least sit down."

Josh nodded and followed her into the family room. She had only enough room for one bookshelf, a love-seat with end tables and lamps and a rocking chair. Josh tugged her down into the loveseat, and then kept hold of her hand.

"So you're a virgin?" he asked in that bald, shocking way of his. "That's not a crime, you know. Especially these days."

Many times in her life, Amanda had forced herself to face her accusers, to face the truth while trying to apologize, to make amends even when she knew that to be impossible.

She could force herself to face Josh, and to tell him the whole story. "I told you it's not a moral choice. I tried, several times, but I'm frigid."

He lifted his free hand to stroke her hair, and ended up removing a piece of a twig. He smiled at it while saying, "You didn't seem frigid to me. Just the opposite."

Her reaction to Josh had surprised her, too, but she wouldn't be fooled. Too many times she had thought herself whole—perhaps forgiven—only to be disappointed again.

Shaking her head, Amanda said, "I want what you want, that's not the problem. But you saw what happened. I can only go so far and then I start remembering and then I… I just can't."

"What?" Josh cupped her chin and brought her face around to his. "What do you remember?"

"Josh…are you sure you want to hear this?" She felt she had to give him one last chance to leave without causing an unpleasant scene. It'd be easier for both of them. "You could just let it go," she suggested, "just sign the release and leave."

"I'm not going anywhere, so quit stalling. And quit acting like whatever you have to tell me will horrify me and send me racing out the door. That won't happen, Amanda."

He twisted further in his seat to hold her shoulders and give her a gentle shake. "When I said I cared about you, I meant it. I don't go around saying that to every woman I want to have sex with."

She laughed. He was so outrageously honest about his intentions.

Josh wasn't amused. "When I said scars wouldn't matter, I meant that, too. It doesn't make any difference to me if the scars are on your body or in your heart. They're still a part of you, and so I want to know. All of it."

Well she'd tried. If it took the full truth to make him understand, then she'd give him the full truth. Amanda looked him in the eyes and said, "When I was seventeen, I killed a man."

Josh froze, his expression arrested, disbelieving.

Better to get it all over with quickly, she thought. "I also wounded two others. They're the ones who wear the awful scars, not me. God knows it would have been so much better, and certainly more just, if it had been me. But that's not how it worked out."

"Amanda…"

She shook her head. "There are so many people who will never forgive me, but that's okay, because I won't ever forgive myself."

Chapter 6

Josh shocked the breath right out of her when he yanked her into his arms. He felt so solid, so strong and brave and heroic. He was everything she could never be.

It seemed criminal for her to be with him, but Amanda couldn't stop herself from knotting her hands in his T-shirt and clinging to him.

He sat back and again lifted her into his lap. In a voice gone hoarse with emotion, he said, "Tell me what happened."

That he bothered to ask for details amazed Amanda. A few men had, men she'd tried and failed to be intimate with in college, and when she'd first moved here. But macabre fascination and selfish intent had motivated their queries, because they wanted to know why they were being rejected. Not one of them had asked out of genuine caring.

She *felt* Josh's caring. She felt it in the way he held her, in the steady drone of his heartbeat against her cheek, in the way his large hands moved up and down her spine, offering her comfort. It settled over her like a warm blanket, almost tangible.

Tears pricked her eyes, but she staved them off. She'd cried enough, and besides, she didn't deserve to sit around whining.

Amanda rubbed her cheek against him, breathing in his masculine scent. "You were right—I did come from money. Dad not only has his own company and more stock in other companies than I can remember, but he inherited a fortune from his family. My mother's family isn't quite as well off, but they're definitely upper-crust. Whenever they weren't around, there was a housekeeper or tutor or someone to keep tabs on me and my sister."

"You said you were seventeen? That's a little old to have a baby-sitter, isn't it?"

"I thought so. But my parents were determined that my sister and I would never embarrass them. So many of their friends had kids who had gotten into trouble, unwanted pregnancies, drugs, bad grades. I don't blame them for being extra cautious. Being influential puts you in the limelight, so we had be exemplary in every way."

"Sounds rough."

She started to lift her head, but he pressed her back down and kissed her temple. She subsided. "Don't get me wrong, my parents loved me."

"*Loved* you? As in past tense?"

She didn't want to delve too deeply into the broken ties with her family. It hurt too much. "Things have been...strained since that awful night. I embarrassed them. I caused a huge scandal that still hasn't died down, even though it happened seven years ago. We keep in touch, but I doubt we'll ever be close again."

"Tell me what happened."

Deciding to just get it over with, she said, "One night I slipped out of my house to meet with my boyfriend. We were going to have sex in the woods behind my house. Can you believe that? A very risqué, exciting rendezvous. I felt totally wicked and very grown-up." She lowered her head and laughed though she'd never remember that night with anything but horror. "Looking back, I realize how immature and ridiculous I was."

"You were young," Josh said without censure, "and most seventeen-year-olds are ready to start experimenting, to start pushing for independence. You sound pretty average to me."

If she had ever been average, Amanda thought, she'd been changed that awful night. "He showed up at midnight. I crawled out my second-story bedroom window and shimmied down a tree, and away we went." She absently plucked at a wrinkle in her skirt, not seeing anything, not wanting to see. "While I was gone, making out in the dirt on a borrowed blanket, our house caught on fire. An electrical short or something they eventually decided. Everyone got out of the house by the time the fire trucks arrived, only…"

The muscles in Josh's arms bunched. He was a firefighter, so she knew he could easily picture the scenario. "Only when no one found you, they all thought you were still inside?"

"Yes." She swallowed hard, but the lump of regret remained. "My parents were hysterical. My mother collapsed on the lawn with my sister, both of them screaming. My father tried to get back inside when he couldn't find me. He punched two firefighters who tried to hold him back, but he finally gave up when three of them went inside instead."

Remorse clawed through her, as fresh and painful as the day it had happened. "My bedroom was in the middle of the upstairs floor. While they were searching for me, going on my parents' assurances that I had to be in there, the floor caved in. One man…" An invisible fist squeezed her throat, choking her. God, she hated reliving that awful night.

Josh waited, not saying a word, just stroking her.

"Even in the woods, I heard the sirens. They seemed to be right on top of us and I was afraid they'd wake my family and they'd know what I did, that I'd sneaked out. So I came home."

Shuddering, rubbing at her eyes so she could see, Amanda said, "The fireman fell into the downstairs and got trapped. He was unconscious and the smoke was so thick, they almost couldn't find him. By the time they got him out he was badly burned."

She gave up trying to wipe away the tears and just dropped her hands into her lap. "He only lived three days. Three days of wavering in and out of consciousness, constantly in pain."

Josh still didn't say anything, but there was such a ringing in her head she wouldn't have heard him anyway. She tried to breathe but couldn't. She tried to relax, to be unemotional, but she couldn't do that either. "The other two men are badly scarred, their arms, and their hands."

Pushing herself away from Josh's embrace, she rocked forward and covered her face, ashamed and embarrassed and sick at heart. "They hated me of course. Not that I blame them. And that man's widow…"

She felt Josh touch her shoulder and she lurched to her feet, then paced to the window. She couldn't talk anymore, but there wasn't much else to say. She stared blindly out at the blackness of her yard, and the blackness of her life.

Then Josh was behind her, drawing her into his warmth, wrapping those incredibly strong arms around her so she had no choice but to give him his way.

"Hush now," he said.

Amanda felt her mascara run, knew she needed to blow her nose. "It was on the news," she said, the words coming on their own. "My parents screaming, the firefighters working so hard, dirty and beat but not giving up. They had videos of my mother in her nightgown, curlers in her hair, my sister bawling. And my father, such a stately, dignified man…acting almost insane, fighting the firemen."

"Trying to get to the daughter he loves. That's typical, Amanda."

"They showed the videos of me, too, just standing there, not hurt, not even in the house. My hair was wrecked, a tangled mess, and my blouse was buttoned wrong. There were weeds on my clothes and…everyone knew. They knew where I'd been and what I'd been doing and my parents were just devastated." She squeezed herself tight, but it didn't help. "It wasn't only on the local news, it was on every station everywhere."

Josh turned her.

She couldn't look at him yet so she pushed away and went to the table for a tissue, blowing her nose loudly and then hiccuping. When she did finally look at Josh, she saw his pity, his sad eyes, and she wanted to die.

"My dad took me to the hospital to see the two men who survived." The things she'd seen that night would live with her forever. There were still nights when she couldn't sleep, when she'd close her eyes and relive every frightening, too real moment. "It was so awful. Firemen pacing, wives crying, and they all looked at me like I'd done it on purpose."

"No," Josh said quietly. "I can't believe that."

Memories bombarded her, and she said, "You're right." Amanda recalled an incredible incident. "One of the firemen who'd gone inside for me, Marcus Lindsey, told me he had a daughter my age. He told me kids made mistakes and that he didn't blame me, so he didn't want me blaming myself. He told me I was too pretty to keep crying."

A new wash of tears came with that admission. Marcus Lindsey was an unbelievable man, a hero, like most firefighters. He'd deserved so much better than what had happened because of her.

Josh touched her hair. "And he's right. We know the risks inherent in our jobs. Lindsey did what he's supposed to do."

"He spent weeks in the hospital, and he'll carry the scars for the rest of his life. He's not a fireman anymore. Neither of the survivors are." She blinked and more tears rolled down her cheeks.

Josh plucked another tissue and wiped her face. He was so gentle and tender it amazed Amanda. "What happened was a freak accident," he murmured, "not a deliberate act, definitely not something to keep beating yourself up for."

Amanda couldn't believe his reaction. "How would you feel? If you'd done what I did, if you'd slipped off against your parents' instruction to fool around in the woods and someone had *died* because of it, how would you feel?"

"There's no way I can answer that, honey, because it didn't happen to me." He tucked her hair behind her ear, rubbed her temple with his thumb. "But I can tell you that I've made mistakes, in my job and in my social life. Everybody has—it's one of the side effects of being human. All we can do is try not to make the same mistakes again, to forgive ourselves, and to make amends."

"I'm trying to make amends."

"No, you're driving yourself into the ground with guilt. It's not at all the same thing."

Confusion swamped her. He sounded so reasonable, when there was nothing reasonable about what had happened.

"Tell you what," Josh said. "Why don't you go take a warm shower? Your clothes are dirty and torn and your makeup is everywhere it's not supposed to be."

"Oh." She started to touch her face, but he caught her hands and kissed her forehead.

"You look like a very adorable urchin, so don't worry about it. But I know you'll be more comfortable if you shower and change. While you do that I'll go ahead and make some coffee. Are you hungry? I could maybe rustle you up a sandwich."

Amanda pushed her hair out of her face and looked around her small house in consternation. She'd bared her soul, then prepared for the worst. But not only wasn't Josh disgusted, he offered to fix her food.

He could muddle her so easily. "You plan to make yourself at home in my kitchen?"

"Yes."

Truth was, Amanda didn't want him to leave. She felt spent, wasted right down to the bone, and she didn't want to be alone. He wasn't blaming her, wasn't appalled or shocked or disapproving. He'd listened and offered comfort.

It was so much more than she usually got, so much more than she thought she deserved.

She was selfish enough to want him to stay.

And realistic enough to know it wouldn't make a difference in the long run.

"All right, but no food. I'm not hungry."

Josh gave her a long look. "Can you manage on your own?"

"To shower?" She frowned. "Of course I can."

"Spoilsport."

Amanda stared. Now he wanted to tease her?

Smiling, Josh bent and kissed her softly on the mouth. "I'll be in the kitchen waiting."

Amanda watched Josh stroll from the room, a tall powerful man who had invaded her heart and then her home. Despite what she'd just confessed, he appeared to have no intention of withdrawing.

Amazing. From the start, Josh had seen the worst from her. She'd been first badgering and defensive to gain his involvement in the calendar, then hysterical and tearful while giving him her truths. He knew all her worst qualities and her darkest secret, yet he didn't leave.

From deep, deep in her heart, something warm and happy and unfamiliar stirred.

It scared her spitless, because what would happen when he realized their relationship would never be an intimate one? Would he remain her friend? Somehow, she doubted it. Josh was a very physical, a very sexual man.

That meant that she had to take advantage of every single second she'd have with him.

Amanda hurried to get through with her shower.

Josh waited until he heard the pipes rumble from her shower, then he punched the wall, hurting his knuckles but relieving some of his anger. Luckily, the old schoolhouse was solid so all he hurt was himself.

He couldn't remember ever being so enraged, to the point he'd have gladly horsewhipped a few people, starting with himself. Everything that had happened since first meeting her now had fresh meaning. And it hurt.

He wanted to pass backward in time and save a young lady from a life-altering mistake.

He wanted to redo about a hundred moments with her, times when he'd been too forward, too pushy. Times when he'd made it clear he wanted sex, when actually he wanted so much more.

He wanted to tell Amanda that it would be all right. But he just didn't know.

Thinking of what she'd likely gone through, what he knew she'd felt judging by the expression on her face during the retelling made him ill.

Josh believed Amanda's father loved her, based on what she'd said. He'd seen many people fight to try to save their loved ones, willingly putting themselves at risk. But her father never should have taken her to visit the injured men in the hospital.

He'd probably thought to teach her a valuable lesson, or perhaps he'd gone strictly out of goodwill, wanting to offer thanks as well as his apologies for what had occurred. But putting Amanda through such an ordeal, making her deal with the accusations wrought from grief, had caused her so much harm.

People in mourning, people afraid and worried, were emotionally fragile, not given to clear thinking. Of course family members and friends had at first blamed Amanda—they'd needed a way to vent and she'd been far too handy.

Her father should have protected her from that, not exposed her to it.

While standing in the middle of her kitchen, struggling to deal with his turbulent thoughts, Josh heard the faint tinkle of bells. He paused, lifting his head and listening. The sound came again, louder with the whistling of the wind and he went to the window to look out.

Nothing but blackness could be seen, and a fresh worry invaded his already overwrought mind. Amanda was too alone here, too vulnerable. She literally lived in isolation with no one nearby if she needed help.

Josh searched for a light switch and finally located one by the sink.

A floodlight illuminated the backyard and an incredible display of wind chimes, large and small, brass and wood, colorful and dull. With each breeze, they rang out in soft musical notes.

He also noted the birdhouses and feeders, dozens of them everywhere, on poles and in the trees.

With his head lowered and his eyes misty, Josh

flipped the light back off and leaned on the sink. Damn, he'd never known a woman like Amanda Barker. She was all starch and hard determination one minute, and so soft and needy the next.

The shower turned off, jarring Josh out of his ruminations. He rushed through the coffee preparations, noting the fact that her coffeemaker only made three cups, proof positive that she never entertained guests.

Rummaging through her refrigerator, he found cheese and lettuce and mayonnaise. He remembered how little she ate and made two sandwiches, one and a half for himself, a half for Amanda. He'd just finished putting pickle slices on a plate and cutting the sandwiches when she appeared.

Josh looked up, and smiled. Amanda's face was still ravaged—her eyes were puffy, her nose pink, her lips swollen and her cheeks blotchy. But the oil and blackening was gone, as was her makeup. She'd tied her hair onto the top of her head, but she'd been hasty with it and long tendrils hung down her nape, around her ears.

Though she was bundled up in a white chenille robe, Josh could see her pale yellow thermal pajamas beneath and the thick white socks on her feet.

Her hands clutched the lapels of the robe and she said, "I told you I wasn't hungry."

Josh lied smoothly, without an ounce of guilt. "But I am, and I hate to eat alone. Even you ought to be able to choke down half a cheese sandwich."

While she stood there hovering just out of his reach, Josh cleared her table. He neatly stacked a small mountain of papers and photographs and transferred them to the washer, the only uncluttered surface available.

Evidence of her continued efforts was everywhere;

the papers he'd just moved, contracts, old calendars, fundraising schedules and event planners.

"Can I ask you a few things, Amanda?"

She braced herself as if expecting an inquisition on the fires of hell. "Yes, of course."

Her guilt was so extreme, he knew she wouldn't give it up easily. She'd been living with it for seven years and it was now a part of her. "If you're not interested in getting cozy with a guy, why do you dress so sexy?"

Even without makeup, her big brown eyes looked lovely, soft with long lashes that shadowed her cheeks when she blinked.

"I don't. I wear business suits."

Business suits that in no way looked businesslike. They had nipped waists and above the knee thigh-hugging skirts. And those sexy shoes she wore...

Josh had his own theories, but he wondered if Amanda realized the connection that she'd made.

The night of the fire, by her own account, she'd been caught disheveled, her activities apparent from her rumpled appearance. Now she was always dressed impeccably, polished from her hair to her high heels. With every tidy suit she donned, she made a statement. But she also emphasized that she was a woman.

"Your suits are sexier than a lot of miniskirts." Josh wasn't a psychologist, but it seemed obvious to him. "You also wear stockings and high heels."

She pulled out a chair to sit, and then picked up a pickle slice, avoiding his gaze. "No one knows that I wear stockings."

Josh drew his chair around next to her. "I do."

She glanced at him and away. "You wouldn't have if things hadn't gotten out of hand."

"Okay, let's look at this another way. *You* know what you're wearing. So why do you?"

She chewed and swallowed before answering. Her cheeks colored. "Sometimes," she whispered, measuring her words, "I don't feel much like a woman. I suppose it's my way of…balancing things. For me, not for anyone else."

Josh's heart pounded. She was trusting him, sharing with him. "You make yourself feel more feminine because you're a virgin?"

She shook her head. "No. Because I'm frigid."

He wasn't at all convinced of that, but he'd argue it with her later. "I guess it makes sense. But I gotta tell you, I can't imagine a sexier or more feminine woman than you. With or without experience."

As more color rushed to her face, Amanda stared hard at another pickle slice and then picked it up.

Josh smiled. He had her confused and that was nice for a change. Maybe he'd eventually get her so confused she'd forget her ridiculous guilt.

"What about this house?" he asked. "If your parents are rich, why the tiny home? And why a Volkswagen? I pegged you as more of a Mercedes gal."

She lifted the bread on her half of a sandwich, looked beneath critically, then replaced it. Since she'd only had mayonnaise in her refrigerator, no mustard, he didn't know what she'd expected to find.

"I love this house, so don't go insulting it. I'm just me and I don't need much room. And my car runs great. When other cars won't start in the cold, she always kicks over and gets me where I'm going."

"That's not what I'm asking and you know it."

"I know." She sighed. "Truth is, I live in a small

house and drive an economical car because that's all I can afford. I only have what I earn, and it's not that much. But," she added, giving him a look, "I'd have bought this house regardless. I do love it, and now, after being here for a while, I can't imagine living anywhere else."

"What about your family?"

"You mean what about the family coffers?" She shrugged. "My father and I had a major falling out. Since we weren't close emotionally, I couldn't use him financially. I decided to make it on my own."

"What did your father have to say about that?"

"He was naturally furious that I refused his money, doubly so when I took out student loans to finish paying for my college tuition. He didn't think I'd make it, but I've proven him wrong. I have to keep an inexpensive car and house to do it, but I'm totally independent and I like it that way."

Josh watched her bite into her sandwich and waited until she'd swallowed to ask, "What caused the falling out?"

She waved a negligent hand, but her big sad eyes darkened again. "What I did, the fire and the damage—"

His back stiffened, his muscles tightened. "He blamed you?"

"Oh, no, never that. But he's never understood how I feel, either."

"You didn't cause the fire, Amanda."

"No, but I sure caused a lot of the damage. As my mother used to say, a house can be quickly rebuilt, but a damaged reputation is impossible to repair."

Disgust filled him. Josh was thinking rather insulting things about the mother until Amanda clarified, "My mother said that in regard to herself—she'd been seen on camera, in her robe and her curlers."

"She was worried about her appearance in the middle of the house burning down?"

"My mother wouldn't normally be caught dead without her makeup. She was mortified. My whole family was. And it was my fault." Amanda peered up at him. "What she said was true, at least when applied to me."

Josh frowned. "Your reputation is that of a beautiful, giving woman who works hard at helping others."

"To some. To those who don't know it all."

"To anyone with any sense."

Amanda stared over his shoulder. "All of us had our lives, our backgrounds thrown out there to be scrutinized. Everyone knew the girl who'd been screwing around in the woods while a man died trying to rescue her, and they knew my family, my sister who was younger than me, the mother and father who had raised such an irresponsible child."

"Amanda, damn it…"

"That's what the papers called me, 'irresponsible.' All things considered, it's not such a horrible insult." She picked at the crust on her sandwich, pulling it apart. "Things quieted down when I first went away to college. Problem was, though, after about a year and a half, I got another boyfriend. Big mistake, that."

"Every college kid dates, Amanda." He could already guess what had happened, and it made him want to shout.

"I shouldn't have. I should have learned."

"Bullshit. You were getting on with your life. That's what we're supposed to do."

"Sometimes," she agreed without much conviction. "But not that time. I thought I liked this guy a lot. He was popular and fun and outgoing. When he wanted to make love to me, I couldn't. It literally turned my stomach to go beyond kissing."

Josh remembered how she'd clung to him, how hot and open she had been. He refused to believe that what had happened with a boy in college would hold true with him. She'd been young then, and college boys weren't known for technique or patience.

"I broke things off with him," Amanda explained, "and he got offended. I guess I wounded his male vanity by not getting...aroused by him. He told everyone I was a cold bitch and a tease, and the next thing I knew, someone remembered my name and the whole story was there again."

Hands curled into fists, Josh said, "I gather he spread it around to salve his own ego?"

"Yes. My father was outraged. He wanted me to press charges against him. Sexual harassment, if you can believe that, and slander even though what the guy said was true. I refused, and that's when I took over all my financial obligations."

Josh felt tense enough to explode, but he held it together for Amanda. "Has it been retold since then?"

"No. Well, not until I just told you." She put her sandwich back down and folded her hands on the table. "When I got my job at the mall, right out of college, I met another nice guy. He wasn't like the first. He wasn't overly popular or loud. He was the new manager, shy and studious, eight years older than me. We dated for six months and he was so patient, I really hoped... But I just couldn't."

Talking about it, thinking about her with other men, especially men who had upset her, made him nuts. But there were things he had to know, things he had to ask about if he ever hoped to make headway with her. "Were you sexually attracted to him?"

She looked perplexed by his question. "I liked him."

"It's not the same thing."

"I *wanted* to make love with him."

"Because you wanted him, or because you wanted to prove something to yourself?"

Amanda shoved back her chair so fast it nearly fell over. Josh was on her before she'd taken two steps. He curled his hands around her upper arms and held her still. She was so skittish, forever running from him. "Tell me, honey. Did you want him like you want me?"

"I don't remember. That was two years ago."

"Amanda." He cupped her face and stroked her cheeks with his thumbs. The feel of her soft, warm skin tantalized him. "Don't lie to me, honey."

Her chin lifted. "All right, then no. I didn't want him like I want you. But it doesn't matter."

"I think it does."

"Then you'd be wrong. I can't ever enjoy that part of being a woman. I'm not meant to enjoy it."

Because she didn't deserve it? Josh wanted to shake her. "That's idiotic, Amanda, and you know it."

"I tried after that, Josh. I tried a couple of times. But no matter what, it never worked out. I could only go so far and then I'd hate it."

"Hate it how?"

"All of it, in every way. I hated being touched, looked at. I hated being kissed. It always made me remember…"

He quickly interrupted. "I'm touching you now and you like it. And you didn't mind my kisses at all."

She glared at him and then thumped his chest. "Stop it! You're seeing what you want to see. Odds are if we try this, you'll just be disappointed, too." She thumped him again, then tangled her hand in his shirt and held on tight as she whispered, "Just as I'm always disappointed."

"Like hell." Josh drew her up, kissed her long and hard and held her close. She struggled for just a second or two, and then she clung to him.

Panting, Josh said against her mouth, "Here's what we'll do, Amanda. We'll go really slow. Excruciatingly slow. If at any point you start to feel bad, in any way, you're going to tell me and I swear I'll stop. I won't rush you and never, ever, will I be disappointed. No matter what."

Amanda stared up at him, her gaze filled with hope and excitement—and that damned guilt. Josh had no more doubts. In that single moment of time, he knew he loved her. He also knew he wouldn't tell her yet. She'd get spooked all over again and he didn't want to risk that.

"Can I stay another hour?" he asked, his voice so low and rough he didn't recognize himself.

Amanda nodded and at the same time, asked, "Why?"

"Because I want to kiss you silly." He held her face and put small damp pecks on her chin, her forehead, her ear and the corner of her mouth. He licked her ear and whispered, "I want to lie down in your bed with you and hold you close and feel all of you against me like I did at the park, and I want to kiss you for an hour.

And when I leave, I want you to lie awake at least another hour, missing me and wanting me." He looked into her beautiful brown eyes and added, "The way I'll be wanting you and missing you."

Her lips trembled—with nervousness or excitement or fear, he wasn't sure. "It won't do any good…"

"Just kissing. That's all I want."

She ducked her head, smiling, and said, "Liar."

God he loved her. Josh hugged her close and laughed. "Yeah, that was a lie. An *enormous* lie. I want you all the time, right now especially. What I meant is that for tonight, for maybe a week, all we'll do is kiss."

"*A week?* But why?"

"Because I want you to get used to me. I want you to know that you can enjoy the kissing because it won't go any further so there's nothing to be afraid of. I want you to learn to trust me, and to trust yourself again."

"Ah." Her dark eyes shone with blatant doubt. "And when the week's over and nothing has changed? Just how long do you think this super-human patience of yours is going to last?"

"As long as it takes." Josh smiled at her surprise. "Get used to it, Amanda. I'm not going anywhere, so we've got forever."

Amanda's eyes widened and she pushed back from him. Josh wanted to curse. He hadn't meant to say that, hadn't meant to rush her again. Just because he now thought in terms of a lifelong commitment didn't mean the same applied to her. It wasn't that long ago that she had denied even being attracted to him.

But then she drew a deep breath—for courage he thought—and went on tiptoe to put her arms around his neck. She said, "Yes, all right."

"You're willing to try?"

Looking like she faced the gallows, she said, "If you are, then I'd be a fool to say no."

Slightly insulted, Josh asked, "You're willing because you want to test yourself again, or because you actually want me, *me,* not just any guy."

She smiled. "With you around," Amanda told him, "there are no other guys."

Josh picked her up and headed for the bedroom.

Chapter 7

An hour later, Amanda felt smothered in a cocoon of sensuality. Her heartbeat raced, her skin tingled, her womb ached and pulled and her breasts…her breasts were so sensitive she couldn't bear it.

But Josh only kissed her.

It was wonderful because she didn't have to worry about freezing up, about not being able to perform. She knew how to kiss, and enjoyed it.

But at the same time, it was frustrating because no matter how excited she got, no matter how much she might want him to touch her a little more, he wouldn't break his word. They'd kiss and that would be all, so she tried to relax and enjoy him.

Relaxing, she found, was out of the question.

"Josh," she gasped, as his lips tugged at her earlobe and his hand opened on her belly. Inside her robe. Stroking.

Normally that would have made her nervous, but not tonight. Not with Josh.

"Yeah, baby?"

Mmmmm. The way he said that, she no longer objected to the endearment. "When you said kiss—ah!" His tongue licked into her ear, making her tremble and shattering her thoughts. She stiffened, and he retreated.

"When I said kiss?" Josh trailed damp love bites down her neck to her shoulder, into the hollow of her collarbones.

With an effort, Amanda gathered her wits. "I thought you just meant kiss. You know, on the mouth."

"I love your mouth," he murmured, then feasted on her lips for a good three minutes until she felt nearly mindless again.

He untied the belt to her robe and opened the material wide.

Amanda opened her eyes and watched him curiously.

"I want this out of my way." Josh stared down at her with heated eyes and a smile of promise. "I adore your jammies."

Forcing her head up, Amanda surveyed her body. Her thermal pajamas were warm and soft, a pale yellow trimmed with white daisies on the neck and the cuffs of her sleeves and pants. Josh hadn't asked her to strip. No, instead he'd complimented her very silly sedate nightwear.

It embarrassed her a little, until Josh sat up and jerked off his T-shirt, throwing it off the foot of the bed.

"I want to feel your hands on me," he explained. "Is that okay? You're all right?"

Amanda stared at his hard chest, now smeared a little with the blackening that hadn't yet rubbed off. His shoulders glistened from the residue of baby oil, and muscles bunched and flexed as he waited for her answer.

"Yes, all right."

Josh groaned. "Touch me anyway you want to, anywhere you want to." He lowered himself back to her, once again taking her mouth.

Amanda knew about kissing, but this wasn't just kissing. This was full body contact, hot breath and a soft tongue and so thrilling she'd never expected it. Every man she'd ever known would have been frantic by now, pushing her for more, trying to convince her with arguments and unwanted touches.

But not Josh. He had large hands and they roamed everywhere, up her arms, over her shoulders, sometimes cupping her face tenderly, sometimes stroking her thighs suggestively. Everything he did was geared toward her pleasure, at her level of comfort.

He seemed to know what she felt before she could understand it. If she stiffened even the tiniest bit, he changed direction. If she gasped in wonder, he intensified his efforts.

She loved it when he touched her belly. He touched it a lot. But he stayed away from any place that might push them beyond the kissing stage, and the result was that she felt on fire.

"Josh, please…"

"Please what? Tell me what you want."

Daringly, she tasted the skin on his neck. He was

salty and hot and she wanted more. "I don't know." She glided her hands over his bare skin, rasping his small nipples, tangling her fingers in his chest hair. He felt so hot, so hard. "I'm afraid to say."

He made a low sound of carnal delight at the feel of her tongue on his neck, her hands exploring his flesh. "Afraid the good feelings will go away?"

"Yes." Guilt nudged at her, memories trying to invade, but above it all was the smell and feel and taste of Josh. She'd probably regret it later, but for now she wanted to be a normal woman, not one filled with fears and reservations. It was what Josh deserved, even if she didn't.

She opened her mouth and sucked on the hot skin of his throat while her fingers pressed into the hard tensed muscles of his shoulders. He tasted *so* good.

Josh dropped his head to rest beside hers on the pillow. "Ah...*damn.*"

"Josh?"

"I think we need to stop," he rasped.

She'd disappointed him! She'd been selfish, taking what she wanted while knowing he wouldn't be satisfied. "I... I'm sorry."

Josh leaned up on one elbow to see her face. His expression was hard and tensed with arousal, his eyes glittering. "For what?"

For everything. Amanda bit her lip, then said, "If you want to try..."

"I want more than a quick screw, sweetheart." He smiled and nipped at her bottom lip, stealing it from her worrying teeth, laughing softly when she gasped.

"I want you," he said, "naked and hot, and I want you laughing and I want you crying. I want you now and tomorrow. None of that has anything to do with having sex right now, but it has everything to do with how you'll feel about me forever."

Her heart stumbled. He'd said it again, used that *"forever"* word twice now, as if they had a future together.

His eyes were smiling and happy, not disappointed. But dark color slashed his cheekbones and she could feel the heat radiating off him, making his skin damp.

He offered her so much; he offered her forever.

Amanda couldn't stop touching him, coasting her hands over his hard muscles and long bones. He was big and macho and very sexy. He was a lot of man, and he claimed to want her forever.

In her heart, she knew forever was impossible. But he was here now, and she was just selfish enough to want a small part of him, for now.

"Will you come over again tomorrow?"

A smile curled his mouth and lit his eyes. "Yeah, I'll be here. But I have a long shift. I work till six. How about I bring dinner?"

"How about I cook dinner?" she countered.

"And after you feed me," he teased, rubbing his palm over her belly, "we can neck some more?"

She touched his jaw where beard shadow rasped her fingertips. "I hope so."

"We'll watch a movie, too. I like the idea of lounging here in your bed, making out and just getting familiar. It sounds real cozy."

Amanda looked up at the ceiling and laughed, a little amazed, a lot confused. "I can't imagine any man saying what you just said. Men want to have sex, not just get cozy."

"Some men, maybe. Not me. Not with you."

Every guy Amanda had ever dated had worked hard toward getting her into bed, and when he accepted that wouldn't happen, he'd walked. Men wanted no part of a dysfunctional woman, a woman who couldn't offer sexual satisfaction. To most guys, that disqualified her as a real woman.

To Amanda, they were right.

Josh apparently disagreed.

"You're making me crazy," she said.

"That's the whole idea." He gave her another hard smooch, then pushed himself off the bed. "I want you crazy enough that you can forget everything but me."

She didn't tell him, but she was already halfway there. And she didn't know if that was good—or bad.

Josh was so proud of Amanda. She stood at a podium and directed people to various tables and displays. Her idea of a charity reception to launch sales of the calendar was brilliant, even if he did feel like an idiot strutting around without a shirt, being ogled by females of all ages.

Amanda had insisted all the guys dress in work gear, sans shirts. Of course, they'd all complied, strutting around with their bunker pants slung low, chests bare, their steel-toed boots clunking on the floor as they moved. But she'd also insisted that Josh carry his ax, which was something Amanda found sexy—not that he understood why.

The fun part was that every time a woman got too close to him, Amanda showed up like a fussy White Knight, ready to defend and protect. Josh chuckled to himself, amused by her, and so damn in love he felt ready to burst.

He was also so sexually frustrated he didn't know how much more he could take. Night after night, he'd gone to see Amanda and every time their intimacy grew, though they'd held to the rule of mere kisses. Still, kissing Amanda was wonderful, because her reactions were wonderful. She literally wallowed in her newfound sexual freedom.

And just yesterday, after nearly a full week of pleasurable torture, he'd held her breast in his hand and felt her nipple pressing into his palm. The moment had been so sweet, and he'd felt so triumphant, he'd nearly come in his pants.

Amanda hadn't objected to his familiarity, and in fact her eyes had gone smoky, her breath choppy, her skin warm. She'd arched into him and given a sexy little moan that drove him nuts.

But Josh had forced himself to go no further. It had nearly killed him, but he'd kept control. More than anything, he wanted her to want him—without restrictions, without any bad memories haunting her. When he finally got inside her, he wanted her to be aware only of the pleasure and the heat and the tantalizing friction as they moved together....

Josh groaned. Much more of that fantasy and he'd be making a spectacle of himself. He stared down at his lap and silently ordered his male parts to behave. He'd been giving that damned order since first starting this strange seduction. His body was about to go into full rebellion.

A swat on the butt, followed by a squeeze, made Josh jump. He turned around, and came face-to-face with Vicki. He hadn't seen her since that day outside Marcos, when he'd told her that his free-wheeling days were over.

"Hey, stud," she teased, then went on tiptoe to give him a kiss. Her mouth was soft and warm, and it moved him not even a tiny bit.

Josh said, "Uh," and looked around to see if Amanda had witnessed the byplay. Luckily, she was busy schmoozing a local society matron who would likely grace her with a sizeable donation.

Watching her, Josh appreciated the pretty picture Amanda made today. She'd worn a trim-fitting peach-colored skirt that sported a jaunty little matching jacket and made her skin look velvety. The hem of the skirt landed well above her knees and showed the sexy length of her calves and part of her thighs. Josh knew damn good and well she had a garter and silk stockings on underneath, and knowing it made him sweat.

Pearl studs decorated her delicate ears and a triple-strand pearl collar circled her throat. Her rich hair was swept up with a studded comb.

She looked…edible, Josh decided. Especially since she wore very high, high heels and he could too easily imagine her without the dress, standing there looking delectable in nothing more than her soft skin, nylons, heels and pearls.

Vicki stroked his bare chest, letting her fingertip stroke a nipple. "Yoo-hoo, Josh?"

He jerked around, feeling mauled, like fresh meat. He wanted a shirt, damn it.

He wanted Amanda.

"Sorry." He stepped out of reach. "What did you say?"

Her smile was slow and wicked. "Look at you, all warmed up. I recognize that hot expression in your eyes."

That expression was for Amanda, not that Vicki would ever believe it when she stood so close and was acting so suggestive.

"Glad to see me?" she asked. "Things with Ms. Snooty not working out?"

Josh frowned. "She's not snooty."

"No? She comes across that way."

"She's...timid."

"Yeah, right."

Josh rolled his eyes. "Okay, so she's not timid. What are you doing here, Vicki?"

"I'm giving my fair share, of course. I ordered two dozen of the calendars—one for myself, and the rest for female relatives. They'll be thrilled."

"Thanks." Josh felt like a dolt, but what else could he say?

"Thanks? That's it?"

He sighed. "What do you want, Vicki?" She opened her mouth and with a grin, Josh waggled his finger at her, knowing exactly what she'd say. "Other than me."

Vicki laughed. "You know me too well." She touched his chest again so Josh caught her wrist and held it. He felt exposed enough bare-chested in a room full of people dressed in casual evening wear, without having a woman play with him.

Looking up at him through her lashes, Vicki said, "We had some good times together, didn't we?"

Because he knew women, Josh saw the vulnerability in Vicki's eyes. She needed to be reassured, so he did just that. He kissed her knuckles and said, "We had a terrific time. I always enjoyed your company, hon, you know that."

"But?"

Gently, because he hated to hurt anyone, Josh reiterated, "But it's over. I really am a one-woman man, now. That hasn't changed."

Vicki looked beyond him and winced. "Well, your one woman looks ready to string you up by your toes. I suppose I should get out of the line of fire."

Josh turned and sure enough, Amanda was fuming. He smiled and gave her a wave, still holding on to Vicki with his other hand, though Vicki did her best to edge away from him. Amanda huffed and turned her back on him.

Finally releasing her, he said to Vicki, "I should mingle."

She just shook her head and gave her farewells. He knew Vicki considered his actions strange, but he couldn't help being flattered every time Amanda showed her jealousy. He was used to women who were openly admiring, women who said what they thought and felt—especially about him.

He had to work hard to get any kind of commitment from Amanda—except when she saw him with another woman.

Mick wandered up next, his suit coat open, his hands shoved in his pants pockets. "Doing a little flaunting tonight, huh?"

Josh made a face. "Amanda's idea. All the guys from the calendar are shirtless, but I swear, some of them are enjoying it more than others."

"Others meaning you?"

"I can think of things I'd rather be doing."

Mick glanced around the crowded room. "Not having any fun here, huh?" It was in his nature to be forever on the lookout. Being cautious was partly his nature, partly his job.

Josh felt like an idiot, but he wouldn't tell Mick that. It wasn't that he was ashamed of his body, but it seemed ridiculous to make such a big deal of it. "I'll survive."

"Since you appear to be the theme of this bash, you better."

Everywhere Josh looked, there hung poster-size pictures of himself as Mr. November. Women would see the pictures, then either seek him out with their eyes and start twittering, or rush to buy the calendar. It was humiliating. "If it'll help make money for the charity, then what do I care?"

Mick looked over the buffet table filled with hors d'oeuvres donated by a local caterer. He chose a cracker piled with pinkish cheese, then eyed it closely. "It's for a great cause," he agreed. "I'd think you'd be enjoying yourself with all this attention."

"Would you?"

Mick snorted. "Okay, this is a little overdoing it. But the thing is, it seems you've given up completely on having fun."

Josh frowned at Mick as he held the cracker eye level and scrutinized it. "Meaning?"

"Meaning you just sent a little 'fun' packing."

Confused for the moment, Josh asked, "Vicki?"

"Yeah, Vicki. I remember her as one of your favorites. Any reason you've decided to become celibate?"

"Ha!" Josh crossed his arms over his bare chest and smirked. "Not in this lifetime."

"Oh?" Mick popped the whole cracker in his mouth and made appreciative noises. "Not bad."

"Just what the hell are you getting at, Mick?" Both Mick and Zack knew he was involved with Amanda. Hell, he'd been with her every available moment. He was here now, dressed in bunker pants and steel-toed boots, toting that damn ax she seemed so fond of, just for her. That should explain it all right there.

Mick searched the table for another cracker. Josh thought about hitting him in the head. "Damn it, Mick…"

"Zack is a little worried about you."

That set him back. "The hell you say!"

"Yeah, seems you've been…distracted." Mick glanced at him, then gave his attention back to the cracker. He sniffed at the cheese and made a face. Glancing around, hoping no one would notice, he set it back on the table.

"Distracted how? And if you pick up another bite to eat," Josh warned, "I'll take the ax handle to you."

Mick grinned and held up his empty hands. "Distracted at work. Zack says it's dangerous for you not to give your full attention to the job. We both figured you were just antsy over things with Amanda, but I gotta admit you have me confused. You two seem tight, but here you are, all jittery. And if you're not tight with Amanda, then why did you turn Vicki away?"

Josh sat the ax against the wall and rubbed his face. "Things are…difficult. Different. That's all. Amanda is…" He shook his head, unwilling to betray Amanda's trust, but wishing he had someone to talk to.

"She's what? Not falling at your feet?"

"Of course she wouldn't do that! She's…"

Mick raised a brow and waited.

"Oh hell, I love her, all right?" The words left his mouth and then he grinned. "I really do. I'm crazy about her."

Mick looked as if that was the last thing he'd expected to hear. It rattled him so much that he picked up the smelly cheese and ate it without thinking, then choked and had to grab for a drink.

Wheezing, he said, "You're in love?"

"Yeah."

"With *Amanda?*"

Eyes narrowed, Josh asked, "Any reason you're saying it like that?"

"No! I mean, she's terrific. Pretty, smart, sexy. It's just that she doesn't…" Mick struggled, then shrugged "…seem your type."

"She's unique."

Mick downed the rest of his drink in one gulp. "God, that cheese was nasty."

Laughing, Josh said, "That's good old American cheese and Swiss down there on the end, with the fruit."

"Thanks." Mick picked up a plate and moved in that direction. Josh followed. "So, uh, does Amanda feel the same way?"

"What is this, Mick? Are you my Father Confessor? Did Zack send you here to pick my brain and make sure I wasn't screwing up my life? Are you supposed to advise me and set me on the straight and narrow?"

"Yeah, something like that." Mick popped a grape into his mouth and smiled. "Now that's good."

His mood quickly turning black, Josh said, "Just let me go get my ax and then I'll…"

Mick caught his arm, laughing. "Don't bludgeon me. I swear, this was all Zack's idea. He'd have been here himself if Dani hadn't gotten sick. Wynn told him to come, but you know how Zack is, a real mother hen when his little girl isn't well."

"Yeah, I know how he is." Josh knew a buildup of sexual frustration had made him a little less than reasonable. He hoped Amanda told him how she felt soon, because he didn't know if he could take too much more.

"So is it true?" Mick asked. "Have you been distracted at work? And don't growl at me! With all the grief you gave us, you're due for some back."

Josh subsided at the truth of those words. He had harassed Mick and Zack plenty when they were trying to figure out the whole love thing.

Of course, Josh had it figured out. It was Amanda who seemed unsure. But damned if he'd tell Mick that.

"We're concerned," Mick continued. "Rightfully so, too. Hell, even Wynn and Del told me you were acting different. Not that I pay much attention to your moods, but now that I am, I see what they mean. And Zack sees you at work. He said everyone was razzing a probie, sending him outside repeatedly to find a hose winder—which I gather doesn't exist—and you never said a word."

All probationary firefighters caught hell on their first week at the station. As a lieutenant, Josh usually did his best to run interference, but true enough, he'd been distracted all week thinking about Amanda. He'd barely noticed the antics going on during his shift.

"Zack also says you've been slower on the drills."

He'd strangle Zack when next he saw him. "I know those drills by heart."

"Yeah, but that's not the point and you know it. So tell me, what's up?"

"It's private."

Mick gave him an incredulous look. "That never stopped you from butting into my business!"

"I know, but this isn't just my business. It's Amanda's business, too. She has some things to work out, and until she does, we're not...that is, I haven't..."

Aghast, Mick said, "Damn. You *are* celibate."

"It's temporary."

At the look on Josh's face, Mick sputtered and quickly snatched up a napkin. "Oh, this is priceless," he said, shaking his head while continuing to chuckle.

Through his teeth, Josh said, "It's not a big deal, damn it. I know what I'm doing."

"Hey, I'm not the one who thinks sexual variety keeps you young. That's your mantra, not mine."

Josh reached for his own drink. It was that or Mick's throat. "You always were a particular bastard."

"And you never were, not where women are concerned. But now you're hooked and she's making you work for it instead of throwing herself at you." Mick grinned. "This is great. I love it."

"Shut the hell up, will you?" Josh saw nothing amusing in the situation. Of course, if it had been Mick or Zack, he might have seen the humor.

"Damn, you're testy. Okay, okay!" Mick held up his hands when Josh started to reach for him. "Don't start foaming at the mouth. I wanted to get serious for a second, anyway."

His tone made Josh uneasy. "What? More unsolicited advice?"

Mick gave him that dark-eyed look he used to bring

criminals low. "I didn't think *you* knew any other kind."

Remembering the hell he'd put Mick through when Mick had fallen in love with Delilah, Josh had to agree. He'd handed out advice—and aggravation—left and right.

"You need to be more careful at work," Mick said. "I know women troubles can rattle any guy, but if there's a fire, you have to be thinking with the right head, and I'm not talking about the one you let make most of your decisions."

Josh bristled. "You saying I can't control myself sexually?" Ha! What a joke. If only Mick knew, he'd be applauding his iron control.

"I'm saying I don't want to see you get hurt."

"I'm damn good at my job." Feeling defensive, Josh squared off and waited for Mick to dare disagree.

Mick didn't give him the satisfaction.

"I'm not questioning that," he said, "just your frame of mind. Being lovesick is all well and good—hell, I personally think you're past due. But don't let your mind wander when your life is at stake, okay? That's all I'm saying."

Josh started to agree, when suddenly he felt a familiar tension. He was so attuned to Amanda, so aware of her on every level, he instinctively felt her presence.

He turned, already knowing she stood behind him.

Hands clasped together and her cheeks pale, Amanda stared up at him. She looked equal parts furious and mortified.

Covering his uneasiness at being caught while discussing her, Josh pulled himself together and reached for her. She felt rigid under his palms, but she didn't fight him when he tugged her to her tiptoes and kissed her lips. "Hey, sweetheart. Finally got a break, huh? It's about time. I was feeling sorely neglected."

She said, "Yes of course. You've only got every woman here following you around, trying to get your attention."

Josh said, "You noticed," and he grinned.

Amanda stared beyond him at Mick, who looked as uncomfortable as a dark, enigmatic undercover cop could look.

Mick drummed up a sad excuse for a casual smile and said, "Hello, Amanda. It's nice seeing you again."

"Mr. Dawson. Thanks for coming."

"Mick, please." Mick glanced at Josh, probably looking for assistance though Josh had none to offer. There were still times when he couldn't figure Amanda out at all, when her moods were a total mystery to him.

This was one of those times.

Mick forged on manfully. "Your reception here is a hit. The, uh, crackers are great."

Josh snickered at that and took pity on Mick. "Go mingle. Go buy a calendar. Just go."

"Delilah already bought several. But mingling sounds nice."

"Coward."

Mick saluted him and wandered off.

Turning back to Amanda, Josh said, "It amazes me how such a small woman can make grown men quake in their boots."

She sniffed. "That's utter nonsense, and you know it. You certainly aren't quaking."

Josh lifted his brows. Acrimony? That told him something, like she was pissed. More jealousy, maybe?

Somehow, he didn't think so. "Do you have any idea how badly I want to kiss you?"

Her gaze skipped away from his and her shoulders stiffened. "I wanted to talk to you about that."

"About kissing me? You been having the same naughty thoughts as me?"

"I... No! That's not what I meant at all." She frowned, chewed her lower lip, and then said, "I think we should calm things down a little."

Damn, she had overheard. Josh pretended he didn't understand. "Now why would you want to do that? Especially when last night was so nice?"

Nice, what an understatement. They'd lain together on Amanda's bed after watching a science-fiction movie and they'd kissed for an hour. Josh, feeling as randy and naughty as a teenager in the back seat of his dad's Chevy, had nonetheless enjoyed holding her close. He'd relished the way she'd gradually relaxed with him, and he'd enjoyed listening to her talk about her work and the stupid calendar and her plans for shade-loving flowers in the spring.

Hell, he just loved listening to her—because he loved her.

Amanda shook her head. "I saw you with that woman."

"Vicki?" He squeezed her shoulders, unconsciously caressing her, hoping to ease her just a bit. "She's an old girlfriend. I already explained things to her."

Stepping away from him, Amanda avoided his direct gaze. "Perhaps you were hasty with that," she said.

Josh crowded close to her back, refusing to let her put a physical or emotional distance between them. He'd worked too hard for the headway he'd gained to just give it up. "Mick already has me edgy. Don't piss me off more by suggesting I go to another woman, okay?"

Her head dropped forward as she tidied the table-cloth on the buffet table and sorted the silverware. Whenever Amanda got nervous, her hands got busy. "This isn't right, Josh. None of it is."

He kissed the ultrasoft skin beneath her ear. "Mmmm. Feels right to me."

"It's not fair."

"Yeah? To who?"

"To you." She whirled around and flattened both hands on his bare chest. She started to speak, then noticed the attention she drew to them. Plenty of women who'd been watching Josh all along now stared openly. "I'm making a spectacle of us both."

He didn't mind, but apparently, she did. "So let's find someplace to be alone."

"There's no place here. Besides, I can't just sneak off. I'm trying to successfully drum up interest in the calendar. Too many people donated too many things for me to simply…"

"Take time with me?" He knew that shot wasn't fair, but still couldn't stop himself from saying it. "Yeah, that'd be a waste, wouldn't it?"

Her eyes widened. "Josh! That isn't at all what I meant."

He ran a hand through his hair, regretting his hasty words, feeling his frustration rise. But damn it, she was trying to pull away. "I know it. I'm sorry."

"Don't apologize, either. It's just…" She looked around. "You're right. We should talk. Let's go into the office in the back." She lifted her wrist and Josh saw a coiled band with several keys on it. "I can get us in."

The idea of a private talk no longer appealed. Josh had a terrible suspicion that she wanted to dump him. The damn calendar was done, and God knew the thing was a hit. Local groceries, bookstores and gift shops had agreed to sell them. Orders were coming in faster than they could be filled. The hall she'd gotten donated for the night was now crowded with interested parties, and the firemen who'd posed were considered local celebrities.

Amanda had no more use for him.

Josh marched behind her, cautiously holding the damn ax away from other people, feeling more ridiculous by the moment. He'd let her draw him in, let her use him...

The lock on the door clicked open and she stepped inside. Josh pushed in behind her and before she could find a light, he turned her and pressed her against the door.

He'd always been a breast man, and now, with Amanda's plump breasts pressed to his bare chest, he felt all his repressed lust boil over.

"Josh!"

He kissed her. He kissed her with a week's worth of frustration and with the fear that she'd reject him now. He kissed her the way he'd been wanting to for a long time. He dropped the ax with a clatter and caught her rounded behind with one hand, urging her closer. With the other hand, he sought her breast, squeezing and cuddling, searching for and finding her nipple, wanting to groan when it puckered tight. He stroked her, then caught her straining nipple between his fingertips and plucked, rolled.

Filled with explosive urgency, he ate at her mouth, devouring her.

Until he felt her frantic hands trying to push him away.

Chapter 8

"Josh, please!" Amanda could barely catch her breath under the impact of that intense kiss and the experienced touch of his hands. She'd been thinking about him all day, stewing each and every time she saw another woman get close to him. She shouldn't care. The whole point of the reception was to share Josh's appeal so more calendars would be purchased.

All the men had shown up shirtless, as she'd directed. One by one, they'd stepped up to the podium with her to be introduced. Amanda had given their names, told what month they could be found, and then they'd removed their outer coats to reveal their hard muscled chests and shoulders. The women had "oohed" and "aahed" as each upper body was bared.

None of them had affected Amanda at all. She'd done her self-assigned job, seeing the men as a means to an end, a way to build up the donation to the burn center, a way to repay her debt.

They were a gorgeous lot, and Amanda was proud of each of them, but she barely noticed them as men.

Until Josh. As she'd suspected, he got the lion's share of attention. When he'd slipped off his jacket, looking chagrined and put out with the whole affair, the women had roared their approval.

All night long, she'd had to watch while the women ogled him and wanted to touch him and competed for his time and attention. His old girlfriend had been especially brazen, but Amanda wasn't surprised. No woman would want to give up on Josh easily, and knowing that, knowing what each woman thought while looking at him, drove Amanda crazy.

He drove her crazy.

She'd barely had a chance to talk to him, but now that they were alone, Josh seemed intent on kissing her senseless.

Amanda pressed his shoulders again and suddenly he cursed and pulled away from her, then cursed again when he stumbled into a chair and sent it skidding onto its side.

With shaking hands, Amanda hastily searched the wall for the switch. Bright fluorescent light shone down on Josh's naked back and shoulders, which he had turned toward her. He stood over the fallen chair, the ax on the floor beside it. His tawny head was down, his large hands curled into fists at his sides.

Her chest hurt just looking at him—and then she remembered what she wanted to talk to him about.

Because of her, Josh was no longer being as cautious at work as he should be. He was thinking of her, of being forced into celibacy, when he should have been concentrating on the job. That would never do. His job was dangerous enough without her adding to it.

She knew what she had to do.

"If you want," Amanda said, her voice sounding hollow in the silent enclosed room, "we can have sex tonight."

Josh snapped his head around. His green eyes blazed with some emotion she didn't recognize. "What the hell did you say?"

Amanda swallowed hard and took a step back. He didn't look particularly pleased by her offer. After the way he'd just been kissing her, after the way he'd kissed her and touched her all week, she'd thought...

"I heard what Mick said," she admitted, hoping he would understand. "I don't want you to get hurt." His narrowed gaze searched hers and she added with a whisper, "If you did, it would kill me."

He took two long strides toward her, then wrapped his long fingers around her upper arms, lifting her. "Why? Why would you care, Amanda?"

Her feet left the floor. She grabbed his biceps, holding on in the awkward position. This wasn't at all what she'd expected. Why couldn't he ever once do as she anticipated? She'd thought...what? That he'd be happy? Anxious?

Her thoughts were in a jumble, but she did her best to explain. "I've hurt enough people. You've been too good, too helpful... Josh, you're a *hero*." Surely he knew that, accepted it. "We need you. Everyone needs you."

For the briefest moment, his hands tightened almost

to the point of pain. There was such a look of raw emotion in his green eyes, she flinched away.

Abruptly he set her on her feet and took two steps back. He seemed remote, even angry, when he said, "Why do you want to sleep with me, Amanda? Or should I ask if you *do* want to sleep with me? You made the offer, but then, that doesn't tell me much."

She licked her dry lips and tried to order her thoughts. It wasn't easy with him standing there half-naked, looking so sexy while glaring at her. "We've been fooling around all week."

"Not me." His jaw hardened. "I was dead serious."

"Oh." Her brain seemed a wasteland, not a clear thought to be found. "I mean, with all the kissing and the touching we've been doing, I assumed... In fact, you've told me!" Her head cleared and she crossed her arms defiantly. "You said you wanted to have sex with me!"

"No, I told you I wanted to make love. There's a difference." He shrugged one massive, hard muscled shoulder. "But either way, so what?"

This whole situation got more difficult by the moment. Had he changed his mind about wanting her? Amanda didn't think so, especially given that hot kiss just a minute before. He'd so taken her by surprise, her knees had nearly buckled.

So why had she thought to make the suggestion? Oh yeah, his well-being. "You've been distracted at work," she pointed out, "and not thinking clearly, and Mick seemed to think it's because you're..."

"Not getting any?"

He made it sound so crude. Well, she wouldn't let

him bully her or embarrass her. She met his gaze head-on and raised her chin. "Yes."

Josh laughed. He looked at her and then he laughed some more. But it didn't sound like a happy laugh. Just the opposite. "I guess that answers my question, doesn't it? You didn't offer to sleep with me because you want me, not because everything we've done has gotten to you as much as it has to me."

It had, but he didn't give her a chance to explain that. Everything he'd done, every moment with Josh, had been wonderful. Sometimes she couldn't sleep for wanting him. Her need for him increased every day, with every sight of him, every touch, every kiss, until now it was a constant ache. She dreamed of having him inside her, and it was always so good…and then she'd wake up and feel embarrassed and guilty as she remembered that awful night long ago.

But still she wanted him. Her emotions were so conflicted these days, she didn't know what to think or feel. She only knew that Josh was important to her and she couldn't tolerate the thought of anything happening to him.

He bent for the ax, straightened, and looked at her with an expression of emptiness. "I'm not interested in screwing a martyr."

Amanda reeled backward, bumping into the door, then had to move quickly when Josh reached for the handle.

On his way out, he said, "Thanks, but no thanks," and he left the door standing open behind him. His stomping footsteps were drowned out by the noise of the crowd in the outer room.

For a minute, Amanda just stood there, her body and

mind thankfully numb so that she barely felt the quaking of her legs, the riotous pounding of her heart, the constriction of her lungs. Her eyes burned with hurt and humiliation.

That *"thanks but no thanks"* had sounded pretty final. But then what had she expected? That he'd wait around forever for her to change? For her to get over her silly phobias and be a real woman? No other man had; no other man would.

She was still standing there, unable to assimilate anything except her sense of loss, when Josh reappeared. He stomped in, cursing under his breath, his face tense.

He took one look at her, groaned and stepped into the room, slamming the door behind him. He propped the ax against the wall and turned the lock.

Amanda stared stupidly at the doorknob.

"Come here." Josh said it gently and reached for her at the same time.

"But…"

"God, I'm sorry." Then he was holding her close to his bare warm chest and rocking her a little and it felt so good, Amanda got angry.

She pushed back and asked with a good dose of suspicion, "What does this mean? Just what are you doing, Josh?"

He smiled and opened his big hand on the small of her back, urging her close again until her belly was against his pelvis and her breasts flattened against his hard abdomen. "Hell if I know," he groaned, and propped his chin on top of her head.

Amanda could feel the solid thumping of his heartbeat vibrating throughout his big body, and the warmth radiating off his skin. She also heard the smile in his tone.

"It's not funny!" Her nose got squashed into his sternum and she inadvertently breathed his scent.

"No," he agreed in a gravelly tone, "it's really not."

"Then why do you sound so amused?"

"Are you kidding?" He kissed the top of her head. "If it was Mick or Zack floundering around like a fish out of water, I'd be laughing my ass off."

Furious and cold one minute, teasing and tender the next. And they said women were fickle. Amanda shook her head and strained away to see him. "I don't understand you."

"I know. Most of the time I don't understand myself." He made that sound like a grave confession. "But damn it, Amanda, I am not going to give up on you."

She frowned. "I didn't ask you to." Then she muttered, "Though I probably should. This whole thing—"

"What *thing?*"

"Us. Me. It's bad enough that you're having to woo me as if I'm a Victorian maiden, instead of a modern mature woman, but..."

Once again annoyed, he asked through his teeth, "But what?"

If he wanted the whole truth, she'd give it to him. "But now, instead of using your...assets to garner more sales for the calendar, I'm warning women away from you."

Josh straightened and his brows shot up. "You are?"

"Yes, I am. Half the women out there are single and, of course, they just have to ask me about you. As if I'm supposed to help set you up or something! If I'd been thinking straight, if I'd been doing what I

should be doing, I'd have encouraged them to buy another calendar and get you to sign it, sort of as a way
to break the ice."

He crossed his arms over his chest and scrutinized
her with great curiosity. "So what'd you do instead?"

Amanda couldn't quite look at him. "I told them
you were taken," she murmured.

"Come again?"

Amanda knew good and well that he'd heard her,
he just wanted to make her say it again. Well fine. She
glared at him and almost shouted, *"I told them you
were taken."*

"Ah." Josh flexed his jaw, whether because she'd irritated him or because he was trying to hide a smile.
She wasn't sure. "Why, Amanda?"

"Because I didn't want you to get involved with
any of them."

"Yet you made me that ridiculous, unemotional
offer."

Angry, remorseful and now insulting. She'd about
had enough of his mood swings. She reached out and
smoothed her hand over his broad chest. Her fingers
found a soft curl there in the middle of his pectoral
muscles where the hair was thickest. She smiled up at
him, and yanked hard.

"Ow, damn it!" Josh lurched, yowled again when
she didn't release him, then caught her wrist and held
her hand still. "That hurt!"

"Did it ever occur to you," she asked, retaining her
hold on his chest hair in a threatening manner, "that
I'm not sure how to go about offering? I've never had
much practice. Every other guy I've been close to has
been the one pressing me, so I never had to offer!"

Now Josh frowned. "I haven't pressed you because I want you to want me. What I don't want is you making some damn offer like a sacrifice. Like you'd be doing me a favor."

Sacrifice. So, that's what he thought? And it had insulted his macho pride?

Her eyes narrowed again. "It'd be nice if you explained all this to me instead of being insulting and mean."

Josh softened. He worked her fingers loose and carried her hand up to his neck, safely away from his chest. "I was mean?" he asked apologetically.

"Yes." Amanda put her other arm around his neck and laced her fingers together at his nape. His dark blond hair felt cool and silky on her knuckles. "I didn't know what to think. You're a very confusing, complex man."

Josh chuckled, then squeezed her close. "That's the pot calling the kettle black, sweetheart." She started to object and he kissed her, a softer, gentler kiss this time. "And here I used to think I knew women."

"You do." Boy, did he ever. Josh knew how to look at her, how to touch her just the right way to make her hot and needy. He also had an uncanny ability to read her mind on occasion. It unnerved her.

"Not you," he denied. "You're a mystery, Amanda, always keeping me guessing. I never know what's going through that head of yours."

"I love kissing you," she said. "That's what's going through my head right now."

His eyes darkened, turning a rich forest green. With her gaze snared in his, Josh very slowly brought his hand up over her waist to her ribs, then higher, just

below her left breast. Her heart galloped—in anticipation and excitement.

"You liked me touching you, too, didn't you?" he
asked.

Breath catching, Amanda murmured, "Yes."

He leaned down, his mouth touched hers, and his
hot palm slid up and over her until he held her breast
securely. His long fingers were gentle, molding over
her, weighing her, caressing. Against her mouth, he
said, "I've always loved breasts."

A laugh caught Amanda by surprise, even as she
closed her eyes to absorb more of his touch. "As I understand it," she breathed, "most men do."

"Some of us like them more than others." And he
growled, "Damn, you have great breasts."

It was the most absurd conversation she ever could
have imagined. Josh touched her nipple, rubbing the
very sensitive tip, and her voice broke as she said,
"Thank you."

"It's not just your incredible rack that turns me on,
though."

Amanda couldn't keep up with his verbal nonsense, not while he was deliberately arousing her. She
dropped her head onto his chest and groaned.

"No," he said, still enticing her. His fingers closed
on her nipple in a soft pinch, and even through her
blouse and bra, it was enough to make her muscles
brace, her breath catch. "Talking to you, hearing you
laugh, smelling you, hell even thinking of you gets
me hard."

Her hold on his neck was now a necessity. Without
it, she might have slid to the floor in a puddle.

"I want to touch you between your legs, okay?"

Her eyes snapped open and everything inside her clenched and curled against a wave of heat. They were at a reception, hidden away in an empty office with over a hundred people only a few yards away. "Josh…"

"Shhh. Tell me if you like this."

He pressed his hand to her belly, then pushed lower until his fingertips just touched her in a barely there caress. His palm was on her lower belly, his fingers together, not moving. There was only that fleeting press, nothing more. Her wool skirt felt nonexistent. Her body rocked with her heartbeat.

He didn't move any further.

Panting, held in suspense, Amanda rasped, "Josh?"

His mouth touched her temple. "Everything okay?"

His voice was low and rough and added to her urgency. She bobbed her head, anxious to reassure him. "Yes. Fine."

"Good." He kissed her ear. "How about this?"

"Ohmigod." Amanda squeezed her eyes shut as his big hand pushed lower, dipping down between her thighs, stroking, seeking through the layers of material to find just the right spot. She felt hot on the outside, wet on the inside.

"Is that good?"

"Yes." Better than good. Astounding, really.

Other than her aborted attempt at sexual satisfaction the night of the fire, she'd never felt so aroused. And even then, it wasn't the same. She'd been just seventeen, more excited about doing the forbidden and feeling grown-up than about the boy she'd been with.

Those thoughts were morbid and Amanda did her best to block them from her mind. She wanted to concentrate on Josh, not the past. Yet, the past was there, forever a part of her…

"Imagine how it would be," Josh whispered, interrupting her disturbing retrospection, "with nothing between my hand and your body. My fingers are rough from the work I do, but I'd be really careful, Amanda. A woman is so soft here, so tender."

Her body jerked in reaction to those words.

Josh made a sound of pleasure. "I bet you're silky wet right now, aren't you? I'd love to feel my fingers inside you. Or my tongue slipping over you. Or my—"

A fine tension began to build inside her. Her nails sank into his shoulders and she arched against him with a raw groan.

Josh moved against her protectively. He still toyed with her nipple, continued to put warm damp kisses on her face, her ear, her neck while saying such tantalizing, provoking, *stimulating* things to her.

And his hand… Josh's hand was between her legs making her feel incredible things.

"Yeah, that's it," he encouraged, stroking her, pushing her.

A loud rapping rattled the door, making them lurch apart. Amanda barely stifled a small yelp. Josh cursed.

"Josh?" called a familiar, hushed voice. "Are you in there?"

Josh froze, his body taut and hot, his nostrils flared. "I'll kill him."

"Ohmigod," Amanda whispered, then covered her mouth with shaking hands. She was in charge of this project, responsible for its success. And instead of supervising things, she was hidden away, being pawed. Just the way she'd been seven years ago…

She drew up on that awful thought. No, Josh made it all different. He made it all…special, not ugly.

"I swear," Josh muttered, rubbing his hands up and down Amanda's back as if to soothe her, "I'm going to—"

"You have my profuse apologies," Mick said through the door, "but there's at least a dozen people out here looking for Amanda and they'll be checking back here in another two minutes."

"Damn it." Josh held her away from him, his gaze searching, concerned. Frustration vibrated through him, shone in his eyes and in the set of his mouth. "Amanda, are you okay?"

Okay? She felt weak with mortification and shaky with arousal—and on the verge of discovering something truly wonderful. "Yes."

"Don't look like that, Amanda," he snapped, misinterpreting her expression of wonder. "What we did—"

"Josh, I can hear you," Mick called, "every damn word. I'll leave if you'll just tell me what to tell everyone else?"

Without looking away from her, Josh shouted, "Give me a minute!"

Regretfully, Mick said, "That's about all you've got before the posse is sent out."

With a heated curse, Josh told Amanda, "Don't move," and turned away to open the door. In a nasty tone that more than gave away his frustration, as well as what they'd been doing, if it hadn't already been painfully apparent, he barked, "What the hell is it?"

Mick answered in a rush. "A whole group of secretaries and assistants from the office complex down the street just showed up, but all the calendars Amanda had out are sold. Some women already left because the calendars were gone, but the secretaries are a little tougher. They're eyeing the ones other women have bought and gotten signed, especially if anyone is holding more than one. You know a bunch of people bought more than one so they could give them away as gifts. Anyway, I'm afraid you're about to have a riot on your hands if you don't get more calendars out here and fast."

Struggling past an amalgam of rioting sensations, Amanda stepped around Josh and forced herself to face Mick. "I'll be right there," she assured him. "If you could let everyone know I'm getting more calendars right now...?"

Mick looked her over, then quickly averted his eyes. Was it that obvious? Amanda wondered. Could Mick tell so easily that she'd been fooling around with Josh at the most inappropriate time? That rather than tending to her obligations and pushing sales of the calendar to earn more money for the burn center, she'd been getting groped instead?

Wonderfully groped, Amanda corrected herself. Almost groped to the point of oblivion.

Her face flushed.

Evidently, her situation was very obvious, because Mick rubbed a hand over his jaw and stared at the ceiling. "Yeah, sure," he said, sounding ill at ease. "I'll tell them. That ought to buy you a few minutes at least, as long as they know more calendars are on the way."

"Thank you."

"I could, ah, fetch them for you," Mick offered to the ceiling, "if you want to tell me where they're at?"

Amanda wondered if she had a big red *G* on her

forehead for "groped." The way Mick acted, she wouldn't be at all surprised. "Thank you, but I need to get back anyway."

Mick glanced at Josh, and Amanda saw their shared man-to-man look. Mick's expression said, "I tried," and Josh returned a silent "thanks for the effort."

"All right." Mick headed off, saying over his shoulder, "I'll go appease the mob. Just don't be too long."

The second he was gone, Josh closed the door and turned to stare down at Amanda with his fists propped on his lean hips. "Don't you dare start feeling embarrassed," he ordered.

She all but sputtered a laugh. "Josh, *anyone* would be embarrassed right now! Mick knew exactly what we were doing."

"So?" Josh shrugged, the picture of unconcern. "Now he knows we're human. Big deal. He's not exactly a choirboy himself."

Amanda wasn't about to discuss all this with Josh now, not with people waiting for her. Besides, she was embarrassed, but she wasn't exactly ashamed. And not for one single second did she fool herself into thinking *she'd* have called a halt to what they were doing. If it hadn't been for Mick's interruption, they might have ended up being caught in a much more compromising position.

That thought brought another, and Amanda wondered just what position Josh might have initiated. No doubt, he knew dozens of positions appropriate to making love in an empty office.

"What?" Josh asked. A crooked smile tilted one side of his mouth as he leaned closer. His eyes warmed. "What naughty things are you thinking, Ms. Barker?"

Amanda bit her lip, chagrined once again that he could so easily read her. But she was too curious not to ask. "How would we have…you know. In here?"

Josh froze, then groaned and ran his hand through his hair, leaving the dark blond locks on end. "You're killing me." He pretended his knees were weak and slumped against the wall. "That's a loaded question, honey, guaranteed to give a guy a boner. That is, if I didn't already have one, which I do."

Amanda's eyes widened, but she managed not to look. She ended up with a dazed, goggle-eyed stare, but she kept her attention fixed firmly on his face.

Josh laughed and reached for her. "Tell you what. Tonight, when we finish this damn reception, I'll show you."

Her heart lodged in her throat at that promise. "Yes, all right."

Amanda smiled at him, then edged toward the door. If she didn't leave now the damn posse might find her accosting Josh. Seeing him look so disheveled, she paused and reached for her hair with a sudden concern. Would everyone know what she'd been doing? Or was Mick just more intuitive because he knew Josh and his sexual propensities? "Do I look okay?"

Josh touched her cheek with an unsteady hand. "Babe, no woman could look better."

Amanda was still high on that compliment when she slipped from the room and hurried down the back hallway to the rear door. She assumed Josh would present himself out front shortly, and would buy her enough time to restock the calendars.

The frigid wind cut right through her suit jacket and blouse when she stepped into the lot where her car was parked. Silvery light from streetlamps lent an eerie glow to the cold dark night and reflected off the falling sleet, which now covered her car and was turning the lot into a slick treacherous sheet of ice.

The driver's door was frozen shut and Amanda had to work to get it open. She looked around and saw ice hanging heavily from every phone wire and tree branch. The crackling of sleet peppering the pavement mingled with the sound of the howling wind.

It was a miserable night.

Her hands and nose felt numb and her knees were knocking together by the time Amanda headed back in. She wished she'd had enough sense to grab her coat, but she'd been daydreaming about Josh and that carnal promise of his instead. Shivering uncontrollably, arms laden with boxes, she struggled with the heavy back door.

A second later the door flew open and she almost toppled over. *Josh.*

"What the hell are you doing out there alone?" he demanded.

Her uncontrollable shriek of surprise echoed up and down the hallway. Josh relieved her of the cumbersome boxes and Amanda thanked him by punching him in the shoulder. "You scared me half to death," she accused, once she'd caught her breath.

"You need scaring." He caught her arms and hugged her close, sharing some of his warmth. Amanda noticed he was now wearing a shirt and coat.

Through chattering teeth, she said, "I had to get more calendars. You already knew that."

His scowl darkened. "I thought you had them somewhere in the building, not outside. You should have sent me, or let Mick go when he offered."

Her face was still pressed against him. He felt warm and smelled delicious and she said without thinking, "I needed to cool down anyway."

His hands, which had been coasting up and down her back, paused. Then he squeezed her and groaned. "I must be cursed."

Amanda tilted back to see him and got an awful premonition. "Josh, what's wrong?"

"I have to go into work."

Her heart sank. *"Now?"*

"Unfortunately, yeah." He began rubbing her again, in apology, in regret. "One of the supervisors has the flu. He's heading home, so I need to finish out his shift."

Amanda wanted to cry. Her body still buzzed with need, every part of her felt too sensitive, too…ready. She said, "Damn."

Josh smiled. "I know. Believe me, if I had any other choice, I'd grab it."

Her next thought was whether or not he'd come over after he'd finished the shift. She knew she'd gladly wait up. She finally felt ready to take the big step. Tonight could be the night. Sure, she'd had a few ill moments, thinking of that long-ago fire and what had resulted from her irresponsibility, but she still wanted Josh. Fiercely.

As usual, Josh read her mind. "I won't be off till sometime in the morning. Probably around three." Then he cupped her face and tipped it up and kissed her. His tongue moved softly, deeply into her mouth until her shivers were all gone and she felt feverish.

"Think about me tonight," he murmured against her mouth, "and tomorrow I swear I'll make the wait worth your while."

With those provocative words, Josh turned and stalked out through the door she'd just entered. Amanda was left with only the churning of lust.

Lust, and something so much more.

Chapter 9

Josh stared through the thick, angry black smoke and gave a silent curse. Long before they'd arrived on the scene, they'd smelled the acrid scent and he'd known, he'd just *known,* this particular fire was going to be a bitch.

His muscles hurt, his head pounded and he was so hot it felt like his skin was roasted beneath his turn-out coat. His gear, including the S.C.B.A., or air-pack, seemed to weigh more than the usual fifty pounds, thanks to his exhaustion.

They'd first gone in without hoses, intent only on rescue. They'd accomplished that much while neighbors all shouted at once, pointing, telling them about the shy quiet single lady still inside on the upper floor. The woman, who Josh had carried out himself, was now in the back of the ambulance being tended. She was a skinny little thing, in her late thirties, disoriented, probably suffering some smoke inhalation and shock, but she'd live.

Given the frigid temperatures and general nastiness of the frozen night, it was one of the worst fires Josh had ever encountered.

They worked their asses off with little success.

The fire spread too quickly, feeding off piles of old newspaper and accumulated junk, licking across dry rotted carpet and up the blistered walls. The howling wind seemed to spur it on, rushing in through shattered windows.

Josh's flashlight flickered over a faded floral couch, now turning orange in flames, then over a pile of books, what looked like an antique desk, a rickety footstool. The place was cluttered, proving the small female being treated outside was a pack rat. Josh searched through the house, seeing objects take shape, forming in the dark as he approached them.

He felt his way through the blackness, checking carefully, watching for a hand, the reflection of pale flesh, anything that might prove to be human.

The narrow flashlight beam bounced off a moving object and Josh crawled closer, then heard a cat's warning yowl. Twin green eyes glowered at him from beneath a small round table tucked into a corner. The cat looked panicked, ready to attack.

Josh's thick gloves provided some protection when he snagged the fat animal and hauled it protectively close to his body. The smell of singed fur burned his nostrils and he crooned in sympathy.

His croon turned to yell a second later as sharp

claws managed to connect with his flesh. Josh was barely able to maintain his tight hold on the feline.

Three loud blasts of the rig horn penetrated the crackle and hiss of the surrounding fire.

"Let's go," Josh said, and signaled the retreat. Three blasts of the horn meant the house was compromised. It was get out now, or maybe not get out at all. Everyone began exiting, Josh a little awkwardly given he had a furious cat tucked into his side.

The second he stepped into the snow-covered yard, the fresh cold air hit him like a welcome slap. Josh flipped up his visor and removed his air mask. There were reporters everywhere, mingling with the noisy neighbors. A flashbulb temporarily blinded him and enraged the cat. It lurched out his arms and shot up a nearby tree in a blur of breakneck speed. Perched on an ice-covered branch, out of harm's way, it took to yowling again.

Josh heard his name called and turned. More pictures were taken, but he didn't even have the chance to get annoyed. The woman they'd pulled from her bed hung on the arm of one of the firefighters. She was now wrapped warmly in someone's coat and a blanket, her thin legs shoved into heavy boots to protect her feet from the cold. Her hair stood on end, and she stumbled toward Josh, her eyes wide and unseeing, her face utterly white in the glow of the moon and the reflecting flames.

"My baby!" she screamed, nearly beside herself. "You have to get my baby!" And she lurched toward the house, falling to her knees in the snow, sobbing, trying to crawl.

Josh went rigid. He looked back at the house, glowing red from within. His heart struck his ribs, his muscles clenched. *Goddamnit, no!*

"Please," the woman moaned, "oh please," and she fought against the restraining hands, as vicious in her upset as the poor cat had been.

Josh locked his jaw, trying to think in the two seconds he didn't really have. His senior tailboard firefighter, fists clenched, shoulders hunched, said, "I'll go."

Josh felt sick. This was the type of decision he didn't like to make. "You're volunteering for a blind, left-hand search in a totally involved fire?"

The firefighter nodded grimly. "Damn right."

Josh understood. He'd already decided to go back in himself.

Then, almost like a gentle stroke, he remembered Amanda. Men had thought she was inside, when she wasn't. During the trauma of a fire, it was difficult as hell to be rational, but that was his job, and now Amanda had helped him.

The probability seeped into him, easing past the exhaustion and fear and the rush of adrenaline, beyond his instinct to charge back inside to save a child, regardless of the odds. It helped him to think above the roar of the fire, the consuming heat, the shouting of all the neighbors, the local media and the wailing of the panicked woman.

A *single* woman. Living all *alone,* the neighbors had said. In her late thirties…

Josh took three long strides to the frightened woman, dropped to his knees so he could hold her shoulders. "Where's the baby?" he asked, and got nothing but hysterical sobs in reply.

He caught her thin, ravaged face in his dirty gloved hands and made her meet his probing gaze. "Where," Josh demanded, "is the baby?"

She blinked tear-swollen eyes, sniffed, then covered her face. Her voice quavered and rose as she wailed, "Upstairs. I think he's still upstairs!"

I think. Josh drew an unsteady breath, silently praying. "Give me a description."

Wiping her eyes on the edge of the blanket, she nodded. "He's fat, mostly black with a white tip on his tail." She shuddered. "Oh please, please find him for me."

Josh collapsed. All the strength left his body and he slumped onto his ass with a great sigh of relief.

"The cat," he said, and smiled. Without giving it another thought he caught the woman and pulled her into him, hugging her close. "I got your cat, miss. He's fine, I promise. Look there in the tree." Josh, still supporting her, turned her with his body and pointed. "See him? He's plenty peeved, and howling to raise the moon, but he's not hurt."

With a cry, the woman stumbled away from Josh and ran awkwardly in the too-big boots and long coat. Two men, concerned because she was so frail, raced behind her. Josh laughed out loud, then scrubbed his hands over his face. "Oh, God."

"You okay?" Another firefighter, a friend, put a hand on Josh's shoulder.

"Hell yeah." Josh looked up at the starless sky, felt the prickling of frozen rain on his face, the bite of a cutting wind. "Hell yeah," he said with more energy. "I'm great."

It was another two hours before they'd finished raking the charred insides of the house out to the sidewalk.

It all had to be broken apart and hosed down. Normally that was the hardest part for Josh, seeing someone's life reduced to a black heap on the curb. Furniture, clothing, memories, all gone.

But this time what he saw was the woman sitting in the back of the ambulance, dirty and disheveled, wearing someone else's clothes—and cuddling her "baby" wrapped in a thick warm blanket.

Josh was amazed to see her smiling, occasionally singing, and even from where he swung his ax several yards away, he could have sworn he heard that big cat purring in bliss.

Tears stung his eyes, not that Josh gave a damn. If anyone noticed, he'd blame it on the smoke. But in that moment, he made up his mind. When they finished, he wouldn't go home to get some much-needed sleep as he'd intended. He'd go to Amanda, where he belonged. He'd tell her how much he loved her, how much he needed her, and it would have to be enough.

He'd make it be enough—for both of them.

Amanda jerked her front door open the minute she heard the rumbling of the approaching car. Josh! She'd watched the unfolding details of the fire on the news, fretting, sick at heart, wanting and needing to be with him. At first she just hoped he'd come to her when his shift was over. Then she'd decided if he didn't, she would go to him.

Snow and ice crunched beneath her slippers as she ran through the twilight morning to greet him, unmindful of the cold frosting her breath, the wind howling through her robe.

Josh turned off his car lights, and Amanda noticed

the sheer exhaustion that seemed to weigh him down as he sat a moment behind the wheel.

Then he saw her.

Quickly stepping out of the car, Josh said, "Hey," and he caught her as she launched herself against him. "What is it, babe?"

He was warm and hard and alive, so big and so strong. Amanda wanted to touch him all over, to absorb him and his strength and his goodness. She needed to know that he was all right, that the fire hadn't touched him.

Her arms locked around his neck and she squeezed him when he hauled her off her feet, out of the snow. She couldn't speak at first, but then he must have decided that was okay. He lifted her into his arms, cradled her to his chest and stalked to her front door with a type of leashed urgency.

Once inside he kicked her front door closed and went straight to the bedroom and the bed, stretching out with her. Amanda just held on, aware of the tension in his muscles, in his mood. He trembled, his face buried in her neck, his breath coming too fast. His thick arms were steel bands, circling her, getting her as close as possible.

Her throat felt tight and she tried to soothe him. "Josh."

Had something happened to him? Just the thought made her frantic, but she kept her tone calm and easy for him. Smoothing her hand through his thick, still damp hair, she said, "Please, tell me you're all right."

He nuzzled into her. "Yeah." His voice was thick with emotion. Rolling to his back and pulling her into his side, he said, "You heard about the fire?"

"It was on the news." They didn't look at each other. Amanda pushed his coat open so she could touch *him,* not leather. He wore an untucked flannel over a soft thermal shirt and he felt warm and hard and—she wanted him naked.

The thought came out of nowhere, but it was true. She wanted to assure herself that he wasn't hurt in any way.

Josh groaned. "I'm sorry. I didn't even think of that."

Amanda went to work on the buttons of his shirt, almost popping them in her haste. "You're not supposed to think of me. Not on the job, not when it's dangerous."

Josh started to protest and she sat up to work his coat off him. He obliged her, twisting his arms free, then giving a raw chuckle when she did the same with his flannel. Amanda tossed them both to the floor. She eyed his thermal shirt, caught the hem and tugged it upward.

"What are you doing, baby?" Josh asked, even as he rose up to help her get it off.

"Undressing you." The second the shirt was free, she saw the red, welted scratches on his neck. Her breath caught. "Oh, God. Are you all right?" She bent closer, touching his hot skin carefully.

Josh smoothed the backs of his knuckles over her cheek. "Yeah, I'm fine. I got that tangling with a fat cat who didn't have the sense to know I was his savior."

Amanda melted. He was the finest man she knew, and right now, he needed her.

She put several gentle kisses on his injured neck and then turned, straddling his legs with her back to him. His boots were lace-up and took her a minute, but she got them free and tossed them into the pile on the floor.

Josh's hands moved up and down her back. While her touch was agitated, his was more so. "When I'm naked," he asked, "will you get naked, too?"

"Yes."

He went still, then suddenly he was as busy as she, yanking at her robe, distracting her from her efforts as he tended his own. Amanda had to leave the bed to remove his jeans. Josh stood to help her. They bumped heads when they both bent at the waist to push the denim down his long muscled legs. Josh kicked free and reached for her, wanting to remove her nightgown.

Amanda didn't give him a chance. She pushed him onto the bed and stretched out over his tall, naked body. She kissed him, holding his face and feasting on his hot mouth, his throat, then down to his smooth shoulders and broad chest. He was alive, unharmed, and for now, he was hers.

The night had been endless and horrifying. She hadn't slept. Instead, she'd sat in bed watching television while waiting for the occasional update on the fire. Knowing Josh was good at his job, that he was well trained, hadn't helped. She just kept remembering how a man had died for her in just such a fire....

The memories had a different effect this time. Rather than filling her with shame that caused her to withdraw emotionally and physically, they spurred her on. They made her want to grab everything she could, every special moment so that not a single second of her life was wasted.

Josh risked himself every day on his job. He never knew when he'd be called upon to fight a fire, never knew which fire might be his last. He was a hero in the truest sense of the word, and he wanted her.

For that, she was very grateful.

Amanda licked at his hot smooth flesh, biting and sucking, hungry for him in a way she had never experienced, not even seven years ago. She wanted to give him pleasure. She wanted him alive with it.

Josh groaned and put his arms out to his sides, making himself a willing sacrifice.

"I was so scared," Amanda said between kisses and touches and deep breaths that filled her with Josh. It still wasn't enough. She didn't know if she'd ever have enough of him.

His abdomen contracted sharply when she put her mouth there, taking a gentle love bite of a sharply defined muscle. He settled one big hand in her hair, caressing, encouraging. "I was, too," he rasped. "I didn't want to go home alone." He paused to groan, then added, "I want to spend the day with you, Amanda."

"Yes." Amanda could smell him, fresh from a recent shower, but still with the lingering scent of smoke clinging to him. She saw traces of soot under his nails, and remembered him telling her how hard it was to remove, even though he wore gloves.

The hair on his chest, narrowing to a silky line down his abdomen, was brown rather than dark blond. But the hair at his groin was darker still, and thick. Amanda looked at him in fascination and awe and barely suppressed excitement.

His erection rose thick and long, a drop of fluid at the head, proving that he was excited, too.

With her heart pounding, Amanda touched him, exploring the hot, velvet-soft skin over tensile steel. She saw him flex with pleasure. Aware of his accelerated breaths, the intent way he watched her, she wrapped her hand around him in a firm hold. Gently, cautiously, she stroked up his length and back.

Josh's body strained from the mattress—and abruptly dropped when she bent and pressed a kiss just above where her fingers held him. It was a light kiss, tentative, but his wild response and guttural groan lured her. She licked up and over the tip, tasting his salty essence.

A sound of pleasure and pain exploded from his chest. His entire big body quivered. While her mouth moved over him, she cupped his testicles in her other hand, cradling him.

"Damn," he said, twisting on the sheets, "I like that, sweetheart."

"Me, too." She breathed in the strong musk scent of his sex, feeling swollen with emotion. It was nearly painful, feeling this way about a man.

"Take me into your mouth," he whispered urgently, "as much of me as you can."

Aroused by the carnal command, Amanda parted her lips wide and drew him in. Both his hands settled in her hair, tangling there, pressing her closer.

"Suck," he growled, arching his hips at the same time.

Amanda squirmed around for a better position to do as he needed her to. It was wonderful, tasting him like this, making him lose control, knowing he enjoyed her efforts. Long before she was ready to quit, Josh pulled away from her. His movements were clumsy, rough and fast and she found herself on her back on the bed, Josh between her thighs, in a matter of seconds.

He stared down at her, heaving, his face hard and dark and his eyes glittering. Not giving her a chance to speak, he took her mouth in a demanding, tongue-thrusting kiss.

His long fingers were between her legs, petting her, quickly parting her. She could feel her own slippery wetness, heard his low murmur of satisfaction. Her heartbeat thundered in her ears, a riot of emotions clamored for attention.

"I need you *now*," he panted into her mouth. Against her sensitive flesh, she felt the broad head of his penis, and then his penetration, unrelenting, forceful, going deeper and deeper.

She gasped, and he kissed her fiercely again, swallowing the sound of surprise and wonder.

Amanda twisted as he filled her, a little uncomfortable, a lot turned-on. She'd never had a man inside her and she found it to be an amazing thing, given the man was Josh.

He didn't allow her time to absorb the new sensations. No sooner was he all the way inside her than he began thrusting, sliding all the way out and then driving in deep again, harder and faster with each stroke.

With a groan, he pushed to his knees, forced her thighs wider apart and levered himself on one arm. Using his free hand he touched her everywhere, her breasts, her belly, down between her legs where he circled her, feeling himself as he pounded into her, feeling her stretched taut around him, holding him so tightly.

Amanda felt a scream of intense sensation building. She lifted her legs and locked them around Josh's waist—and he was a goner.

He cursed, long and rough and lurid and then he gripped her close, so close she couldn't draw a breath.

His face pressed hard into her shoulder and he said, *"Amanda,"* on a broken whisper.

She knew he was coming, could feel the spasms of his erection inside her, the jerking of his taut muscles, the stillness of his thoughts in that suspended moment. His broad back grew damp, heat rising off him in waves. His buttocks were tight, his thighs rigid. It went on and on and Amanda just held him, so pleased, so awed, until he dropped heavily against her, breathing hard, his heartbeat rocking them both.

Long minutes passed and Amanda relished his limp body cradled against her own. Finally, Josh lifted his head. His movements were slow and sluggish. He looked at Amanda, smiled tenderly, then shook his head. "I'm an ass," he said, his eyes twinkling lazily.

Startled, Amanda frowned. "No you're not. You're wonderful."

He smiled again, then stretched and moved to his back with an earthy groan. "Oh, hell." He put his forearm over his eyes. "That didn't go at all as I meant it to."

Amanda touched his sweaty chest. She couldn't *not* touch him.

"I should be horsewhipped," he complained.

"No, you should sleep here with me." She loved the feel of him, the sleek skin, now damp from exertion, over hard planes and hollows. He was so impressive in every way. "Stay all day, and then tonight again. Let me take care of you, Josh. I don't have to go into work and I assume you won't either now."

"I'm off for the next forty-eight hours." He lifted his arm and looked at her with heavy, sated eyes. "C'mere," he murmured, pulling her onto his chest, "let me show you 'wonderful.'"

It was almost six in the morning and they'd both been up all night. Amanda had spent the night worrying and waiting, but Josh had worked hard. She knew he had to be exhausted, going on lost reserve, but instead of sleeping, he kissed her forehead and asked, "Are you okay?"

"I'm astounded," she told him, and rubbed her cheek against his shoulder. "I'm also a little…messy."

"Mmm." Josh stroked his hand down her back, over her bottom, and between her legs. "Messy with me. And with you."

The things he did, the things he said never failed to shock Amanda. She was engorged, her flesh still tingling, and his rough fingertips rasped over her, gently exploring. She caught her breath and he pushed slightly inside her. The careful prod of his finger only served to exacerbate already sensitized nerve endings.

"I didn't use anything," Josh whispered, and began kissing her ear, her neck. He didn't sound apologetic so much as matter-of-fact.

Amanda couldn't assimilate the repercussions, not while his fingers were there, making her crazy.

"I still don't want to use anything," he told her, but rather than explain why, he pushed his middle finger deep inside her, making her gasp and stiffen.

Amanda nodded. She didn't want him to use anything, not if he didn't want to.

Her quick agreement drove him to action. "Spread your thighs wide around me."

She did, and felt him catch her knees to draw them up so she literally sat astride him, but with her cheek

still to his chest. It was an awkward position, forcing
her behind up.

"Hmm," Josh growled in satisfaction. "Now I can
get to you better."

And he did. Feeling open and vulnerable, Amanda
curled her fingers on his shoulders and held on. All
the tension began building again, quicker this time,
making her vision blur, her skin burn. She squeezed
her eyes shut.

"Stiffen your arms so I can get to your nipples."

Amanda moaned. She wasn't sure she could move.

"Amanda," he scolded in a rough throaty purr.
"Trust me, honey. Rise up. You'll like this."

Swallowing hard, she forced her arms straight.

With heated eyes, Josh surveyed her breasts. "Beautiful. Damn, honey, let me taste you." So saying, he
lifted his head and closed his mouth around her nipple to suckle.

A tearing moan escaped her. She was already so
aroused, but now his mouth drew at her breast and his
finger moved gently in and out of her, easily because
her lust and his climax had made her very slick. She
trembled. "Josh..."

He seemed to have all the patience in the world now
that he'd come. He licked a path to her other nipple
and put that breast through the same sensual torment.

Amanda hovered over him, her belly drawing tight,
her nipples aching, her vulva hot and pulsing. Josh released her breast with a last leisurely lick and looked
up at her. "You're close," he said with a tender smile.
"I can feel you contracting. Almost there."

Amanda couldn't answer him. She bit her lip and
concentrated on breathing.

"Do you want to come, sweetheart?"

She nodded.

"Tell me how this feels." He pulled his wet fingers from her and found her clitoris, gently stroking.

Amanda tipped back her head, moaning, so close...

Using his free hand, Josh positioned his erection against her and slowly pressed upward. He sank in to the hilt on the first stroke. "Let's sit you up," he said.

Amanda was too mindless with newfound carnality to do anything, so Josh gently guided her. The new position left her filled, impossibly stretched, and it was wonderful.

Josh bent his knees to support her back, cupped her left breast firmly in his hand, and started the rhythm that she knew would make her wild.

"You're so damn beautiful," he whispered, looking at her belly as it pulled tight, at her breasts as they bounced. She flushed, her muscles tensing and she did her best to stifle a scream.

Locking his intent gaze with hers, Josh licked his middle finger, wetting it, then reached down to toy with her turgid clitoris again.

The scream broke free.

Amanda reached back, clutching his thighs for support as her body shook and bowed with her first orgasm. Josh was so high inside her, filling her up, encouraging her, she felt shattered.

It was her turn to drop onto Josh, and she did so just as he cupped her hips, held her to him tightly, and gave into his second release with a rumbling groan.

Their hot sweaty skin felt fused, their heartbeats mingling. In slurred tones, Josh mumbled, "Sleep."

Mindless, Amanda reached out with a limp hand,

snagged the corner of the sheet and pulled it up and over their bodies. Just as Josh began to breathe evenly in sleep, she felt him slip from her body. Smiling, she realized she was really messy now, but she didn't care. She closed her eyes on a sigh, and fell asleep.

Chapter 10

Josh woke with a groan and without even thinking, he reached for Amanda. He found an empty bed.

His head fuzzy from lingering exhaustion, he looked toward the bedside clock. It wasn't even noon yet, but it felt like he'd been out cold for two days. His body was lethargic, his brain sated for the first time in weeks.

And he smiled, knowing why he was sated, remembering Amanda's scream as she'd climaxed, how her sexy brown eyes had gone all soft and vague in her pleasure. She'd been a virgin, so snug and warm his brain had almost shut down. She was all his—he'd given her her first climax.

At that thought Josh frowned and jerked upright. His head spun, but he ignored it. *Her first time.* God, he hadn't been gentle and coaxing and understanding. He hadn't eased her into lovemaking.

He hadn't even insured her pleasure that first time.

He'd been a pig, concerned only with his own pleasure. He'd coerced her into giving him a blow job! He'd been wild, like a crazy man, pushing her and...

Naked, Josh threw his legs over the side of the bed and cupped his head in his hands. For weeks he'd been planning to make Amanda limp with pleasure while utilizing iron control over his own urges. She was emotionally fragile where sex was concerned, and more than a little wary about commitment.

He'd hoped to woo her with sex, to show her how beautiful it could be between them. *Ha!* He remembered the way she'd taken him in her mouth, the way he'd instructed her, and he squeezed his eyes shut. What they'd done had been raw and uncontrolled and just remembering made his blood boil.

He pushed to his feet, going over in his mind all the things he'd say to her, how he'd explain and try to make it right.

A quick trip to the bathroom was top of the list. He recalled Amanda saying she was messy, and what had he done? He should have bathed her, cherished her. He should have used his mouth to bring her to orgasm. It was one of the most intimate methods of making love, and it was something he especially enjoyed. But he hadn't tasted Amanda, hadn't shared that with her.

Instead, he'd had her ride him, and he'd been so deep... Josh groaned. At least that second time she'd gotten her own orgasm.

Josh washed up, splashing his face with cold water to clear away the cobwebs. Though he now smelled more like sex than smoke, he still felt coated in soot. God knew he'd scrubbed long enough under the shower before coming to Amanda early that morning. He hadn't wanted any reminders of the fire for fear it would trigger her memories.

Last night he'd needed her more than he'd needed air.

He needed her still.

Josh located his jeans, now neatly folded over the foot of the bed, and he stepped into them. He didn't bother with the zipper or the snap and despite the chill of the air, he never gave his shirt a second thought. The moment he entered the small living room, his eyes were drawn to her.

She sat at the tiny kitchen table, the morning paper open before her and a blank, almost shocked look on her face.

Damn, damn, damn. Josh strode to Amanda and pulled her from the chair. He'd tell her he loved her and she'd just have to accept it. Sex was great, damn it, not something to shy away from, not something to mentally link to a bad memory. Sex between them was so incredible he didn't know how he'd survived.

So what that he'd shown her the more carnal side to sex, rather than the gentle beauty of it? He was a man, and he didn't see a thing wrong with enjoying a woman's body in every way possible.

Those thoughts had him shaking.

"Amanda..." he started, but she looked at him and there were tears in her big brown eyes that stopped his heart. She glanced away at the paper, opened to an article about the fire. Accompanying the text was a large color picture of him, carrying that ungrateful cat. He was backlit by the fire, and the photo looked more staged than anything.

Josh released her to pinch the bridge of his nose. His head pounded. "Sweetheart..."

With shaking fingers, Amanda touched his mouth. "I have to tell you something."

He felt sick. "Me first." He drew a bracing breath. "I love you."

Her eyes opened wide in shock. Her mouth moved, but nothing came out.

"I love you, damn it!"

She blinked at his raised voice and stepped away from him. Even rumpled from a night of debauchery, wearing only a robe, Amanda managed to look elegant. Her hair had been brushed and her nails were pink and he wanted her again. Right now. He eyed the cluttered kitchen table. Probably not sturdy enough, he decided. He shook his head.

"Amanda," he warned, about ready to lose his cool, "you better say something and fast."

She nodded, and gestured at the paper without looking at it. "I saw that and realized I should use it to help promote the calendar. You're a remarkable hero and the whole town knows it by now. It's...great publicity."

Josh locked his thighs. The hell she would. The hell he'd let her! Last night had been—

"But I knew I couldn't."

His anger died a rapid death.

She turned her face up to him, appearing dazed again. "I don't want to share you anymore. That damn reception was hard enough, having all those women fawn over you and knowing what they were thinking because I was thinking it, too."

His tension eased. Cautiously he asked, "What were you thinking?"

"How much I wanted you. How sexy you are, how heroic and wonderful and—"

"I'm just me, babe." And he reiterated, "And I love you."

She swallowed. "I need to start getting things set up for the next calendar."

"The *next* calendar." Her verbal leaps made his head spin. Two more seconds and he was carrying her back to bed for more of that primal mating that made *him* feel a whole hell of a lot better.

"I'd like to make it a yearly event. All kinds of possibilities occurred to me, only…" Amanda bit her lip, then forged on. "Only I can't stand the thought of sharing you."

Josh smiled and explained, "You don't have to share me."

She put a hand to her forehead and looked away. "I don't own you."

"Marry me." He made the offer with a racing heart and a lot of uncertainty. "That's close enough isn't it?"

Amanda whipped around to face him, dropped into her seat, and watched him with the same fascination she might have given a snake. "You want to marry me?"

Josh went to his knees in front of her. He really had to make her understand. "I've known a lot of women—"

She put her hands over her ears, and he pulled them away. Amanda was such a jealous little thing—and he loved it.

"I've had a lot of fun, Amanda," he explained. "But no one has ever made me feel like you do." He carried her hand to his chest, held it there over his heart. "I *love* you. I want to make babies with you and plant gardens and go on family vacations and all that." Josh frowned with sincerity. "I want us to grow old together. And I damn well want you to tell me you love me, too."

She started to speak, but he wasn't ready for her to yet. He had a few more points to make. "Amanda, you do love me, you know. Last night you were incredible. I'm sorry I lost my head there, but you're just too much—"

"I'm just me!"

"—and once you touched me, well, baby, I went a little nuts." Josh shrugged. "There's nothing wrong with us having great sex. I'd meant to be really gentle and romantic, but it didn't work out that way. I'd been thinking about you all night and I guess I was half-cocked before I got here."

Amanda choked at his wording, and then sputtered, "I told you, you shouldn't think about me when you're working!"

"You," Josh told her, "are never far from my mind." He pulled her from the chair and into his lap on the floor. Any space between them was too damn much. "Besides, thinking about you is what saved the day."

Josh explained about the cat and how her experience made him stop and think. "If it hadn't been for loving you, I'd have followed my gut instinct and gone back in that house last night, looking for an infant. Then who knows what might have happened to me."

"No!" Amanda curled around him, desperate and sweet, protective even though he outweighed her by over a hundred pounds.

Cradling her head to his chest, Josh said, "What

happened to you was awful, sweetheart, but it's in the past and I'm here now. *I love you.*"

"I love you, too."

Josh froze. He grabbed her shoulders and tried to lever her away so he could see her face, but she clung like a stubborn vine. "Amanda!"

He felt her smile against his throat. "That's what I was going to tell you. Last night, you needed me. Not just a body, not just any woman. You came to me and I knew you needed *me.*"

"Hell, yes I need you! Isn't that what I've been saying?"

"You didn't have to work at getting me into bed because I'd already decided I wanted you there. Everything was different because you're different and how I feel about you is different."

His chest expanded, with love and a dozen other elusive emotions. "You love me?"

"Yes. So how can making love with you be anything but wonderful?"

Josh squeezed her until she squeaked. "You little sneak! I've been in agony here, trying to figure you out, trying to decide how to get you to say 'I do,' and all along you knew you loved me."

"You wouldn't let me tell you."

"You only wanted to talk about another damn calendar."

Now she pushed back to see him, and she grinned. "I will."

He frowned suspiciously. "You will what?"

"I will marry you."

"Oh." Josh wanted to shout, to jump up on the table

and dance, to drag Amanda to the bedroom and strip her naked. He just nodded. "Good. What a relief."

"And I will do another calendar—"

He groaned and started to topple to the floor.

Amanda laughed and pulled him upright "—but you won't be in it."

"Thank God."

"I want new blood," she said, making him scowl with his own share of budding jealousy. "This is turning out even bigger than I'd first planned. The amount of money we made last night was astronomical. I have all kinds of ideas for letting women in on choosing the models for next year. This time we'll include the paramedics, and maybe we'll even be able to talk Mick into…"

Josh pulled Amanda down to the floor as he reclined, arranging her on top of him.

"Josh! What are you doing?"

"I want you to make love to me again."

"Oh." She relaxed.

"And I want you to quit talking about other men. I don't like it."

"I am doing the calendar." She levered herself up, digging her pointy elbows into his chest to scowl at him, just in case he didn't hear the seriousness in her tone. "I'm good at it and I enjoy doing my share to help."

Josh slanted her a look. "You aren't doing it for retribution? This isn't your idea of donning a hair shirt?"

"I'll always feel horrible over what happened that night, Josh. There's no way that'll ever change."

"I'll always love you," Josh whispered. "There's no way that will ever change."

Amanda smiled, bent and kissed him sweetly. "No," she said, "I'm not mentally flogging myself. Not anymore. I just want to help a worthy cause. I've seen now how much the money helps."

"Okay. I'll help too—just not by posing ever again." Josh caressed her behind. "Can we live here?"

Amanda had just started to stretch out over him again, but drew herself back up. "What?"

"After we're married," he explained. "I'm thinking we could do a large addition, something that would work well with the existing structure and the grounds. We'll need room for babies and all my stuff, a bigger kitchen and another bathroom."

Amanda laid down on him and hugged him tight. "Yes, I'd love that. Living here with you would be perfect."

He held her hips against his growing erection. "You wanna have a baby right away?"

She laughed, leaned up to look at him, then laughed some more. Her body shook atop his and Josh had to smile. Her laughter was such a turn-on, he started inching up the hem of her robe to get to her luscious behind.

"My parents won't believe this."

"Hmmm?"

"That after everything, I've fallen crazy nuts in love…with a firefighter."

Epilogue

"Mick, you have to move your hand so I know which guy to vote for."

"I'll cast the vote for you. Hand me your card."

Amanda laughed as she watched Mick and Zack doing their best to keep their wives from viewing the strutting men on stage. They'd paid big money in the name of charity to get front row tables for the event, but now they were turning into prudes. Amanda had every faith that Del and Wynn could hold their own.

Josh was backstage with the men, directing them on when to showcase their assets, while constantly heckling and provoking the young men. He enjoyed his role as assistant and supervisor much more than being a model.

Amanda couldn't imagine being happier. She was now the president of the Firefighter's Calendar yearly production, and as he'd promised, Josh freely gave his help. He was, as she'd accepted from the first, a most remarkable man. And he was all hers.

They'd married two months ago. Their wedding was a huge elaborate celebration and Wynn and Del had teased her mercilessly about her fancy lace and pearl dress, her long train, her veil. But when they'd appeared in their own lacy, feminine gowns, as part of the procession, Mick and Zack had nearly fallen over. Their eyes had glazed and their shoulders tensed and Josh laughed out loud at them.

Amanda learned that the men didn't see their wives dressed up very often, and apparently, seeing them thus was a huge turn-on. She'd heard Wynn whisper to Del that dressing up more often might not be such a bad idea. They'd both turned to Amanda, and said she'd have to give them some tips. Amanda really liked them both and valued their friendship.

Her parents had attended the wedding, along with her sister, and of course, they all loved Josh. He charmed them easily, all the while holding Amanda close.

To Amanda's surprise her father had gotten teary eyed when he hugged her. They'd had regular, friendlier contact since.

Josh stepped up behind Amanda and put his large hot hands on her belly. "You feeling okay?"

She leaned her head back on his shoulder. "I feel fabulous."

"No sickness?"

Amanda laughed. "Josh, I just found out I'm pregnant two days ago!"

He kissed her temple. "I'm going to take such good care of you."

"Mmmm."

"Mick tells me pregnant ladies are always horny."

Amanda sputtered a laugh. Del was in the family way too, but then, Amanda doubted that had anything to do with her heightened sexuality. As far as she'd been able to tell, both Wynn and Del were always willing to indulge in a little physical love-play with their husbands.

Now that she'd been with Josh, Amanda totally understood that sentiment. All he had to do was look at her and her knees went weak. She felt weak now, and they were in the middle of a special program!

With that thought, Amanda gave her attention back to the stage.

"If I'd have put you up there," Amanda said, eyeing the young firefighter now flexing his muscles and grinning at the feminine catcalls, "we'd have made a fortune."

"You'll make a fortune anyway and you know it. Besides, my wife is territorial. She hates having me ogled by other women, and I love her too much to upset her."

Amanda turned into his arms and hugged him fiercely. The past, for her, was just that. In the past. All the hurt, all the guilt, were now faded memories, buried beneath the incredible love she shared with an incredible man.

He was a hero. He was *her* hero. And working together on the calendar benefit, they'd make a big difference to a lot of people. She couldn't ask for anything more.

* * * * *

RIDING THE STORM

Brenda Jackson

Chapter 1

"Jayla? What are you doing in New Orleans?"

A gasp of surprise and recognition slipped from Jayla Cole's lips when she quickly turned around. Her gaze immediately connected with that of the tall, dark and dangerously handsome man towering over her as they stood in the lobby of the Sheraton Hotel in the beautiful French Quarter.

There stood Storm Westmoreland. The man had the reputation of being able to talk the panties off any woman who caught his interest. According to what she'd heard, even though Storm sported a clean-cut, all-American-kind-of-a-guy image, he was a master at providing pleasure without promises of forever. The word was that he had the uncanny ability to turn any female's fantasy into reality and had created many memories that were too incredible to forget. Many women considered him the "Perfect Storm."

He was also a man who, for ten years, had avoided her like the plague.

"I arrived in town a couple of days ago to attend the International Organization for Business Communicators convention," she heard herself saying, while trying not to be captivated by the deep darkness of his eyes, the sensual fullness of his lips or the diamond stud he wore in his left ear. And if all that weren't bad enough, there was his skin tone that was the color of semi-sweet chocolate, hair that was cut low and neatly trimmed on his head and the sexiest pair of dimples.

He was dressed in a pair of khakis and a pullover shirt that accentuated his solid frame. His chest was broad and his butt was as tight as she remembered. He always looked good in anything he wore. Her heart accelerated at the memory of her mischievous teenage years when she'd once caught him off guard by boldly brushing up against him. She had thought she'd died and gone to heaven that day. And just like then, Storm was still more than just handsome—he was drop-dead, make-you-want-to-scream, gorgeous.

"What about you?" she decided to ask. "What are you doing in New Orleans?"

"I was here for the International Association of Fire Captains meeting."

She nodded, doing a remarkable job of switching her attention from his strong male features to his words. "I read about your promotion in the newspapers. Dad would have been proud of you, Storm."

"Thanks."

She saw the sadness that immediately appeared in

his eyes and understood why. He hadn't gotten over her father's death, either. In fact, the last time she had seen Storm had been at her father's funeral six months ago. He did, however, on occasion call to see how she was doing. Adam Cole had been Storm's first fire captain when he had joined the squad at twenty, over twelve years ago. Her father always thought of Storm as the son he'd never had.

She would never forget the first time her dad had brought him to dinner when she was sixteen. Storm had made quite an impression on her. Not caring that there was a six-year difference in their ages, she'd had a big-time crush on him and would never forget how she had gone out of her way to make him notice her. But no matter how much she'd tried, he never did. And now as she thought back, some of her tactics had been rather outrageous as well as embarrassing. Thank goodness Storm had taken all of her antics in stride and had rebuffed her advances in a genteel way. Now, at twenty-six, she was ten years older and wiser, and she could admit something she had refused to admit then. The man was not her type and was totally out of her league.

"So, how long will you be in The Big Easy?" he asked, breaking once again into her thoughts.

"I'll be here for the rest of the week. The conference ended today, but I've made plans to stick around until Sunday to take in the sights. I haven't been to New Orleans in over five years."

He smiled and it was a smile that made her insides feel jittery. "I was here a couple of years ago and totally enjoyed myself," he said.

She couldn't help wondering if he'd come with a

woman or if he'd made the trip with his brothers. Everyone who'd lived in the Atlanta area for an extended period of time was familiar with the Westmoreland brothers—Dare, Thorn, Stone, Chase and Storm. Their only sister, Delaney, who was the youngest of the siblings, had made news a couple years ago when she married a desert sheikh from the Middle East.

Dare Westmoreland was a sheriff in a suburb of Atlanta called College Park; Thorn was well-known nationally for the motorcycles he raced and built; Stone, who wrote under the pen name of Rock Mason, was a national bestselling author of action-thriller novels and Chase, Storm's fraternal twin, owned a soul-food restaurant in downtown Atlanta.

"So how long do you plan on staying?" she asked.

"My meeting ended today. Like you, I plan on staying until Sunday to take in the sights and to eat my fill of Cajun food."

His words had sounded so husky and sexy she could actually feel her throat tighten.

"How would you like to join me for dinner?"

Jayla blinked, not sure she had heard him correctly. "Excuse me?"

He gave her what had to be his Perfect Storm sexy smile. "I said how would you like to join me for dinner? I haven't seen you since Adam's funeral, and although we've talked briefly on the phone a couple of times since then, I'd love to sit and chat with you to see how you've been doing."

A part of her flinched inside. His words reminded her of the promise he had made to her father before he'd died—that if she ever needed anything, he would be there for her. She didn't relish the thought of another domineering man in her life, especially one who reminded her so much of her father. The reason Storm and Adam Cole had gotten along so well was because they'd thought a lot alike.

"Thanks for the offer, but I've already made plans for later," she said, lying through her teeth.

It seemed that turning down his offer didn't faze him one bit. He merely shrugged his shoulders before checking his watch. "All right, but if you change your mind give me a call. I'm in Room 536."

"Thanks, I'll do that."

He looked at her and smiled. "It was good seeing you again, Jayla, and if you ever need anything don't hesitate to call me."

If he really believed she would call him, then he didn't know her at all, Jayla quickly thought. Her father may have thought of Storm as a son, but she'd never considered him a brother. In her mind, he had been the guy who could make her all hot and bothered; the guy who was the perfect figment of a teenage girl's imagination. He had been real, bigger than life and for two solid years before leaving Atlanta to attend college, he had been the one person who had consumed all of her thoughts.

When she returned home four years ago, she had still found him totally irresistible, but it didn't take long to realize that he still wouldn't give her the time of day.

"And it was good seeing you again, too, Storm. Just in case we don't run into each other again while we're here, I hope you have a safe trip back to Atlanta," she said, hoping she sounded a lot more excited than she actually felt.

"And I ditto that for you," he said. He surprised her when he grasped her fingers and held them firmly. She'd shivered for a second before she could stop herself. His touch had been like a shock. She couldn't help noticing how strong his hand was, and his gaze was deep and intent.

She remembered another time their gazes had connected in such a way. It had been last year, when the men at the fire station had given her father a surprise birthday party. She distinctly remembered Storm standing across the room talking to someone and then suddenly turning, locking his gaze with hers as if he were actually seeing her for the first time. The episode had been brief, but earth-tilting for her nonetheless.

"Your father was a very special man, Jayla, and he meant a lot to me," he said softly before releasing his grip and taking a step back.

She nodded, putting how intense Storm's nearness made her feel to the back of her mind while holding back the tears that always flooded her eyes whenever she thought of losing her father to pancreatic cancer. He had died within three months of the condition being diagnosed.

Although while growing up she had thought he was too authoritative at times, he had been a loving father. "And you meant a lot to him, as well, Storm," she said, through the tightness in her throat. "You were the son he never had."

She watched him inhale deeply and knew that her words had touched him.

"Promise that if you ever need anything that you'll call me."

She sighed, knowing she would have to lie to him for a second time that day. "I will, Storm."

Evidently satisfied with her answer, he turned and walked away. She watched, transfixed, trying to ignore how the solid muscles of his body yielded beneath the material of his shirt and pants. The last thought that came into her mind before he stepped into the elevator was that he certainly did have a great-looking butt.

When the elevator door swooshed shut, Storm leaned back against the back wall to get his bearings. Seeing Jayla Cole had had one hell of an effect on him. She had been cute and adorable at sixteen, but over the years she had grown into the most breathtaking creature he'd ever set his eyes on.

"Jayla." He said her name softly, drawing out the sound with a deep, husky sigh. He would never forget the time Adam had invited him to dinner to celebrate Jayla's return to Atlanta from college. It was supposed to have been a very simple and quiet affair and had ended up being far from it. He had walked into the house and felt as if someone had punched him in the stomach. The air had miraculously been sucked from his lungs.

Jayla had become a woman, a very beautiful and desirable woman, and the only thing that had kept him from adding her to his To Do list was the deep respect he'd had for her father. But that hadn't kept her from occasionally creeping into his dreams at night or from being the lone person on his Would Definitely Do If I Could list.

He sighed deeply. She had the most luscious pair of whiskey-colored eyes he'd ever seen, medium brown hair that shimmered with strands of golden highlights and skin the color of creamy cocoa. He thought the entire combination went far beyond classic beauty. And he hadn't been able to ignore just how good her body looked in the shorts and tank top she'd been wearing and how great she'd smelled. He hadn't recognized the fragrance and he'd thought he knew them all.

She had actually trembled when he'd reached out and touched her hand. He'd felt it and her responsiveness to his touch had given his body a jump-start. It had taken everything within him to pretend he wasn't affected by her. Since he was thirty-two, he calculated that Jayla was now twenty-six. She was now a full-grown woman. All woman. But still there was something about her that radiated an innocence he'd seldom found in women her age. It was her innocence that confused him most. He was an ace at figuring out women, but there was something about her that left him a bit mystified and he couldn't shake the feeling. But one thing he was certain about—as far as he was concerned, Jayla was still off-limits.

Maybe it had been a blessing that she'd turned down his invitation to dinner. The last thing he needed was to share a meal with her. In fact, spending any amount of time with her would only be asking for trouble, considering his attraction to her. He released a moan, a deep throaty sound, and realized that the only thing that had changed with the situation was that Adam was no longer alive to serve as a buffer and a constant reminder of the one woman he could not have.

"Damn."

Just thinking about Jayla sent a jolt of desire straight from the bottom of his feet to the top of his head, leaving an aching throb in his midsection. Storm rubbed a hand down his face. Nothing had changed. The woman was still too much temptation. She'd been a handful while growing up; Adam had been faced with the challenge of raising his daughter alone after his wife died, when Jayla was ten.

Adam had been a strict father, too strict at times, Storm thought, but he'd wanted to keep his daughter safe and not allow her to get into the kind of trouble other teenagers were getting into. But Adam had also been a loving and caring father and had always placed Jayla first in his life. Storm had always admired the man for that.

Storm's thoughts went back to Jayla and the outfit she was wearing. It hadn't been blatantly sexy, but it had definitely captured his interest. But that was as far as he would allow it to go, he thought with a resigned sigh. Jayla was definitely not his type.

He enjoyed his freedom-loving ways too much and no matter what anyone thought, he knew the main reason he lived a stress-free life was because of his active sex life. In his line of business, you needed an outlet when things got too overbearing. And as long as he was responsible and made sure all his encounters didn't involve any health risks, he would continue to engage in the pleasures of sex.

Okay, so he would admit that he was a man with commitment issues, thanks to Nicole Brown. So what if it had been fifteen years, there were some things a man didn't forget and rejection was one of them.

He and Nicole had dated during his senior year in high school and had even talked about getting married when he finished college. He would never forget the night he had told Nicole that his future plans had changed. He decided that, unlike his brothers, he didn't want to go to college. Instead, he wanted to stay in Atlanta and attend the Firefighters Academy. Nicole hadn't wasted any time in telling him what she thought about his plans. A man without a college education could not provide adequately for a family, she'd told him, and had broken up with him that same night.

He had loved her and her rejection had hurt. It had also taught him a very valuable lesson. Keep your heart to yourself. You could have sex for sex's sake, but love and marriage would never be part of the mix. So what if his uncle Corey, who had pledged to remain a bachelor for life, as well as his older brothers Dare, Thorn and Stone, had all gotten married in less than a year? That didn't mean he or his twin Chase would follow in their footsteps.

His thoughts shifted back to Nicole. He had seen her at a class reunion a few years back and had been grateful things had ended between them when they had. After three marriages, she was still looking for what she considered the perfect man with a good education and plenty of money. She had been surprised to learn that because firefighters made it a point to constantly study to improve their job performance and prepare for promotional exams, he had eventually gone to college, taking classes at night to earn a bachelor's degree in fire science and later a master's degree in public administration.

His thoughts left Nicole and went back to Jayla. He remembered when she had left Atlanta to attend a college in the north. Adam had wanted her to stay closer to home, but had relented and let her go. Adam would keep him updated on how well she was doing in school. He'd always been the proud father and when she had graduated at the top of her class, Adam had taken all the men in his squad out to celebrate. That had been four years ago....

The chiming of the elevator interrupted his reverie. The elevator opened on his floor and Storm stepped out. He had reached the conclusion that, incredible-looking or not, the last woman he would want to become involved with was Jayla Cole. But once again he thought about how she looked downstairs in the lobby. Incredible. Simply incredible...

The next morning, Jayla leaned back in her chair at the hotel restaurant, sipped her orange juice and smiled brightly. The call she had received before leaving her hotel room had made her very happy. Ecstatic was more like it.

The fertility clinic had called to let her know that everything had checked out and they had found a sperm donor whose profile met all of her requirements. There was a possibility they could schedule the procedure in less than a month.

She felt downright giddy at the thought of having a child. Her mother had died when she was ten, and her father's recent death had left her suffering with occasional bouts of loneliness. She had been an only child; she never had a sibling to share that special closeness with and now more than ever she wanted a child to love and to add special meaning to her life.

At first, she had looked at the pool of guys she had dated over the past couple of years, but for the most part they left a lot to be desired—they'd been either too overbearing or too overboring. So she'd decided to try a fertility clinic. After doing a load of research she had moved ahead with the preliminary paper work. Now in less than two months, she would take the first steps in becoming a new mother. A huge smile touched her lips. She couldn't wait to hold her baby in her arms. Her precious little one would have chocolate-colored skin, dark eyes, curvy full lips, cute dimples and...

"Good morning, Jayla. You seem to be in a rather good mood this morning."

Jayla looked up and met Storm's gaze. Although she had decided to avoid him for the remainder of her time in New Orleans, she wasn't upset that they had run into each other again so soon. She was too elated with life to let anything or anyone dampen her spirits today.

"I *am* in a good mood, Storm. I just received some wonderful news," she said smiling brightly. She saw the curiosity in his eyes, but knew he was too well-mannered to ask her for any details. And she had no intention of sharing her plans with him. Her decision to venture into single parenthood was personal and private. She hadn't shared it with anyone, not even Lisa, her best friend from work.

"Mind if I join you?"

Her smile widened. "Yes, have a seat."

She watched as he sat down and noticed his outfit complemented his physique just as it had the day before. He definitely looked good in a pair of cutoff jeans and a T-shirt that said Firefighters Are Hot.

"So what are you having this morning?" he asked, glancing over at her plate.

"Buffet. And everything is delicious."

He nodded. "Umm, I think I'll try it myself."

No sooner had he said the last word, a waiter appeared and Storm informed the man that he would be having the buffet. "I'll be back in a minute," he said standing.

Jayla watched as he made his way across the room to where the buffet was set up. She couldn't help but watch him. She knew there was no way she could feel guilty about being drawn to him, since she had always been attracted to him. And at least she wasn't the only one, she thought, glancing around and seeing that a number of admiring women had turned to check him out. However, it appeared he was more interested in filling his plate than in all the attention he was getting.

Jayla blinked when she suddenly realized something. Storm's features were identical to those she had requested when she'd filled out the questionnaire for the fertility clinic. If the clinic filled her request to the letter, the donor whose sperm she would receive would favor Storm and her baby would almost be his clone.

She shook her head, not believing what she'd subconsciously done. When she blinked again, she noticed that Storm had caught her staring at him, lifted his brow in question and then stared back at her.

Jayla's heart thudded in her chest as she watched as he crossed the room back to her with a plate filled to capacity. "Okay, what'd I do?" he asked sitting down. "You were staring at me like I'd suddenly grown an extra nose or something."

This time, Jayla had to force herself to smile. "No, you're fine. I just couldn't help but notice how much food you were piling on your plate," she said instead of telling him the real reason she'd been staring.

He chuckled. "Hey, I'm a growing boy. All my brothers and I eat like this."

Jayla took another sip of orange juice. She had met his brothers a while back and remembered all four of them being in excellent shape. If they routinely ate that much food, they must also work out…a lot. "Your parents must have had one heck of a grocery bill."

"They did, and while we were growing up my mom didn't work outside of the home, so it was up to my dad to bring home the bacon. And not once did he complain about the amount of money being spent on food. That's the way I want it in my household *if* I ever marry."

Jayla lifted a brow after taking another sip of orange juice. "What?"

"I don't want my wife to work outside of the home."

Jayla gazed at him as she set down her glass. She had heard that very thing from several people who knew him. It was no secret that when Storm Westmoreland married, he would select a domestic diva.

"I have deep admiration and respect for any woman who works inside the home raising her family," she said truthfully.

His features showed signs of surprise. "You do?"

"Yes, raising a family is a full-time job."

He leaned back in his chair and studied her for a moment before asking, "So you would do it? You would be a stay-at-home-mom?"

"No."

He sat up straight. "But you just said that you—"

"Admired women who did it, but that doesn't necessarily mean that I would do it. I believe I can handle a career and motherhood and chose to have both."

"It won't be easy."

Jayla chuckled as she pushed aside her plate. "Nothing about being a parent is easy, Storm, whether you work in the home or outside the home. The most important thing is making sure the child is loved and well taken care of. Now if you will excuse me, I think I will try some of that fruit."

Storm watched as she stood and crossed the room. Wasn't it just yesterday that he had decided to stay away from her because she was too much of a temptation? When he had walked into the restaurant, he had sensed her presence even before he had actually seen her. Then he had glanced around and his gaze had locked in on her sitting alone at a table, drinking her orange juice with a huge smile on her face, completely oblivious to anyone and anything around her. Even now, he couldn't help but wonder what had put her in such a good mood.

He took a sip of his coffee, thinking she evidently didn't want him to know since she hadn't shared whatever it was with him. Electricity shot through him as he continued to watch as she put an assortment of fruit into a bowl. He liked the outfit she was wearing, a fuchsia sundress with spaghetti straps and a pair of flat sandals on her feet. She had gorgeous legs, and her hair flowed around her shoulders, emphasizing her beauty from every angle. She looked the very image of sexiness and at the same time she looked comfortable and ready for the New Orleans heat that was normal for a September day.

"The food in this place is good," she said returning to the table and digging into the different fruits she had brought back with her.

He lifted his dark head and his stomach tightened as he watched her slip a slice of pineapple into her mouth and relish it as if it were the best thing she'd ever eaten. She chewed very slowly while his gaze stayed glued to her mouth, finding the entire ordeal fascinating as well as arousing.

"So, what are you plans for today?"

Her question reeled him back in. He set his fork down and leaned back in his chair. He met her gaze, or at least tried to, without lowering it to her mouth again. "Take in the sights. I checked with the person at the concierge's desk and he suggested I do the Gray Line bus tour."

Jayla smiled brightly. "Hey, he gave me the same suggestion. Do you want to do it together?"

Innocent as it was, he wished she hadn't invited him to join her sightseeing expedition in precisely those words. *Do it together.* A totally different scenario than what she was proposing popped into his head and he was having a hard time getting it out of there. "You sure you don't mind the company?" he asked searching her face. Although he got very few, he recognized a brush-off when he got one and yesterday, after asking her to dinner, she had definitely given him the brush-off.

"No, I'd love the company."

He wondered what had changed her mood. Evidently the news she'd received had turned the snotty Jayla of last night into Miss Congeniality this morning.

"So what do you say, Mr. Fireman? Shall we hit the streets?"

Hitting the sheets was more to his liking, but he immediately reminded himself just who she was and that she was still off-limits. "Sure. I think it would be fun." *As long as we keep things simple,* he wanted to add but didn't.

She chuckled, a low, sexy sound, as she leaned forward. "And that's what I need, Storm, some honest-to-goodness fun."

He looked at her for a moment, then suddenly understood. The past six months had to have been hard. She and her father had been extremely close, so no doubt the loneliness was finally getting to her.

A jolt of protectiveness shot through him. Hadn't he promised Adam that he would look after her? Besides, if anyone could show her how to have fun, he could. Because of his attraction to her, over the years he had basically tried to avoid her. Now it seemed that doing so had robbed him of the chance to get to know her better. Maybe it was time that he took the first step to rectify the situation so that a relationship, one of friendship only, could develop between them.

Having fun with a woman without the involvement of sex would be something new for him, but he was willing to try it. Since there was no way the two of them could ever be serious, he saw nothing wrong with letting his guard down and having a good time. "Then I will give you a day of fun, Jayla Cole," he said and meaning every word.

A smile touched the corners of his mouth. "And who knows? You just might surprise yourself and have so much fun, you may not ever want to get serious again."

Chapter 2

A rush of excitement shot through Jayla's blood-stream when the bus made another stop on its tour. This time to board the *Steamboat Natchez* for a cruise along the Mississippi River. So far, she and Storm had taken a carriage ride through the French Quarter, a tour of the swamps and visited a number of magnificently restored mansions and courtyards.

The *Natchez* was a beautiful replica of the steamboats that once cruised the Mississippi. Jayla stood at the railing appreciating the majestic beauty of the river and all the historical landmarks as they navigated its muddy waters. She was very much aware of the man standing beside her. During the boat ride, Storm had kept her amused by telling her interesting tidbits of information about riverboats.

As he talked, she tipped her head and studied him,

letting eyes that were hidden behind the dark lenses of her sunglasses roam over him. She enjoyed looking at him as much as she enjoyed listening to him. Soft jazz was flowing through several speakers that were located on the lower deck and the sound of the boat gliding through the water had a relaxing effect on Jayla.

When Storm fell silent for a few moments, Jayla figured she needed to say something to assure him that he had her full attention, which he definitely did. "How do you know so much about riverboats?" she asked, genuinely curious. She watched his lips curve into a smile and a flutter went through her stomach.

"Mainly because of my cousin Ian," he replied as he absently flicked a strand of hair away from her face. "A few years ago, he and some investor friends of his decided to buy a beauty of a riverboat. It's over four hundred feet long and ninety feet high, and equipped with enough staterooms to hold over four hundred passengers."

"Wow! Where does it go?"

Storm leaned back against the rail and placed his hands in the pockets of his shorts. "Ian's riverboat, *The Delta Princess,* departs from Memphis on ten-day excursions along the Mississippi with stops in New Orleans, Baton Rouge, Vicksburg and Natchez. His crew provides first-class service and the food he serves on board is excellent. In the beginning, business was slow, but now he has reservations booked well over a year in advance. It didn't take him long to figure out what would be a drawing card."

Jayla lifted a brow. "What?"

"Gambling. You'd be surprised how many people

have money they figure is worth losing if there's a chance that they might win more."

Jayla could believe that. A couple of years ago, she and Lisa had taken a trip to Vegas and had seen first hand just how hungry to win some people were.

When there was another lull in the conversation, she turned away from him to look out over the river once more. It was peaceful, nothing like the tempest that was raging through her at the moment. Storm had kept his word. She'd had more fun today with him than she'd had in a long time. He possessed a fun-loving attitude that had spilled over to her. There were times when he had shared a joke with her that had her laughing so hard she actually thought something inside her body would break. It had felt good to laugh, and she was glad she'd been able to laugh with him.

She tried to think of the last time she had laughed with a man and recalled that it had been with her father. Even during his final days, when she'd known that pain had racked his body, he'd been able to tell a good joke every now and then. She heaved a small sigh. She missed her father so much. Because he had kept such a tight rein on her, she had been a rebellious teen while growing up. It was only when she'd returned from college that she had allowed herself to form that special father-daughter relationship with him.

After his death, at the encouragement of the officials at the hospice facility, she had gone through grief counseling and was glad she had. It had helped to let go and move on. One of the biggest decisions she'd been forced to make was whether to sell her parents' home and move into a smaller place. After much soul-searching, she had made a decision to move. She loved her new home and knew once she had her baby, it wouldn't be as lonely as it was now. She was getting excited again just thinking about it.

"So what are your plans for later?"

Storm's question invaded her thoughts and she tipped her head to look over at him. "My plans for later?"

"Yes. Yesterday, I invited you to join me for dinner and you turned me down, saying you'd already made plans. Today, I'm hoping to ask early enough so that I'll catch you before you make other arrangements."

Jayla sighed. She knew her mind needed a reality check, but she wasn't ready to give it one. Spending the day with Storm had been nice; it had been fun and definitely what she'd needed. But she didn't need to spend her evening with him as well. The only thing the two of them had in common was the fact they both loved and respected her father. That would be the common link they would always share. But spending more time with Storm would only reawaken all those old feelings of attraction she had always had for him.

She took off her sunglasses, met his gaze directly and immediately wished she hadn't. His eyes were dark, so dark you could barely see the pupils. The jolt that passed through her was so startling she had to remind herself to breathe.

"I was wondering when you were going to stop hiding behind these," he said, taking the sunglasses out of her hand when she was about to put them back on. He gave her a cocky smile. "But I didn't mind you checking me out."

Jayla couldn't hide the blush that darkened her

cheeks. Nor could she resist easing her lips into a smile. So he'd known she had been looking him over. "I guess it probably gets rather annoying to you after a while, doesn't it?"

He arched a brow. "What?"

"Women constantly checking you out."

He smiled again. "Not really. Usually I beat them to the punch and check them out, so by the time they decide they're interested, I know whether or not I am."

A grin tilted the corners of Jayla's lips. "Umm, such arrogance." She took her sunglasses from him and put them back on, preferring her shield.

"Instead of arrogance, I see it as not wasting time," he said simply. "I guess you can say I weed out those who won't make the cut."

Jayla sighed deeply and struggled with good judgment as to whether to ask her next question. Although she may have struggled with it, curiosity got the best of her. She couldn't help but ask, "So, did I make the cut?"

For a moment, she thought he would not answer. Then he leaned forward, pulled off her sunglasses and met her gaze. "With flying colors, Jayla Cole. I'm a hot-blooded man and would be telling a lie if I said I didn't find you attractive. But then, on the other hand, I have to respect who you'll always be to me."

"Adam's daughter?"

"Yes."

Jayla had to resist grinding her teeth in frustration. She doubted he realized that he'd hit a sore spot with her. Not because she was Adam Cole's daughter, but because being her father's daughter had been the reason Storm had always kept his distance from her. A part of her had gotten over his rejection years ago, but still, it downright infuriated her that he had labeled her as "hands off" because of his relationship with her father.

She watched as he pointedly checked his watch, as if to signal their topic of conversation was now over. "You never did say whether or not you had plans for later."

Jayla almost reached out to snatch her sunglasses from his hand again, then changed her mind. Instead, she decided to have a little fun with him. She stepped close to him, reached out and took hold of the front of his shirt. "Why, Storm? What do you have in mind for later?" she asked, in a very suggestive tone of voice.

She watched as he studied her features with a well-practiced eye before he said, "Dinner."

She pressed a little closer to him. "Dinner? That's it?"

He glanced around. There were only a handful of people about. Most had gone up on deck to listen to the live jazz band that was performing. His gaze returned to hers. "Yes, that's it. Unless…"

She lifted a brow. "Unless what?" she asked, then watched as his mouth curved into a smile. A very sexy smile.

"Unless you want me to toss you into the river to cool off."

Jayla blinked. His smile was gone and the dark eyes staring at her were serious. She stared back, willing him to get the message she was sending with her eyes. His words had ticked her off. "Do you think I need to cool off, Storm?"

The smile that returned to his lips came slow, but it

came nonetheless. "I think you need to behave, brat," he said, playfully tweaking her nose.

She frowned. Those were the same words he had spoken to her ten years earlier when she had made that pass at him. She knew he'd been as right then as he was now, but, dammit, it really annoyed her that he was still using her father as an excuse to keep her at arm's length. A part of her knew it was ludicrous for her to be upset, especially when she should probably be grateful, considering his "wham, bam, thank you, ma'am" reputation.

His Don Juan exploits were legendary. Even so, a part of her hated his refusal to acknowledge she was not a child any longer. She was a full-grown woman and it was up to her to decide whom she was interested in and whom she wanted a relationship with. After all, pretty soon she would be a woman with the responsibility of raising a child alone.

"So, what about dinner, Jayla?"

Time seemed to stop as Jayla considered her options. On the one hand, having dinner with him was a really bad idea. She sure didn't need someone like Storm in her life, especially with her plans with the fertility clinic and her future as a single mom a definite go. That's what the rational part of her brain was trying to get through to her. On the other hand, there was that irrational part, the one that resented him for being all knowing and too damn caring. That part of her head said that one little dinner would do no harm. She knew she should leave well enough alone, but part of her just couldn't.

She met his gaze. "I'll think about it." And without

saying anything else, she took her sunglasses from his hand and walked away.

Storm shook his head as he watched Jayla stroll across the deck. She'd had a lot of nerve asking if she made the cut, as if she hadn't felt the sparks that had flown between them yesterday as well as most of the morning. Fortunately for him, it was an attraction that he could control. But he had to admit that when she had pretended to come on to him a few moments ago, he had almost broken out in a sweat.

He remembered her teen years. During that time Adam had described her as headstrong, free-spirited and an independent thinker. It seemed not much about her had changed.

Storm watched as she moved around the tables that were filled to capacity with an assortment of food and knew he had to rethink his relationship with her. A lot about Jayla *had* changed and he was looking his fill, taking all those changes in at that very moment.

He couldn't remember the last time any woman had gotten his attention the way Jayla had. She didn't know how close she'd come to getting a kiss from him when she had molded her body to his. His gaze had latched on to her lips. They had looked so soft that he'd wanted to find out for himself just how soft and kissable they were.

He sighed. Her ploy had been no more than teasing, but his body was still reeling from the effects. However, no matter what, he had to keep her best interests at heart, even if she didn't know what her best interests were and even if it killed him.

Why couldn't he keep his eyes off her? Hadn't he

decided she was off-limits? He glanced away and tried
to focus on the beauty of the river as the riverboat continued to move through it. It was a beautiful September day and he had to admit he was enjoying Jayla's
company. She had a knack for making him want to
see her smile, hear her laugh; he could honestly say he
had relished his time with her more than he had any
woman in a long time.

He wondered if she was romantically involved with
anyone. He recalled Adam mentioning once that he
felt she was too nitpicky when it came to men and that
she would never meet the "perfect man" that met her
satisfaction. That conversation has taken place years
ago and Storm couldn't help wondering if her attitude
had changed. Had she found someone? Something or
someone had definitely had her smiling when he'd
first seen her at breakfast that morning. All she'd said
was that she had just received some wonderful news,
news she hadn't bothered sharing with him. Did the
news have anything to do with a lover?

"Storm, don't you want something to eat?"

The sound of her voice grabbed his attention and
he glanced back over to her, met her gaze and had to
swallow. The hue of her eyes seemed to pull him to
her. And he didn't want to think about her mouth, a
mouth that now contained a pulse-stopping smile. It
seems the feathers he had ruffled earlier were now all
smoothed. When he didn't answer quickly enough, she
quirked a brow and asked, "Well, do you?"

He fought the urge to tell her yes, that he was hungry, but what he wanted had nothing to do with food.
Instead of saying anything, he strolled over to join

her at the table and took the plate she offered him. "Yes. Thanks."

"You're welcome. You might want to try these, they're good," she said popping a Cajun cheese ball into her mouth.

Storm's breath hitched. He watched her chew, seeing her mouth barely moving. He quickly decided it wouldn't be that way if they were to kiss. He definitely intended to get a lot of movement out of that mouth. He continued to stare at her mouth for a moment and then sighed. Thinking about kissing her was not the way to go. He needed to concentrate on sharing a platonic relationship with her and nothing more,

"If you eat enough of these, there might not have to be a *later.*"

Her words reclaimed his attention. "Excuse me?"

She smiled. "I said if you eat enough of these you might be able to forgo dinner later. They're so delicious."

His first instinct was to tell her that to him, food was like sex—he rarely got enough of it. But he decided telling her that wasn't a good idea. After they had both filled their plates, they walked up the steps to the upper deck where tables and chairs were located.

His attention shifted to claiming a table close to the rails so they could continue to enjoy the view of the river while they ate. When they were both seated, he turned his attention back to her. Her hair was blowing in the midday breeze and he stared at the magnitude of her beauty once again. While his attention was on her, her attention was on her food. Most people who came to New Orleans appreciated its culinary excellence and he could tell by the way she was enjoying her bowl of seafood gumbo that she was enjoying the cuisine, too.

Instead of concentrating on his food, Storm was becoming obsessed with a question. When he realized that he wasn't going to be able to eat before he got an answer, he decided to come out and ask her the one question that was gnawing at him.

"So, are you seeing anyone seriously, Jayla?"

He watched her lift her head and met his gaze. She smiled. "No, I've given up on men."

Storm frowned. Her answer was not what he had expected. "Why?"

She leaned back in her chair. "Because there're too many out there like you."

He leaned forward, lifting a dark brow. "And how am I?"

"The 'love them and leave them' type."

He couldn't dispute her words since he was definitely that. But still, there was something about hearing it from her that just didn't sit well with him. "Not all men are like me. I'm sure there are some who'd love to get serious with one woman and make a commitment."

She tipped her head back and grinned. "Really? Any recommendations?"

His frown deepened. There was no way he would ever introduce her to any of his friends. Most of them were players, just like him, and his only unmarried brother was too involved with his restaurant to indulge in a serious relationship. His thoughts then fell on his six male cousins, eight now if you counted the most recent additions to the Westmoreland family—the two sons his uncle Corey hadn't known about until recently. But still, he wouldn't dare introduce her to any of them either. If she was off-limits to him, then she was off-limits to them, as well.

"No," he decided to answer. "There aren't any I can recommend. Where have you been looking?"

She chuckled as she went back to her gumbo. "Nowhere lately, since I'm no longer interested. But when I was interested I tried everywhere—bars, clubs, blind dates and I even used the Internet."

Storm's mouth fell open. "The Internet?"

She smiled at the look of shock on his face. "Yes, the Internet and I have to admit that I thought I had gotten a very promising prospect...until I actually met him. He was at least fifteen years older than the picture he had on the Web site made him seem and instead of having two hands, it seemed he had a dozen. I had to almost deck him a few times for trying to touch me in places that he shouldn't."

Storm's hands trembled in anger at the thought that she had done something so foolish as to place herself in that situation. No wonder Adam had asked him to look out for her. Now he regretted that he hadn't done a better job at it. He could imagine any man wanting to touch her body, since it was so tempting, but wanting to touch her and actually doing it were two different things. "Don't ever date anyone off the Internet again," he all but snarled.

Jayla grinned. "Why, Storm, if I didn't know better, I'd think you were jealous," she said playfully.

Storm wasn't in a playful mood. "Jealous, hell. I'm just trying to look out for you. What if that guy would have placed you in a situation you couldn't get out of?"

Jayla raised her gaze upward. "Jeez, give me the

benefit of having common sense, Storm. We met in a public place and—"

"He was groping you in a public place?"

She took a sip of her drink and then said, "We were dancing."

Storm took a deep, calming breath as he tried reeling in his anger. "I hope you learned a lesson."

"I did, and there's another reason I've given up on men."

He raised a brow. "Yeah, what's that?"

Her eyes turned serious. "Most are too controlling, which is something I definitely don't need after having Adam Cole for a father. I didn't start dating until I was seventeen, and I wasn't allowed to do sleepovers at my friends' homes."

Storm frowned. "There was nothing wrong with your father wanting to protect you, Jayla. I'm sure it wasn't easy for a single man to raise a daughter, especially one as spirited and defiant as I'd heard you could be at times."

Jayla shrugged. "Well, whatever. You wanted to know the reasons I'd given up on men and I've just told you why I don't date anymore. I figured what the hell, why bother. Men are too much trouble."

The eyes that were gazing up at him were big, round, sexy and serious. He shook his head. To tell the truth, he'd often thought women were too much trouble, too, but at no time had he considered giving them up. "I don't think you should write men off completely."

The jazz band that had taken a break earlier started back up again and conversation between him and Jayla ended. While she became absorbed in the musicians, he sat back and studied her for a long time. Being concerned about his late mentor's bratty daughter meant he was a good friend and not a jealous suitor as she'd claimed. He never cared enough about a woman to become jealous and Jayla Cole was no exception... or was she?

Jayla sipped her drink and half listened to the musicians who were performing a very jazzy tune. Of course she had recognized Storm's concern as a protective gesture but still, she couldn't resist ribbing him about being jealous.

He was so easy to tease. Charming, gorgeous and sexy as sin. But what she'd told him had been the truth. She had basically written men off. That's why she had decided to use the fertility clinic instead of a live donor.

She had made up in her mind that marriage wasn't for her. She enjoyed her independence too much to have to answer to anyone, and men had a way looking at their wives as possessions instead of partners, a lover for life, his other half and his soul mate. Her time and concentration would be focused on having her baby and raising it. Then later, if she did meet someone who met her qualifications, he would have to take the total package—her and her child.

She glanced over at Storm and saw his full attention was focused on the musicians. There was a dark scowl on his face and she wondered if he was still thinking about her and the Internet man.

Running into him in New Orleans was definitely an unexpected treat. She decided to enjoy the opportunity while it lasted. So far, their day together had been so much fun…at least for half the time. The other half of their time together she'd been too busy fighting her attraction to him to really enjoy herself. He was no different from the other men she had dated—possibly even worse—but that didn't stop that slow sizzle from moving through her body whenever he looked at her.

A part of her couldn't help but wonder if all the things she'd heard about him were fact or myth.

"The riverboat has returned to dock, Jayla."

His words, spoken low and in a husky tone, intruded into her thoughts. She glanced around and saw that the riverboat had returned to the Toulouse Street Wharf. "We returned sooner than I thought we would," she said, forcing down the lump of disappointment that suddenly appeared in her throat.

"We've been cruising the Mississippi for over three hours," he said, returning the irrepressible smile that had recently vanished from his lips. "Don't you think it's time we got back?"

She shrugged, wondering if he'd gotten bored with her already. Without saying a word, she stood and began gathering up the debris from their meal. He reached out and stopped her. She looked up and met his gaze.

"I'm not one of those men who expects a woman to clean up after him."

She opened her mouth to speak, but the words wouldn't come out. His hand was still on hers, holding it immobile, and she could feel the sensuous heat from his touch all the way down to her toes. She pressed her lips together to fight back the moan that threatened to escape. How could he overpower her senses in such a way that she couldn't think straight?

Frowning, she blew out an aggravated breath as she pulled her hand from his and resumed what she was doing. "I don't consider it as cleaning up after you, Storm. It's an old habit. Whenever Dad and I ate together, I always cleared the table afterward. We had a deal. He cooked and I cleaned."

"Really?" he asked, studying her intently as his lips quirked into a smile. "And why was that? Can't you cook?"

She glanced up at him and the deep dimples in his cheeks did things to her insides that were totally beyond her comprehension. She figured it would have been a lot easier for her to understand if she wasn't a twenty-six-year-old virgin. While in college she'd *almost* gone all the way with a senior guy by the name of Tyrone Pembrooke. But his roommate had returned unexpectedly, interrupting things. For her, it had been fortunate since she'd later discovered he had made a bet with his fraternity brothers that he would get into her panties in a week's time. She had almost learned too late that the name the senior guys had given the freshman girls was *fresh meat*.

"Yes, I can cook," she finally answered Storm. "Dad loved home cooking. He thought food wasn't worth eating if it wasn't made from scratch. He just couldn't get into those little microwave dinners that I was an expert at preparing."

Storm chuckled as he helped her gather up the remaining items off the table. "Hey, I can understand your father's pain since I like home-cooked food, too."

They walked over to the garbage container and tossed in their trash. "You cook for yourself every day?" Jayla asked as they headed toward the lower deck to depart.

"No. Since my shifts run twenty-four on and forty-eight off, I eat at the station when I'm working and the days I'm off I eat at Chase's Place, my brother's restaurant."

She nodded, remembering that his twin brother, Chase Westmoreland, owned a restaurant in downtown Atlanta. It was a really popular place; she had been to it several times and always found the food delicious. She glanced down at her watch. "When we get back to the hotel, it will be nap time for me."

"Umm, not for me. There's still more for me to see. I think I'll go check out that club on Bourbon Street that's located right next to the drugstore. I hear they have good entertainment."

Jayla lifted a brow. She knew exactly what club he was referring to, since a group of the guys who'd also attended the convention had visited there. And if what she'd heard about it was true, its only entertainment was of the striptease kind. She frowned wondering why the thought of Storm watching women bare all bothered her. Why did men fail to realize that there was more to a woman than what was underneath her clothes?

"Well, I hope you enjoy yourself," she said. Her tone had been more curt than she had intended.

"Oh, trust me, I will."

And she knew, just as clearly as he'd said it, that he would.

Chapter 3

Storm was having a lousy time, but when he glanced over at his cousin Ian, it was evident that he was enjoying himself. Ian had contacted him last night and told him that *The Delta Princess* would be making a stop in New Orleans and suggested they meet for drinks at this club.

A few seconds later, Ian must have felt him staring and looked over at him. "What's the matter with you, Storm?"

Storm decided to be honest. "I'm bored."

Ian lifted a brow. "How can you be bored looking at women take off their clothes?"

He shrugged. "It all looks basically the same."

A smile curved the corners of Ian's lips. "Well, yeah, I would hope so."

Storm couldn't help but return the smile. He and

Ian were first cousins—their fathers were brothers. While growing up, they had always been close. They were the same age and one thing they'd always had in common was their appreciation of the opposite sex. Storm wasn't surprised that his cousin thought the fact that his lack of interest in women stripping naked was strange.

"Okay, who is she?"

Storm looked confused. "Who's who?"

"The woman who's ruined your interest in other women."

Storm frowned. He glared at Ian. "Where on earth did you get a crazy idea like that from? No one has ruined my interest in other women."

Ian met his glare. "And I say you're lying."

Storm released a frustrated sigh. Ian was damn lucky he hadn't hauled off and hit him. But that was his brother Thorn's style. Thorn was known for his moody, ready-to-knock-the-hell-out-of-you temperament. At least, that had been his attitude until he'd gotten married. Now Tara had unruffled Thorn's feathers and the last few times he'd seen him, Thorn had actually been easygoing. Marriage had certainly made a happy man out of Thorn, as well as his brothers Dare and Stone. Storm found it downright sickening. He'd also been curious as to why his brothers were smiling all the time. As far as he was concerned, they weren't getting anything at home that he wasn't getting out there in the streets.

Or were they?

"I can't believe you just sat there calmly after I called you a liar, so it must be true," Ian said, taking another sip of his beer.

Storm rolled his eyes. "I just don't feel like knocking the hell out of you right now Ian, so back off." What he preferred not to let his cousin know was that he had pretty much hit on the truth. For the time being, Jayla *had* ruined him for other women and he couldn't understand why. He certainly hadn't ever been intimate with her and he never ever intended to be. And yet, here he was bored to death at the sight of these half-clad dancers, while the thought of Jayla taking off her clothes made him break into a sweat.

"Want another drink, cuz?"

He glanced over at Ian. What he wanted was to go back to the hotel and call Jayla to see what she was doing. "No, I'll pass. When will you be back in Atlanta?"

Ian leaned back in his chair and smiled. "In a few weeks. I promised Tara I'd be in town for that charity ball she's working on. Why?"

"I'll check you out then." Storm stood and tossed a couple of bills on the table. "I'll let Uncle James and Aunt Sarah know you're doing okay."

Ian nodded. "And for heaven's sake if Mom asks if I was with a woman when you saw me, please say yes. With your brothers getting married, she's starting to look at us kind of funny."

Storm grinned. His mother was beginning to look at him and Chase kind of funny, too. He glanced around the room before turning his attention back to Ian. "I guess I can tell her that and not feel guilty about lying, since this place is full of women. I'll just leave out the part that the woman you were seeing was naked."

Ian chuckled. "Thanks, I'd appreciate that."

Storm turned to leave.

"Hey, Storm?"

Storm turned back around. "Yeah?"

Ian met his gaze directly. "I know it's just a temporary thing, man, but whomever she is I hope she's worth all the hell you're going through."

Storm frowned, opened his mouth to give his cousin a blazing retort that no woman was putting him through hell, changed his mind and turned and walked out of the club.

Jayla heard the phone ring when she had finished toweling herself off and slipped into the plush hotel bathrobe. She quickly left the bathroom and picked up the phone on the fourth ring. "Hello?"

"How was your nap?"

Jayla frowned. The last thing Storm needed to know was that she hadn't been able to sleep, thanks to thoughts of him being surrounded by naked women. Each time she'd tried closing her eyes, she saw women, taking off their clothes, heaving their breasts in his face, skimming panties down their legs and giving him an eyeful of all their treasures. She'd even heard there were some women who were bold enough to sit naked in a man's lap if he tipped her well enough.

"My nap was fantastic," she lied. "How was the entertainment at the club?" she asked then wished that she hadn't.

"It was definitely interesting."

Jayla's frown deepened. A part of her wanted to slam the phone down, but she had too much pride to do so. Besides, she took great care of herself and thought she looked rather decent, in or out of her clothes. As far as she was concerned, there was nothing those women who'd stripped off their clothes had on her other than that none of them was Adam Cole's daughter.

"I called to see if you're free later."

She rolled her eyes upward. So they were back to that again. "Dinner, you mean?"

"Yes."

In her present frame of mind, he was the last person she wanted to see. It was on the tip of her tongue to suggest he invite one of the "ladies" from the club to dine with him. But she thought better of making the suggestion, since he might very well do it. "I think I'll pass on dinner. I'm not hungry."

"Well, I am, so how about keeping me company?"

She lifted a brow. "Keep you company?"

"Yeah, I enjoy being with you."

Jayla dropped down on the bed, feeling ridiculously pleased by his admission. Although she knew that she shouldn't read too much into his words, she suddenly felt confident, cocky and in control. "Well, I hope you know that my company is going to cost you," she said, breaking the silence between them.

"In what way?"

She rubbed her fingers over the smooth wood-grain texture of the nightstand next to the bed. "I'm not hungry for anything heavy, but I'd love to have a slice of K-Paul's mouthwatering strawberry cheesecake."

She could hear him chuckle on the other end. "K-Paul's Louisiana Kitchen? I've heard of the place, but have never eaten there. I'm going to take your word that I won't be disappointed," he said.

She grinned. "Trust me, you won't be."

"How long will it take for you to get ready?"

"I just got out of the shower so it won't take me long to slip into something."

It was close to forty-five minutes before Jayla appeared in the lobby.

But the moment she walked off the elevator, Storm knew she had been well worth the wait. His chest grew tight as he watched her walk toward him, thinking she looked absolutely incredible.

He'd known he was in trouble when she had mentioned on the phone that she had just gotten out of the shower. Immediately, visions of her naked had swam his mind, which was a lot better than any live scene he had witnessed at that club earlier.

Common sense told him to pull himself together and remember who she was. But at the moment, all his senses, common or otherwise, were being shot to hell with every step she took toward him. He stood practically unmoving as he watched her, enraptured, while hot desire surged through his bloodstream.

She was dressed in a short dress that totally flowed over her figure, emphasizing the gorgeous shape of her body as well as her long beautiful legs. His gaze lowered slightly to those legs. It had been hard to keep his eyes off them this morning, and it seemed this evening wouldn't be any different. She had the kind of legs any man would just love to caress and have wrapped around him.

He drew in a deep breath, not wanting to think such thoughts but discovering he was hard-pressed to stop them from coming. Whether he liked it or not, he was undeniably attracted to Jayla Cole.

"Sorry I kept you waiting," Jayla said when she came to a stop in front of Storm.

"You were worth the wait. Ready to go?"

"Yes."

They took a cab over to the restaurant and Storm was glad he'd gotten the hotel to make reservations for him. The place was packed. "Something smells delicious," he whispered to Jayla as a waiter showed them to their table.

"Everything in here is delicious," she said smiling.

Including you, Storm was tempted to say. He wondered how he could assume that when he'd never tasted her, but he just knew that she would taste delicious.

The waiter presented them with menus. "Just coffee for me now and I'll wait for later to order dessert," she said handing the menu back to their waiter.

Storm glanced over at her. "Since you're familiar with this place, what do you suggest?"

Jayla caressed her upper lip with the tip of her tongue as if in deep thought. "Umm, I'll have to recommend Chef Paul's Duck & Shrimp Dulac. I had it the last time I was here and it was totally magnificent."

Storm nodded and returned the menu to the waiter. "Then that's what I'll have and I'd like a bottle of sparkling mineral water."

"Great choice, sir," the waiter said before walking off.

Storm leaned back in his chair. "So, do you return to work on Monday?"

Jayla shook her head. "No, I won't officially return to work until a week from Monday. Then on Tuesday of that same week, I have a meeting with a Dr. Tara Westmoreland. Is she a family member of yours?"

Storm smiled. "Yes, Tara is my sister-in-law. She and my brother Thorn tied the knot a few months back. Why would you need to meet with Tara? She's a pediatrician and you don't have a child."

Not yet, Jayla thought to herself. "The reason I'm meeting with Dr. Westmoreland is for business reasons—in fact, we're doing lunch. The company I work for, Sala Industries, is picking up the tab for the caterers the night that the Kids' World calendar is unveiled at a charity ball, and Dr. Westmoreland is on the committee. It will be a huge event, and we expect well over a thousand people to attend."

"I understand the ball will be next month," he said, after the waiter had returned with their drinks.

"Yes, the second weekend in October, in fact. And I understand your brother Thorn is Mr. July."

"Yes, he is." Storm couldn't forget how Tara had been given the unlucky task of persuading Thorn to pose as Mr. July. Doing so hadn't been easy, but things had worked out in the end, including Thorn's realizing that he loved Tara and the two of them getting married. Kids' World was a foundation that gave terminally ill children the chance to make their ultimate dream—a visit to any place in the world—come true. All proceeds for the foundation came from money raised through numerous charity events.

"I understand the calendar turned out wonderfully and the sale of them will be a huge success," Jayla said smiling, interrupting his thoughts. She gazed across the table at him for a second, then said. "Tell me about your family."

Storm raised a brow after taking a sip of his water. "Why?"

She smiled. "Because I was an only child and whenever you mention your siblings or your cousins I can tell you all share a special closeness. It was lonely growing up without sisters or brothers and I've already made up my mind to have a large family."

Storm chuckled. "How large?"

"At least two, possibly three, maybe even four."

Storm nodded. He wanted a large family as well. "The Westmoreland family is a big one and we're all very close. It started out with my grandparents who had three sons, one of which was my father. My parents had six kids, all boys until Delaney came along. Dare is the oldest, then Thorn, Stone, Chase and me. As you know, Chase is my twin brother. My father's twin brother's name is James and he and his wife Sarah also had six kids, but all of them were boys—Jared, Spencer, Durango, Ian, Quade and Reggie. My father's youngest brother, Uncle Corey, never married, so it was assumed he'd never fathered any kids, but we discovered differently a few months ago."

Jayla placed her coffee cup down, curious. "Really?"

"His sons, who never knew he was their father, just like he never knew he had sons, had an investigator track him down. Uncle Corey is a retired park ranger in Montana and that's where they found him."

Jayla was fascinated with the story Storm was sharing with her. "But how did he not know that he was a father?"

"It seems a former girlfriend found out she was pregnant after they'd broken up and never bothered telling him. Unknown to Uncle Corey, the woman gave birth to triplets."

"Triplets?"

"Yes, triplets. Multiple births are common in our family. Like me and Chase, Ian and Quade, and my father and Uncle James are fraternal twins."

Jayla inhaled, trying to absorb all this. "And your uncle's former girlfriend had triplets?"

"Yes, the first in the Westmoreland family. It seems that she told them their father had died when they were born and only revealed the truth on her deathbed. Although Uncle Corey never married the woman, she had moved out west to Texas and had taken his last name, so fortunately, her kids were born as Westmorelands."

"So your Uncle Corey has three sons he didn't know a thing about?"

"No, two sons and one daughter." He shook his head, chuckling. "And all this time we all thought Delaney was the only girl in the Westmoreland family in two generations. Last month Uncle Corey suprised us and got married!"

They suspended conversation when the waiter brought out Storm's food. Storm surprised Jayla when he handed her a fork. "There's too much here for one person. Share it with me."

She glanced at his plate. He did have a lot and it looked delicious. "Umm, maybe, I'll just take a few bites," she said taking the fork from him.

"Help yourself."

And she did. The picture of them sharing a meal played out a rather cozy and intimate scene in her mind, one she tried to ignore. She licked her lips after they had finished. The food had tasted great. "Now you're going to have to help me eat that cheesecake."

"Hey, I can handle it."

His words triggered a flutter in the pit of her stom-

ach. There was no doubt in her mind that Storm Westmoreland could handle anything. And he did. They
finished off the strawberry cheesecake in no time.

Storm checked his watch after he signed the check
for their bill. "It's still early. How would you like to
go dancing?"

His words echoed through Jayla's mind. She knew
the smart thing to do would be to tell him, no, but
for some reason, she didn't want to think smart. She
didn't want to think at all. She was in the company
of a very handsome man and she was in no hurry for
them to part ways.

She met his gaze. "I'd love going dancing with you,
Storm."

The club that had come highly recommend from
one of the waiters at K-Paul's was dark, rather small,
and crowded. Storm and Jayla were lucky to find an
empty table inside Café Basil, which had a reputation of being the undisputed king of nightlife in the
French Quarter.

Storm doubted that another couple could fit on the
dance floor. Already, the place was jam-packed, but
he was determined that they would squeeze in somehow. There was no way he would leave this place tonight without molding Jayla's body to his and holding
her in his arms.

He glanced across the table at her, barely able to
make out her features in the dimly lit room. Her body
was swaying to the sound of the jazz band that was
playing and as he watched her, he had to restrain the
emotions that were pulsing inside of him.

He had been with numerous women before and each

one had met his specific qualifications—whatever they'd been at the time. And every single one of them had known the score. He promised nothing other than a good time in bed. He wasn't interested in satisfying emotional needs, just physical ones. But there was something about Jayla that was pulling at him. The pull was definitely sexual, but there was something about it that was emotional, too.

And Storm Westmoreland didn't do anything with women that hinted of the emotional so why was he here, bursting at the seams to take Jayla into his arms on that dance floor?

Before he could ponder that question, the tune that was playing stopped and another started. Some of the dancers went back to their seats, clearing the way for others to take their turn. "This is our number," he said to Jayla, standing and reaching out for her hand.

She smiled and placed her hand in his. Immediately, he felt a tug in his gut that he tried ignoring as he led her onto the dance floor. He took a deep breath, then exhaled slowly the moment she came into his arms and molded her body to his.

"I like holding you," he said truthfully into her ear moments later, wanting her to hear his words over the sound of the band.

She leaned back and searched his face a moment before asking, "Do you?"

"Hmm..."

She smiled and he thought it was the most beautiful smile he'd ever seen on a woman and felt good that his words had brought a smile to her lips. Speaking of lips...

His gaze shifted to her mouth and he couldn't help

but take in their proximity to his. All he had to do was inch a little closer and—

"You smell good, Storm."

He inhaled deeply and slowly shook his head. She could say the damnedest things at times. They should be concentrating on small talk that was socially acceptable for platonic friends and not the sultry murmurings of lovers. "Thanks, but you shouldn't say that to me."

"Why not? If you can tell me that you like holding me, then I should be able to tell you that I think you smell good."

His hands were around her waist, holding her tight, and her arms were draped about his neck. The music playing was slow and their bodies were barely moving. He knew it and she knew it, as well. He was also certain that she was aware that he was aroused. With her body so close to his, there was no way that she didn't know it.

He wanted her to feel all of him and pulled her closer into his arms. Automatically, she placed her head against his chest and he closed his eyes as they swayed to the sound of the music. If she thought he smelled good, then he thought likewise about her. The scent of her perfume was intoxicating, seductive and a total turn-on. Moments later, the music faded and they stopped dancing, but he refused to release her. He needed to continue to hold her in his arms.

Jayla lifted her face and met Storm's gaze. The look in his eyes was intense and purely sexual. "I should try and continue to fight this," he said as if the words were being forced from him. She could clearly understand what he meant.

She did. "Don't fight it," she said softly.

He narrowed his eyes at her. "You're not helping matters, Jayla." His words were a low growl in her ear.

She narrowed her eyes right back at him. "Why should I?"

He stared at her for a long time. Then he glanced around. It seemed they were the center of attention. He looked back at her. "But you deserve more than just—"

"A one-night stand? Shouldn't I be the one to make that decision, Storm? I'm twenty-six years old. I work and pay my own bills. I'm a woman, not a child, and it's time you realized that."

He stared at her for a long moment, then said, "I just did." He tightened his hand on hers and tugged her along with him out of the club.

"Where are we going?" Jayla asked, almost out of breath as she tried keeping up with Storm's long strides as he tried hailing a cab.

"Back to the hotel."

A few moments later, Storm cursed. There were few cabs around and the ones he saw were already occupied. He glanced across the street and saw a parked horse-drawn coach. Evidently, someone had used it for a wedding and it reminded him of the coach that might be used as a prop in *Cinderella*. "Come on," he said, keeping a firm hold on Jayla's hand.

They quickly crossed the street and approached the driver, who was holding the reins to keep the horses from prancing. "We need a ride back to the Sheraton Hotel on Canal," Storm said, nearly out of breath.

The old man raised a bushy brow. "My rates are by the hour."

"Fine, just get us there quick and in one piece."

The driver nodded his head, indicating that he understood. Storm then turned and opened the carriage door. When Jayla lifted her leg to climb inside, Storm swept her into his arms and placed her inside on the seat. He then climbed in and shut the door.

As the coach lurched forward, anticipation and sexual desire the likes he had never known before gripped him and he could think of only one thing that could relax him.

He paused, wondering if he had lost his mind and then quickly decided that he had. There wasn't a damn thing he could do about it. He would worry about the consequences of his actions tomorrow. He was too far gone tonight.

He glanced over at Jayla where she sat on the other side of the seat. The interior lighting provided him with barely enough illumination to see her features, but he heard her breathing and it was coming out as erratic as his own.

"Come here, Jayla."

She met his gaze before sliding across the seat to him. He curved his hand about her neck and drew her to him. Leaning forward, he captured the lips he had been dying to taste for over ten years. He took possession and staked his claim. He couldn't help himself.

He felt the shiver that flowed from her body to his when she surrendered her tongue to his. He took his time to savor what she offered, relentlessly mating his mouth with hers as he tried to satisfy what seemed to be an endless hunger. Her taste was like a drug and he felt himself getting addicted to it as his controls were pushed to the limit, wanting more and determined to get it. He lapped up every moan she made while glorying in the feel of her kissing him back.

He deepened the kiss and she proved that she could handle him, tongue for tongue, lick for lick, stroke for stroke. It seemed that he had also tapped a hunger inside of her that she hadn't fed in a while. He intensified the kiss, knowing she wanted him as much as he wanted her.

They felt a jolt when the coach came to a stop and they broke off the kiss, pulling apart. He glanced out the window, then glanced back at her. They were at the hotel. Would she change her mind or would they finish what they'd started?

Knowing the decision was hers, he leaned over and placed a kiss on her lips. "What do you want, Jayla?" he asked, his breath hot and ragged against her ear. He hoped and prayed that she wanted the same thing that he did.

He watched as a smile touched her lips. She then reached out to run her hand down his chest, past his waist to settle firmly on his arousal that was pressing hard through his pants.

He swallowed hard, almost forgetting to breathe. His mind was suddenly filled with scenes of all the things he wanted to do to her.

She met his gaze and in a soft voice whispered, "I want you to make love to me, Storm."

Chapter 4

Storm's knuckles gently brushed across Jayla's cheeks just moments before his mouth descended on hers. The words she'd just spoken were what he wanted to hear, and at that moment he needed to taste her again.

He was swamped with conflicting emotions. A part of him wanted to pull back, unable to forget she was Adam's daughter, but then another part of him accepted and acknowledged what she'd said was true. She was old enough to make her own decisions. Even Adam had pretty much conceded that before he'd died.

He slowly, reluctantly, broke off the kiss and took a deep breath. Her eyes glinted with intense desire and he was suddenly filled with a dangerously high degree of anticipation to give her everything she wanted and needed. Without saying a word, he took her hand. Together, they got out of the coach and went into the hotel. The walk across the lobby to the elevator seemed endless, and all Storm could think about was what he would do to her once they were alone. That short dress she was wearing had driven him crazy all night. More than once, his gaze had been drawn to her bare legs, legs he wanted wrapped around him while they made love.

"My room or yours," he asked, moments before the elevator door swooshed open before them.

Their eyes met and held. "Whichever one is closest," she said as desire continued to flicker in her eyes.

"That would be yours."

They stepped into the elevator and after the door closed behind them, he leaned against the wall. They were alone and he tightened his hands by his side. The temptation to pull her into his arms and devour her mouth again was unbearable, and when she swept the tip of her tongue nervously across her top lip, his stomach clenched and he swore beneath his breath.

"I want you so damn much," he had to say. The scent of her perfume was soft and seductive.

"And I want you, too, Storm."

That statement didn't help matters, either. He had wanted to pull her into his arms the moment the elevator came to a stop on her floor, but taking a deep breath, he held the door as she stepped out off the car before him. Holding hands, they walked silently down the corridor to her hotel room. Intense sexual need was closing in on him. He had to admit he'd never wanted a woman this badly.

When they reached her room, he leaned against the wall as Jayla opened her purse, pulled out her key and inserted it into the lock. She opened the door with ease and walked into the room. He didn't waste any time following and closing the door behind them. She flipped a switch that brought a soft glow of light to the room, then turned slowly to him, meeting his gaze.

They didn't say anything for a brief moment; then he reached out and pulled her into his arms. His mind told him to take things slowly but the moment he touched her and desire swept through his body, he threw the thought of taking things slowly out the window. The only thing he could think of was lifting her short dress and becoming enfolded in her feminine heat.

He tightened his arms around her as his mouth greedily devoured hers and his chest expanded with the solid feel of her breasts pressing against it. His tongue again made a claim on her mouth while his hands skimmed across her backside, making him intensely aware of just how shapely she was. He deep his arms and walked towa... he placed her in the center of it and tumbled down beside her, his hands immediately going to her camisole to remove it from her body.

He sucked in air through clenched teeth when he pulled back and looked down at her, completely naked. At that moment he felt an unbearable desire to feel his mouth on her skin. Leaning toward her, his tongue traced a path down her neck to her breasts, where it stopped and drew a hard, budding nipple into his mouth and feasted, licking, sucking.

He felt her tremble again and heard the purring sound that came from deep within her throat. She wanted more and was letting him know it. He took his hand and ran it across the flat of her stomach, it increased his need to make love to her to the point where his veins throbbed.

Storm lifted his head just long enough to reach out and whip the short dress over Jayla's head, leaving her standing before him clad in a silky black camisole. He suddenly became dizzy with the sight of her standing before him, lush and sexy. Her scent was seductive and the pale lighting in the room traced a faint glow across her dark skin. His temperature went up another notch and he knew at that moment what he was about to share with Jayla went way beyond his regular routine of "wham-bam, thank you, ma'am." And for a mere second, that thought bothered him. But like everything else that was out of the norm for him tonight, he placed it on the back burner. He'd deal with his confusing thoughts tomorrow.

He reached out and pulled her back to him, capturing her mouth at the same time he picked her up in ened the kiss and a hoarse sound of pleasure erupted from his throat. Moments later, he broke off the kiss and pulled back. He wanted her with an intensity that bordered on desperation.

"You sure?" he asked, wanting to make certain she knew exactly what she was getting into.

"I'm positive," she said, drawing up close to him.

"Hell, I hope so." He pulled her back to him and his mouth came down on hers with a ferociousness that he didn't know he possessed. Fed by the raging storm that had erupted within him, his mouth plundered hers, sweeping her breath away and tasting the sweet, deep and delicious taste that was distinctively hers. He felt the tremor that passed through her and

moving lower until he found the moist heat of her. He touched her there, glorying in her dampness. Deftly, expertly, his fingers went to work.

Jayla felt her breath rushing in and out of her lungs. Although there was light in the room and her eyes were open, she felt her world was on the edge of blackness. She felt light-headed, dizzy, dazed, and she was feeling things that she'd never felt before. Storm's fingers were driving her out of her mind, and what his mouth was doing to her breasts was pure torture. Her body felt hot, on fire, in need of something it had never had before, but something it desperately needed.

She groaned deep in her throat. It was either that or scream out loud. So she clamped her mouth shut, but couldn't stop from releasing a sound that was alien to her ears. At the moment, nothing mattered but the feel of Storm's mouth and hands on her.

"I can't wait any longer," she heard him say, as he eased away from her. She watched as he stood next to the bed and quickly removed his shirt, almost tearing off the buttons in the process. Then he wasted no time in removing his pants and briefs. She continued to watch him when, with the expertise of a man who had done it many times before, he ripped the condom from the packet he had taken from his pant pockets and slid it over his erection.

She blinked at the size of him and before she could form the words to let him know of her virginal state, he had returned to the bed, pulled her into his arms and captured her mouth with his, once again giving in to the thirst of her desire; a desire that only he could quench. Want and need spiraled through her, making blood pump fast and furious through her veins. It

seemed his mouth and hands were everywhere. Her insides were churning, her stomach was spinning and her brain had turn to mush. She didn't know what was driving him, but whatever the source, it was driving her, too. She felt the tip of his erection pressing against the entrance to her feminine mound in such a way that beckoned her to part her legs for him.

Then he kissed her again, long, hard, as his tongue plowed hers in breath-stealing strokes. She savored all the things he was doing to her, all the ways he was making her feel and wondered if the feelings would ever end, hoping and praying that they wouldn't, yet at the same thing knowing there was something else she needed, something she had to have.

She felt him place his body over hers, felt the strength of his thighs entwining with hers and relished the strong beat of his heart against her breasts. He lifted her hips into his hands.

He broke off their kiss and met her gaze, looked down at her the moment he pushed himself inside of her, with one deep, hard thrust. Her body stiffened and she gasped as a surge of pain ripped through her.

He immediately went still as total disbelief lined his features. "Jayla?"

Her name was a low rumble from deep within his throat. She saw the shock that flared in his eyes and felt the tension coiling within him. A spurt of panic swept through her at the thought that he wouldn't finish what he'd started, so she decided to take action.

"Don't ask," she said, then leaned upward and recaptured his mouth with hers. Her hands clutched at his shoulders and her legs wrapped solidly around him, locking him in place. She felt his resistance and began

kissing him in all the ways he had kissed her that night, letting her tongue tangle relentlessly with his. He slowly began moving, easing in and out her, claiming her, taking her, making love to her in a way she always dreamed that lovemaking was supposed to be. The only thought on her mind was the strength of him driving back and forth, rocking her world and sending her over the edge. She knew she would remember every moment of this night for as long as she lived.

A groan eased from Storm's lips as Jayla's body met his, stroke for stroke. His hand reached down and lifted her hips to him for a closer fit, as if they weren't already close enough. She was tight, sensuously so, and his body surged in and out of hers, back and forth, massaging her insides the same way and with the same rhythm that her breasts were massaging his chest.

He had recovered from shock at discovering she'd been a virgin and decided since he was the one initiating her into lovemaking, that he would do it right. And the little whimpering sounds coming from her lips told him that he was definitely making an impact.

"Storm…"

He felt her body jerk at the same time she pressed her head into his shoulder to stifle a scream. The intensity of her climax jolted him, nearly stealing his breath before he followed her in his own release, yanked into the strongest and most mindless orgasm he had ever experienced in his entire life. And it was destined to be the longest…or perhaps he was having multiples, back to back. There was no way to tell since the earth-shattering sensations were hitting him all at once in every form and from every possible angle. The feeling was unique, incredible, out of this world and once in a lifetime. He hadn't expected this and was caught off guard by the magnitude of what was happening to him. He was being hurled into something he had never before experienced.

"Jayla!"

Her name was torn from his lips and he threw his head back as he continued to pump rapidly into her when he felt another climax claim him—his third, possibly a fourth. With a growl that came low from deep within his throat, he leaned down and pressed a kiss to her mouth as his body continued to tumble into oblivion, and he knew what they had shared was nothing short of heaven.

"I did as you requested and didn't ask then, but I'm asking now, Jayla."

Storm's words gave her pause. She let out a deep breath and wondered why he couldn't be one of those men who just accepted things as they were?

She looked up at him and saw the intensity in the depth of his dark eyes. She also saw the impressive shape of his lips and his well-toned, broad chest that was sprinkled with dark curly hair. And it wasn't helping matters that they were both naked in bed, with him leaning on his elbow and looming over her. She closed her eyes and shook her head. The man was too handsome for his own good…or for hers.

"Tell me," he whispered, then leaned down and placed a soft kiss on her bare shoulder. "Tell me why, in this day and age, a twenty-six-year-old woman would still be a virgin."

She met his gaze. "Because women in this day and

age have choices," she said slowly, then asked. "Have you ever taken a love compatibility quiz?"

Storm arched his brow. "A what?"

She smiled at the confused look on his face. "A love compatibility quiz. There's a site on the Internet where you can go and take this quiz if you're looking for Mr. or Miss Right. Well, after a few dates with losers—men who lacked confidence but had plenty of arrogance and who also acted as if it was a foregone conclusion that our date would end in my bed—I decided to take the quiz and my results indicated that my Mr. Right didn't exist."

Storm frowned down at her. Would he ever understand women? "You've been avoiding a serious relationship because of some quiz?"

"Pretty much…yes. I discovered like oil and water, me and relationships don't mix because I have a low tolerance when it comes to men who expect too much too soon."

It took Storm a minute to analyze everything she'd said. "What about those guys you dated off the Internet?"

Jayla released a single, self-deprecating chuckle. "That was my way of trying to prove the quiz wrong. From then on, I never wasted my time going on a guy hunt."

"But…but didn't you date in college?" Storm sputtered. Why hadn't her going off to college assured her returning to town with her hymen no longer intact?

She smiled again, a bit sadly this time. "Yes, but unfortunately, not long after I got there I met a guy name Tyrone Pembroke."

"What happened? He broke your heart?"

She chuckled derisively. "On the contrary. Actually he did me a favor by showing me just what jerks some guys were. He opened my eyes to the games they played, games I wasn't interested in. After Ty, I made it a point not to get serious about any one guy and since I wasn't into casual sex, I never felt pressured into sleeping with anyone."

Storm nodded. "So why now and why with me?

To Jayla's way of thinking, that was an easy question. "Because of timing. I know you and I like you. I also know your position on relationships. I'm not looking for anything beyond what we shared tonight and neither are you, right?"

Storm held her gaze. "Right." The last thing he needed was a clingy woman who wanted to occupy his time. Still, although he didn't want to feel it, he felt a special connection to Jayla since he had been her first. He couldn't recall ever taking a woman's virginity before.

"Now that I've answered your question, do you think I can get some sleep? I'm exhausted." Jayla asked softly.

Storm glanced down at her. Was she dismissing him? "Do you want me to leave?"

She smiled. "Actually…" she began, as she snuggled closer to him. "I was hoping you'd want to stay all night."

A grin spread across Storm's lips. Hell, yeah, he wanted to stay all night. "I think that can be arranged," he told her as he leaned down and placed a kiss on her lips. "Excuse me for a second while I go into the bathroom to take care of something. I'll be right back."

"All right."

There was just enough light in the darkened room to let Jayla admire Storm's nude form as he crossed the room to the bathroom. She inhaled deeply as heated sensations shot through her. He'd been the perfect lover. He was confident, secure in who he was, but not arrogant. She felt tired and yet exhilarated at the same time. Slightly sore, but still smoldering from his lovemaking. Funny how things worked out. Storm was the man she'd been trying to get to notice her since the time she had started noticing boys. She was beginning to believe the cliché that good things came to those who wait. Now timing had not only finally worked for them, it was working against them as well. At any other time, she would have loved to take what she'd shared with Storm tonight to a whole other level, but not now. What she had needed was him out of her system so she could focus on the baby.

Her baby.

"I'm back."

Her nipples peaked in instant response to his words. She watched as he made a casual stroll over to the bed, totally at ease with his naked state. Seeing him that way stirred up desires within her again and she no longer felt as tired as she had earlier.

"Do you want me to prepare you some bath water to soak in for a while before you go off to sleep?" he asked coming to sit on the side of the bed next to where she lay. "If you don't, you might wake up feeling a lot sorer than you probably do now."

Jayla leaned back against her pillow, seriously doubting that most men were as considerate as Storm was being. She pressed her lips together, liking his suggestion. "You're right, a soak in the tub sounds wonderful."

He smiled as he stood up. "I'll be back when your bath is ready."

"All right."

Again she watched him cross the room, finding it hard to tear her gaze from the sight of him, especially his tight behind. She smiled, feeling downright giddy at the thought that he'd agreed to spend the night with her. She might as well stretch this out for as far as she could because when they returned to Atlanta, things would be different. She would go her way and he would go his. They would both resume a life that had nothing to do with each other. He would go back to being a hero by fighting his fires and saving lives and she would eagerly prepare for the most life-altering experience she'd ever encountered—pregnancy.

"Ready?"

Hearing the sound of his voice, she glanced across the room. A thick surge of desire shot through her veins at the sight of him leaning in the doorway, naked and aroused. If she wasn't ready, he certainly was.

"Yes, I'm ready," she said, barely able to voice the words. She moved to get out of bed and then he was there, sweeping her up into his arms. The heat of his skin seeped through the heat of hers and the feeling was electrifying. She immediately knew the meaning of the words *raging hormones*. Hers were totally out of control. She quickly decided that she needed to get back in control of things.

"I can walk, Storm."

"Yes, but I want to carry you. That's the least I can do."

She clamped her lips tight, deciding not to tell him that he had done quite a lot. He had turned their night into more than a one-night stand. It had become a romantic interlude, one she would remember for the rest of her life.

As he carried her into the bathroom, her breasts tingled from the contact with his skin. And when he leaned down, shifting her in his arms to place her into the bubbly water, sliding her body down his, the sensations that rocketed through her almost took her breath away.

"The water might be a little warmer than what you're used to, but it will be good for your muscles," he said, in a voice that let her know he, too, had been affected by the contact of their bare skin touching.

She nodded as he placed her in the water. He was right. The water was warm, but it immediately felt good to her body. She glanced up at him as he stood beside the tub looking down at her. She tried to keep her attention on the top part of his body and not the lower part. "You seem to be good at this, Westmoreland. Is this how you treat all your virgins?"

He chuckled and his gaze captured hers. "Believe it or not, I've never done a virgin before."

She lifted a brow. "Never?"

His smile widened. "No, never. You're my first, just like I was your first."

Jayla watched as his features shifted into a serious expression as if he had to really think about what he'd just said for a moment. "Do you need my help?" he asked her.

She shook her head. "No, I can manage. Thanks."

He nodded. "Call me when you're ready to get out."

She smiled. "Storm, really, I can manage things."

"Yeah, I know you can but I want you to call me anyway." Then he left, closing the door behind him.

Storm poured himself a glass of ice water and tipped it to his mouth, wishing it was something stronger but appreciating the cool liquid as it soothed his dry throat.

He had sworn off having anything to do with Jayla years ago; yet now, after finally making love to her, he was aching so badly for her again that it actually hurt. To make matters worse, the taste of her was still strong on his tongue and, before he could contain himself, he groaned, which was followed by a growl that erupted from deep within his throat. Jayla Cole had no idea just what a desirable and sexy woman she was. Even being a novice at making love, she was every man's fantasy. He could see her attracting the wrong kind of men and felt a heartfelt sense of pride, as well as relief, that she had kept her head on straight and had not been taken in by any of them.

But was he any better? His no-commitment, hands-on-but-hearts-off, no-strings-attached policy left a lot to be desired, but he and Jayla had been struck by that unique kind of passion that had sent her straight into his arms and had propelled him unerringly into her bed.

And he had no regrets.

Frowning, Storm took another huge swallow of water. No woman had ever gotten to him like this. It was time for him to start building a defense to the passion she aroused in him. He pulled on his pants and did his best to reorder his chaotic thoughts and unruly emotions.

He heard a sound and turned around. Jayla was standing in the doorway wearing one of the hotel's complimentary bathrobes. His heart fluttered as he assessed her from head to toe. She looked refreshed. She looked incredible, blatantly sexy. With a steadying breath, he asked, "Why didn't you call me when you were ready to get out of the tub?"

She smiled and his pulse kicked up a notch. "Because although I was tempted, it wouldn't be a good idea to start becoming dependent on you."

For him, it wasn't an issue of dependency. He'd known she could manage on her own but he had wanted to be there to help her anyway. There was something about her that pulled at his protective instincts...among other things. "Do you feel better?"

"Yes," Jayla said, blowing out a ragged breath as her gaze roamed over him, noticing that he had put his pants back on. What a shame. She was beginning to get used to seeing him naked.

She met his gaze again and couldn't help but notice that his eyes were dark, very dark, and her body's reaction to it was spontaneous. "I, ah, need to get a nightgown out the drawer," she said in a voice that sounded soft and husky even to her ears. She swallowed deeply when he slowly crossed the room to her.

"Have you ever slept in the nude?" he said, reaching out, opening her robe and sliding his hands over her bare skin, beginning with her waist, moving to her hips and then reaching around to cup her bottom.

"Ah, no," she said, barely getting the words out.

He gave her that killer smile. "Would you like to

try it? I can't think of anything I'd like better than to have your naked body next to mine all night."

A small purring sound left Jayla's throat when he leaned forward and his tongue licked the area underneath her right ear, then the left. A sensuous shudder ran all through her, and she thought that a woman could definitely become dependent on his kind of treatment. And then she ceased to think at all when he stopped messing around with her ears and shifted his focus, opening his mouth hotly over hers.

Images of how intimate they'd been less than an hour ago flooded her mind. They had been together in bed with him on top of her, their legs entwined, their bodies connected while making love the same way they had done numerous times in her dreams. But this was no dream; it was reality. And the scent of his body heat and the sound of his breathing while he was kissing her did more than stir up her desire; it was stroking her with an intensity that shook her to the core, forging past those emotions she kept tightly guarded.

The thought that Storm was seeping through the barriers she'd set around her emotions disturbed Jayla, but she was too absorbed in the way his tongue was stroking the insides of her mouth to worry about it. This kiss was so full of greed and sensuality that she could feel the air crackling around them, and she was returning with equal vigor everything he was putting into their kiss.

And then slowly, reluctantly, he pulled back and his gaze locked to hers. "So, do we get naked?"

She swallowed. The huskiness in his voice made her want to do a lot more than get naked. "Yes," she managed to get out in a shaky breath.

"Good," he murmured, then reached up and pushed the robe off her shoulders, letting it fall in a heap at her feet. "Let's go back to bed."

Taking her hand into his, he lifted it to his lips and placed a warm kiss against the center of her palm. And then he picked her up in his arms and carried her to the bed. He placed her in the middle and then stood back to remove his pants.

Jayla watched him while thinking that nothing, other than a fire alarm going off, could distract her at that moment. She wanted to see every inch of him again, especially that part that had given her so much pleasure. He kept his gaze on her as he slowly eased down his pants. Then she watched as he pulled a condom packet out of his pants and went through the process of sheathing himself.

When he had finished, he glanced over at her and smiled. "Although I don't plan for us to do anything but sleep, there's nothing wrong with playing it safe."

She sighed and it took a lot of effort to concentrate on his words and not on him. "Umm, yes, that's smart thinking."

He quickly got into the bed, pulled her into his arms and felt her shiver. "You're cold?" he asked in a low, husky voice.

She shook her head. "No, quite the contrary. I'm hot."

He smiled. "I know a way to cool you off," he said, shifting his position to reach down between her legs to slide his fingers back and forth through her feminine curls.

She closed her eyes and moaned as he slowly but thoroughly began stroking a fire within her. "I—I don't think that's helping, Storm," she murmured, barely able to get the words out.

"Sure it is," he whispered close to her ear. "Just relax, feel and enjoy."

And she did.

His fingers literally drove her crazy. The sensation of his fingertips as they intimately skimmed her feminine folds at a sensuously maddening and erratic pace had her purring and moaning.

She made the mistake of opening her eyes and meeting his gaze. Something she saw in the depths of his eyes took her breath away. Her senses suddenly became filled with an emotion that caused a tightening in her chest at the same time that her body lost control, exploded. The sensations that shot through her made her cry out, call his name and then he was capturing her mouth with his, kissing her deeply while he continued to skim the tip of his fingers between her legs.

Moments later, she felt her body become weak and she could barely reclaim her breath as he cuddled her limp body next to his, holding her tightly. She knew if she wasn't careful, that she was going to fall—

No! She couldn't go there. She couldn't even think such a thing. The only thing she wanted to focus on was how he was making her feel. She had made plans for her future and Storm Westmoreland wasn't a part of those plans. But here, now, at this very moment, he was part of her present and was giving her undiluted pleasure. She could not refuse what he was offering and when they parted in two days, she would always have these memories.

Chapter 5

Storm drew in a long breath as he looked down at the woman asleep in his arms. His chest tightened and he forced back the surge of desire that swept through him. She was an unbelievably beautiful woman.

Bathed in the rays of predawn light that spilled through the hotel's window, Jayla's hair, a glossy medium brown with strands of golden highlight, was spread across the pillow and shone luxuriously against the darkness of her creamy skin.

Sharing a bed with her hadn't been easy. In fact, he doubted that he'd gotten any sleep. While trying to find that perfect sleeping position, she had twisted and turned most of the night. And he had been tormented with each and every move she'd made. At one time, she had lain facing him, with her leg thrown over his, with his arousal pressing against her center.

Then there had been that time when she had shifted around, placing her back to his chest, her sweet delectable backside right smack up against his groin. More than once during the course of the night he had been tempted to just say, "To hell with it," and ease inside of her. His mind had been filled with numerous possibilities. Instead, he had fought the urge and had wrapped his arms around her waist, pulled her close and thought about the time when he *had* been inside of her.

He would never forget how it felt, the moment he'd realized that she was a virgin. At first he'd been shocked, stunned and then panic had set in. But the notion of ending their lovemaking session had fled his mind when she pulled his mouth down to hers and kissed him with a hunger that he had quickly reciprocated.

And now he wanted her again. If truth were told, he hadn't stopped wanting her but had held back to give her body time to adjust to him. Now he was driven with an undeniable need to bury himself deep within her welcoming warmth again. He glanced over at the clock. It was just past six. He wanted to let her sleep but couldn't. He had to have her. Now.

He leaned over, close to her lips. "Jayla?" he whispered. A few moments later, she purred his name and slowly lifted one drowsy eye. Then she opened the other eye and blinked, as if to bring his face into focus.

"Storm," she murmured in a voice that was muffled with sleep, but to his way of thinking sounded sensuous as hell. Little tendrils of hair had drifted onto her face and graced one of her cheeks. He pushed the hair back from her face before sliding that same hand down the length of her body. Shifting slightly, he wanted her to feel his arousal pressing against the curve of her pelvis.

"I want you," he whispered and wondered if she could hear the urgency in his tone. The need. The desperation. She must have because she inched her lips closer to his for him to take control of her mouth, mate with it.

And he did.

His every muscle, his every nerve, felt sensitized as their tongues tangled with a hunger that was driving him crazy. The sweet, honeyed taste of her consumed his mind, sent a flame through his body and made him quickly lose touch with reality.

"Storm," she said softly, breaking off their kiss as her hands reached down, tentatively searching for him. When she captured him in the warmth of her hands, he thought he had died and gone to heaven. "I want this."

He definitely knew what she was asking for and didn't waste any time rolling her beneath him. He reached down and touched her, finding her hot, wet and ready. Lowering his head he needed to taste her breasts and drew one hardened nipple into his mouth, gently pulling it with his tongue, glorying in the shivers he felt going through her.

And then with her hands still holding him, she placed him at her opening and, slanting her hips upward, began easing him inside her. At this stage of the game, his arousal didn't know the meaning of slow and he pushed deep inside, finding her body still tight, but not as tight as it had been the night before. He stopped to give her time to adjust to him, but her soft moans and the rotation of her hips let him know she didn't want him to stop.

He thrust harder, buried himself to the depth they both wanted, and then he kissed her again, needing the contact to her mouth. And then he began to move inside of her as intense, dizzying, mind-boggling desire consumed him, sending him on a voyage that was out of this world. And Jayla was right there, taking the trip with him, as they flew higher and higher to the place where passion was taking them. A place that was a potent blend of exultation and euphoria, a place where he wanted to think that few people went—at least not to this degree and certainly not this level.

"Wow," he whispered huskily, for lack of a better word, and then he increased his pace, established their rhythm and like finely tuned musical instruments they played together in absolute harmony. Each movement added sensation and increased their pleasure. He dragged in a deep breath, feeling as if he were seconds from toppling over the edge, moments from exploding.

He clamped his hands down on her hips while he mated relentlessly with her. Her feminine muscles began gripping, clutching him with every thrust he took. And when he heard the sharp cry that was torn from her lips and felt her body jolt at the same time she arched her back, then shattered in his arms, he let go and began drowning in his own release.

"Jayla!"

He threw his head back, as something, everything, inside him broke free. If he thought he'd experienced pure, unadulterated ecstasy inside her body before, then this was a pleasure so raw and primitive that he doubted he would ever be able to recover from it. It was as if this was where he belonged, where he was supposed to be.

He quickly banished those thoughts from his mind as they continued to move together. He felt as if every cell within him was electrified, energized as they were propelled even deeper into the sensuous clutches that held them.

And then, before they could recover, it happened again, just as fast and just as potent. They were hurled into another orgasm so powerful that he actually felt the room spin and wondered if he would ever regain his equilibrium. A cry tore from his throat, only to be drowned out by the sound of hers as once again they were plunged into the throes of pure ecstasy.

With a shuddered sigh, he pulled her closer to him, felt himself getting hard all over again and knew this woman was doing more than draining his body. She was draining his very soul and at the moment, he couldn't do a damn thing to stop her.

Jayla couldn't move, so she lay still, feeling sated, exhausted and caught up in the aftereffects of remarkable sex. She stared up at the ceiling as she tried to calm the rhythm of her breathing. She smiled as she forced herself onto her side and faced Storm. He was lying flat on his back with his eyes closed. He, too, took long, deep, steadying breaths. When she saw he was once again aroused, the sight of him sent her senses into a mindless sensuous rush all over again. He was as hard as a rock, seemingly ready for another round. How on earth was that possible?

She sighed deeply. "Everything I've heard about you is true, Storm." She watched as he slowly lifted his eyes, slightly turned his head and looked over at her.

"What have you heard about me?"

Every bone in her body felt as if it had melted, so she chuckled huskily. "That you're perfect in bed. Did you know some women call you, The Perfect Storm?"

Storm frowned. For some reason he didn't want her to think about the other women he'd been with. And he didn't want to think about them, either. The only woman he wanted to think about was her. Instead of answering her question, he leaned over and kissed her deeply, thoroughly, and moments later, when he pulled back, he reached down and touched her intimately. "I didn't mean to be rough."

A huge smile touched the corners of her lips. "You weren't. I got everything I asked for and then some."

"Yeah, but you're new at this."

"And enjoying every minute." She studied him for a moment, then said. "I was curious about you when I was sixteen. You were the first guy I was really interested in."

"Was I?"

"Yes."

Storm held her gaze. He could vividly recall how, whenever he dropped by to visit Adam, her whiskey-colored eyes would seek him out and convey her every youthful emotion. She'd had a crush on him. He had been aware of it and he had a feeling that Adam had been aware of it as well. Storm had known that around her he would have to tread lightly, because she was the boss's daughter who was noticing boys for the first time; but unfortunately, instead of a boy, she had set her sights and budding desires on a man. To make matters worse, she fully intended for him to notice her and he had tried like hell not to.

"Do we stay in bed for the rest of the day or do we

get up and do something else?" she asked, interrupting his stroll down memory lane. "Just to let you know, the thought of staying in bed all day doesn't bother me."

Storm couldn't help but laugh. "What have I created here, a monster?"

She lifted a brow. "Like you can talk. I'd say you're up for it," she said, pointing out his aroused state.

"Well, yeah, but some things can't be rushed. Just give me some time, will you."

"Sure, if you think you need it, but from what I understand most men need time to get it up, not down."

One corner of Storm's mouth lifted. He was enjoying this turn in their conversation, but he knew if they didn't get out of bed really soon, their conversation might turn into something else. Forcing himself to move, he slowly sat up. "I guess I need to go back to my room and take a shower." He glanced over at the clock. "Do you want to meet me downstairs for breakfast?"

"Yeah, I'm starving."

He nodded knowingly. "And after breakfast, how about if we do some more sightseeing today?" *Anything to keep them out of their hotel rooms.* "When does your flight leave tomorrow?" he asked. Suddenly, reality of how short their time together would be began to seep in. From the expression on her face he could tell that she felt it, too.

"In the morning, around eight. What about yours?"

"Tomorrow evening, around three."

She nodded. "Too bad we aren't on the same flight," she said quietly.

He'd been thinking the same thing. "Yeah, it's too bad." But then, maybe it was for the best. Too much more of Jayla Cole would go to his head and right to a place he wasn't quite ready for.

He sighed deeply. So much had happened between them in the last forty-eight hours. "Nothing has changed, right Jayla? Neither of us is looking for a serious relationship."

Jayla glanced at him, understanding his need to reestablish ground rules. "Yeah, right, nothing has changed. Trust me, a serious relationship with anyone is the last thing I want or need right now. I'm going to be so busy over the next few months that an involvement of any kind will be the furthest thing from my mind."

He lifted a brow as he slid out of bed. "Oh? What will you be doing?"

Jayla nervously licked her lips. There was no way she could tell him that she would be preparing for motherhood. "There's this project that I'm going to start working on."

"Oh, and what kind of project is it?"

She sighed deeply; he would ask. She decided to brush off his question and forced out a chuckle, saying, "Nothing you'd be interested in, trust me."

He smiled as he studied her for a long moment, then said. "I might surprise you. If you ever need my help, don't hesitate to call."

She smiled. "Thanks for the offer, but I have everything under control."

"All right. I'll be back in a second."

She watched as he walked into the bathroom and closed the door. She rolled over on her stomach and buried her face in his pillow, enjoying his lingering scent. Had she been dreaming or had Storm just offered to help with her project? She felt it was pretty safe to assume that the last thing Storm Westmoreland would want was to be a daddy. Besides, she had no regrets in going solo. A man like him as the father of her child would definitely cramp her style. He'd already stated his belief that a woman couldn't work outside the home *and* raise a family. She didn't envy the woman he would end up marrying, since it was evident that he would be a controlling husband.

She got out of bed, slipped into her robe, walked over to the window and glanced out to watch the impending sunrise. Tomorrow, she and Storm would bring an end to their short affair and she hoped when they returned to Atlanta that they didn't run into each other anytime soon. It would be difficult to see him and not think about the intimacy they had shared here in The Big Easy. There definitely wouldn't be anything easy about that.

Storm slid his hands around Jayla's waist and pulled her snugly against him. "An hour?" he asked with a puzzled lift of his brow. "Are you saying it will take you an entire hour to pick out an outfit for tonight?"

She smiled up at him. "Yes. Already I see a number of things in this dress shop that I want to try on. It has to be just perfect."

"Jayla," he began, but she cut him off.

"Please, Storm. I want a new outfit for tonight."

He studied the excitement in Jayla's face, thinking she was even more beautiful than before, if that were possible. When he had met her for breakfast, he'd told her of the phone call he had received from his cousin Ian. Ian, a good friend of New Orleans's mayor, had been invited to a huge gala being given in the man's honor. Ian had invited Storm as his guest and Storm had gotten the okay to bring Jayla as his date. Instead of going sightseeing as they had originally planned, Jayla had insisted that the first thing she needed to do was go shopping for something to wear that night.

"All right, I guess I can find something to kill time while you shop," he said releasing her. "But I'll be back in a hour, Jayla."

She grinned, nodding. "And I'll have everything I need by then."

A short while later, Storm took his time as he strolled around Jackson Square. It was a beautiful day and a lot of tourists were out and about. He smiled when he thought of how excited Jayla had been when he'd mentioned tonight's affair. He had enjoyed seeing her happy. He was also enjoying her company... almost a little too much. She was definitely someone he liked being with, both in and out of bed. More than once he had to remind himself not to make more of what they were sharing than there was.

It was no big deal that over the past few days, they'd discovered that they enjoyed many of the same things. She liked jazz, and so did he; she enjoyed watching bone-chilling thriller movies and so did he. She was one of the few people who lived in Atlanta whose favorite football team *wasn't* the Atlanta Falcons. His favorite team was the Dallas Cowboys and she was a fan of the Philadelphia Eagles.

It seemed the only thing they didn't agree on was his belief that a woman's place was at home raising her kids and not in an office all day. Jayla insisted that a man who held such traditional views would be too controlling in a marriage. He didn't see himself as wanting to control, but rather he saw himself as someone who wanted to be the sole provider for his family in the purest sense of the word.

He glanced at his watch. He still had over forty-five minutes to go before he went back to that dress shop for Jayla. Damn, but he missed her already. A warning bell suddenly went off in his head. He'd never admitted to missing a woman before, so why was he doing it now? He sighed deeply, deciding to be honest with himself. The honest truth was he liked having Jayla around and for him that didn't bode well.

He frowned as he continued to walk around Jackson Square, wondering what was there about her that was getting to him and playing games with his mind? They were games he had no desire to play. She knew the score and so did he. Neither of them wanted anything beyond what they were sharing here in New Orleans. Getting together and developing some sort of relationship when they returned to Atlanta was unacceptable, totally out of the question, a definite bad idea.

Then why was he allowing such thoughts to invade his mind?

"You're confused, aren't you?"

Storm turned to the sound of the craggy voice and saw an old woman sitting on the bench less than five feet from where he stood. He lifted a brow. "Excuse me. Did you say something?"

The old woman smiled serenely. "Yes. I said you're confused. Nothing like this has ever happened to you before has it?"

Storm tilted his head to the side as he studied the woman, wondering if she was operating with a full

deck. She was talking as if she knew him. "I think you
might have me mixed up with someone else."

"No, I don't," she muttered with a shake of her head.
"And I'm not crazy," she said, as if reading his mind.
"I'd tell you more if you let me look into your future."

Storm nodded as understanding dawned. The old
woman was a fortune-teller. New Orleans was full
of them. He crossed his arms over his chest amused.
"And what do you think you can tell me that I don't
already know?"

"Oh, you'd be surprised."

Storm didn't think so but decided to humor the old
woman. "Okay, then surprise me. What do you have
to work with? Tarot cards or a crystal ball?"

The older woman met his gaze and looked at him
with a scrutiny that Storm found unnerving. Finally,
she responded. "Neither. I'm a palm reader."

Storm nodded. *That figured.* "Okay, how much to
read my palm?"

"Twenty dollars."

He sighed as he reached into his pocket and pulled a
twenty-dollar bill while wondering why he was wasting his time. He glanced at his watch. He still had a
good thirty minutes left before Jayla was ready and
having his palm read was just as good as anything else
to pass the time away.

He sat down next to the woman on the bench and
stretched out his hand to her. "Okay, what does my
palm say?"

He watched as the woman took his hand into her
frail one and studied his palm. Moments later, when
she lifted her gaze, the intensity in the depth of her

dark eyes almost startled him. She smiled sympathetically. "I can see why you're confused."

He frowned. "Meaning what?"

"You are about to make unexpected changes in your life and although you yearn for peace, turbulence is in your future. Keep your sights high, be patient and let destiny take its course."

Storm's frown deepened. He had just gotten a promotion three months ago, so what changes was the woman talking about? He had thought about moving out of his present house and buying a larger one, but what problems could a decision like that bring on? There had to be more.

He lifted his brow. "Is that it?"

She stared at him and sighed deeply. "Trust me, son. That will be enough."

He shook his head, a part of him found the entire thing outright amusing. "Ahh, can you be a little more specific?"

"No, I've told you everything you need to know."

He slowly stood. He couldn't wait until he and his brothers had their next card game so he could tell them about this experience. Knowing them, they would probably find the whole thing hilarious. "Well, it was nice getting my palm read," he said, not knowing what else to say.

She shook her head slowly. "I wish you the best of luck."

Storm looked at the woman. She'd said it like she had truly meant it. "Thanks," he said before walking off, not sure just what he was thanking her for.

"Tell her you like the red one."

He turned back around and lifted a brow. "Excuse me?"

The old woman smiled. "Tell her you like the red one the best."

Storm frowned, not understanding what she meant. He decided it would be best not to ask, so he nodded, turned back around and kept walking. Moments later, when he returned to the dress shop, he saw Jayla standing at the checkout counter waiting for him. His face lit into a smile as he walked over to her. "Did you find anything?"

"Yes," she answered excitedly. "I found two really nice outfits and they're both beautiful. I want you to pick out the one you like the best."

He watched as she turned and grabbed two dresses off the counter, one blue and the other red. Storm blinked twice and his throat suddenly went dry when he remembered what the old woman had said. *Tell her you like the red one.* He stared at the two outfits that Jayla was holding up in front of her.

"Well, which do you like the best, Storm?" she asked, looking from one dress to the other.

"The red one," he replied promptly, feeling somewhat dazed, like he was a participant in *The Twilight Zone.*

Jayla didn't notice his consternation as she handed the red dress to the smiling saleswoman behind the counter. A huge grin touched her lips. "I like the red one best, too."

Later that night, Storm had to admit that he definitely liked the red dress, especially on Jayla. His tongue had nearly fallen out of his mouth the moment she had stepped off the elevator to meet him in the lobby.

Instantaneous. Immediate. A jolt of mind-wrenching desire had shot straight to his groin. There was nothing like an eye-catching, incredulously sexy, tight-fitting dress on a woman who definitely had sleek and delectable curves. Her silver accessories made her look sophisticated, elegant and hot, all at the same time. The dress was short, really short, but then she had legs that transformed the dress from provocative to mind-blowing. Her breasts sat high and looked full, lush and ready to tumble out of the low-cut neckline at any given moment.

"I had a lot of fun tonight, Storm, and I like your cousin Ian."

He glanced at her. They were sitting in the back of a cab on their way back to the hotel. It was dark, but the moonlight, as well as the bright lights from the buildings they passed, provided sufficient light for them to see each other's features clearly. But even if he hadn't been able to see her, he would have definitely been able to smell her. The perfume she was wearing was a luscious, blatantly sensual scent and it was doing downright crazy things to his libido.

"Yeah, and I could tell he liked you," he responded huskily. *Almost a little too much,* he thought. He smiled when he remembered the look on his cousin's face the moment he and Jayla had walked into the party. Ian's expression of appreciation was also shared by most of the other men present. His heart had swelled with pride that she was with him.

And he couldn't forget how Ian had pulled Jayla to him and planted a kiss on her lips when they'd been leaving. He grinned, knowing Ian had intended to give him a dose of his own medicine. Ian had wanted to get a rise out of him, the same way he enjoyed getting a rise out of his brothers whenever he kissed their wives. Now he knew how it felt.

"I can't wait to get to the hotel to get out of these shoes. They are killing my feet."

Storm smiled and was glad that because of the darkness, Jayla couldn't see the heated gleam in his eyes. He couldn't wait to get her back to the hotel to get her out of something else. The sight of her in that dress had nearly driven him mad all night. He couldn't wait to see just what she had or didn't have underneath it.

"Lift your feet into my lap and I'll be glad to give you some temporary relief," he murmured, wanting to touch her any way he could. She didn't waste time taking him up on his offer and she shifted her body to slide her legs across his lap. He knew there was no way she could not feel the hardness of his groin with her legs resting across his thighs.

He went about removing the silver stiletto heels and began massaging her feet. Her panty hose felt smooth and silky to his touch, and the thought that he'd never pampered another woman this way suddenly hit him. He tossed the thought from his mind as he continued to gently and methodically stroke her feet, thinking there was nothing like a great pair of legs and she had a pretty nice pair.

"Umm, I could get used to this. You have gifted hands, Storm."

He smiled. "Anything to make you happy." He thought about what he'd said and shook his head. He wondered what it would take to make a woman like her completely happy.

"We got back too soon," Jayla said, and he glanced out of the cab's window to see they had arrived back at the hotel. He strapped her shoes back on her feet and felt an immediate sense of loss when she pulled her legs out of his lap.

He glanced over at her, determined to remove that disappointment from her voice. He leaned over, pulled her against him and captured her lips. The taste of her was arousing...as if he needed to be aroused more than he already was. In minutes, he had her groaning and liked the sound of it.

"My room or yours?" he whispered softly against her lips.

She stared at his mouth a moment before answering in a voice that increased his heart rate another notch. "I've never been inside a man's hotel room before and since this trip to New Orleans has been a first for me in a lot of ways, let's go to your room tonight."

He kissed her again, devouring her soft lips and thinking he could definitely get used to this.

Jayla awoke when she heard the ringing of the telephone. A quick glance at the clock on the nightstand indicated it was the wake-up call she had ordered. She watched as Storm reached over, picked up the receiver and, without answering, hung it back up. He then met her gaze and for a moment she thought she saw a quick instant of regret in his eyes when he said, "I guess it's time."

"Yeah, it seems that way," she said softly, not wanting to get out of bed and get dressed, although she knew that she should. She needed to go to her room and pack. Her flight was scheduled to leave in a few hours and she had to make sure that she arrived at the airport on time.

Heat spread low in her belly when Storm continued to look at her. Whenever he looked at her, it did things to her. She would remember every moment of last night. She had entered his hotel room and he had closed the door behind them. She had walked into his embrace and the kiss they'd shared had been blazing and within seconds he had removed her dress and panty hose, leaving her wearing only a thong.

She would never forget the way he had looked at her, how he had swept her up into his arms and carried her over to the bed and made love to her as if pleasing her were the most important thing in his life. The lovemaking that they had shared had been simply amazing.

"Do you need help packing?" he asked, looking breathtakingly handsome, sleep-rumpled and delicious. He smiled as he braced himself up on one elbow and looked down at her. He reached out and gently touched the nipples of her breasts. They hardened with his touch and she felt a warmth begin to build between her legs.

She returned his smile, knowing if she were to take him up on his offer she would never finish packing. "Thanks for the offer, but I believe I can manage."

She felt her smile slowly fade away as reality set in. Although she did not regret any of the time she had spent with him, she knew it was about to end. There was no other way, and it would be for the best. She had to shift her focus away from Storm and back to the baby she wanted more than anything. As soon as she got home, she would schedule an appointment with the fertility clinic to get things started. A continuation of Storm in her life would only complicate things and she didn't do well with complications. Besides, she knew there was no Mr. Right for her, especially one by the name of Storm Westmoreland.

So why was it so hard for her to get out of his bed? And why did she want to make love to him again, one last time before she finally walked out the door?

"I enjoyed our time together, Jayla."

His words interrupted her thoughts and she met his gaze, studied his eyes. "I did, too, and still no regrets, right?"

He reached out and threaded his fingers through her hair. "No regrets. We're adults and we did what we wanted to do."

A smile curved her mouth. "Thank you Storm for showing me how great lovemaking can be."

He looked at her, countered her smile. "You're welcome."

"But life goes on," she decided to say when more than anything she wanted to kiss him.

He nodded. "Yes, life goes on, but it won't be easy. If I were to run into you anytime soon," he said, gently smoothing his fingertips across her cheek, "there's no way I'll see you and not think about that red dress and those killer high heels, not to mention the only thing you were wearing under that dress."

She chuckled. "Shocked you, huh?"

A huge smiled tipped one corner of his mouth. "Yeah, you shocked me. You also pleased me."

Storm decided that what he couldn't tell her was that she was unlike any woman he had ever known. She was someone who could laugh with him, tease him and talk to him just about anything. And the sex had been amazing and there was no way he could let her go without making love to her again. He needed this one last time to seal the memory of their time together into his mind forever.

Forever.

That was a word he had never included in his vocabulary, one he had never associated with a woman. He didn't do forever, and never thought about it. But he had to admit that with Jayla Cole, he thought of things he had never thought of before. And he was glad for the time they had spent together. He had learned things about her that he otherwise might not have known, such as her passion for strawberry cheesecake and how she volunteered her spare time at Emory University Hospital's Cancer Center.

"Storm, I need to get up, get dressed and leave."

He stared at her, feeling a sense of finality and a part of him felt a sense of loss he'd never experienced before and one he couldn't explain. And then, suddenly, he wanted her with an urgency he had never wanted her or any woman before. Blood rushed through his veins and he breathed in deeply.

"Storm..."

He looked at her and his breath stopped. He had to have her again, this one last time. He eased her beneath him the same moment that he lowered his head and captured her lips, tasting her, mating his tongue over and over with hers. She had stamped her mark on him and now he was going to make sure he stamped his on her.

For just a little while, he would make her *his,* and

if he lived a hundred years, there would be no regrets. What he would have were memories to last a lifetime.

And from the way she was returning his kiss he could tell she wanted those memories, too.

Chapter 6

"So, how was your trip to New Orleans?" Lisa Palmer asked as she sat back in her chair at Jayla's kitchen table.

Jayla looked up and met her best friend's curious stare. "It was fine. Why do you ask?"

"Because I've noticed that since you've been back, you haven't said much about it."

Jayla drew in a deep breath and wished she could ignore Lisa's curious scrutiny. It was just like Lisa to pick up on her reference about the trip. She knew that sooner or later she would have to come clean and tell her friend everything, including her planned trip to the fertility clinic.

"Umm, why do I get the feeling that you're not telling me something?"

Cupping her chin in her palm, Jayla forced a smile. "You're imagining things."

Lisa shook her head. "No, I don't think so." She gazed at her thoughtfully, then said, "There's something different about you. You look more relaxed and well-rested which can only mean one thing."

Jayla swallowed, wondering if she really had a different look about her. "What?" she asked softly.

Lisa's lips tilted into a deep smile. "That you got plenty of rest this trip, which is a good thing that I didn't go with you. Had I gone I would have worn you out with endless shopping and—"

"I ran into someone."

Lisa lifted a brow. When seconds ticked off and Jayla didn't say anything else, Lisa scooted closer in her chair. "Okay, are you going to keep me in suspense or are you going to tell me?"

Jayla took a sip of her lemonade before responding. "I ran into Storm Westmoreland."

Lisa placed her glass of lemonade down on the table. "Storm Westmoreland? The Perfect Storm?"

Jayla chuckled. "Yes, that Storm."

Lisa stared at her for a moment as she recalled Jayla once telling her about the crush she'd had on Storm Westmoreland at sixteen. And, like most women in the Atlanta area, she also knew about his reputation as a womanizer, and that's what bothered her the most. "What was Storm Westmoreland doing in New Orleans?" she asked, having a feeling there was a lot more to the story.

Jayla chuckled again. "He was attending a conference."

"And…?"

Jayla was quiet for a moment. She knew Lisa had a thousand questions and decided she might as well tell her everything or else she would get grilled to death. "And we ran into each other and one thing led to another and we ended up having an affair."

She almost grinned when she saw Lisa's jaw drop. She then watched as Lisa picked up her glass and drained it as if it contained something stronger than lemonade.

Lisa then turned her full attention to her. "You're no longer a virgin?" she asked as if her mind were in shock.

Jayla did grin this time. "Nope."

Lisa then slumped back in her chair and pinned her with a look. Jayla was well aware of *that* look. It was a look that said you'd better tell me everything and start from the beginning.

"Like I said," Jayla said, before she was hammered with relentless questions, "Storm and I ran into each other, decided to spend time together and one thing led to another."

"Evidently."

Now it was Jayla who pinned Lisa with a look. "And don't expect me to tell you *everything* because there are some details you're better off not knowing." Her mind was suddenly filled with thoughts of everything she and Storm had done. They had made love so many times she had lost count, and each time had been better than the last.

What she held special was the first time and how, afterward, he had drawn her bath water, gently picked her up into his arms and carried her into the bathroom. But it was the last time they'd made love on the morning she'd left, that stood out in her mind more than the others.

With a loving tenderness that had almost brought tears to her eyes, he had used his hands and mouth to drive her over the edge, making her body burn out of control for him. And it was only when she was about to come apart in his arms did he fill her and begin moving back and forth inside her, combining tenderness with compelling need, and sending her escalating into a sharp, shattering orgasm that had taken her breath away and had left her sated, exhausted and spent. And as much as she'd tried to stay awake, she had drifted off to sleep. They both had. When they had awakened, she'd dressed quickly and returned to her room to pack.

He had gone to her room with her to help her pack and the last kiss he had given her before she had walked out of the hotel room door for the airport had been off-the-charts fantastic. She knew that if she never made love to another man, she would always remember having that time with Storm. It had been more than just good, mind-blowing sex. For three days, he had made her feel special, as if knowing he'd been her first had been extraordinary and he was still in awe of the gift she had given him.

"Jayla?"

She jumped when Lisa snapped a finger in front of her face. "What?"

"You haven't answered my question."

Jayla frowned. "What question?"

"Do you have any regrets?"

Jayla immediately shook her head. "No. Twenty-six years was long enough to be a virgin, but I'd never met a man I felt worthy of giving myself to until Storm."

Lisa raised a dark brow. "With Storm's reputation, you thought he was worthy?"

"Yes, because he didn't try to snowball me into doing it with him. In fact, at first he actually tried resisting my advances. I'm the one who came on to him. And he always behaved like a perfect gentleman, giving me choices and not assuming anything."

Lisa nodded, and then a curious glint shone in her dark eyes. "Is everything we've heard about him true?"

Jayla tried to ignore the heat that was settling between her legs when she thought about just how true it was. When it came to lovemaking, Storm Westmoreland was a practiced and skillful lover. She couldn't help but smile. "Yes, everything we've heard is true."

A silly smirk appeared on Lisa's face and she sat back in her chair. "Damn. Some women have all the luck," she said with envy. She then smiled. "So when will the two of you see each other again?"

Jayla tried to ignore the ache that suddenly settled around her heart, convincing herself it was only indigestion. "We won't be seeing each other again. What we shared was nothing more than a no-strings-attached affair, and since neither of us is into relationships, we decided that when we returned to Atlanta, he would continue to do his thing and I would continue to do mine."

Lisa lifted a brow. "You don't have a 'thing' to do. You basically live a boring life. All you do is go to work and come home, except for those days when you're volunteering at the cancer center."

Jayla knew what Lisa said was true, but in a few weeks all of that would change. She smiled. "Well, I want you to know that my life will no longer be boring. I've decided to take the first step in doing something I've wanted to do for a long time."

"Oh, and what's that?"

"Have a baby."

Jayla watched Lisa's expression. She looked as if someone had just pulled a chair out from under her. Lisa looked at her long and hard before finally saying something. "What do you mean, have a baby?"

"Just what I've said. You of all people know how much I love children."

Lisa shrugged. "Hey, I love them, too, but I'm not planning to have any until Mr. Right comes alone and I'm ready to settle down and get married."

Jayla raised her eyes to the ceiling. "Well, yeah, but for some of us there is no Mr. Right, so I've decided not to wait any longer."

Lisa was quiet for a moment as she pinned Jayla with that look again. "Tell me you didn't deliberately try and get pregnant by Storm Westmoreland."

Jayla couldn't help but laugh. Lisa's question was so ridiculous. Storm Westmoreland would be the last man she would want to father her child. He was too controlling. "Trust me, that thought never crossed my mind. Besides, I would never trick any man that way. I made all the necessary arrangements before I left for New Orleans, and I'm going to go to a fertility clinic and have the procedure done."

Lisa quickly held up her hand. "Time out. Back up. What are you talking about?"

Jayla smiled. The expression on Lisa's face was both endearing and maddening. They were as close as sisters and she knew her best friend well enough to know that she would not agree with her decision regarding the fertility clinic. But then, Lisa didn't have any problems finding a Mr. Right since she was already involved in a serious relationship with a wonderful guy. Added to that was the fact that Lisa came from a big family, so she didn't know the meaning of loneliness.

"I'm talking about my decision to have a baby. I've already done the preliminary paperwork and they'd located a potential donor who fits the profile I've requested. All that's left is for me to take another physical, which is scheduled for next Friday. Once it's determined when I'm most fertile during my cycle, I'll be going in to have the procedure done. If I'm not successfully inseminated on the first try, then there will be another try and if necessary, a third or however many times it takes. I'm sure my eggs will eventually be ripe for some donor's sperm," she said smiling.

Lisa, Jayla noticed, wasn't smiling back. In fact, she looked mortified. "Tell me you're joking about this, Jayla."

Jayla sighed deeply. She then worked her bottom lip between her teeth several times, which was something she tended to do when she was bothered by something. Over the years, Lisa may not have agreed with everything she did but had always supported her. Jayla knew because of her friend's traditional beliefs, this would be a hard sell, which was why she had put off telling Lisa about her plans.

She lifted her chin. "No, I'm not joking, Lisa. I've made up my mind about this. You may not agree with what I'm doing, but I really do need you to support me on this. I want a baby more than anything."

"But there are other options, Jayla."

"Yes, and I considered those other options and none will work for me. I want a baby not an involvement with a man who may not be Mr. Right, and I don't have time to wait until I finally get lucky. Times have changed. A woman no longer needs a man to get pregnant or to raise a child, and that's the way I want to do things."

Lisa didn't say anything for a long moment, then she reached across the table and captured Jayla's hand in hers. "Although I can understand some women having the procedure done in certain situations, your case is different, Jayla, and what you plan to do goes against everything I believe in. When it's possible, I think a child should benefit with the presence of both the mother and father in the home. But if you're hell-bent on going through with it, then I'll be there to do whatever you need me to do."

Jayla blinked back the tears in her eyes. "Thanks."

"Hey, Storm, get your mind back on the game, stop daydreaming and throw out a card."

Thorn Westmoreland's words recaptured Storm's attention and he threw out a card then leaned back in his chair and frowned. "I was not daydreaming and my mind *is* on the game," he said throwing out a card.

After another round of bid whist, Stone Westmoreland shook his head. "If your mind is on the game then you're a lousy card player since you just threw out a diamond instead of a heart which means you've reneged." A huge smile tilted the corners of Stone's lips. "But I'm not complaining since that puts me closer to winning."

Storm pushed back his chair and stood, glaring at

his four brothers. Apparently they'd found his lack of concentration amusing but he didn't find a damn thing funny about it. "I'm sitting out for a while. I need some fresh air."

While he was walking away he heard his brother Thorn ask the others, "What's wrong with him?"

"Don't know," his brother Dare replied. "He's been acting strange ever since he got back from that conference in New Orleans."

"Maybe the pressures of being a fire captain is getting to him," he heard his brother Chase add. "There's nothing worse than letting a job stress you out."

"Yeah," his other brothers agreed.

Storm shook his head when he opened the door and stepped out on the lanai. His brothers didn't know how wrong they were. His new promotion or work-related stress had nothing to do with the way he'd been acting since returning from New Orleans.

He glanced up and noticed a full moon and the stars in the sky. It was a beautiful night and he was glad he had come outside to appreciate the evening for a little while.

After Thorn and Tara had gotten married, they had moved into Tara's place since it was larger than Thorn's, but only temporarily. They were building their dream home on a parcel of the Westmoreland family homestead, which was located on the outskirts of town. It was a pretty nice area if you liked being out in the boon-docks and cherished your privacy.

Storm shook his head as an image of a woman forced its way into his head. It was the same image he'd been trying like hell to forget the past week. Jayla Cole.

He balled his hands into fists at his side as he wondered what was wrong with him. He'd had affairs before but none had affected him the way this one had. No woman had ever remained in his thoughts after the affair had ended. He'd known there would be memories, hell he had counted on savoring them. But he had wanted them safely tucked away until he was ready to revisit them. He hadn't counted on having no control of his own memories.

Visions of Jayla in the red dress were taking him to the cleaners and wringing him out. And then there were those images of the sway of her hips whenever she walked, whether she was in heels or flats. It didn't matter. The woman was sensuality on legs. She was a mouthwatering piece flat on her back as well. All he had to do was close his eyes and he was reliving the evenings filled with their mind-boggling, earth-shattering lovemaking.

She had fired up and completely satisfied a need within him that he hadn't known existed. Each and every time he had taken her to bed they had made incredible love. He could get her so wet, so hot, so ready, and likewise she could get him so hard, so needy, so out-of-his-mind greedy, to the point where getting inside her body was all he could think about; all he wanted.

And then there was the look on her face whenever she came. It was priceless. It was as if the force of what she felt stole her breath and the intensity of it exploded her world into tiny fragments as she tumbled into mindless completion. Seeing that experience on her face would then push him over the edge into the most potent climax he'd ever experienced; usually more than one—back to back.

"Damn," he let out a low growl and wiped a sheen of perspiration from his forehead with his hand. He was used to sexual experiences, but getting seduced by memories was something that he was not used to or comfortable with. Hell, he had even thought about dropping by her house to make sure she was all right. If that didn't beat all. He had never checked up on a woman after the affair ended.

"Storm, are you okay?"

He inhaled deeply when he heard his sister-in-law's voice and quickly decided that although it was dark, it wouldn't be a good idea for him to turn around just yet. There was a glow of light filtering out from the living room and he had gotten hard just thinking about Jayla.

"Storm?"

"Yeah, Tara, I'm fine." Seconds later when he was sure he had gotten his body back under control he turned around and smiled.

Tara Matthews was beautiful and had nearly blown Storm and his brothers away the first time they had seen her at their sister Delaney's apartment in Kentucky. And he might have even considered having a relationship with her, but he'd soon discovered that Tara was a handful. He and his brothers had quickly concluded that the only man who could possibly handle her was their brother Thorn, so they had deemed her Thorn's challenge. Now, a little more than two years later, she was Thorn's wife. But she still held a special place in his heart as well as the hearts of his brothers because in the end though Thorn may have handled her, Tara had proved that she was capable of handling Thorn, which wasn't an easy task.

He met her gaze and saw concern in her eyes. "I was worried about you," she said softly. "When I passed through the dining room and saw you missing, your brothers said you had needed fresh air. I didn't know if you were coming down with something, especially when they'd said you'd been playing badly tonight."

Storm laughed, then gave her a playful grin. "Hell, they claim I play lousy even when I'm winning."

Tara nodded smiling. "So, how was your trip to New Orleans?"

Funny you should ask, he thought as he slumped back against a column post. He sucked in a deep breath when another vision of Jayla floated through his mind. He envisioned his mouth finding her most sensitive areas, especially her ultra-hot spot and tilting her up to his mouth and making her scream.

"Storm?"

"Huh?"

"I asked how was your trip." She took a step closer to him and looked deeply into his eyes. "Are you sure you're okay, your eyes seemed somewhat dazed."

And my body is hard again but we won't go there, he thought, thinking the best thing to do was go back inside and play cards and hope that this time he could keep his mind on the game. "I'm fine and I had a great time in New Orleans. I even saw Ian while I was there and he mentioned that he would be in town for that charity benefit that you're working on."

A smile touched the corners of Tara's lips. "Really," she said excitedly. "That's the night we'll unveil the charity calendar for Kids' World and everyone will get to see Thorn as Mr. July."

Storm laughed. "I don't think that's the only reason Ian is coming, Tara," he said, thinking that maybe if he kept talking he wouldn't have to worry about visions of Jayla intruding. "The main reason Ian's coming is because you asked him to, but there's another reason."

Tara lifted her brow. "And what reason is that?"

A grin appeared on Storm's face. "He figures there will be a lot of pretty, single women in attendance."

Tara shook her head smiling, finally getting the picture. "Well, I'm sure there will be plenty of single women there since eleven of the men who posed for the calendar are still single. Thorn is the only one who has gotten married since those photos were taken."

Something suddenly pulled at Storm's memory. He remembered Jayla mentioning that she would be meeting Tara for lunch the Tuesday after returning to work. Unless those plans had changed, that meant the two of them would be meeting tomorrow. There was no way he could ask Tara about it without her wondering how he'd known. But if they were to meet tomorrow for lunch and if he knew where, he could unexpectedly drop by and pretend that he'd been in the area. For some reason he wanted to see Jayla again and if they *accidentally* ran into each other, she wouldn't think he had intentionally sought her out…although in essence, he would be doing just that.

"So, Tara, how about if I took you, Madison and Shelly to lunch tomorrow?" he suggested. He knew Dare's wife Shelly hadn't returned from visiting her parents in Florida, Stone's wife Madison would be leaving with Stone tomorrow on a book-signing trip to Kansas City, and if Tara had made other plans for lunch then he would find out soon enough.

"Thanks, Storm, that's really sweet of you, but Shelly and Madison will be out of town and besides I already have a lunch date. I'm meeting with a woman who's working with me on the charity benefit. Her company has agreed to pick up the tab for all the food and drinks that night."

Bingo. He was suddenly beginning to feel pretty good now. Confident. Cocky. Smug. He straightened from leaning against the post. "Oh, that's too bad. Where are you going?"

Tara lifted a brow. "Excuse me?"

He inhaled slowly, knowing he couldn't appear too inquisitive. The last thing he needed was for Tara to get suspicious of anything. "I asked where are you going for lunch? It might be a place where I've eaten before. Perhaps I can tell you whether the food and service are good."

Tara smiled. "Trust me, I know you've eaten at this place plenty of times and can definitely vouch for the food and service being the best. My lunch date left it up to me to select a place and although I haven't told her yet, I'm going to suggest that we have lunch at Chase's Place."

His heart suddenly did a back flip and his mouth curved into a huge smile. Things couldn't have worked out better if he was planning things himself. Tara was taking Jayla to his brother's restaurant, a place where he ate lunch on a regular basis, so it wouldn't seem out of the ordinary if he showed up there tomorrow. "I think that's a wonderful choice."

She shook her head smiling and before she could say anything, Thorn's loud voice roared through the air. "Storm, get back in here if you're in this game, and you better not be out there kissing my wife."

Storm laughed. "He's a jealous kind of fellow, isn't he?" he asked, taking Tara's hand as they walked back inside

She grinned and he could see her entire face light up with absolute love for his brother. "Yes, but I wouldn't have him any other way."

"Chase's Place?" Jayla asked, making sure she had heard correctly.

"Yes," Tara said brightly on the other end of the phone. "It's a soul-food restaurant that's owned by my brother-in-law Chase Westmoreland, and the food there is wonderful."

Jayla rose from behind her desk, no longer able to sit. She knew the food there was wonderful but at the moment that wasn't what was bothering her. She recalled Storm saying that he routinely ate at his brother's restaurant. She was tempted to suggest they go someplace else but quickly remembered that she had been the one to suggest that Tara select the place for lunch. She sighed deeply. "I've eaten there before and you're right the food is wonderful."

"And he's promised to take good care of us."

Jayla raised a dark brow. "Who?" She heard Tara chuckle on the other end before answering.

"Chase. He's good at taking care of people."

"Oh." It was on the tip of Jayla's tongue to say it must run in the family because Chase wasn't the only

Westmoreland who was good at taking care of people. She vividly remembered the way Storm had taken care of her, fulfilling and satisfying her every need.

She tried forcing the memories to the back of her mind. "What time do you want us to meet?"

"What about around one-thirty? That way the noon-day lunch crowd won't bombard us. But if you think you'll be hungry before then we can—"

"No, one-thirty is fine and I'll meet you there." After ending the call, Jayla sat back at her desk. If she saw Storm again, what was the correct protocol to handle the situation? Women and men had affairs all the time and she was sure that at some point they ran into each other again. Did they act casually as if nothing had ever happened between them and they were meeting for the first time? Or were they savvy enough to accept that they had shared something intimate with no regrets, moved on and didn't make a big deal about it? She decided the latter would work. It wasn't as if they had been total strangers.

She glanced at her watch. One-thirty was less than five hours away. Although Atlanta was a big town, she and Storm were bound to run into each other soon or later, but part of her had been hoping it was later. She had expected to see him at the charity benefit, but had figured she would be prepared to see him by then. It was more than a week since they had been together, nine days, if you were counting, and unfortunately, she was.

She closed her eyes and exhaled a deep breath. If she saw him, she would play it cool, take the savvy approach and hope and pray that it worked.

* * *

"Is there a reason why you're hanging around here?"

Storm shrugged and shot his twin a beguiling smile. "I like this place."

The expression he read on Chase's face said he knew better, since he only dropped by to eat and rarely hung around to socialize. He usually was too busy pursuing women to visit with his brother for very long. His answering machine had maxed out while he'd been out of town and his phone hadn't stopped ringing since he'd been back. But for some reason, he wasn't interested in returning any of those women's calls.

"Well, if you don't have anything better to do with your time, how about waiting tables?" Chase said, interrupting his thoughts. "One of my waitresses called in sick and we're shorthanded."

Storm glanced at his watch while shaking his head. "Sorry. I like you, Chase, but not that much." He turned and glanced at the entrance to his brother's restaurant and wondered if perhaps Tara and Jayla had changed their minds and decided to go someplace else since it was past lunchtime. No sooner had that possibility crossed his mind, than the door swung open and the two women entered.

His breath caught at the sight of Jayla. Because he was sitting at the far end of the counter, he knew she wouldn't be able to see him but he could definitely see her. She was dressed differently than she'd been in New Orleans. Today, Jayla was Miss Professional in her chic navy blue power suit. She still looked stunning and as sexy as sin. Storm could feel his libido going bonkers. He swung around to Chase. "Hey, I've changed my mind. I will help you out after all."

Chase raised a suspicious brow. "Why the change of heart?"

"Because if a man can't depend on his twin brother in a time of need, then who can he depend on?" Storm asked, giving Chase a boyish grin.

Chase cast a speculative glance over Storm's shoulder and said dryly, "I hope the person you're all fired up at seeing is the woman with Tara and *not* Tara. I would hate for Thorn to kill you."

Storm chuckled. "Relax. I got over Tara a long time ago. I just like getting a rise out of Thorn."

He leaned over the counter and snagged a pencil from Chase's shirt pocket and tucked it behind his ear. He then picked up a pad off the counter. "Who's working the table where they're sitting?"

"Pam."

Storm smiled. "Then tell Pam to take a break or, better yet, tell her to find another table to work. I got that one covered." Before Chase could say anything, Storm stood and headed over to where Tara and Jayla were sitting.

"We made perfect timing," Tara said smiling. "Had we arrived any earlier this place would have been packed." The menus were in a rack on the table and she passed one to Jayla.

Jayla nodded as she opened the menu. She was tempted to glance around but decided not to. Chances were if Storm had been there earlier as a part of the lunch crowd he would have already left.

After they had looked over the menus for a few moments, Tara glanced up, smiled and asked, "So what are you going to get?"

Tara's question recaptured her attention and she couldn't help but return the other woman's smile. Already she'd decided that she liked Tara Westmoreland. They had spoken several times on the phone, but this was the first time they had actually met in person. Jayla thought the woman was simply gorgeous and could quickly see how she had captured the heart of motorcycle tycoon, Thorn Westmoreland.

"Umm," Jayla said smiling as if in deep thought as she glanced back down at the menu and licked her lips. "Everything looks delicious, but I think I'll get—"

"Good afternoon, ladies, what can I get you?"

Jayla's head snapped up and she blinked upon seeing Storm standing beside their table. "Storm!" Without thinking, she said his name as intense heat settled deep in her stomach.

Storm's mouth curved into a devilish grin, and that grin reminded her of sensations he could easily elicit, tempting her into partaking in any number of passionate indulgences. "I'm not on the menu, Jayla, but if I'm what you want, I can definitely make an exception."

Chapter 7

"I take it the two of you know each other," Tara said curiously as a smile touched her lips. She glanced from Storm to Jayla.

Jayla cleared her throat, wondering how much she should say. Before she could decide on how to respond, Storm spoke up.

"Jayla's father was my first fire captain and was like a second father to me," he said, giving them his killer-watt smile. "So, yes, we know each other."

Jayla swallowed deeply, grateful for Storm's timely and acceptable explanation.

"It's good seeing you again, Jayla."

She smiled. "It's good seeing you, too," she said, meaning every word, although she wished that she didn't.

"And you look good, by the way."

Her smile widened. "Thanks." He looked rather good, too, she thought. He was dressed in a pair of khaki trousers and a polo shirt. And he smelled good. His cologne could always jump-start her senses. It was a good thing she was already sitting down because she could actually feel her knees weaken. Everything about Storm was a total turn-on—the rippling muscles beneath his shirt, his extraordinary butt, long legs, his too-hot grin and eyes so dark they reminded you of chocolate chips…. Had she forgotten that she had a weakness for chocolate chips just as bad as her weakness for strawberry cheesecake?

She glanced over at Tara and saw that she was still watching them and Jayla decided it wouldn't be a bad idea to go ahead and place her order. She cleared her throat. "I'll have today's special with a glass of iced tea."

"All right." Storm scribbled down Jayla's order, not knowing and not really caring what today's special was. The only thing on his mind was that he was getting the chance to see her again.

He then turned his attention to Tara and smiled. "And what will you have Mrs. Westmoreland?"

Tara lifted a brow. "An explanation as to why you're waiting on tables."

Storm chuckled. He was busted. Leave it to Tara to ask questions. She'd been hanging around his brother Thorn too long. "Chase was shorthanded so I thought I'd pitch in and help him out."

Tara nodded, but the look she gave let him indicated that she knew there was more to the story than that. He wondered if parts of their conversation last night were coming back to her. "That was kind of you,

Storm, and I'll have today's special, as well, with a glass of lemonade."

Storm wrote down her order, then said, "I'll go ahead and bring your drinks." He winked at them and then walked off.

Jayla watched him walk away. When she returned her attention back to Tara she knew the woman had been watching her watch Storm. "Small world, isn't it?" she asked trying to pull herself together before she actually started drooling.

Tara smiled. "Yes, it is a small world," she agreed as she studied Jayla. Storm had been blatantly flirting with the woman, which was nothing surprising. Tara had seen Storm in action many times before. But something was different with the way he had flirted with Jayla; however, at the moment she couldn't put a finger on just what that difference was.

"I'm looking forward to the charity benefit," Jayla was saying, rousing Tara from her musings and reminding her of the reason for their meeting.

"So am I, and the committee appreciates Sala Industries agreeing to be our food and beverage sponsor. Kids' World will benefit greatly from their contribution. The money raised from the calendar will be more than enough to make the children's dreams come true."

Jayla smiled in agreement. "Doesn't it bother you that your husband is Mr. July on that calendar?"

Tara laughed as she remembered how she'd maneuvered Thorn into posing for the calendar. Actually, they had come to an agreement only after Thorn had made her an offer she couldn't refuse. "No, I'm not bothered at all. It will be nice knowing other women will find my husband as sexy as I do."

Jayla nodded. She had seen Thorn Westmoreland before in person and the man was definitely sexy. But she didn't think anyone was sexier than Storm. She couldn't help but glance to where he had gone. He was behind the counter preparing their drinks and, as if he knew she was looking at him, he lifted his head, met her gaze and smiled.

It was a smile that sent shivers all the way through her body. It was also a smile that seemed to say, *I remember everything about those days in New Orleans.* She couldn't help returning his smile as she also remembered everything about their time together.

When she turned her attention back to Tara, Jayla realized that Tara had noticed the silent exchange between her and Storm. "Umm... I, well—" she started to say, feeling somewhat embarrassed that Tara had caught her ogling Storm.

Tara reached across the table and touched her hand. "No need to explain, Jayla. I'm married to a Westmoreland so I understand."

Jayla pulled in a deep breath, wondering how could Tara possibly understand when she didn't understand her feelings for Storm. "It's nothing but simple chemistry," she decided to say to explain.

Tara smiled, thinking of her reaction to Thorn Westmoreland the first time she had seen him. "Happens to the best of us, trust me."

Jayla laughed, suddenly feeling relaxed and thinking that, yes, she really did like Tara Westmoreland.

Chase shook his head as he stared at his brother. "Are you going to stand there all day and stare at that woman with Tara?"

Storm met Chase's gaze and grinned. "I like watching her eat. I love the way her mouth moves."

Chase's gaze followed Storm and he didn't see anything fascinating about the way she was eating, although he would be the first to admit that she was good-looking. He turned his attention back to Storm. "Who is she?"

"Adam's daughter."

Chase snapped his gaze back to the table where Tara and the woman were sitting. "Are you saying that's Adam Cole's girl, all grown up?"

"Yes."

"Wow. I haven't seen her since she was in high school. He would bring her in here every once and a while for dinner." He let out a low whistle. "Boy, has she changed. She was a cute kid, but now she is definitely a looker. I'd say she is a woman who looks ripe for loving."

Storm turned and glared at his brother as he leaned against the counter and shoved his hands deep into his pants pockets. "I'm going to ignore the fact that you said that."

Chase smiled. "Hey, man, I didn't know things were *that* way with her," he offered by way of apology.

Storm's glare deepened. "And what do you perceive as *that* way?"

Chase's smile widened. Storm was so used to getting a rise out of people that he couldn't recognize when someone was trying to get a rise out of him. "You're interested in her. *That's* obvious."

Storm shrugged. "Of course I'm interested in her. Adam was someone I cared a lot about. He was like a second father to me. He was—"

"We're not talking about Adam, Storm. We're talking about his daughter. Come on and admit it. You're interested in her as a woman and not as Adam's daughter."

Storm frowned. "I'm not going to admit anything."

Chase chuckled. "Then why did you get jealous a few minutes ago?"

Storm blinked, then looked at his twin as if he were stone crazy, definitely had gone off the deep end. "Jealous?" he repeated, wondering how Chase could think such a thing. "The word *jealous* is not in my vocabulary."

Chase studied his brother's face and knew he had pushed him enough for one day, but couldn't resist taking one final dig. "Then it must have been added rather recently. Not only is it now in your vocabulary, you should spell the word with a capital *J*. And I thought the reason you were acting strange had to do with work. The way I see it, that woman sitting over there definitely has her hook in and is reeling you in."

Storm drew in a deep breath, squared his shoulders. The eyes that stared at his twin were hard, ice cold. "You're going to regret the day you said that."

Chase laughed. "And I have a feeling that you're going to regret the day you didn't figure it out for yourself."

Jayla slipped off her pumps as soon as she walked into the house and closed the door behind her. She let out a deep breath. Lunch with Tara Westmoreland had gone well and they had finalized a lot of items for the charity benefit. But what stood out in her mind more than anything was seeing Storm again.

More than once she had glanced his way. The heat in his eyes had ignited a slow, sensual burn within her. Across the distance of the room, he had silently yet expertly aroused her, almost making concentration on her discussion with Tara impossible.

And when he had placed their meals on the table, her eyes had been drawn to his hands and it didn't take much to remember how skilled his fingers were, and how those fingers had known just the right places on her body to touch to drive her crazy. It was only when he had left the restaurant, shortly after serving their lunch, that her mind had become functional. Only then had she been able to zero in on the business that she and Tara had needed to accomplish.

On her drive back to the office, she had to remind herself several times that there was nothing between her and Storm and that any future involvement with him was out of the question. They each had a different agenda. To consider a possible relationship between them would only complicate things. What they had shared in New Orleans, just great sex, was over.

Placing her purse on the counter that separated the kitchen from her dining room, she started sorting through the mail she had retrieved from her mailbox and smiled when she saw a letter from the fertility clinic.

Tearing it open, she quickly scanned the contents and her smile widened. It was a letter reminding her of the physical that was scheduled for the next week and information about the insemination procedure.

Placing the letter in the drawer, she laughed, feeling elated, happy beyond words. She anxiously awaited that day—after the procedure was done—when a doctor would confirm she was pregnant. Although Lisa didn't totally agreed with what she planned to do, at least her friend would be there to support her. And, of course, Lisa had agreed to be her child's godmother.

In her heart, Jayla believed things would work out. She had a good friend who would stand by her and she had a good job. And as she had told Lisa, if the artificial insemination didn't work the first time around, she would try a second and, if need be, a third time. She would repeat the procedure as many times as it took to get pregnant whatever the cost. Thanks to the trust fund her father had left for her, as well as the insurance funds that had been left after all the burial expenses had been taken care of, she could afford making her dream of having a baby come true.

She decided to take a shower and relax before fixing dinner. Later, she would find a comfortable spot on her sofa to sit and prop her feet up on her coffee table and enjoy a good book. She tried shaking off the lonely feeling that she suddenly felt. Lisa had a date with her boyfriend Andrew tonight, which meant she wasn't available for a chat.

She tried not to recall that this time nearly a week and a half ago, she had been in New Orleans with Storm. Nor did she want to think about how much she had enjoyed his company. Of course, the time they had spent in bed had been great, but there had been more than that. She had discovered a fun side to Storm. Before New Orleans, she'd always assumed that he was a really serious sort of guy.

She had enjoyed laughing with him, talking to him, dancing with him, sharing food with him and going sightseeing with him. He had been full of surprises in more ways than one. She couldn't help but compare him to the last guy she had dated, Erik Turner. Erik had turned out to be an A-number-one bore and had expected they'd go straight to her bedroom when he'd brought her home from their first date. He had actually gotten pissed off when she'd turned him down.

Frowning, she headed for her bedroom as she remembered how angry she had gotten, too, that night. Angry for having such high expectations that most men would treat a woman like a lady, decently respectable and not assume anything—especially on the first date. Erik had been included in a long line of disappointments for her, but he had definitely been the last straw and had been an eye-opener. That night Jayla realized that she didn't want to be one of those women who were in such a frenzy to be involved in a relationship that they failed to look at the signs that said, "This may not be the best person for me."

Another pitfall she had avoided, which was the main reason she had remained a virgin for so long, was the mistake some women made of equating sex with love. She'd learned from listening to the women she worked with, that some women still believed that if a man slept with her, it meant he loved her. She definitely hadn't assumed such a thing with her and Storm. It had been her hormones and not her heart that had been raging out of control. Storm didn't love her and she didn't love him. She hadn't expected anything from him and he hadn't expected anything from her. They had communicated well both in and out of bed, and the one thing they understood and agreed upon was that their affair would be one that led nowhere.

Sighing, she began removing her clothes for her shower. But as much as she didn't want to think about it, she couldn't get the memory of Storm and the way he had looked at her today out of her mind.

Drawing in a deep breath, Storm raised his hand to knock, then pulled back as he asked himself, for the umpteenth time, why he was standing in front of Jayla's front door. And no matter how many times he asked the question, the answer always came up the same.

He still wanted her.

Seeing her today had done more harm than good and what Chase had said hadn't helped matters. The notion that Jayla had hooked him was preposterous. Okay, he would admit she was still in his system. He had discovered that a man didn't have sex with a woman at the magnitude that he'd had with Jayla and not have some lingering effects. Lingering effects he could handle; the notion of some woman reeling him in, he could not.

Tonight, and only tonight, he would break his rule of not performing repeats after an affair ended. But he had to make sure that the only thing that was pulling him back to her was the incredible sex they'd shared. Physical he could handle, but anything that bordered on emotional he could not.

Taking another deep breath, he finally raised his hand and knocked on the door. As he waited for her to answer it, he hoped to God that he wasn't making a huge mistake.

He was about to knock again when he heard the sound of her voice on the other side. "Who is it?"

"It's me, Jayla. Storm."

She slowly opened the door and the anticipation of the removal of the solid piece of wood that stood between them sent a shiver of desire up his spine and down to his midsection. When she opened the door enough for him to see her, the sight of her nearly knocked him to his knees like a gale-force wind. It was obvious that she had just gotten out of the shower. Her hair was loose, flowing around her shoulders, and there were certain parts of her, not covered by her short bathrobe, that were still wet. He itched to take the robe off her to see what, if anything, she was wearing underneath it.

"Storm, what are you doing here?"

Her voice, low in pitch yet high in sensuality, rapidly joined forces with desire that had already taken over his body. He was almost afraid to stand there and look at her. Too much longer and he might be driven to topple her to the floor and make love to her then and there.

"Storm?"

Claiming that he just happened to be in the neighborhood would sound pretty lame when she lived in North Atlanta and he resided in the southern part of town. Believing that honesty was the best policy, he decided to tell her the truth as his gaze locked on hers. "Seeing you today made me realize something," he murmured softly as he leaned in her doorway.

He watched her throat move when she swallowed. "What?"

"That I didn't get enough of you in New Orleans. I want you again."

He heard her inhale sharply and the sound triggered the memory of how her voice would catch just seconds before she came. His mind was remembering and his body was, too. He was tempted to pull her close and let her feel just how hard she was making him. "May I come in?" he decided to ask when she didn't say anything.

"Storm..."

"I know I shouldn't have come and I'm just as confused about showing up here as you are," he quickly said. "But seeing you today *really* did do something to me, Jayla, and it's something that's never happened to me before. It was as if my body went on overload and you're the only person who can shut it down. Since returning from New Orleans, I've been constantly reminded of the best sex I've ever had, and tonight I couldn't handle things any longer."

He sighed deeply. There. He'd said it. He'd been honest and upfront with her, although it had nearly killed him to admit such a thing. Even to his ears his predicament sounded almost like an addiction. His blood was pumped up a notch. Every muscle in his body ached at the thought of making love to her again and a part of him knew the look in his eyes was just shy of pleading. He might even go so far as to follow the Temptations' lead and sing out loud, "Ain't Too Proud To Beg."

It was all rather pathetic, but at the moment there wasn't a damn thing he could do about it. Jayla Cole was under his skin...at least temporarily. Just one more time with her should obliterate this madness. At least, that's what he hoped.

He watched her as she tried to make up her mind

about him, but patience had never been one of his strong points and he couldn't help asking, "So are you going to let me in?"

Silence filled the air.

Moments later, Jayla sighed deeply. Her mind was in battle over what she *should* do versus what she *wanted* to do. She knew what she should do was send Storm packing after reminding him of their agreement. But what she really wanted to do was give him what she knew they both desired.

Just one more time, she decided. What could possibly be wrong in giving in to an indulgence just one more time? However, more than just once would be a complication she didn't need. Her heart hammered hard in her chest. She knew once he stepped inside and closed the door behind him, that would be the end of it…or the beginning. But as her body began to slowly tremble, her control began slipping. She knew that tonight she needed him just as much as he seemed to need her. He was right. This *was* madness.

"Yes," she finally said, taking a step back. "You can come in."

He entered and closed the door behind him. Locked it. The click sounded rather loud in the now awkward silence between them. That small sound was enough to push her heart into overdrive, making it beat that much faster.

"Thirsty?" she asked, deciding she should at least offer him a drink.

"Yes, very."

She turned toward the kitchen and was surprised when he reached out, gently grabbed her, pulled her close to him and wrapped his arms around her. "This is what I'm thirsty for, Jayla. The taste of you."

When her lips opened on a breathless sigh, his tongue swept into her mouth as if he needed to taste her as much as he needed to breathe. His lips were hot and demanding, and his tongue was making love to her mouth with an intensity that overwhelmed her. Helpless to do anything else, she looped her arms around his neck and held on while the heat of him consumed her, breaching any barrier and snatching away any resistance she might have had.

Too late. He was inside and intended to fill her to capacity in more ways than one.

She pushed good judgment, initial misgivings and any lingering doubts aside. She would deal with them later. Right now, being in Storm's arms this way was most important and demanded her full concentration. And everything about him—his scent, his strength, his very sensuality—permeated her skin, seeped into her blood and sent her senses spinning.

When he tore his mouth away from hers, she drew in a long audible sigh. She looked up at him and the air surrounding them seemed to crackle with ardent awareness. He reached out and traced a slow path down the center of her neck, then slowly pushed aside her robe to reveal what was underneath.

Nothing.

She heard his sharp intake of breath and he pushed the robe off her shoulders to the floor. "A few moments ago, I was thirsty for your mouth, but now I'm starving for this," he said reaching out and stroking her between the legs. "Once I get you in bed, I plan to make love to you all night."

His voice was low, uneven and so sexy that it sent shock waves all through her body. She met his gaze, saw the deep darkening of his eyes and any grip she had on reality slipped, joining her robe on the floor.

"That's a promise I intend to hold you to, Storm Westmoreland," she said on a breathless sigh, just seconds before he swept her into his arms.

Chapter 8

"Which way to your bedroom?"

"Straight ahead and to your right."

Storm didn't waste any time taking her there and immediately placed her naked body in the middle of the bed. He took a step back to look at her. For a moment, he couldn't move, too overwhelmed by her beauty to do anything but to take it all in…and breathe. He ached to make love to her, and sink his body into the wet warmth of hers.

Love her.

Air suddenly left his lungs in a whoosh and he summoned all the strength he could not to fall flat on his face. The thought that he wanted to love her had been unintentional, absolutely ridiculous, outlandish and totally absurd. He only did non-demanding relationships and short-term affairs. He wasn't into strings, especially the attached kind. He suddenly felt a tightening in his chest at the same time that he felt a bizarre quickening around his heart.

Hell! Something was wrong with him. Then, on second thought, maybe nothing was wrong with him. He was merely imagining things. He was aching so badly to be with Jayla again that he wasn't thinking straight. That had to be it. When he got home later tonight, on familiar turf, his mind would be clear. And spending a day at the station tomorrow around the guys would definitely screw his head back on straight.

"Are you going to stand there all night, Storm?"

He blinked, attempting to clear his mind and immediately became entranced with the warmness of Jayla's smile and the teasing heat of intimacy in her eyes. He swallowed deeply and tried to get a grip, but all he got was a harder arousal. "Not if I can help it," he said, suddenly needing to connect with her that instant. He needed to touch her, taste her, mate with her.

Right now.

He yanked his T-shirt over his head and then began fumbling with the fastening of his jeans, and became irritated when the zipper wouldn't slide down fast enough because of the size of his erection. Finally, he was able to tug his jeans down his legs and quickly stepped out of them. He reached down and took a condom packet out of the back pocket of the now discarded garment.

After he took the necessary steps, he looked at her and one corner of his mouth quirked up. "Now to keep that promise."

* * *

Simply looking at Storm caused Jayla's blood to pump rapidly through her veins. The look in his eyes said that he would hold nothing back. Her pulse quickened as he slid his body onto the bed. He moved, with the grace of a leopard, the prowl of a tiger and the intent of a man who wanted a woman. Overhead, the glow from the ceiling light magnified the broad expanse of his chest. He was perfectly built, his flesh a chocolate brown and every muscle well defined.

When he joined her on the bed she couldn't stop herself from reaching out to touch him. Her fingers trembled as she ran them through the dark, tight curls on his chest, and she smiled when she heard his breathing hitch. Hers did likewise when she felt the hardness of him press against her thigh. Her gaze was drawn to his nipples. They were hard, erect, and she wanted to know the texture of them under her tongue. He had tasted her breasts many times, but she'd never tasted his.

Leaning forward, her mouth opened over a stiff bud and her tongue began sliding around it, tasting it, absorbing it, sucking it. But for her, that wasn't enough. Reaching down she took hold of his hard heated flesh and her thumb and forefingers began caressing the hot tip. This was the first time she had ever tried to bring a man pleasure, to drive him insanely wild with desire with her hands. And from the sounds Storm was making, it seemed she was doing a good job.

When she heard him groan her name, the sound forced from deep within his throat, she lifted her head, but continued to let her hand clutch him, caress him, stroke him. "Umm?" she responded as she moved her mouth upward to take a tiny bite of his neck, branding him.

"You've pushed me too far, Jayla," Storm growled, as the need within him exploded. With one quick flick of his wrist, he tumbled her backward, ignoring her squeal of surprise. But she didn't resist and instead of moving from him, she moved to him, reaching up and looping her arms around his neck as he placed his body over hers, pressing his erection against the heat of her feminine core.

"Gotta get inside," he whispered brokenly as his hand clutched her waist, his thighs held hers in place. Taking her arms from around his neck, he captured her wrists and placed them above her head. He looked down at her, met her gaze at the same time he pushed himself inside of her.

He gasped. The pleasure of being inside of her was almost too much. He tipped his head back and roared an animalistic sound that mirrored the raging need within him. Then he began moving, in and out, straining his muscles, flexing his pelvis, rolling his hips while holding her in a firm grip, rocking her world, just mere seconds away from tumbling his own.

The bed started to shake and the windows seemed to rattle, but the only storm that was raging out of control was him, pelting down torrents of pleasure instead of sheets of rain. He didn't flinch when he felt her fingernails dig deeper into her flesh, but he did groan when he felt her inner muscles squeeze him, clench him, milk him. The woman was becoming a pro at knowing just what it took to splinter his mind and make him explode. No sooner had he thought the word, he felt her body do just that.

"Storm!"

And while she toppled over into oblivion, he continued to move in and out, claiming her as his.

His.

The thought of her belonging to him, and only to him, pushed him over the edge in a way he had never been pushed before. He thrust deep into her body, burying himself to the hilt, as his own release claimed him, ripped into him—not once, not twice, not even three times. The ongoing sensations that were taking over his body were more than he could stand.

"Jayla!"

And she was right there with him, lifting her hips off the bed, opening wider for him, moving with him, as they drove each other higher and higher on waves of excruciating pleasure.

The first light of dawn began slipping into the windows, fanning across the two naked bodies in bed. Jayla slowly awoke and took a long, deep breath of Storm and the lingering scent of their lovemaking.

It was there, in the air, the scent of her, of them—raw, primitive—the aftermath of her crying out in ecstasy, clutching his shoulders, pushing up her hips while he drove relentlessly into her, going as far as he could go, then tumbling them both over the edge as their releases came simultaneously.

She closed her eyes as panic seized her. What on earth had she done? All she had to do was open her eyes and glance over at Storm who was lying on his side facing her, still sleeping with a contented look on his face, to know what she had done. What she needed to really ask herself was how had it happened and why.

Storm had a reputation of not being a man who looked up a woman for a second helping. Once an affair ended, it was over. If that was the case, then why had he dropped by? What was there about her that had made him come back for more?

Jayla's features slipped into a frown. Although most women would have been ecstatic that Storm had deemed them special enough to grace their bed a second time, to her he was a distraction. And a distraction was the last thing she needed now, especially with her upcoming appointment at the fertility clinic. If he were to find out about her plans, like Lisa he would probably try and talk her out of it. But unlike Lisa, he wouldn't understand her decision, or support her anyway, even if he disagreed with her.

She took a quick glance at him and wondered why it mattered to her that he might not support what she planned to do? Jayla was pretty sure Storm would frown upon the idea of her having a baby by artificial insemination. Like her father, Storm was a traditionalist. He believed in doing things the old-fashioned way. She had to admit that at least in the bedroom she found Storm's old-fashioned, always-remain-a-gentleman ways endearing. Being a gentleman didn't mean he wouldn't engage in some off-the-charts, blow-your-mind hot sex like they had definitely shared last night. It simply meant that he would never try anything that made her feel uncomfortable. Nor would he ever assume anything. The only reason he was still in her bed at the crack of dawn was because he had asked if it was okay for him to stay the night. He hadn't just assumed that it was. If only she could shake his belief that a woman could not manage both a career and motherhood. How primitive was it for someone to think that way in this day and time?

She shook her head as she quietly slipped out of bed thinking Storm had definitely earned his rest. The man had energy that she wished she could bottle. No sooner had they completed one climax, he was going down for another, and somehow he always managed to take her with him. It was as if his orgasms—and the man had plenty—always triggered hers. Multiple orgasms were something she'd read about and at the time, the thought of it happening to anyone seemed too far-fetched to consider. But she was living witness that it was possible. She smiled thinking Storm had spoiled her. She wouldn't know how to act if another man ever made love to her.

Her smile slowly died at the thought of making love to another man. Would she spend the rest of her life comparing every future lover to The Perfect Storm? She shook her head as she made her way into the bathroom for a shower. She was getting in deeper by the minute.

Storm woke slowly to the sound of running water and the scent of jasmine. He smiled, closing his eyes again as visions of what he and Jayla had done played through his mind like a finely tuned piano.

He reopened his eyes, thinking he was just as confused now as he'd been the night before. He wasn't sure why he was here in Jayla's bed instead of his own bed. Then he remembered. He'd had to be with her last night. He had been willing to say or do anything to get back into her bed. Even if it had meant begging.

He glanced at the clock on her nightstand. It was

early, but time for him to go. He had to report to the station today to pull a twenty-four hour shift. He thoroughly enjoyed his new position of fire captain. To move from the ranks of lieutenant had meant many nights and weekends of studying for the fire department's promotional exam. During that time, he had given up a lot of things, including women. And even then, the thought of going without one hadn't bothered him. There hadn't been one single woman that he could name that he had missed making love to during all that time.

He closed his eyes again, not ready to move, not sure that he could if he wanted to. But the thought of Jayla, naked, wet and standing beneath a shower of water suddenly made him go hard, as if his body could do anything else around her.

He sighed deeply and suddenly the features of that old woman, the one who had read his palm in New Orleans, flitted across his mind at the same time the words she had spoken rang through his ears: *You are about to make unexpected changes in your life and although you yearn for peace, turbulence is in your future. Keep your sights high, be patient and let destiny take its course.*

He opened his eyes, quickly sat up and glanced around the room. It was as if the old woman's voice were right there. He shook his head, thinking he was definitely losing it.

He turned when he heard the sound of a door opening and glanced over his shoulder to see Jayla walk out of the bathroom with a towel wrapped tightly around her. She gave him a soft smile that immediately made him go hard…as if he wasn't already. And no matter how much he thought he was crazy this morning, he didn't have one single regret about last night.

"You should have woken me up and I would have joined you in the shower," he said standing, and crossing the room to her.

He watched as her gaze took in his nakedness, as it left his face to slowly roam down his chest, down past his stomach to settle…yeah, right there. He felt his erection get larger, become harder and saw her eyes grow dark with desire and her cheeks become flushed.

"You like being in your natural state, don't you?" she asked, lifting her gaze back to his.

He smiled. "Yes, and I like you being in your natural state, too."

She shook her head and chuckled. "I think we need to talk."

"I'd rather do something else." His smile widened. All she had to do was to drop her gaze back to his midsection to know what he had in mind.

She cleared her throat. "Well, unfortunately we both have jobs to go to this morning, right?"

"You would have to remind me of that, wouldn't you?" he asked, pulling her into his arms. "Have dinner with me at Anthony's tomorrow night."

She quickly pulled back. "Dinner?"

He dipped his head and captured an earlobe in his mouth. He'd heard the surprise in her voice. Hell, he was even surprised that he had suggested such a thing. "Yes, dinner. We can talk then, okay?" He knew what she wanted to talk about. She wanted to know why he was not adhering to their agreement. He hoped when he saw her again he would have some answers.

"Storm… I don't think that we—"

He lifted her chin with the tip of his finger so their eyes could meet. "Like you said, we need to talk, Jayla, and we can't do it here or at my place."

She nodded, understanding. At least at Anthony's, there wouldn't be any bedrooms around. "Okay."

Then Storm captured Jayla's mouth in a kiss that he definitely needed. The taste of her was like a drug to which he was addicted. She was a problem that needed a solution, but for now...

Wednesdays had always been referred to as over-the-hump day and it wasn't until today that Jayla actually understood what it meant...at least in terms of her and Storm.

It was almost lunchtime and Jayla was still besieged with constant memories of the night she'd spent with Storm. She glanced around to make sure no one noticed the blush that had to have appeared on her face, even with her dark skin tone.

She was in a room with, of all people, the vice president of the company, as well as the sales and advertising managers for Sala Industries. It was that time of the year when she needed to prepare the annual public relations report that the company distributed to the general public, interest groups and stockholders to make everyone aware of the company's activities and accomplishments the previous year. One of Sala's main goals for the year had been to increase their involvement in community affairs. Being a part of the charity benefit for Kids' World was one of the many projects they had undertaken to do just that.

Jayla had worked for the company since college and up until recently, the job had been the single most important thing in her life outside of her relationship with her father. After his death, she had moved her job up to the number one spot, which was why she had made a decision to have a baby. She had needed a life outside of work and someone to share that life with her. She smiled, thinking that she had only eight days to go before she went to the fertility clinic for her physical, the first step toward making her dream come true.

She glanced across the conference table and saw Lisa looking at her strangely. She lifted a brow and Lisa surreptitiously lifted one back. Jayla couldn't help but smile. Evidently, Lisa had seen her blush a few times.

As soon as the meeting was over, Lisa pulled her back the moment she was about to walk out the room and whispered, "We need to talk."

Playing dumb she smiled and asked, "What about?"

"Like the fact you sat through most of the meeting like you were zoned out. It's a good thing Mr. McCray didn't notice."

Jayla sobered quickly as she came to her senses. Having erotic flashbacks on her time was one thing, but having them on her employer's time was another. "Sorry."

Lisa laughed. "Hey, girlfriend, don't apologize. I'd trade places with you in a heartbeat. You've been with Storm Westmoreland again haven't you?"

Wondering how Lisa could know such a thing, Jayla asked innocently, "What makes you think that?"

Lisa raised a dark brow. "It's either that or you're reliving some dynamite memories. My guess is that you're reminiscing about the past twenty-four hours."

Jayla sighed as she closed the door so that she and

Lisa could have total privacy. She sat back down at the table and Lisa joined her. She met her best friend's curious gaze. "Storm dropped by last night."

Lisa leaned back in her chair and grinned. "That's a first. I heard that once an affair was ended, Storm Westmoreland never looked back. Booty calls are not exactly his style."

Jayla shot her a frown and Lisa held up her hand apologetically. "Sorry. I was just making an observation."

Jayla let out a breath. That was one observation she didn't need. "He wants to take me out tomorrow night. To dinner. At Anthony's."

Lisa smiled. "Real classy place, so what's the problem?"

Jayla returned the smile. Lisa could be so good for her at times. "The problem is what you indicated earlier. Storm is not a man who looks up women from his past. I knew that in New Orleans and he knew that, and it was understood that when we returned to Atlanta we would have no reason to seek the other out."

Lisa nodded. "And he's seeking you out."

"Yes, and I can't let it happen."

Lisa sat up and leaned in closer. "Is it okay for me to ask why?"

Jayla dragged a hand through her hair, and drew in a frustrating breath. "Because it's lousy timing. My life is about to undergo some major changes, Lisa, for Pete's sake. My physical is set for next Friday and soon after that, I plan to get inseminated. The last thing I need is Storm deciding, for whatever reason, that I'm a novelty to him."

"Hey, Jayla, don't sell yourself short. There might

be another reason that Storm Westmoreland finds you interesting, other than you being a novelty. The guy might actually like you. I mean really, really *like* you. There's a chance that you've blown him away."

Lisa's comments gave Jayla pause. She thought about that possibility all of two seconds and shook her head. "Impossible. Even if there was a remote chance that was true, Storm and I could never get serious about each other."

Lisa lifted a brow. "Why?"

Jayla frowned. "He's too much like my father. He would want to keep a tight rein on me. He actually believes a woman should be a stay-at-home mom. I guess he thinks the ideal woman is one he can keep barefoot and pregnant."

Lisa smiled. "Hey, I could do barefoot and pregnant with a man like him," she said, wiggling her eyebrows.

"Well, I can't. I have my life mapped out just the way I want, thank you. I'm having a baby without the complications of a man. The last thing I need is someone dictating how I should live my life and there's no doubt in my mind that Storm would be very domineering."

Lisa's smile widened. "Yeah, but also very sexy."

Jayla raised her gaze to the ceiling. "But I can't think of sexy when all I can see is domineering."

Lisa laughed. "Evidently you could last night if those blushes were any indication. But if you feel that way, you should let him know. It should be simple enough to tell him you aren't interested and to stop coming around."

Jayla nodded. Yes, that should be simple enough and she would tell him tomorrow night at dinner.

* * *

Storm walked into Coleman's Florist Shop and glanced at the older woman who was standing behind the counter. Luanne Coleman was considered one of the town's biggest gossips, but he still enjoyed doing business with her. And besides, none of the women he ever ordered flowers for lived in College Park, the suburb of Atlanta where he and the majority of his family resided and where his brother Dare was sheriff.

"Good morning, Ms. Luanne."

She glanced up from looking at the small television screen that was sitting on the counter. Her soaps were on. "Oh, hello, Storm. You want to send the usual?"

He smiled. By the usual, she meant a bouquet of fresh-cut flowers. "No, I want to send something different this time."

He knew that would grab her attention. She stared at him for a long moment, then raised her brow over curious eyes and asked, "Something different?"

"Yes."

She nodded. "All right, what do you have in mind?"

He glanced around. "What do you have that will last a while?"

"I have plenty of live plants and they make beautiful gifts."

Storm nodded. He didn't recall seeing a live plant in Jayla's home and thought one would be perfect, especially in her bedroom for her to look at and remember. "Good. I want you to pick out the biggest and prettiest one, and this is the person I want it delivered to," he said, handing her a slip of paper.

She took it and glanced at the name. She then

looked at him and smiled. "How much do you want to spend?"

A huge grin touched his lips. "The cost isn't important. Just add it to my account. And make sure it's delivered this afternoon."

She nodded and smiled as she quickly began writing up his order. "She must be very special."

Storm sighed heavily. There. He had heard someone else say what he'd been thinking all day, so the only thing he could do was smile and agree. "Yes, she is."

Jayla blinked at the man holding the huge potted plant in front of him. The plant was almost larger than he was. "Are you sure you're at the right address, sir?"

"Yes, I'm positive," the older man said, peeping from behind the bunch of healthy green leaves of a beautiful and lush looking areca palm. "It's for you."

Jayla nodded as she stepped aside to let the man bring the plant inside, wondering who on earth could have sent it. When the man had placed it down, he turned to leave. "Wait, I need to give you a—"

"The tip's been taken care of," the man said. And then he was gone.

Jayla quickly pulled the card from the plant and read it.

Whenever you look at this, think of me.
Storm

Jayla's heart skipped a beat. No it skipped two, possibly three. She blinked, then sank down on her sofa.

Storm had sent her a plant, a beautiful, large, lush green plant and for the first time in a long time, she was at a loss for words.

Chapter 9

"Thanks again for the plant, Storm. It's simply beautiful."

"You're welcome and I'm glad you like it."

"And thanks for bringing me here, tonight. Everything was wonderful."

"You're welcome again."

Then she glanced around Anthony's, the stunning and elegant antebellum mansion that had a reputation of fine service and delicious food. Being here reminded her of New Orleans, and she wondered if perhaps that was the reason Storm had chosen this place.

She glanced back over at Storm and their gazes met. He'd been watching her, something she noticed he'd been doing all evening. He had arrived at her house promptly at seven and since she'd been ready, she had only invited him inside long enough for her to grab her purse and a wrap.

At least, that's what she had assumed.

The moment he had stepped inside her home, he had pulled her into his arms and kissed her, making her realize that although she wished otherwise, there was definitely something going on between them, something that had not ended in New Orleans.

She regarded him with interest and although she knew that she should broach the subject of why they were here, she wasn't ready to do that yet. Tonight was too beautiful to bring up any unpleasantries just yet. "So, how are things going at work?" she asked, after taking another sip of her wine.

In New Orleans, he had told her that he had made the transition from lieutenant to captain rather well, but hadn't gone into much detail. Because her father had been a fire captain for years, she was familiar with all the position entailed. She was well aware that today firefighters needed more training to operate increasingly sophisticated equipment and to deal safely with the greater hazards that were associated with fighting fires in larger, more elaborate structures, as well as wild fires.

In her eyes, all firefighters were heroes, but she knew being a fire captain also required strong leadership qualities. A captain had to possess the ability to establish and maintain discipline and efficiency, as well as direct the activities of the firefighters in his company.

"Work is fine, and how are things at Sala Industries?" he asked rousing her from her musings.

She smiled. "Things are great. In addition to working with Tara on the Kids' World charity benefit, I'm working on another project that involves an environmental agency."

He nodded. "And what about that project you were excited about? How is it going?"

She swallowed, knowing exactly what project he was referring to. She worked her bottom lip between her teeth several times before responding. "I haven't started it yet."

She decided it was time to discuss the reason they were there. They had dodged the subject long enough. She met his eyes and a shiver ran through her when she saw the desire in their dark depths. Wanting to make love with him seemed natural. Too natural. It was a good thing they were in a public place.

Her body continued to stir and an unbearable heat spread through her. Trying to ignore her torment, she considered him for a long moment, then spoke, her voice barely above a whisper. "You said you would explain things tonight, Storm."

I did say that didn't I? Storm thought as his gaze continued to hold Jayla's. The only problem was that he wasn't any closer to answers today than he had been yesterday. The only thing that he was certain of was that he wanted to continue to see Jayla. He enjoyed being with her, taking her out and having fun with her and wanted to continue to do all those things they had done together in New Orleans. For some reason, she had his number and he was helpless to do anything about it.

"Storm?"

He blinked and realized while he'd been thinking

that he had been staring at her like some dimwit. He cleared his throat. "Jayla, is there a possibility for us to start seeing each other?"

It was evident from the look on her face that his question surprised her. "Why?" she asked, regarding him as if the question were totally illogical.

"I like you."

She blinked, then threw him a grin that caught him off guard. "Storm, you like women. I know that much from your reputation."

He didn't like hearing her say that. They weren't talking about other women; they were talking about her. He didn't place her in the same category with those other women he'd dated before. To him, none of them could be compared to Jayla.

He watched as she leaned over the table and, with a curious arch of her brow, whispered, "It's the virginity thing, isn't it?"

Storm nearly stopped breathing. He blinked, not understanding just what she was asking him. Seconds later, it dawned on him just what she'd insinuated and he frowned. "Why would you think something like that?"

She straightened back in her chair and shrugged. "What else could it be? I was your first virgin. You said so yourself. So I'm a novelty to you." She picked up her wineglass to take another sip, smiled, then said, "Trust me, you'll get over it."

His frown deepened. "Tell me something," he said, leaning back in his chair. "When did you figure that out?"

Her smile widened. "What? That I'm a novelty to you or that you'll get over it?"

"That you're a novelty to me."

She licked her lips and Storm felt his gut catch. "The night you showed up at my place. Seeking me out was so unlike how you're known to operate, so I figured there had to be a reason, since any woman can basically please a man in bed. It slowly dawned on me why I was different."

Storm inhaled deeply. He was glad they were sitting at a table in the rear of the restaurant in an area where they were practically alone. He would hate for anyone to overhear their conversation.

He shook his head slowly. Everything she'd said had sounded logical. With one exception. It was so far from the truth that it was pitiful.

He smiled. "First of all, contrary to what you think, Jayla, any woman cannot please a man in bed. When making love to a woman, most men…and women for that matter, experience various degrees of pleasure. On a scale from one to five, with five being the highest, most men will experience at least a three. In some situations, possibly a four, and only if they're extremely lucky, a five."

She lifted a brow. "How did I rate?"

Storm's smile widened. He'd known the curiosity in Jayla would give her the nerve to ask. In fact, he'd hoped that she would. "You rated a ten."

She blinked, then a smile touched the corners of her lips. "A ten?"

He chuckled. "Oh, yes, a ten."

He watched as she thought about it for a second, then she shook her head, perplexed and confused. "But—but how is that possible if a ten isn't on the chart?"

He reached across the table and captured her hand in his. "Because you, Jayla Cole, were off the charts." He watched her smile widen, evidently pleased with herself. Then he added, "And it had nothing to do with you being a virgin, but had everything to do with the fact that you are a very passionate woman."

He tilted his head and said, "It also had a lot to do with the fact that the two of us are good together. We click. When we make love, I feel a connection with you that I've never felt with another woman." What he didn't add was that when he made love to her, he felt as if they were made for each other.

"Wow, that's deep, Storm," she said regarding him seriously.

He sighed as he nodded. "Yeah, it is deep and that's why I'd like for us to continue to see each other."

Jayla inhaled. She would like to continue to see him, too, but she knew that wouldn't be a wise thing to do. In less than a month, she would be getting inseminated and hopefully soon after that, she would become pregnant. The last thing she needed was to get involved with anyone, especially Storm, no matter how tempting the thought was.

"Jayla?"

She met his gaze. "I don't think that would be a good idea, Storm. This new project will take up a lot of my time, and I won't have time for a relationship."

He considered her words. He was still curious as to what kind of project she would be working on. He had asked her about it in New Orleans and she had danced around an answer. The only thing he could come up with was that it involved her job, perhaps a confidential, top-secret assignment. "And there's no way we can work around this project?"

"No."

Her response had been quick. Definite. "When will you start?"

She shrugged. She would have her physical next Friday and then hopefully within three weeks after that, she would go in to have the procedure done. "Possibly within a month."

He met her gaze levelly. "Is there any reason we can't continue to see each other until then?" Slowly, he raised her hand to his lips and kissed it.

Jayla swallowed and knew what she should say. She should tell him yes, there were plenty of reasons why they couldn't continue to see each other for the next month, but for some reason she couldn't get the words out. What Storm had said earlier was true. They were good together. They clicked and they connected. And deep down, a part of her felt she needed this time with him. Afterwards, at least she would have her memories of their time together.

"No, there's no reason," she finally said. "But you will have to promise me something, Storm."

He kissed her hand again before asking. "What?"

"When I say it's over, then it's over. You won't drop by and you won't call."

He shook his head. "I can't agree to that, Jayla. I promised your father that I would periodically check on you and—"

"I'm not talking about that, Storm. I'm taking about you dropping by or calling with the intention of us becoming involved again. You have to promise me when I say it's over, that it will be over. No questions asked."

Storm stared at her for a long moment as emotions tumbled inside of him. They were feelings he didn't understand, but he knew that no matter what, things would never be over between them, project or no project. He would see to it.

"All right," he agreed. "You'll be calling the shots and I'll abide by your wishes."

"Hey, Storm, are you in this game or not?"

Storm glanced over at Thorn and frowned. "Yes, I'm in."

"Well, keep your mind on the game. You're day-dreaming again."

Storm's frown deepened. "Yeah, whatever." He glanced across the table at his four brothers who had smirks on their faces. "What's so funny?"

It was the oldest brother, Dare, who answered. "Word's out on the streets that some woman has finally caught the eye of the Storm. I pulled old man Johnson over the other day for running a Stop sign, and he said that he'd heard you were so besotted with some gal that you can't pee straight."

When Storm narrowed his eyes, Dare held up his hand. "Hey, those were Mr. Johnson's words, not mine."

Chase chuckled. "And I've heard that you're sending so many flowers to this woman that the money Coleman Florist is making off you is the reason Mrs. Luanne has that new swing on her front porch."

"And I heard," Stone piped in, as a huge smile touched his lips, "that you've been seen all over Atlanta with her and that she's a beauty. Funny that we haven't met her yet."

Thorn added, "Hey, Storm, what happened to your 'love them and leave them' policy?"

Storm leaned back in his chair thinking that Thorn's question was a good one, but one he didn't intend to answer.

"I've seen her," Chase said grinning. "She came into the restaurant one day to have lunch with Tara."

"Tara?" Thorn asked, raising a curious brow. "Tara knows her?"

Chase nodded. "Evidently, since they had lunch together that day. However, I don't know if Tara knows that Storm has the hots for her."

"Excuse me, guys," Storm said interrupting his brothers' conversation. "I don't appreciate you discussing my business like I'm not here."

Stone chuckled. "All right, then we'll discuss your business like you're here." He then looked at Chase. "So, is she as good-looking as everyone claims she is?"

Chase grinned. "Yeah. She's Adam's daughter all grown up."

Thorn frowned. "Adam? Adam Cole, Storm's boss who died a few months back?"

"Yep."

Stone glanced over at Storm. A curious glint shone in his eyes. "You're actually seeing Adam Cole's girl?"

Angrily, Storm stood and threw down his cards. "That's it. I'm out of the game."

Dare stared up at his youngest brother. Being the oldest, he had to occasionally bring about peace... and in some situations, order. "Sit back down, Storm, you're getting overheated for nothing. And to be quite honest with you, for all intents and purposes, you've been out of the game since you got here. You haven't been concentrating worth a damn all night."

One of Dare's dark eyebrows lifted. "And what's wrong with us wanting to know about this woman that you're seeing? As your brothers, don't you think we have a right to at least be curious?"

Storm inhaled deeply as he glanced around the table and glared. "I don't appreciate any of you discussing her as if she's like the other women I've dated."

Dare nodded. "If she's not like the other women you've dated, then it's up to you to tell us that. There's nothing wrong with letting us know that you think she's special, instead of trying to keep her a secret," he said in a low voice.

Storm sat back down and glanced around at his brothers. They were staring at him, waiting expectantly. He sighed deeply. "Her name is Jayla Cole and yes, she's Adam's daughter all grown up and we're seeing each other. We're taking things slow, one day at a time, and yes, she's special. Very special."

Stone smiled. "When will we meet her?"

Storm leaned back in his chair. "I'll introduce her to everyone the night of the charity benefit for Kids' World. Her company is a corporate sponsor and she's working closely with Tara to pull things together for that night."

Dare nodded. "And all of us will look forward to meeting her then." He glanced around the table and grinned. "Now let's play cards."

Jayla sat curled up on her sofa and glanced around her living room, thinking the past week had been like a scene from a romance novel. Storm had sent her flowers practically every single day and had wined and dined her to her heart's content.

On Saturday night, they had gone to a laser show on Stone Mountain and then on Sunday evening, he had taken her to a movie. Because he had been at the station all day Monday, she didn't see him again until Tuesday night, when he'd dropped by with Chinese food. They had sat eating at her kitchen table while she had told him about how her day had gone and how things were coming together for this weekend's charity benefit.

They had talked about his day, as well. He had told her that he had been selected to head up the city's fire prevention program for the coming year and that he was excited about that.

She glanced down at the letter she had in her hand, the same letter that had arrived last week from the fertility clinic reminding her of tomorrow's appointment. Seeing it and rereading it had reaffirmed her decision to have the procedure.

She nearly jumped when she heard the phone ring. Thinking that perhaps it was Storm, she placed the letter on the table, then quickly moved across the room to answer it. He had called earlier and said he would be playing cards tonight with his brothers rather late and that he would see her tomorrow. "Yes?" she said, after picking up the phone.

"It's Lisa. How are things going?"

Jayla smiled. Lisa had been out of town most of the week on business. "Everything's going fine. How was your trip?"

"Wonderful. I love Chicago. You know that."

Jayla chuckled. Yes, she did know that. Lisa enjoyed shopping and Chicago was her favorite place to shop.

"So, are you planning to keep your appointment tomorrow?"

Lisa's question immediately silenced Jayla's thoughts. She frowned. "Of course, why wouldn't I?"

"Because from what you told me every time I've called this week, you and Storm have been seeing a lot of each other."

Jayla shrugged. "So? What Storm and I are sharing is short-term. I know that and so does he."

"But it doesn't have to be that way, Jayla. I believe things could last if you gave them a chance."

Jayla rolled her eyes to the ceiling. "Lisa, trust me, they won't. What Storm and I share is physical. I'm enjoying his company and he's enjoying mine. Why does it have to be more than that?"

For a long moment, there was silence. Then Lisa asked softly, "What are you afraid of, Jayla?"

Jayla flinched. "I'm not afraid of anything."

"I think that you are. Storm Westmoreland is everything a woman could want in a man and you are in a good position to be that woman. Why are you willing to turn your back on such a wonderful opportunity?"

Jayla closed her eyes. She could never be the kind of woman Storm wanted. Besides, he wasn't what she wanted, either. At the moment, no man was. She wanted a baby and not a complicated relationship. She'd long ago given up on finding Mr. Right. The "married with children" routine was a fairy tale that might never come true for her. Her biological clock was ticking and she had made the decision to start a family sooner rather than later.

She turned when she heard a knock at the door. "Look Lisa, there's someone at the door. I'll talk with you later. Bye."

After hanging up the phone, she glanced at the clock on the wall, then crossed the living room to the door. It was late, after midnight. The only reason she was still up was because she had taken the morning off for her physical at the fertility clinic. Since her appointment wasn't until nine, that meant she would get to sleep late.

She knew before she got within a foot of the door that her late-night visitor was Storm. That would explain the reason her heart was beating so fast and her senses were getting heated. She tried forcing her conversation with Lisa out of her mind. Her best friend was wrong and she wasn't afraid of anything, especially a serious relationship with Storm. She merely chose not to have one.

"Who is it?"

"Storm."

She quickly opened the door and he stood there, staring at her. His eyes were dark, intense, and she immediately recognized the look in them. Her lips curved into a smile. "Hi."

He returned her smile and the heat infiltrating her senses kicked up another notch. "Hi, yourself. The card game ended and I wasn't ready to go home."

"Oh?"

"I had to see you, Jayla."

A teasing glint shone in Jayla's eyes. "Okay, you see me. So now what?"

He slowly took a couple of steps forward, and she took a couple of steps back. When he was completely inside the house, he closed the door behind him and locked it. He walked the few feet over to her, cupped her shoulders in his hands and pulled her to him, her mouth just inches from his. "Now this," he breathed against her lips.

Then kissed her.

As soon as their mouths touched, Storm felt something hot rush through his bloodstream. The scent of Jayla, as well as the taste of her, was getting to him and the only thing he could think of doing was devouring her, making love to her. Suddenly, some emotion that he'd never felt before flared within him, almost bringing him to his knees, and he finally acknowledged it for what it was.

Love. He loved her.

Storm drew back and stared at her for a quick second before his mouth came back down on hers again. His hands were everywhere as he began removing her clothes, and broke off the kiss just long enough to remove his own. Then he swept her into his arms and carried her into the bedroom.

What should have been a no-brainer had been hard as hell for a staunch bachelor like him to figure out. The reason he had wanted a relationship with Jayla had nothing to do with them being great together in bed, but everything to do with emotions he hadn't been able to recognize until tonight.

He was in love with Jayla Cole. She had caught more than the eye of the Storm. She had captured his heart.

Chapter 10

Anchoring himself above Jayla on his elbows, Storm looked down at her and smiled. Dang, she always looked beautiful after experiencing an orgasm. What more could a man ask for than to be right there to experience each one with her.

He sighed deeply. Now that he knew he loved her, he had to figure out a way to get her to fall in love with him as well. First, he would have to gain her complete trust, and then he had to make sure she clearly understood that he was her Mr. Right and wanted a long-term relationship with her, one that ended in marriage. A smile curved his lips. Yeah, that's what he wanted, Jayla as his wife.

"Why are you smiling?"

He met her gaze. Her eyelids were heavy and her cheeks had a sated flush. Leaning down, he brushed a kiss across her lips. "After what we've just shared, how can you ask me that?"

As usual, everything had been perfect. The way their bodies had come together while a trail of fire had blazed between them. It was a fire he hadn't wanted to put out, but instead had done everything within his power to ignite even further, to make it burn out of control.

And it had.

By the time he had entered, she had been delirious with desire, begging breathlessly for him to make love to her; she'd been a she-cat, clawing his back and nipping his shoulders. And when they had finally come together, she had cried out his name and he had continued to move inside of her, taking them to heights of profound pleasure.

He loved her, he thought in wonder, as he leaned down and murmured her name against her cheek. "Mind if I stay the night?"

He felt her smile against his lips. "Umm, I would be highly disappointed if you didn't," she said softly.

He chuckled. "In that case, I'll stay." He pressed his mouth to hers and kissed her, needing the taste of her again. Moments later, he slowly pulled back and flicked his gaze over her features. Heat immediately surged through his groin. If he didn't get out bed, he would be making love to her all over again, and she needed her rest.

"I'll turn off the lights," he whispered.

"All right, but hurry back."

He grinned as he eased out of bed and slipped into his jeans. And just think he'd assumed that she needed her rest. He glanced at the huge plant that sat in the corner. It was just where he'd wanted it, in her bedroom so she could think of him whenever she saw it.

As he walked out of the bedroom, the image of Jayla's sexy smile when she'd told him to hurry back filled his mind and made him want to do just as she'd requested. When he got to the living room, he leaned down to turn off the lamp near the sofa and his gaze caught sight of a letter lying on the coffee table. It was a letter from a fertility clinic.

Without thinking that he didn't have any right to do so, he picked up the letter and read it. A few seconds later, he sank down on her sofa, not believing what he had just read. He felt stunned. Confused. Jayla had sought out the services of a fertility clinic to get artificially inseminated with some stranger's sperm? Why?

He reread the letter, thinking there must be a mistake but again the contents were the same. She was scheduled to have a physical tomorrow—which actually was today—and then, when it was determined her body would be most fertile, she would go in to have the procedure done.

"You were supposed to hurry back."

Storm stood when Jayla walked out of the bedroom. When she saw the letter in his hand, she quickly crossed the room and snatched it from him. "You had no right to read that, Storm."

He just stared at her as every muscle in his body vibrated. Confusion gave way to anger. "Then how about you telling me what this is all about."

She glared at him. "It's private and personal and doesn't concern you."

"Doesn't concern me? Like hell, it doesn't. If it concerns you, then it concerns me. Are you actually considering having your body inseminated with some man's sperm?"

Jayla tipped her head back; her anger clashed with his. He'd made it sound as if what she planned to do was something filthy and degrading. "It's not what I'm considering doing, it's what I will be doing. I made the decision months ago."

Taken back by Jayla's statement, he wiped a hand down his face as if doing so would erase his anger. When he looked over at her, she was standing with her hands on her hips, glaring at him. A thought suddenly popped into his head. "Wait a minute. Is this the project you've been so excited about lately?"

"Yes."

He shook his head, not believing the conversation they were having. "I understand the need for that procedure in certain situations, but not with you. Why would you even consider doing such a thing, Jayla?"

Her eyes were consumed with fire. "Because I want a baby that's why! I want a baby more than anything."

Storm was shocked by that revelation. She had once mentioned she wanted to have kids, but she had never given him the idea that she'd been obsessed with having one. "And you want a child to the point where you would actually consider having a baby from someone you don't know?"

"Yes. In fact, I prefer it that way. I want a baby and not the baby's father. I don't want a man coming in my life trying to run things."

"Run things how?"

"Like telling me how to live my life, forcing the issue of whether I can have a career outside of my home, a man who'd try to control me and keep a tight rein on me."

Of all those things she'd named, Storm recognized only one that he might eventually become guilty of.

"And what's wrong with a man wanting the sole responsibility of taking care of his wife so she won't have to work outside the home?"

Her glare thickened. "For some women, nothing, but I prefer taking care of myself. I don't want to depend on anyone."

Storm frowned and crossed his arms over his chest. "So, for your own selfish reasons, you're willing to deny your child a father?"

"If it means not wasting my time looking for a Mr. Right who doesn't exist, then yes."

Storm tried to keep his anger in check. Why couldn't she see that he was her Mr. Right? He slowly shook his head again. "If you want a baby, then I'll give you *my* baby."

"What!"

"You heard me. I'll be damned if I'll let another man get the woman I love pregnant."

Jayla was shocked at the words he'd spoken. "The woman you love?"

Silence shredded the air and Storm knew he had to get her to understand the depth of how he felt. He crossed the room and with his fingertip, lifted her chin to meet his gaze. "Yes. I love you, Jayla, and if you want a baby, then we'll get married and I'll give you one."

She stared at him as if she didn't believe he'd suggested such a thing. And then she took a step back from him. "Things wouldn't work between us, Storm.

You would want more from a wife than I'm willing to give."

"And what about the fact that I love you?"

She shrugged. "I believe you like sleeping with me, but I find it hard to believe that you really love me, Storm."

She sighed deeply when he didn't say anything but continued to stare at her. "We agreed that we would end things between us whenever I was ready," she finally said to break the silence. "Well, I'm ready. For us to continue seeing each other will only complicate matters."

"Complicate matters like hell!" he said, his voice rising. "I tell you that I love you and that I want to marry you and give you the baby you want, and you're telling me that you don't believe a word of it and to get out of your life? And to top things off, you plan to continue with this crazy scheme to have a baby from a man who not only doesn't love you, but a man *you* don't even know?"

"I don't owe you an explanation for anything I do, Storm. And considering everything, it would be best if you left."

Storm stared at her for a moment, then moved past her to the bedroom. Moments later, fully dressed, he came back into the living room. He stood in front of her and said softly, "I hope that one day you'll take your blinders off. Maybe then you'll recognize your Mr. Right when he comes and stands right in front of you."

He then turned and walked out the door.

When Storm left, Jayla moved around the house trying to convince herself that she was glad they would no longer be seeing each other. The last thing she needed was a man trying to control her life.

After closing things up and turning off the lights, she slipped back into bed, and tried to ignore the scent of Storm that still lingered there. She closed her eyes.

I love you, Jayla...

She opened her eyes, flipped on her back and stared up at the ceiling as she tried to convince herself that she wasn't the one with blinders on, he was. Couldn't he see that what he was feeling wasn't really love but lust? Die-hard bachelors like Storm didn't fall in love in a blink of an eye or after a few rolls between the sheets.

She turned to her side and closed her eyes, trying to force thoughts of Storm from her mind. But she couldn't. Steeling herself, she sighed, knowing the memories of the times they'd spent together were too deep, too ingrained in her memory.

Getting over him wouldn't be easy, but dammit she would try. She would shift her focus elsewhere and appreciate the good things that were happening to her. Everything she'd wanted was falling in place. Tomorrow, she would go to the fertility clinic for her physical and then she would wait eagerly for the day when she would be inseminated.

Storm was not the most important thing to her—having a baby was.

"Hey, Captain, you got a minute?"

Storm glanced up from the stack of papers on his desk. After having a sleepless night, he had gotten up at the crack of dawn to come into the station. Most of his men hadn't arrived yet. Although it wasn't a requirement, he was one of those captains who preferred working the same hours as the firefighters he supervised.

"Sure, Cobb, come on in. What can I do for you?"

Darryl Cobb had recently become a father again. Four months ago, his wife Haley had given birth to their third child. Darryl was a few years younger than Storm and they had known each other since their high school days. He'd also known Darryl's wife, Haley, from high school, as well, and remembered Darryl and Haley dating even back then. Evidently, Haley hadn't had a problem recognizing Darryl as her Mr. Right since the two of them had been married for over ten years now and always seemed happy together.

"I was wondering if I can take a few hours off today. The baby has a doctor's appointment and Haley just called. Her boss called an important meeting for later today."

Storm nodded. Haley was a computer programmer for a financial management company. "That shouldn't be a problem," Storm said, turning to check the activity board. "You're supposed to teach a class on fire prevention at that elementary school today. Do you have a replacement?"

Darryl smiled. "Sure do. Reed has agreed to cover for me."

Storm nodded. The one thing he liked about the men he supervised was that they got along and were quick to help each other out when something unexpected came up. "In that case, your taking a few hours off won't be a problem," he said making a notation on the activity sheet.

He glanced back over at Cobb. "So how has it been going since Haley returned to work?"

Darryl chuckled. "Crazy."

"Then why did she go back?" he asked, then quickly felt he'd been out of line for asking such a question. But from the laugh Cobb gave him, evidently he hadn't been surprised by the question. From Storm's early days as a firefighter, it had been a joke around the station that his views on women working inside the home were unrealistic and so outdated they were pitiful. He'd been told that it would be hard as hell to find a woman who'd agree to do nothing but stay at home, barefoot and pregnant.

"Well, that humongous house we just bought in Stone Mountain was one good reason for her to return to work," Darryl said, still chuckling. "But another reason is that Haley enjoys what she does and I'm not going to ask her to give it up." He looked pointedly at Storm and said, "That's where a lot of men make their mistakes."

Storm raised a brow. "Where?"

Darryl smiled. "In assuming that they are the only ones who have it together. I personally think it's women who really have it together, and we're merely bystanders looking in. Besides, with Haley and me both sharing equally in the raising of our kids, I feel I'm playing just as an important role in their lives as she is, and that's important to me. It has nothing to do with which one of us is bringing home the bacon, but mainly how the both of us are serving the bacon. Together, we're forming a deep, nurturing attachment to our children and are giving them all the love we have, which is a lot. And to me that's the most important thing."

A few moments later after Cobb had left, Storm stood at the window in his office and looked out as he thought about what Darryl had said. Was one of the reasons Jayla hadn't recognized him as her Mr. Right was because in her mind he was all wrong?

Had what Nicole done to him all those years ago driven his beliefs that a husband should be sole provider for his wife and family? He would be the first to admit that because of Nicole's rejection, he'd always wanted to prove the point that a man, highly educated or not, could take care of his household. His father had done it and had raised a family on a construction worker's salary.

He thought of his brothers and their wives. Even married to a sheikh, his sister Delaney was still working as a pediatrician and doing one hell of a job raising their son Ari, who was beginning to be a handful. But then her husband Jamal also played an equally important role in raising their son. Then there were his sisters-in-laws, Shelly, Tara and Madison. Although Shelly and Dare were the only ones who had a son, eleven-year-old AJ, Storm was fairly certain that if Tara and Madison were to get pregnant, they wouldn't consider giving up their careers.

He closed his eyes and remembered the scene that had played out in Jayla's living room last night. The woman he loved was planning to let another man get her pregnant only because she was convinced there wasn't a Mr. Right for her. She actually believed there wasn't a man who could and would understand her need to be in control of her life.

He opened his eyes and glanced down at his watch. According to that letter he'd read last night, she had a physical at nine this morning at that fertility clinic. After the physical, it would probably be two to three weeks before the actual procedure could be performed. Hopefully that would give him time to convince Jayla that he really did love her, and that he would satisfy all her needs, including her need to remain independent...to a certain degree. Changing his conventional views wouldn't be something he could do overnight, but it was something he could definitely work on, especially for Jayla.

The most important thing was to show her that he was the right man for her. The only man for her. For the second time since returning from New Orleans, the old fortune teller's words crept into his thoughts.

You should keep your sights high, be patient and let destiny take its course.

He smiled. Perhaps the old woman hadn't been a flake after all and had known exactly what she'd been talking about. Tomorrow was the night of the charity benefit and because of her involvement, he knew Jayla would be there. He would start wooing her with the intensity of a man who had one single goal in his mind.

To win the love of the woman he intended to marry.

"You can go ahead and get dressed, Ms. Cole," the nurse said smiling. "The doctor will return in a few minutes to go over the results of your tests."

"Thanks."

Jayla sighed deeply as she began putting her clothes back on. She'd had a sleepless night and hadn't been as excited about the appointment this morning as much as she'd wanted to be because of thoughts of Storm. And it hadn't helped matters that she'd been crying most of the morning.

She walked over to the mirror in the room and looked at herself. She looked pathetic. Her reflection revealed a woman who was truly drowning in her own misery. And it was a misery well deserved. Even Lisa hadn't given her any slack when she'd called this morning and she'd told her about the argument she'd had with Storm. And when she'd mentioned that Storm had told her that he loved her and wanted to marry her, her best friend had actually gone off on her. But then, what was a best friend for if she couldn't give you hell when you needed it?

The sad thing about it was that everything both Storm and Lisa had said was true. She wouldn't recognize her Mr. Right if he came to stand right in front of her.

She sighed deeply as she slipped back into her panty hose. So what if Storm was one of those men who wanted to take care of his woman? Wasn't it better to have a man who wanted to take care of you than to have a man who expected you to take care of him? And was it so awful that he was a little on the conventional side? She would be the first to admit that she found some of his old-fashioned ways sweet. Besides, if his conventional way of thinking became too much for her, couldn't she just make it her business to modernize him? And so what if he had ways like her father? Adam Cole had been a great parent and a part of her could now say she appreciated her strict upbringing. A couple of the girls she had wanted to hang around with in high school had either gotten pregnant before graduating or had gotten mixed up with drugs.

Upon waking this morning, it had taken several hours of wallowing in self-pity, as well as being forced to listen to Lisa's tirade, before she'd finally taken the blinders off. Storm loved her and he was her Mr. Right and she loved him. She couldn't fight it, nor could she deny the truth any longer. She loved him and had always loved him.

Oh, she understood now why he had kept his distance so many years ago but still, it had been a bitter pill for a young girl to swallow. A part of her had built up an immunity against ever being rejected by him again. But now she was a woman and she wanted what any other woman would want—a man to love her. And that man had offered to marry her and give her the baby she wanted. How blessed could a woman be?

Her feeling of euphoria quickly disintegrated when she remembered she had thrown his words of love back in his face. She had a feeling that Storm was a man who wouldn't take rejection well. What if he never wanted to see her again?

She quickly slipped into her skirt, thinking she had to work fast to correct the mistake she'd made or she would lose him completely. And the first thing she had to do was to cancel her plans to get inseminated. The only man she wanted to father her child was Storm.

She turned when she heard a knock at the door. "Come in." She smiled apologetically when Dr. Susan Millstone walked in. Before the doctor could say anything she quickly said, "I've changed my mind."

After closing the door behind her, Dr. Millstone

tilted her head and looked at her. "You've changed your mind?"

"Yes. I've decided not to go through with the artificial insemination procedure after all."

The doctor leaned against the closed door. "May I ask the reason you've changed your mind?"

Jayla smiled. "Yes. The man that I love wants to marry me and give me his child, and I want that, too, more than anything." *And I hope and pray I haven't lost him,* she thought.

Dr. Millstone chuckled as she shook her head. "What you've just said will make what I have to tell you a little easier."

Jayla raised a brow. "Oh?"

"I just went over the results of your physical and it seems you're already pregnant."

The news was so shocking that Jayla dropped into a nearby chair. She looked back up at the doctor, not believing what she'd been told. "I'm pregnant?"

The doctor chuckled again. "Yes. You're almost a month along."

Jayla shook her head, as if trying to keep it from spinning. She was almost a month pregnant! "New Orleans," she said softly, as a smile touched her lips.

"Excuse me?"

She met Dr. Millstone's grin. "I said New Orleans. I got pregnant in New Orleans. But how is that possible when we were careful?"

A smiled played at the corner of Dr. Millstone's mouth. "I deliver a lot of babies whose parents thought they were careful, too. No birth control is one hundred percent."

Jayla chuckled. "Evidently not."

"So, can I assume that you're happy with the news?"

Jayla jumped up as the feeling of euphoria took control of her again. "Yes, I'm happy! I am ecstatic!" she said, laughing joyously. She just hoped and prayed that Storm would be happy and ecstatic, as well, when she told him that she loved him and was having his baby.

Chapter 11

Everyone who was somebody in Atlanta had turned out for the Kids' World charity benefit. There were politicians, CEOs of major corporations, celebrities and well-known sports figures, all of whom considered Atlanta home.

There was also a sheikh in attendance, the very handsome Prince Jamal Ari Yasir, who was dressed in his native Middle Eastern attire and causing quite a stir among the ladies, single or otherwise. Jayla smiled, knowing the stir was a waste of time and effort since it was well known that Prince Yasir was happily married to the former Delaney Westmoreland, Storm's sister.

Jayla glanced across the room at the group of men standing together laughing and talking. Although Storm hadn't arrived yet, it didn't take much to recognize the men as Westmorelands. Their kinship was clearly evident in their facial features, their height as well as their sex appeal.

She began wondering if perhaps Storm had changed his mind about coming. After leaving the clinic yesterday, she had decided to take the rest of the day off. Too excited to work, she had gone home and called Lisa and invited her to lunch.

She'd barely gotten the words out after Lisa arrived when she burst into tears of happiness. Then she told Lisa of her fears about telling Storm. What if he no longer loved her? What if her rejection had killed his feelings for her?

Lisa, in her usual optimistic way, had assured her that although Storm might be a little angry with her right now, she doubted his love could have died so quickly.

Jayla had wanted to call and ask him to come over, but then she'd remembered he was on duty at the fire station. So, instead of talking to him yesterday, she had walked around the house wondering what she would say when she saw him tonight.

"Everything looks beautiful, doesn't it?"

Jayla turned when she recognized the voice of Tara Westmoreland. Tara was accompanied by three other women whom Jayla didn't immediately recognize. At first, Jayla thought each of the women was beautiful in a unique way. Like Tara, they were smiling and each of their smiles reflected a sincere friendliness. Jayla returned their smiles as Tara made the introductions.

The women were Shelly Westmoreland, who was married to Sheriff Dare Westmoreland; Madison Westmoreland, who was married to Stone Westmoreland and Storm's sister, Delaney Westmoreland Yasir. Jayla swallowed deeply. All three women, like Tara, were part of the Westmoreland clan. Somehow, Jayla found her voice to respond to Tara's earlier comment. "Yes, everything is beautiful and your committee should be proud of what they've accomplished."

Tara chuckled. "Yes, but your company also played a huge role. The food is wonderful. Everyone is talking about the catering service that is being used. It's quite evident that Sala Industries went out of their way tonight."

"Thanks."

"And I have to say the dress you're wearing looks simply gorgeous on you," the woman who had been introduced as Madison Westmoreland said.

"Thank you," Jayla said smiling, beginning to feel more relaxed.

She and the women launched into a discussion of styles in clothing and movies they'd recently seen when they heard a sudden buzzing from a group of single women standing not far away. A quick glance at the entrance to the ballroom revealed why. Storm and his cousin Ian had walked in and were crossing the ballroom floor to join the other Westmoreland men. Both men looked dashing and handsome dressed in black tuxedos.

Part of Jayla wished Storm would look her way; then, seconds later, she decided maybe it would be best if he didn't when she overheard the conversation between two women standing not far away.

"Hey, I'm going to make it my business to go after 'The Perfect Storm' tonight," the more statuesque of the two said.

The other women giggled and said. "Storm Westmoreland has a reputation of not doing the same woman twice."

"Yeah, but I heard that just once is all it takes to blow your mind and I definitely intend to have that one time," the statuesque one countered.

A flash of jealousy raced through Jayla, and she started to turn to the woman and tell her that when it came to Storm, hands off. But she couldn't do that. She didn't have the right.

She glanced up when she felt someone gently touch her arm. "I wouldn't worry about what the 'hottie duo' are saying if I were you," Shelly Westmoreland whispered, smiling. "I heard from a very reliable source that Storm has found a special lady and only has eyes for her."

Jayla blinked in surprise at Shelly's words and glanced at the other women standing beside her. They all nodded; evidently, they'd heard the same thing. Was it possible that they knew she and Storm had been seeing each other? And who was this reliable source Shelly Westmoreland was talking about? Had Storm mentioned her to members of his family?

Her heart stopped and she wasn't sure what to say to the four women who were staring at her with such genuine and sincere smiles on their faces. Tears pressed at the corner of her eyes.

"I may have lost him," she whispered, as her mind was suddenly filled with doubt and regret.

Delaney Yasir chuckled and placed an arm around Jayla's shoulder. "I doubt that. My brother hasn't taken his eyes off of you since he arrived."

Hope ran through Jayla. "Really?" She was standing with her back to Storm so she couldn't see him.

Madison Westmoreland grinned. "Yes, really."

"Hey, Storm, you want something to drink?" Jared Westmoreland asked his cousin as he grabbed a glass a wine off the tray of a passing waiter.

"Storm doesn't want anything to drink," Ian said, grinning. "The only thing Storm wants is that woman who's standing over there talking to the Westmoreland women."

Stone Westmoreland lifted a brow and glanced across the room. The woman's back was to them, so he couldn't get a look at her. "You've met her?" he asked in surprise.

Ian chuckled. "Yes, Storm introduced us in New Orleans."

That comment got everyone's attention. Chase stared at Storm. "You took her to New Orleans with you?"

Before Storm could respond, not that he would have anyway, Ian spoke up. "Of course he didn't take her to New Orleans with him," he said, as if the thought of Storm taking any woman out of town with him were ludicrous. "They just happened to be in the same place at the same time. Her father was Storm's old boss, Adam Cole."

Thorn Westmoreland took a slow sip of his drink and said, "Her parentage is old news, Ian, but her being in New Orleans with Storm is definitely something that we didn't know about."

"And something all of you are going to forget you heard," Storm said. The tone of his voice matched the look on his face. Highly irritated. Totally annoyed. Deadly serious. "And I thought I told you guys that I don't like you discussing my business like I'm not here."

Chase gave his twin a dismissive shrug and said, "Yeah, whatever." He then turned his attention back to Ian. "So what else can you tell us about Storm's lady?"

Ian met Storm's gaze and got the message loud and clear, although it was obvious his brothers hadn't… or they chose no to. Ian grinned and decided to play dumb. "I forget."

Storm smiled. He knew he could count on Ian to keep his secrets, just as Ian knew he could count on him to keep his. Things had always been that way between them. He then turned his attention back to Jayla and wished the crowd would thin out so his view wasn't as blocked, or that she would at least turn around so he could see her. He wanted to look into her eyes to let her know that no matter how much she might want him out of her life, he was there to stay.

Moments later, as if he had willed it to be so, the crowd thinned out and she turned and met his gaze. His heart almost stopped when he saw how radiant she looked. And what made her even more beautiful was the fact that she was wearing that red dress.

His dress.

It was the same one he had picked out for her in New Orleans. He wondered, hoped and prayed that there was a hidden meaning behind her wearing that dress. Could he dare hope she might realize that he was her Mr. Right? Knowing there was only one way to find out, he walked away from the group.

His destination was the woman he loved.

* * *

Jayla's breath caught in her throat when she saw Storm heading toward her. She couldn't tell from his expression whether he was glad to see her or not, but one thing was certain—he wasn't going to avoid her. But maybe she was jumping to conclusions. Although he was headed to where she was standing, he might be coming over to say hello to his sister and sisters-in-law since they were standing next to her.

"Here comes Storm Westmoreland," she overheard one of the women from the "hottie duo" say. "And I think he's seen my interest and is coming over to talk to me."

"Fat chance of that happening," Tara whispered. Jayla couldn't help but smile and hoped Tara was right. As Storm got closer, her hope went up a notch when she saw he was still holding her gaze. She sighed deeply when he stopped in front of her.

"Hi, Jayla."

She smiled up at him and tried to keep her heart from pounding erratically in her chest. "Hi, Storm."

It was only then that he released her gaze and glanced at his sister and sisters-in-law. "Good evening, ladies, and, as usual, all of you look beautiful and bestow much pride upon the Westmoreland name."

He glanced back at Jayla. "And you look beautiful, as well, Jayla."

"Thanks." And before she lost her nerve, she asked, "Is there a chance I might speak with you privately for a moment?" The man standing before her looked so irresistibly handsome, so utterly gorgeous that it almost took her breath away.

Her pulse quickened when he stared into her eyes

with an intensity that made her shiver. He nodded, then said, "Sure." He shifted his gaze from her to the others and said, "Please excuse us for a minute." After taking her hand in his, Storm led her through the doors and outside into the lobby.

"There're a lot of people here tonight," Storm said, as they continued walking down the elegant and immaculate hallway.

"Yes, there are," Jayla replied. The benefit was being held in the ballroom of the Atlanta Civic Center and the facility was the perfect place to host such an event. She wondered where Storm was taking her. It was obvious that wherever it was, he wanted them to have privacy.

They stopped walking when they came to a beautiful atrium. All the greenery, flowering plants and the huge waterfall added warmth and even more grace and style to their surroundings. Jayla suddenly felt nervous, not sure of herself, but then she knew she had to say her piece. No matter what, he deserved to know about their baby, but she couldn't tell him that now. If he wanted her back, it had to be because he still loved her and not because he would feel obligated because she was carrying his child.

She cleared her throat. "Storm."

"Jayla."

She smiled when they had spoken at the same time. She glanced at him and his features were expressionless and she had no idea what he was thinking.

"Ladies first," he said, meeting her gaze.

Jayla swallowed. She knew that a lot was at stake here, but she remembered the words her father would often say—*nothing ventured, nothing gained.* She cleared her throat. "I kept my appointment at the clinic this morning."

He contemplated her silently for a moment, and then asked, "Did you?"

She expelled a soft breath, still unable to read him. "Yes, but I've decided not to go through with the procedure." She thought she saw relief flash through his gaze but wasn't sure.

He held her gaze steadily, studied her for a moment. "Why did you change your mind?" he asked.

Jayla swallowed again as she lifted her chin. "Because I realized that you were right and that I did have blinders on. So I took them off and when I did, I could see things a lot clearer."

Tension hummed between them; she felt it. "And what do you see, Jayla?" he asked softly.

She breathed deeply and decided to tell him just what she saw. "I see a tall man who is so strikingly handsome I can barely think straight, who has eyes so dark they remind me of chocolate chips and a voice so sexy it sends shivers down my spine. But most importantly, since taking my blinders off, I can see my Mr. Right standing right in front of me. Now. At this very minute. And I pray that I haven't ruined things, and there's a possibility that he still wants me, because, since taking off my blinders, I've also discovered just how much I love him and just how much I want him in my life."

Jayla held her breath, not knowing what he would say, not knowing if he would accept her words. Then, she saw a slow smile come into his face and spread from corner to corner on his lips. And those lips leaned down and came mere inches from hers and whispered. "I'm glad you quickly came to that conclusion, Jayla Cole, because I love you and there was no way in hell I intended to let you go."

Before she could say anything, he captured her mouth in a kiss. It was a kiss that was so powerful and tender that it immediately brought tears to her eyes. Storm loved her and she loved him and she believed in her heart that everything would be okay. Together, they would make their marriage work because love was the main ingredient and she believed they had plenty of that.

He reluctantly broke off their kiss. "I know you can't leave until everything is over, but I have to get you alone."

Jayla grinned and glanced around. "We're alone now, Storm."

He chuckled. "Yeah, but this place is too public for what I want to do to you." His features then turned serious. "But more importantly, Jayla, we need to talk and come to an understanding about a few things, all right?"

She nodded. "All right. But no matter what, we'll work things out."

He pulled her back into his arms. "Most definitely."

It was well after midnight when Jayla entered Storm's home. The evening had been perfect and a lot of money had been raised for Kids' World, which meant that plenty of terminally ill children's dreams would be coming true. It wasn't hard to guess that the calendars would sell like hotcakes. Over one hundred thousand calendars had been sold, and an order had already been placed for that many more.

And it hadn't come as a surprise to anyone that the single women had gone wild over the twelve men who had posed for the calendar, especially Mr. July, Thorn Westmoreland. However, any women who might have given thought to the possibility that she had a chance with Mr. July, married or not, discovered just how wrong they were when, after receiving the plaque that had been presented to all twelve men, Thorn crossed the room and kissed his wife, proclaiming to all that Tara Westmoreland was all the woman he wanted and needed.

And, Jayla thought as she inwardly smiled, Storm had made a number of declarations himself tonight. That single woman who'd vowed that she would get at least one time with Storm had been brazen enough to approach him while he and Jayla had stood together talking. Storm had smoothly introduced Jayla to the woman as his fiancée. The woman had congratulated them and walked off, thoroughly disappointed.

He had also introduced her to his parents and the rest of his family. She even got to meet the newest additions to the Westmoreland clan, his cousins Clinton, Cole and Casey. She had quickly decided that the Westmoreland family was a very special one and they all stuck together like glue.

"Would you like something to drink, Jayla?"

She turned and watched as Storm closed the door and locked it. "No, thanks." She nervously glanced around and stopped when her gaze came to rest on a framed photograph that sat on his fireplace mantle. It was a photo that the two of them had taken with her father at his last birthday party, the one the men at the fire station had given him. Her father had insisted that she and Storm stand next to each other while he stood in the background. Because of Adam Cole's six-seven height, he appeared to be towering over them. And he was smiling so brightly that she couldn't help wondering if perhaps he'd known about her feelings for Storm and, in his own special way, had given them his blessings that night, because less than five months after that picture was taken, he'd died.

Storm followed her gaze and after a few moments said, "Whenever I look at that picture and really study it, I think that your father was a lot smarter than either of us gave him credit for being."

Jayla nodded. Evidently their thoughts had been on the same page. She inhaled deeply and then met Storm's gaze. "I agree." She broke eye contact with him and continued her study of his home. With earth-toned colors and basic furnishings, it was clearly a bachelor's place. But everything was neat and in order. "Nice place."

"Thanks. A few months ago, I decided to sell it and get a bigger place," he said as his gaze roamed over her from head to toe. "Thanks for wearing that dress. It's my favorite."

Jayla smiled. "That's the reason I wore it. I was trying to give you a sign, or at least make you remember the time we spent together in New Orleans. I figured the only other person who would know I'd worn this dress before was Ian, and I counted on him not noticing."

Storm lifted a brow. He hated to tell her, but Ian had noticed. In fact, every man who'd been present tonight had noticed Jayla Cole in *that* dress. And each and every time he saw a man looking at her, even when trying not to, he was inwardly overjoyed that she belonged to him.

And now with her standing in the middle of his living room, there was nothing he was itching to do more than to take that dress off her because chances were, like before, the only thing underneath that dress was a pair of thongs. But he knew before they could get to the bedroom, there were issues that needed to be resolved between them.

Sighing, he slowly crossed the distance that separated them and took her hand in his. "Come on, let's sit down and talk."

She nodded and then he led her over to the leather sofa and they sat down. "I've done a lot of thinking, Jayla, and you're right. There's nothing wrong with a woman working outside the home if she wants to do so. The reason I was opposed to it was because years ago, while a senior in high school, I thought I was in love with a girl who threw my love back in my face when I told her of my decision not to go to college but to attend the Firefighters Academy instead. She said that a man without a college education could not properly take care of the needs of his family. When she said that, something snapped inside me and I intended to prove her wrong and, with college or not, I wanted to be a man who could sufficiently provide for all of my family's needs."

Jayla nodded. She could see the pride of a man like Storm getting bruised with a woman saying something like that. She sighed, knowing it was time to get rid of her emotional baggage as well.

"Because Dad was so strict on me while I was growing up," she started off by saying, "I had this thing against marrying a man who I thought would try and control me. But now I see that Dad had the right approach in raising me, or no telling how I might have turned out."

She inhaled in a deep breath, then added, "I believe all those times I thought I was looking for Mr. Right I failed miserably because it wasn't time to find my Mr. Right. It wasn't time until I saw you again in New Orleans."

Storm lowered his mouth to hers and the kiss he gave her was filled with so much intensity and passion, Jayla couldn't help the groan that purred from her throat. Nor could she ignore the sudden rush of heat that threatened to consume her entire body as Storm continued to claim her mouth, staking a possession all the way to the darkest recesses of her soul. She kissed him back, putting into the kiss all the love and feeling that he did, claiming his mouth as well and staking her possession.

He pulled back, stood and pulled her into his arms. "Will you marry me, Jayla Cole? Will you love me for better or worse, richer or poorer, in sickness and in health, till death do us part?"

Tears gathered in Jayla's eyes. "Yes! Oh, yes! I love you."

Storm grinned. "And I love you, too." His gazed locked with hers and smiled. "Tell me again what you see."

She smiled up at him, knowing it was time to tell him her other news. "I see my Mr. Right...and," she whispered softly, "I also see the man who is the father of my baby."

Jayla watched Storm's expression and knew the exact moment it dawned on him what she'd said. For a moment, he continued to gaze at her, his dark eyes clouded with uncertainty, hope. "Did you just say what I think you said?" he asked breathlessly.

She smiled. If there was any doubt in her mind that he wanted a baby, their baby, it evaporated when she saw the look of sheer happiness in his eyes. "Yes. After taking my physical, I told the doctor that I had changed my mind about the insemination procedure and she said it was a good thing since I was already pregnant."

Jayla chuckled. "By my calculations, I got pregnant in New Orleans but I still can't figure out how that happened when I know for certain that protection was used every time we made love."

Storm laughed. "Yeah, but a condom can only hold so much, sweetheart. When a man is driven to have multiple—"

Jayla placed a finger to Stone's lips and grinned. "Okay, I get the picture."

He swept her into his arms and chuckled. "I'm glad that you do and I guess you know what your pregnancy means," he said as he moved toward his bedroom.

"What?"

"There's no way we'll have a June wedding, even if you wanted one. We're getting married as soon as possible."

She laughed. "How soon?"

"Tomorrow isn't soon enough for me."

"What about in a month?"

"Umm, that's negotiable," he said as he placed her in the middle of his bed.

When he stood back, Jayla's gaze swept over him. When she saw the magnitude of his arousal, she inhaled deeply. "I have a feeling I might not be able to move in the morning."

He smiled as he began removing his clothes. "I have a feeling you just might be right. And I have a feeling that if you weren't pregnant now, you would very well be in the morning."

Jayla smiled and her gaze met his. "And you're sure you're okay with becoming a father, Storm? It's a lot for a devout bachelor to take on a wife and child at the same time."

His smile widened. "But I won't have a ordinary wife and child," he said coming back to her, completely naked. "They will be extraordinary because they are mine. And I promise to take very good care of them, Adam's daughter and grandchild, just as I believe he knew that I would."

He leaned over and slowly peeled the dress from Jayla's body. Then he quickly removed her shoes and panty hose. Finally, he removed her thong. "I really like that dress, but I like you naked a lot better."

He then joined her on the bed. "Do you know what is about to happen to you, Jayla?"

She laid a hand against his cheek. "No, tell me," she implored softly, seeing the dark, heated look of desire in his eyes. It was a look that sent sensuous shivers all through her body.

He smiled. "You're about to be taken by *Storm*."

Jayla smiled. She was definitely looking forward to that experience.

Epilogue

A month later

"You may kiss your bride."

As the Westmoreland family looked on in the back-yard of his parents' home, Storm smiled as he turned to Jayla and captured her mouth in the kind of a kiss that everyone thought should have been saved for later, but one he was determined to bestow upon his bride anyway.

"At least he has his own woman to kiss now," Dare whispered to Thorn.

"It's about damn time," Thorn Westmoreland replied, grinning.

Finally, Storm tore his mouth away from Jayla and smiled. He then leaned over and whispered something

in her ear and whatever he said made her blush pro-
fusely.

"Umm, I wonder what he said that made her blush
like that, considering the fact she's already pregnant,"
Stone whispered to Chase.

Chase shrugged. "You know Storm. Nothing about
him surprises me."

"Well, hell, I'm still in shock," Jared Westmoreland
said, shaking his head. "Storm was the last Westmoreland I thought would marry, and just think in less than
nine months he'll be a daddy."

Jared then chuckled as he glanced at Dare, Thorn,
Chase and Stone. "What is it with your side of the
family? All of you are tying the knot."

Chase frowned. "Not all of us."

Stone smiled. "Your time is coming, Chase." He
then glanced over at his cousins, Ian, Jared, Spencer, Durango, Quade, Reggie, Clint and Cole. "And
all of yours."

Durango narrowed his eyes. "Don't try putting a
damn curse on us like that old woman put on Storm."

Dare shook his head laughing. "She didn't put a
curse on Storm, she merely read his palm. Besides,
if it's going to happen, then it's going to happen. The
big question is who's next."

He studied his remaining single brother and his
eight male cousins. He smiled, having an idea just
who the next Westmoreland groom would be, and he
couldn't wait to see it happen.

He grinned. "All I have to say is that when it happens, don't fight it. You'll find out later that it will be
the best thing to ever happen to you."

Quade Westmoreland frowned. "No disrespect,

Sheriff, but go to hell." He turned and walked off, and the other single Westmoreland men did likewise.

Dare laughed and he kept on laughing while thinking there would definitely be another Westmoreland wedding before long. He would bet on it...if he were a betting man.

* * * * *

We hope you enjoyed reading
MR. NOVEMBER
by *New York Times* bestselling author
LORI FOSTER
and
RIDING THE STORM
by *New York Times* bestselling author
BRENDA JACKSON

Both were originally Harlequin® Desire stories!

Powerful heroes…scandalous secrets…burning desires.

From passionate, suspenseful and dramatic
love stories to inspirational or historical,
Harlequin offers different lines to
satisfy every romance reader.
Up to eight new books in each line
are available every month.

www.Harlequin.com   NYTHRSLF0218

Get 2 Free Books,
<u>Plus</u> 2 Free Gifts –

just for
trying the
*Reader
Service!*

STRS17R2

"You'll get to meet my brother tonight."

Penelope was embarrassed she didn't know a thing about another Ferguson sibling. She'd only been in Texas for a year, and between juggling her new business, moving into her apartment and handling crises for the Dallas elite, she hadn't climbed the Ferguson family tree any higher than Chase and Stefanie.

"Perfect timing," Chase said, his eyes going over her shoulder to welcome a new arrival.

"Hey, hey, big brother."

Now, that…that was a drawl.

The back of her neck prickled. She recognized the voice instantly. It sent warmth pooling in her belly and lower. It stood her nipples on end. The Texas accent over her shoulder was a tad thicker than Chase's, but not as lazy as it'd been two weeks ago. Not like it was when she'd invited him home and he'd leaned close, his lips brushing the shell of her ear.

Lead the way, gorgeous.

Squaring her shoulders, Pen prayed Zach had the shortest memory ever, and turned to make his acquaintance.

Correction: reacquaintance.

She was floored by broad shoulders outlined by a sharp black tux, longish dark blond hair smoothed away from his handsome face and the greenest eyes she'd ever seen. Zach had been gorgeous the first time she'd laid eyes on him, but his current look suited the air of control and power swirling around him.

A primal, hidden part of her wanted to lean into his solid form and rest in his capable, strong arms again. As tempting as reaching out to him was, she wouldn't. She'd had her night with him. She was in the process of assembling a firm bedrock for her fragile, rebuilt business and she refused to let her world fall apart because of a sexy man with a dimple.

A dimple that was notably missing since he was gaping at her with shock. His poker face needed work.

"I'll be damned," Zach muttered. "I didn't expect to see you here."

"That makes two of us," Pen said, and then she polished off half her champagne in one long drink.

Don't miss
LONE STAR LOVERS
by Jessica Lemmon, the first book in the
***DALLAS BILLIONAIRES CLUB** trilogy!*

Available March 2018 wherever
Harlequin® Desire books and ebooks are sold.

www.Harlequin.com

HDEXP0218

HARLEQUIN *Desire*

Powerful heroes…scandalous secrets…burning desires.

Save **$1.00**

on the purchase of ANY Harlequin® Desire book.

Available wherever books are sold, including most bookstores, supermarkets, drugstores and discount stores.

Save **$1.00**

on the purchase of any Harlequin® Desire book.

Coupon valid until May 31, 2018.
Redeemable at participating outlets in the U.S. and Canada only.
Not redeemable at Barnes & Noble stores. Limit one coupon per customer.

THE WORLD IS BETTER WITH

Romance

Harlequin has everything from contemporary, passionate and heartwarming to suspenseful and inspirational stories.

Whatever your mood, we have a romance just for you!

Connect with us to find your next great read, special offers and more.

f /HarlequinBooks

🐦 @HarlequinBooks

www.HarlequinBlog.com

www.Harlequin.com/Newsletters

⬦ HARLEQUIN®

A *Romance* FOR EVERY MOOD™

www.Harlequin.com